The
Silence

The
Silence

Kristi Buckel

NEF HOUSE PUBLISHING

The Silence
Copyright © 2024 Kristi Buckel

ISBN 978-1-965393-01-7

This book is dedicated to my mother, Linda Blanc, who has never failed to support me and rally the troops behind me; to my father, Peter Buckel, without whom I would have never found my love of writing; and to my spouse, Joshua Bader, who is the rock I turn to when the zombies are eating my brains.

Prologue
~ Kiera ~

I had long since stopped running. My feet hurt, and my companions huffed and puffed, struggling to regain their breath. I sat down in the middle of an office with several hanging ferns, some of which were clearly dying. I closed my eyes. It was too much. Without Sean, I didn't know who I was. I wasn't part of a *we* anymore. It was just me, a dog, and some random "friends" I'd just met.

Maybe I could form a new "we." Maybe . . . after all of this, I would come out on the other side to see the CDC with some kind of miracle cure. Maybe I'd see Sean again.

I didn't think I'd ever see Sean again.

I reached down and pet Grace around her doggy armor, ignoring the conversations around me. I had never felt so lonely, so down in front of a group of people. Normally it energized me, got me excited to talk; this little ragtag bunch looked up to me for some reason. Normally groups energized me, got me excited to talk, but I had no idea what we were supposed to do. Why was I the one they looked up to, when clearly Brett was the better leader? How should I lead them? Keep fighting and waiting for the CDC, I guessed. But what was the point? If there was no cure, I'd never see Sean again, and that made me feel like my insides were breaking. I'd never loved someone the way I loved him; hell, I loved him enough to doctor him through the plague. But it wasn't enough. Love wasn't enough to save him.

It never would be.

I stood up slowly, looking at the second-floor office. It seemed to be a real estate office; there were signs everywhere about closing the deal. The one by the door was stained with gore, and I wondered whose blood saturated the cardboard. Grace was glued to my side in her makeshift armor. She was the spikiest dog around, ready to take on the horde with us, and she wasn't a bad fighter, either. The rest of the group stared at me, waiting for something. Some kind of speech, a plan, the answers to questions we were afraid to ask. I had nothing.

"Let's go," I finally said. Evan stood, ready as ever, and got in position next to me. We'd formed a little triangle with myself, Grace and Brett at the front. It occurred to me that I only knew these people because of a disaster; I would never have found them if we hadn't organized training parties on my roof. We passed the bloodstained sign as we went toward the stairs, our little time of regrouping over. It was nice to have a moment that wasn't punctuated by moans.

We left the building, which was strangely devoid of blood and guts, and found ourselves hugging the walls of buildings whenever possible, sliding past alleyways and trash cans. I saw the university in the distance: our goal, which had seemed impossible this morning, but was rapidly becoming a reality. There were at least two hordes in front of us. I held my hatchet-mop close to me, feeling the anxiety and putting Grace behind me. We were as ready as we'd ever be.

I stepped away from the wall, heading for the horde in front of the pharmacy. The rest followed blindly, placing trust in me that I wasn't sure I'd earned. They were my party, my newfound friends, and I led them toward death and destruction. The zombies' gaze locked in and the battle was on. They were shambling and groaning.

One mistake and any one of my teammates could die. I felt their energy around me as we readied our weapons and fanned out. I stepped forward and felt a squelching; I looked down and saw a body. It was mangled, the leg twisted at an unnatural angle, and I'd stepped on it. My sorrow bowled me over, and I realized that this was the real deal: there was a war going on, and there was nothing I could do to fix it.

It was sobering. I wrapped my hands more tightly around the mop; my hands were shaky, and I looked toward the group. Brett was talking quietly to Evan, who clutched his weapon, his hands turning white with the effort. In front of me, I saw one woman whose cheek hung wide open, showing her teeth. Another man was staggering forward, a leg missing from his body. As we moved in toward the horde, I raised my hatchet-mop and Grace steadied herself next to me. Brett signaled for us to move forward.

It was getting easier and easier to kill the things that used to be people. I stopped remembering what it meant to end a life. I didn't feel as guilty. I didn't think of Sean as much.

The first zombie rushed forward and I steadied my weapon, thrusting hard toward his chest. The hatchet was buried deep inside the man's chest, and I had to fight to pull it out, catching on a stray rib that I'd broken. I couldn't help but wonder what Sean would have been like fighting with us. I thought about what he would do when faced with a not-person. I thought about the way he would protect me, and how I wouldn't have to be in charge, their lives would not be in my hands.

I could smell roses. The building in front of us had a clean, white awning with red stripes, and bushes full of beautiful red roses framing the front door. There was a bicycle leaning against the wall, a mint green color with white flowers. It was the kind of place that looked like a therapist's office or a bookstore; I took a second to peer in and saw that it was a cafe, a cafe that I might have used as my home base for studying, if the world had turned a different way. Grace barked and a cloud of birds exploded from the ground, and I thought of the days I'd spent bird watching instead of writing. I steadied my pole and aimed for the heart.

Six Months Earlier

~ Sean ~

Man eats his wife, it said, *News on the murder at six*. Kiera was making breakfast for dinner as I watched the news. The French toast smelled amazing, the sausage was a little questionable, and the news was a blurb on the ticker tape that talked about a mystery murder.

"Hey," I called. "There's a cannibal in town. Think we're next?"

She scoffed, turning around and waving a blue spatula. "He was probably on that acid bath bomb shit," she said. "Didn't that turn people into cannibals a few years ago or something?"

"Drugs or something," I agreed. "But still." We lived in a college town, and normally students couldn't afford the good drugs while the adults were rich enough to buy stuff we'd never even heard of. Bath bombs were not a thing that happened in Richmond. "How fucked up do you have to be to eat somebody? Raw, even. Moving." A chill ran down my spine, but I was more curious than horrified. I wondered what a human body tasted like. Probably chicken.

"Do you not remember that you were dared once to eat a live goldfish your sophomore year?"

"Hey! I didn't do it. I threw up once I put it in my mouth And I was drunk." It was the best excuse I had.

Kiera scratched her face with her fingers, leaving a line of flour up her cheek. It somehow made her look even more beautiful, and my heart melted. She worked so hard for us. Grad school for English, a job teaching the under-grads, *and* making me dinner? I didn't deserve her.

She returned to the kitchen, calling from the door-way. "You're right, though," she said. "That's six kinds of fucked up. Let me finish the eggs and I'll come watch with you."

She plopped a plate down on the secondhand end ta-ble. I turned up the volume as she laid her head against my shoulder, propping herself up. It was almost six. We watched a commercial about a cat balancing treats on its head, and then the news began.

It was so horrible that we had to laugh. They showed video clips, of course: the man had bloodstains and gore plastered across pale white lips. He looked . . . well, crazy.

We watched the video clips in horror. "I . . . don't think that's drugs," said Kiera as she rubbed her fingers over the calluses on my hands. She was shaking. I held her closer, dropping my plate on the end table.

"I don't think that's drugs either," I replied. The picture

of the man's wife was on the screen. She was pretty, a brunette with wide, bright blue eyes, cornflower blue in contrast with the man's neon green. I could see how they would have looked good together, before he'd done it. Before he'd *eaten* her.

It was difficult to watch. I wondered what was driving him to become this monster that hurt his own wife. I wrapped my arms around Kiera more tightly, until she was almost squirming to breathe. I let her go just a little, looking out the cracked window. Our apartment was not very new; we were lucky the window was only cracked and not broken. I remembered that I was going to fix it with duct tape. Duct tape held our apartment together.

"I don't know," she answered, though I hadn't asked my question aloud. "I don't know how he could do it. What's wrong with him, Sean?" She turned her face upward toward mine.

I sighed and looked back at the TV, trying not to think about it. The news didn't share my concern, though. It was a headline, nothing more. There were other news stories to play out over the screen. Other tales to tell. This was nothing more, nothing less.

But I couldn't shake the uncomfortable feeling that those lambent, glowing eyes would follow me for a long time to come.

~

After a few strange dreams that I couldn't quite remember, the headline faded into the depths of my mind, only for Kiera to text me a few days later from school. I was busy at my own job stocking shelves at a sports store;

while I didn't know a lot about sports, I knew a hell of a lot about being alone outside and always joked with Kiera that I'd be a great boyfriend if she ever wanted to flee her finals and go to the mountains.

Somebody's eaten their children this time, she said. *Two kids. Pls tell me this is a joke.*

I stared at my phone for a long time. Images of wailing children, flailing and screaming, kicking and beating at their parent as they were eaten. I gagged and threw myself into the employee bathroom just in time to vomit into the debatably clean toilet. It took me more than a few seconds to clean myself up, and I just thanked God I hadn't puked on my shirt.

How could I go back to selling firepit griddles after that?

The answer was the American dream: don't think about it. Don't imagine it. Pretend it didn't happen, and it won't affect you. Pretend that nothing is wrong, and as long as you can carry on living your life under the ledge of that privilege, you will persevere.

Too bad that lasted about as long as it took me to get another text from Kiera.

Fuck Sean there's an attack on campus come get me now!!!

Kiera wasn't one to exaggerate. She wrote nonfiction, for God's sake. I didn't even think someone *could* exaggerate in a memoir. My mouth went dry and I sucked on my teeth, trying to keep breathing. Campus was exactly thirteen minutes away by motorcycle if I left now. She could hang on for thirteen minutes.

Wait. The American dream. I'd forgotten about the second part of it: it lay on the backs of retail workers. I'd have to tell my boss I was leaving first.

I have to admit that my voice sounded a bit screechy as I hollered. "Kenneth!" I tried for a manly bellow. "Kenneth, where the hell are you?" I held on to my little microphone headset as hard as I could.

I heard his soothing baritone. "Man, calm down. I'm in bikes and rec. I just finished with a customer. What do you need?"

"I need to leave. Now. There's an emergency. It's Kiera."

I skidded around the corner and nearly hung my boxers on the bike rack. I'd forgotten what clotheslining one's balls felt like in the half decade or so since I'd been in high school. I was seeing stars. He stared down at me for a long moment, searching for something he wasn't going to find for as long as I had to stand there clutching my junk like an idiot.

"Inventory's tonight," he said slowly. "Try to be back by six."

Six. I looked at my watch. It was 4:33. If I left now, I could reach campus before five. Hell, I'd make it up from there. I grabbed my phone, nodding frantically. "I'll see what I can do," I said hoarsely. I started to text Kiera to ask if she was okay and I went to the break room to grab my helmet.

On my way. Where r u? Stay where u r!

There was something about emergencies that made me see stupid realizations in the midst of them. For me, it was that I was texting like I was in high school to someone trying to get their master's degree in literature. Maybe, I thought, at some point I could use big boy words and impress her a little.

Bookstore, came the immediate reply. *We locked the doors. SWAT is here. Idk what's going on but it's bad. Pls come!!!*

I could beat thirteen minutes. She was panicking. I could feel it running through the bandwidth, the electronic aether connecting us both when we were so far away. It tasted like gunmetal. It felt like shock, and a bone-chilling shiver.

I hit the parking garage, got on my bike, and started for the streets. We were behind the main thoroughfare, not on it, so it didn't *seem* like a big deal until I hit Richmond Avenue, the cross street that wound its way downtown to campus. I wasn't the kind of guy to swerve in and out of traffic, but the cars were unbelievable.

There was a three-car pileup about as far down as I could see. There was a blue car, torn into two, bisected by a black sedan. I winced, knowing that someone wouldn't be walking out of there okay. The third vehicle was a white van, and I saw men in camo-colored coats milling around the scene like they were cops or something. Like they were in charge.

Okay. That was strange.

What was even more strange was that the cops were listening to them. Intently. Cops did not like it when someone had authority over them. And men in camo coats? Please.

Weaving in and out of traffic, I saw that the cars were busy on the road. I used my relatively small size to my advantage, squeezing between gridlock to the chagrin of drivers on either side. More than one honked as I flew by. I flipped on the Bluetooth radio inside my helmet, hoping that the news was big enough that even the little local radio station I liked would have *some* kind of info about the situation.

There was static.

The radio station was on campus. My stomach dropped.

I gunned it, hauling ass. I made it to campus just two minutes past my self-imposed deadline and almost took a dive over my handlebars trying to pull into the closest parking spot to the bookstore. Since I'd taken the back way, I didn't see the view from the front of campus, not until I walked around to the main doors of the store.

I was surprised they hadn't locked down the little side street, too. SWAT teams were everywhere, scouring the campus, and men in black helmets with massive guns patrolled the pathways. I eased to the side of the doors, managing to wedge myself into a bush, and got out my phone.

By front door. Let me in.

She looked out the window before letting me in. "I think if we tried to leave now, they'd stop us," she said, concerned. I reached out to hold her and we walked toward the back of the store.

I followed blindly, through the shelves and to the break room, where her fellow grad students were holed up. One of her coworkers kept scrolling on his phone, his hair hiding his face. The others stared numbly at the wall. A few people sitting on the floor still had their shopping totes, and the light flickered overhead.

She stood against the lockers while I held her by the shoulders and examined her. She looked all right, just scared. "Baby, what's going on?"

She slumped into my arms, and her tiny body shook against mine. I ripped off my helmet and sent it tumbling to the floor, holding her as tightly as I could. "Please. What happened?"

"There was an attack on campus," she mumbled into my T-shirt. "Or . . . I guess several attacks at the dorms. Whatever it was, a bunch of undergrads started attacking their roommates, and it escalated from there. The last we heard is that there's someone still attacking people on the grounds, but SWAT is looking for them."

"So we can't go outside until SWAT is done?" I asked. Kiera nodded glumly. I looked around the room at dead eyes and pale faces. "All right," I said slowly. "So we're locked in here for a while. At least we're safe and there's snacks. We just have to wait it out, wait for SWAT to come tell us it's okay."

That was about the time that we heard a thud on the break room door.

A girl shrieked, and Grant slapped a hand over her mouth. "Shut up," he hissed, blocking her sobs with his hand. "I don't fucking want to get eaten!"

"Nobody's going to get eaten," I said, attempting to be soothing. "The door is shut. I don't think whatever's happening to people allows them to open doors.

"Besides, why would we get eaten? Everybody that got attacked, like, knew each other. Or were family. Maybe it really is drugs and it makes you want to eat whatever is in front of you. No one's going to get in here, so we're safe."

Thud.

The hinges shuddered and I turned to Kiera. "How sure are you?"

"About what?"

"That we're safe in here." The hinges were bending.

"I'm not."

I pulled at her hand, yanking her toward the front door. "Because something's hell-bent on getting in here, and I'm not about to become an experiment for your thesis. Come on. We're all going to the front door."

The store wasn't that big, and we could get to the front door within a minute or two. It would be easy, I thought. Whatever it was, we could deal with it.

Too fucking funny.

The door burst open and fell in a clatter of dust. An undergrad soccer player stared back at me from the other side of the hole in the wall, his black hair tousled and his clothes covered in grime. As I looked, I saw that his hands—and his mouth—were covered in red paint.

Yeah, I finally figured out that wasn't paint.

"Go! We need to get the hell out of here!"

It was the three car pileup all over again with gridlock at the door as the seven of us all tried to get out at once.

Samantha was shrieking again, and Grant was pushing at her ass in a way that I knew was not socially acceptable in any other circumstance. She finally got the door open, and workers started darting towards the door, shoving each other out of the way. Kiera and I were last, waiting for the room to clear out.

The soccer player gave chase.

I didn't know what the hell was wrong with him, but I wasn't about to find out closer up. We fled, and he fled with us, toward us. *For* us. We ran and I felt a sharp pinch on my forearm, and I kicked blindly, my foot connecting with his body before I slammed the door behind us.

We finally made it to the front doors of the store and near a SWAT team. They were in the cafeteria across the courtyard.

"Get in here!" a man screamed. It always seemed like men in black with guns needed to scream everything they said, I analyzed numbly. I held Kiera's hand like a beacon of hope while we were shoved and pulled into the cafeteria and the doors clicked, locking behind us.

The cafeteria was half-full of sobbing students, and we found ourselves a little corner table, sitting down at last. I didn't think any of us knew what was going on, not yet.

"Sean, you're bleeding," Kiera said, pulling my forearm up to look at it in the dim light.

"It's fine," I said, holding her hand in mine and wiping away the blood with my other hand. It was a deep cut. I knew I should probably do something about it, but what? "I think I got caught on the door on the way out or something."

She sighed and fished around in her purse, coming back with a maxi pad and some electrical tape.

"What even the fuck?" I was a little proud at my MacGyver girlfriend.

"Shut up. You're hurt, I'm fixing it," she muttered, unwrapping the pad and pressing it into my arm. She wound the electrical tape around it and sighed in satisfaction. "At least that's one thing I can fix. All better."

As my nerves buzzed with lightning, I looked down into her soft blue eyes. "Why do you have electrical tape in your purse?" The stupid question was the most reassuring thing I could think to say.

She laughed, and among all the chaos, it sounded like music.

Medic Alert

~ Kiera ~

It took about six hours for the SWAT team to clear us to go home, and I still didn't know what happened to the guy we saw in the bookstore. I was afraid to ask, really—what if he was the one they were looking for after all? I mean, there was a niggling feeling in the back of my mind that he *was*, but there was a niggling feeling in my mind that facing reality on this one was going to be hard. Maybe he was just tired. Yeah. That's it.

I clung to Sean as he eased us both onto his motorcycle and placed the extra helmet on top of my head. It was green, my favorite color—he'd bought it just for me. "Thanks," I mumbled, wrapping my arms around him.

"Hey," he said quietly. I looked up at him, miserable, unsure of what to do. "It's going to be okay. We're going to go home. Your weird coupon addiction has an entire dining room worth of food and toilet paper in our apartment." I blushed, knowing that my coupon obsession was a little much.

"We can just stay there until this is over. It'll be fine." His voice was the most soothing, the most reassuring that I'd ever heard it. I wanted to melt, to fall into him—but something told me that I was going to have to be strong. For me. For him.

I exhaled, closing my eyes. This was a transient crisis. Someone had done something stupid, and a bunch of people had followed suit. Couldn't they contact trace things like this? I was positive that someone, somewhere in the government had been notified and they were coming right this way, like a virus-obsessed Mulder and Scully, and they would save the day before we knew the day needed saving.

As Sean got on the bike, I sighed. I remembered those poor kids that got eaten They'd needed saving from the very people who protected them from what went bump in the night.

We sped off into the night, my arms wrapped tightly around Sean's waist, and settled into a slow pattern of traffic after getting off of the back streets Sean had used to get to the school. It seemed like every other car was in danger of being rear-ended, and we were uncomfortably squeezed between an exterminator van and a hearse. The sick smell of grease wafted toward us from a food truck and I almost gagged, holding onto Sean harder.

He wrapped a hand around mine briefly before easing our way into the next lane, which was moving a little faster. The night was quiet—all I could hear was the sound of the engine, the bark of dogs and the occasional car revving. There were no shouts, no screams of the broken and dying, nothing else to remind me of the crazed green eyes of the soccer player and the people on the news.

We rolled into our parking space behind our apartment building and said nothing as we trudged up the stairs, helmets in hand. I realized how listless I felt as I leaned against the wall, waiting for Sean to open the door.

"Are you gonna be okay?" he asked as he ushered me in. I think he already knew the answer, as he took charge, taking off my coat, pulling me to my favorite couch that I so often used to fall asleep on his lap, and settling me down with a blanket.

He sat next to me. "I know what we saw was scary, but—"

It was then that our phones screeched in unison. *National Emergency Alert. Please remain indoors. If you are outside, seek shelter immediately. Dangerous individuals have been identified nationwide attacking nonviolent citizens. The National Guard has been deployed . . .*

It was the longest NEA that I'd ever seen. Normally, they told you there was a tornado, and good luck with that. I clung to Sean, pressing myself into his arms, and took a deep breath. "No, Sean," I said finally. "I don't think I'm going to be okay."

He was reading his phone, frowning as he scrolled through the entire message. "Okay," he said slowly, rubbing at the maxi pad on his arm. "So we stay inside. We have a ton of food and more toilet paper than God needs,

I think. Fuck, the White House doesn't have as much toi-let paper as we have."

"There was a sale!" I protested weakly. "I had coupons!"

"You have coupons for everything. That's not the point. We lock the door, we wait for the National Guard to fig-ure shit out and tell us what to do, and you get a break to work on your thesis. Excuse me, book-length project. Is that what we're calling it now?" He was itching a little harder.

I made a face. "Just because ONE GUY called it that doesn't mean you can't use the word "thesis." I have to stand up there and read it and defend it and feel like an ass when I can't answer questions about my own book, it's a thesis." I grabbed his arm before he had a chance to pull away and yanked the electrical tape off of him, caus-ing him to howl.

"Hey! What the fuck was that?" he grumbled, but I could see a hint of a smile. He knew that when I took charge, it usually meant things were going to be okay. Or he'd end up on the floor with my karate foot staring him in the face.

"You keep itching. We've got to disinfect that better than we did. Hand sanitizer, a hospital it is not." I care-fully pulled the pad off of him and he winced, cursing in Gaelic. It was his thing. Duolingo had nothing on Sean.

The pad stuck, which worried me . . . weren't they sup-posed to be non-stick for blood? Wasn't that the whole point?

He peered under it before I had a chance and sucked in a breath. "I think it's infected," he said calmly. Too calmly.

Yellow pus stuck to the wound, which oozed blood. The edges were turning colors—I couldn't tell if they were black, blue, or purple. It looked like a bruise around the cut, which was still gaping a little at the middle. It was a pretty good-sized cut. "So I think it's infected," I agreed, my heart leaping in my chest. "What the hell did you cut it on?"

"I told you, I was on the ass end of a train going nowhere as we all shoved each other out the door. I think I hit it on the latch and dug in. I don't even know, but if we don't get some peroxide up in here, I think we're going to have to call *Grey's Anatomy* or something."

"Is that show even still on air?" I asked, trying to sound casual as I went for the brown bottle in my bathroom cabinet. On the inside, I was panicking: this was not normal. I didn't think so, anyway. An infection this fast? It had only been . . . fuck, it had been eight hours since we'd escaped from the bookstore. Maybe infections did set in that fast. I read books and edited words, what the hell did I know?

"Probably, but the one I liked left anyway," he said glumly. "The main one's best friend. The one that hated everybody."

I came back with gauze and peroxide, tape and more tape. I didn't know what else to do; wound care was not my strong suit. Outdoorsy men stuff was Sean's outfit, not mine. And he quit the Boy Scouts a long time ago. "All right," I said cautiously. "This is going to suck. Like, a lot. I have to wipe all the pus out, I think."

He grabbed the bottle from my hand and grunted, heading toward the kitchen sink. "So first, we're not doing this over the couch that your mom bought us for Christmas. And second, no the hell you are not, I've seen you cook, you dig your hands into the hamburger like it's Play Doh. If I have anything to do with this, it's me who's wiping anything out of me, thanks."

As much as I didn't want to admit it, he was sort of right. I'm a bull in a china shop. "All right," I said softly. "But . . . be careful? Don't, like, wipe anything that needs to stay in there?" I bit my lip and followed him to the kitchen.

He wrapped his free arm around me briefly and dove in, pouring the peroxide over it like bleach over blood. "Oh, holy fucking fuck, this was not my best move," he muttered as the peroxide bubbled and fizzed audibly. I could have sworn that the bruise grew larger as he poured. He doused the cut and let it sit, tapping his foot wildly to a tune I couldn't hear, waiting until the frothing stopped. It took a lot of goopy gauze, but he managed to wipe away all of the pus until the wound was angry and bleeding.

"That looks great," I squeaked.

"You would make an amazing EMT, Kiera. Just for the record." He looked at the supplies in my hand and grabbed the tape, using it as makeshift butterfly bandages to pull the wound together. "I think just pulling it closed and leaving the rest to the air will do the best. My mom always said if it's wet, get it dry, if it's dry, get it wet. No Neosporin and air?"

"Yeah. That sounds right. I mean, I could Google it—"

"You'd faint at the first three picture suggestions."

"Okay. Truth. So let it be, and watch TV?"

He turned his smile on me and I melted. This was Sean the way I always wanted to think of him: goofy, happy, and loving me. He scooped me up in his free arm, the other dangling damply at his side, and led me back to the couch. "You can lay your head on my lap, just like every other day, and we can pretend none of this has happened."

"DVD marathon of *Bob's Burgers*?"

"You know I love me some Louise," he said, and we settled on the couch together for a long night of pretending. I couldn't help but look at his arm every time he shifted, wondering if the bruise was getting bigger. If the pus was coming back. If the infection was spreading.

Wondering what we'd do then.

~

When I woke up, Sean was still sleeping beneath me, snoring softly with his hand in my hair, my head on his chest. It had been hard to sleep. My mind was racing, thoughts tumbling over each other like a waterfall, and I was surprised that I actually had fallen asleep. My eyes drifted slowly to the arm that was hanging off the edge of the couch, held together by makeshift tape bandages.

The bruise was . . . probably not a bruise.

And it was much, much larger. I felt trapped in the dream state, unable to move, unable to think past my surface thought of shock and fear, wrapped in a bubble wrap of numbness. I fought to wake up, fought to bring myself back to Sean, and struggled out of the sea of somnolence until I could untangle myself from his fingers and gently take his arm in my hands.

"Fuck," he mumbled in his sleep.

"Sorry," I whispered back. I recalled something I'd seen on a show that Sean and I had watched together. Apparently, venomous snakebites were a thing at zoos sometimes (who knew!) and one way to track bite wounds, or any infection, was with a Sharpie.

Luckily, my couponing had extended to a sale on the markers, and I had an entire case full of Sharpies at my disposal. I grabbed a bright orange one, the farthest away from the bruise colors that I could manage, and carefully began to draw a dotted line around the black and purple skin. Pus oozed from the cracks that weren't held together by the black tape, and it wept amber, trailing down his punished skin. What the hell had been on that door?

His eyes were upon me when I looked up, and he was amused, a half-smile and tousled hair making him more charming with every moment. "What are you doing?"

"Don't you remember the show *Zoos After Dark*? I'm marking your injury so we can tell if it's spreading. It looks bigger than last night. I'm not hallucinating, it's different than it was. I want to prove it. And if we need to go to the hospital," I added as I wrote the date and time under the dotted line, "we have a track record to go by."

"I am not going to the hospital because I got attacked by a door."

"You so are if I tell you to. This is nonnegotiable. I am driving your sulky ass to the doctor if I have to ride your motorcycle myself and tie you to the back."

His amusement grew, his bright, grass-green eyes twinkling as he watched me. "You can't drive a motorcycle."

"I'll figure it out," I muttered, closing the cap on the

Sharpie with a soft *click*. "I think we need to peroxide it again."

"You know that peroxide eats away skin cells, right? You aren't supposed to do it more than, like, once. I think at this point I need to bust out the alcohol."

"Oh. Right." Again, medical pursuits—so not my strong suit. This was a tidbit of knowledge I filed away in my editor's brain, in case I needed to point it out to some future author that was also attempting to keep someone from dying by stupidity. "Well, let's get the tape off, I guess?"

I thought about climbing back into bed and pulling him down into it, to nest in the familiarity of us. We'd been together since our freshman year in college, with me in English, he in Engineering. He was a lot brighter than he gave himself credit for, and I would never understand why he was working retail at an outdoors store rather than getting his Master's.

His jeans began to slide off of his ass as he walked and I laughed, running behind him and tugging them up by the belt loop so he didn't trip. "Have you lost weight?"

He grunted. "No," he said with a short laugh. "They're old jeans, and I'm too lazy and cheap to buy a belt. Put it on my Christmas stocking list."

We had a habit of adding things to Samsung Notes year-round for Christmas: every time someone said "I need X," we wrote it down, because come Christmas, neither one of us remembered what the hell we'd told the other. It was one of our favorite little habits of ours, surprising each other with things we genuinely needed and had forgotten we wanted.

"All right," he said under his breath as he sat down at the toilet. A hiss escaped his lips that sounded as if a kettle was dying: a low, moaning hiss that ended in an abrupt squeak as he pulled the tape off. His skin came with it.

The skin was gooey around the edges, infected and sick, and came off easily with the tape. The wound was bigger now, big enough that the tape wasn't going to hold it. Hell, I wasn't sure even sutures would hold it. I didn't know there was anything about it that could be sutured in the first place. It was gelatinous. "We're going to have to pack that," I said softly.

His eyes were narrowed as he stared at the wound. He licked his lips. "So I stayed up after you fell asleep," he said carefully.

"Okay?" This sounded like a random train of thought that I wasn't prepared for as I stared at his bleeding, pus-ridden flesh.

"They're saying that some of the people, the cannibals? They're giving people who live some sort of infection. A bad one. There was a news story at about three this morning about a guy who got scratched by a cannibal dude . . ." He trailed off.

"What are you saying?" My voice sounded low. Unstable. Not like me.

"I don't think that the door was what bit me." He uncapped the alcohol with one hand, staring up at me with bold green eyes as he poured half the bottle onto the infected flesh, the skin at the corners of his eyes taut and strained. He let it sit, the pus running down his wrist and into the sink, until it ran only pink and clear, until the gelatinous skin was gone, and clean, albeit bruised, flesh remained.

I looked down at the gaping hole the size of a silver dollar in my lover's arm. I could see thin threads of white that I couldn't identify, and a red-black vessel that made me gag. He carefully took a piece of gauze, doused it in alcohol, and packed it into the hole, wrapping the nonstick sterile cloth around the rest of the angry wound and taping it shut. "I think we're past 'keep it dry.'"

"Yeah," I said finally. My stomach muscles were heaving. I stared down at him, feeling a cold sweat burst through my temples. "So what bit you?"

His eyes were unwavering. "I think you already know."

TV Time

~ Sean ~

It wasn't ideal. I had been telling the truth when I told Kiera that I'd woken up in the middle of the night, staying awake while she slumbered peacefully against my chest, scrolling through news articles and clips, playing them on mute with captions so that I didn't wake her. I didn't want to admit to myself what I had figured out at about four in the morning: I hadn't been bitten by the door. I had been scratched by the soccer player.

What I really didn't want to admit to myself is what the blogger-turned-journalists had been calling them: zombies.

Like, really? Zombies? The undead set to rise again and eat the flesh of the living? Who were we kidding? It seemed absolutely ridiculous. For one, I hadn't seen any evidence that any of these cannibals were dead. And then I started reading Reddit.

For the unenlightened, Reddit is a bastion of personal

experience and masturbatory fantasy. It's basically a refuge for all of the knowledge of the Internet piled into one horrible little site. And that's where the bloggers had gone, the ones with real experience with the cannibals, the ones who'd seen them in person. And that's where I saw the video.

It's been three hours since my grandma passed, the captions read. *The coroner's not here yet. He's backed up with how many car accidents there were today on the freeway. My grandma's leg is twitching.*

It was a shaky, grainy video of a woman lovingly wrapped in a shawl, her face peaceful, but her leg was definitely twitching. It took me a long moment to see it: a toe, first. Then her entire foot convulsed. The muscles in her leg spasmed, a tightening that startled me. *I started videoing this ten minutes ago. I thought I was crazy. I thought I was making it up.*

You could see the girl shriek as she dropped the phone, then picked it back up with shaking hands. The grandma's fingertips were twitching. Her mouth was moving. Her eyes are neon green.

Her eyes weren't open a few moments ago.

I was *not* about to tell Kiera that I stayed up until the sun rose because I couldn't close my eyes against the image of a fucking zombie cannibal—is that redundant? Somehow it doesn't seem like it—rising from the dead. She was dead. And then she wasn't.

The video stopped at the point where the grandmother sat up, and no one on Reddit had heard from the girl since. I turned up the volume a little and watched again, hoping to catch the tell that it was fake. No luck. I'd thought it was a weird ass fluke, until I saw the thread beneath it. A mortician chimed in: bodies were moving, ones fresh from the hospital, and she was pretty damn sure she knew how to tell if someone was dead or alive.

That was about the time when I flipped back to the news feed, and my jaw dropped. It was real.

It was real, it was fucking real, and Kiera slept on as I stared at my arm with growing horror. I wasn't stupid enough to think hand sanitizer and a maxi pad had saved me, if this was what I thought it was. The news was reporting that there were at least twenty people, if not more, in the city—four just from Kiera's college—that had been bitten or scratched, and they were showing symptoms of a rapidly advancing infection. Skin that looked bruised until touched, and then burst in a sea of pus and blood. Black, thick blood vessels pounding with your pulse, almost as if you could see each droplet of blood coursing through them. It was too early to say what happened to people that got the infection. So far, an infection was all it was.

An infection is all it is.

"An infection is all it is," I echoed to Kiera as the sun rose softly through the eyelet curtains she'd hung in our living room. An apartment can't be a home without curtains, she'd told me, eyes gleaming with pride as she stood on a chair with a hammer and nails. Apparently curtain rods were optional. "That's all. I'm going to be fine. After all, I have to take care of you, don't I?"

She nodded as she slept, nuzzling into my chest, her

breath sweet against my hand. I smelled her hair, the jasmine and rose shampoo that she used wafting into my nostrils, and I felt my love for her swell to proportions I'd never experienced before. I'd hide this from her, I decided. She wasn't exactly much for news feeds, especially not the up-to-date, hard-hitting news that I liked. She was more of a Facebook feed kind of girl that thought NPR was the best form of news there was. I could keep her ignorant of this. She might threaten to bring me to a doctor, but I knew something she didn't.

If I thought it would break her heart, I knew I could lie to her. Maybe that's a bad thing. Maybe that meant something about my love, something broken and shallow, but I knew that there was no way I could tell her what was happening to me—what had happened to me—without couching it in velvet pillows, cushioning the blow until we knew she wouldn't lose me. She couldn't lose me. I wouldn't accept it.

It would break her.

Her mother was a nurse, and Kiera had a well-stocked pharmacy in the kitchen, its own little pantry cupboard stocked full of antibiotics of all shapes and sizes, as well as steroids and probably some illegal shit I couldn't name. I knew at the very least it had about three different kinds of painkillers, one from Kiera's last dental surgery and one from when I fucked up my knee on my last bike. Between those three, I could contain this.

I would contain this.

"Morning," Kiera said breathily. She was so sweet when she was just waking up. "Any news? How's your arm?" She yawned, nuzzling into me hard, her hair brushing against the bottom of my chin.

"Just the usual. Cannibals eating people, the campus is on lockdown, and we got out of the cafeteria just in time not to be stuck there. The dorms are all locked down. It's a disaster," I said cheerfully. "The interstate is a nightmare, because evidently cannibals mean people can't drive, and there are wrecked cars everywhere. Your mom texted me this morning to make sure we got home safe. I told her we haven't eaten each other yet. Do you want pancakes?"

"Your arm," she said sternly, slowly sitting up and stretching. "It looked bad last night. Lemme see it."

I exhaled slowly, so slowly that I knew she wouldn't see it. I turned my wrist, gazing at her with steady eyes. "Just as bad as yesterday," I said simply. "I think I need antibiotics. What'd your mom send you with the latest care package?"

She held my arm gently, her black acrylic nails brushing against my skin, and I shivered. I loved the way that she touched me. She unwound the tape, and I was glad to see that none of me came with it this time. The gauze was saturated with blood and green pus, graduated from yesterday's yellow. I could feel the skin burning beneath her fingertips. It wasn't pleasant.

"So this looks . . . bad," she said cautiously. She was, in fact, *not* a nurse like her mom, and strictly avoided anything to do with that world. She wouldn't know what blood poisoning was if it smacked her in the face, and I was afraid it was heading in that direction if we didn't do something quickly. "But you're right. I have an assload of antibiotics and I remember the combination I was on in the hospital for that cat bite. I think if we do the same thing, we can get through to where we can get you to a doctor."

"It'll take a while to get me there," I cautioned carefully. "The hospitals are overrun. There are accidents everywhere. The cannibals are getting worse. I don't know, Kiera. I think it's better if we just do this on our own."

She bit her lip thinly, closing her eyes and taking a deep breath. "Okay. We can do this. This is gross. We can do it. Right?"

"Can we stop talking about how gross my arm is and, like, do something about it?" Teasing her was the best part of my day.

"I'll go get antibiotics. You . . . do you. Do whatever you think you need to do with that. YouTube it or something. Somebody's got to be as stupid as you are and put it on video, how to doctor themselves."

She disappeared into the kitchen and I sagged in relief. I carefully pried the gauze ball out of the deeper wound, swearing under my breath. Oh, fucking God, it hurt. It burned, like holding my hand to the stove top, and sliced through me like a scalpel at the same time. It hurt so badly that I couldn't make a sound, couldn't breathe, couldn't think.

It took me more than a second to gather my wits enough to get the hell into the bathroom with the alcohol. The blood vessels that I could see inside the wound were black, as I'd expected. I poured the rest of the bottle on it and bit back a scream, digging my teeth into my lip, watching the whites of my eyes roll in the mirror. I looked like a panicked animal, waiting for my own doom.

I kind of felt like that, too, as I stared numbly at the devastation of my arm. Kiera could *not* see this. It looked bad enough with the gauze packed into it, but without, the crater of green and black purulent drainage was seeping into a lake. I balled up another wad of nonstick gauze—fat lot of good the nonstick seemed to be doing me—and shoved it into the wound, grabbing another pad and wrapping it up tightly with the tape. It was all I could do.

I wiped my face, calmed my shaking hands, went into the bedroom and changed my T-shirt that reeked of sweat and fear. I put a nonchalant smile on my face and strolled into the kitchen, grabbing Kiera by her waist with my good arm and pulling her in for a little kiss.

It was all I could do.

~

We stayed glued to the TV for the better part of the morning, watching with growing horror the stories that were displayed there with gory glee. I was lucky that some of the Reddit stories hadn't made it onto the regular news; at least, not the kind of news that Kiera would trust. They didn't say "zombie" once. "Cannibal," now, that came up so much we were considering making a drinking game out of it.

Couldn't hurt. I grabbed the whiskey and made us some shots, placing the bottle I'd gotten on my junior year trip to Ireland on the black coffee table in front of us. "Every time they say 'cannibal.' Got it?"

"Fuck me," she muttered, and grabbed the glass. "We'll be dead by sundown."

My eyes strayed to the tape that I had purposely applied far wider than my wound actually required. The black was spreading. Dead by sundown. I hoped not.

"Or I'll whiskey and dine you, seduce you and make you forget all about the cannibals," I said softly, running my free fingers through her red hair. The afternoon sun shone through our windows, blazing against her hair, showing me the gold that I so rarely saw. We were night owls by nature; this was a rare vision of my beautiful girl.

She laughed, that tiny, tinkling-of-the-bells giggling that made me swoon, for lack of a manlier term. God, I loved her! I pulled her into my lap and wrapped my bad arm around her, making a show that it was more okay than it really was. I rested it on her belly, injured side up, so she didn't feel the heat radiating through the bandages.

"I love you," she said.

"I will never, ever get tired of hearing that," I said.

"I know. Drink!" She swigged her whiskey with a gasp and a shudder, laughing after the drink passed her lips. "You missed it. He said that the local Walmart was besieged by cannibals while we slept. Or something. It sounded more poetic than that."

I sobered, contrary to the whiskey on my breath. The Walmart wasn't too far from our apartment. We were in the middle of town; there was nowhere to go. As I watched, the news made it sound more and more like this was something that was becoming a major problem, rather than a few rampant cannibals here and there.

"Kiera," I said tentatively.

"Sean," she said back.

I didn't get a chance to make up a story about what was happening, what I'd read the previous night; the news got to it before I did. "OhmyGod," she said in a rush.

It went from "cannibals" to "zombies," just like that. In a single sentence, a blank look by the news reporter followed by: *Excuse me, there's just been an update by the CDC* . . . They didn't actually say the word, but there it was. It wasn't the same video that I'd seen, nor any of the clips that the Redditors had trickled down the thread during the wee hours of the morning.

It was a morgue, of course. Because it had to be a morgue to be real. The feed was from a security camera mounted in the corner on the wall. We watched in tandem silence as the mortician began her examination, going over the cadaver's outward appearance, noting the rather festive neon green eyes.

"Sean," Kiera said nervously. I could see the whites of her eyes.

I squeezed her hand, saying nothing. If I turned it off now, she'd know that I was protecting her from something, and she might make assumptions that I wasn't ready for her to make. She still thought the door had bit me, and I wanted to keep it that way for as long as possible. I wasn't ready to know what would happen to me, and here was a chance I could get better, now that she'd shoved a pharmacy down my throat. She'd even gone so far as to inject my pert little ass with a steroid shot. I didn't even want to begin to think how her mom smuggled that into our pantry.

There's evidence of bite wounds on the upper thigh, the mortician said calmly, as if this was something that she saw every day. Maybe she did; was there a market for TV about kinky autopsies? I shook my head, bemused. The camera didn't give a close-up, of course, it was a fixed position, but I could see the bloodstains dripping down to the man's knee.

A strange sound filled the autopsy room. It sounded like someone opening a door that had been closed for decades and haunted by the ghost of Christmas Past. Kiera's mouth dropped open at about the same time the man's did.

"Oh, holy mother of God," Kiera whispered. She wasn't Catholic; I wondered exactly what Mary would do in a situation like this. Her son came back from the dead. She might have some useful advice.

His brown hair fell over his bushy eyebrows as he slowly sat up, much to the surprise of the autopsy-ist. *The subject is experiencing some muscular contracture post-mortem,* she said quickly. Because of course he was. That was the only explanation a woman of science could have to what was very obviously—

"It's a fucking zombie," Kiera said numbly.

Shit.

"It's a zombie," I agreed, and was surprised at how sad my voice sounded. It wasn't like I was a doomsday prepper or something, but part of me had always been surprised that the world hadn't ended quite yet. I'd never been sure of how we were going to go, but the fall of civilization had to happen sometime, and a niggling little feeling in me prompted me to quit college and start working in a store where I'd learn an awful lot about living off the land.

It's great to know that you're clairvoyant when you've been scratched by a soccer-playing zombie and there's nothing you can do but wait.

The man, who was quite obviously no longer a man but the undead, staggered off of the table and toward the mortician, who was slowly backing up with a scalpel and a bone saw. If she went down, she was going down fighting. As the man approached, I took a breath, finding myself disappointed as the feed switched back to the reporter.

I watched Kiera's face as I listened to the woman with the microphone. She had perky, curly blonde hair and bright blue eyes. She was wearing a black raincoat, looking quite cute under her clear umbrella. Her voice didn't match the severity of the situation. *The CDC has confirmed that what we are seeing is, in fact, the reanimation of corpses that have been bitten by the so-called cannibals. We have no reports on how often the deceased are reanimating, how long it takes them to do so, or what the chances are of someone coming back . . .*

I could see the blood draining from Kiera's face and held her hand more tightly, until my arm throbbed. I pulled my sleeve down subtly, half covering the bandage, as I looked at her. "Kiera. Baby. Talk to me."

She turned to me slowly. "You were right. You were

fucking right. The world is ending." That was when she slapped me across the face.

"Hey! What the hell?" I stared at her, somehow feeling like I deserved it for being scratched.

"Sorry. I'm sorry. It's not your fault. I know it's not your fault. God, Sean, I'm just so scared," she whispered, closing her eyes and resting her head against my shoulder.

I played with her hair gently, stroking with my good hand, and pulled her further into my lap. "We have food for weeks," I reminded her. "You did good. I can boil water without burning the bottom of it, so we at least can rely on both of us to feed each other. We have more toilet paper than anyone can go through in the amount of time it will take for this to be over. You heard her; the CDC is on this. Isn't that exactly who you *want* for this kind of thing?" The reassurances sounded weak even as they slipped from between my teeth.

"Didn't you watch *The Walking Dead?*" she said, clinging to me through her tears. "The CDC, like, fell. They holed up and didn't do a damn thing and said everybody's got the disease so hoorah, become a fucking zombie, and that's just how the world is now. What if this is just how it is? What if we're screwed? What if it never gets to be over?" She was hyperventilating.

I pushed her back gently, looking into her eyes. "You have *nothing* to worry about," I said solemnly. "I will *always* come for you. I will always watch over you. And I will never, ever let anything hurt you."

"Even if we have to live in the forest and pee in the river?" she sniffled.

"I'll even hold up a towel so I can't see you peeing."

"Promise?"

I offered her the only solace I could, and smiled. "I promise." *I promise to protect you, baby. Even if it's from myself.*

Planning for the Apocalypse

~ Kiera ~

It wasn't quite peeing in the river, but I did take stock of our perishables and, well, stock. Math was more Sean's strong point than mine, but I could at least do the bare minimum to ensure our survival for the next . . . what? Few weeks? It had to be over in a few weeks, right?

"Sean," I called thoughtfully from the kitchen.

"Kiera," he replied. "The news is just getting weirder, babe. They just used the word 'zombie' on live, national TV. And the UN just called a travel ban to the US. So apparently it's just an us problem? Get it? US problem?"

Yes, he really did think he was funny. "Okay, we need to revisit the word 'zombie' in a minute, but are those beanie weenie things that you bought actually still good, or is this one of the times that we're going to listen to Kiera and go by the date on the bottom of the can?"

"Listen to Sean," he drawled. "Those are good five

years past the expiration. Promise. The Internet tells me so."

Great. So that meant there was a slight chance of disgusting miniature hot dogs in my future, if I chose those over starvation. I closed my eyes, resting my head against my pad of paper, relishing the cool feel of the pad on my forehead. This was such a mess. I was supposed to be working on my thesis: it was a novel about a girl finding her birth family, vaguely based on Sean's adoption story with Amish people added for flavor. I could be writing thousands—okay, a thousand—words by now. Or selling overpriced textbooks to unsuspecting freshmen.

I typed numbers into my calculator and frowned, tallying the little marks and columns until they made sense. "If we're careful, and don't snack too much, and eat all the perishables by *their real due dates*, then we should have enough food to last us about two and a half months."

I could almost feel his eyes on me from the living room. "Two and a half months? Are you kidding me?"

"There was a sale at Whole Foods," I protested weakly. "And it was my Christmas bonus from the bookstore. My couponing group was going insane. I got the best receipt out of the whole group that participated."

"Did you get a gold star, too?" he exclaimed, launching himself over the couch one-handed and coming to inspect the dining room. I mean, we didn't eat dinner in it, so why *not* use it as extra storage?" He started to read the labels on the boxes that were stacked on the industrial shelving I'd bought from Sam's Club instead of a dining room table.

"Maybe three and a half months, if we're conservative," I added softly.

"So what you're saying is we're good, baby. Your extreme couponing Facebook group has saved us, and I give you full permission to post pictures and tell them that you've won the battle against your significant other. I now endorse your couponing and I was wrong."

I dropped my jaw, turning and wrapping my arms around his waist. "I'm *right?* You're admitting that I'm right?"

"I admit that our storage unit in the basement full of doomsday prepper equipment, that I refuse to call doomsday prepper equipment, is likely less useful to us than your ultra pantry of doom. Yes. You are right. I'm going to buy you a three-inch binder for your coupons for Christmas."

Well, holy crap. Miracles did happen. I grinned, hugging him tightly. "You think this will be over by then?"

"I'm almost sure of it, baby." His eyes were wrinkled around the corners.

I pulled back, studying his face. I knew him better than I knew my own reflection; I could tell that something wasn't right. "What aren't you telling me?"

"I was serious about the zombies. But we also need to be careful; they did . . ." He paused. He was struggling with something.

"Sean, you're scaring me," I whispered, pushing back a tendril of his brown hair. "What is it?"

"We have to make sure not to get bitten or scratched," he said firmly. "I'm not letting you out of my sight. They're saying that there's some kind of wild infection happening, and they're not sure what kinds of antibiotics will treat it yet. That's all. I just don't want you to get infected when I'm taking all the antibiotics we have."

"Oh." I sagged in relief. I had thought he was going to tell me something awful, something life-changing. Something I wouldn't be able to come back from. "Okay. Well, we just won't go outside, then. Right? And not answer the door except for police and EMTs. Just like when we were little. Stranger danger."

"You know, I was never actually taught stranger danger," he said deadpan. "Seeing as how I was adopted by some."

I smacked him on the shoulder. "You know what I mean. The point is, we stay here. I calculated that unless one of us gets really sick, we have enough toilet paper to last us at *least* six months."

Sean shook his head sadly. "You do have a problem when it comes to toilet paper," he said. "There are, what, five different kinds? Seven?"

Sigh.

As he held me, I nuzzled into his throat, sighing, only to pull back and frown. "You're warm," I noticed.

"Yeah," he said. "I don't think the antibiotics have kicked in yet. The steroid shot did, though. I feel pretty good." He tucked my head under his chin, holding me tightly with one arm, loosely with the other.

I tensed. "Sean, what aren't you telling me? I know you better than this. Something's up. Why aren't you telling me the truth?" I reached around behind me and grabbed his arm, pulling up his sleeve.

"Oh, shit, Sean!" There were tiny black lines escaping under the bandages. "You've got a blood infection or something! We have to go to the doctor."

He pulled his arm away, shoving the sleeve down. "No, we don't," he said, his lips pressed thin. "I've been up most of the morning looking at this thing, Kiera, and we aren't. Fucking. Leaving." He grabbed my face with his hands, staring down into my eyes. "I know that we're joking about toilet paper right now, but you haven't been watching the news. The city's in lockdown, Kiera. They quarantined us—and the whole country. New York City. Boston. Everything. Everywhere. No one's allowed in or out of where they are right now. It's not safe out there."

My eyes lingered on his arm. I wanted to tear away the bandages, to look at what we were dealing with. I wanted to channel my mom, to find her inner strength when it came to emergencies, to find my peace and calm and deal with what was in front of me and fix the problem. I could do that, right?

Right?

I swallowed, closing my eyes briefly. My mom could do this. She probably *was* doing this. She worked nights at the ER, and it wouldn't surprise me if she was in the thick of this right now, working on patient after patient with weird infec—

Weird infections. "Sean, if you don't tell me the motherfucking truth right now, I am walking out that door."

He blinked a little. I didn't swear very often. "Wait, what?"

This time I grabbed his arm again, holding on with all

of my strength, and pulled up his sleeve. "The door didn't bite you, did it? You got scratched by that thing. The soccer player. Didn't you?" Oh my God, my boyfriend got scratched by a zombie. What the hell was the right thing to do now? What would Miss Manners say? Hell, what would Betty White say?

He looked like he wanted to lie. My fingers played with the tape, felt the heat of his arm, and my stomach dropped. "Tell me the truth," I whispered. "Please."

Gently disentangling himself from me, he pulled me back toward the couch, guided me to sit down, and held me carefully. His eyes were glassy, as if he were trying not to cry. It was so unlike Sean that I didn't know what to do, didn't know what to say. He was the strong one. He was always the strong one.

"Yeah," he said finally. "I think I did."

"Show me?"

His hand gripped mine, more firmly than I'd ever felt him act against me in our entire relationship. "No," he said. "I got scratched. I'll deal with it. I'm absolutely sure that we caught it early, but I don't want you to see it like this. It's gross, Kiera," he said, almost cheerfully. "You don't do gross. It'll be fine. I promise."

I wanted to believe him so badly that it burned. My heart leapt at his words. He didn't make promises lightly, right? This was the Sean I'd always known. The one who strove to tell me the truth, tell me everything. He was just protecting me from the gross. He didn't want me to throw up on his lap. Something, any excuse. Some reason to believe him, to believe in us above this, us above all things.

"I promise," he said again.

"I believe you," I said.

I wondered how soon I'd regret it.

~

I wasn't sure how Sean was managing to take a shower with the massive bandage across his arm, but there he was, and there I was on the couch, alone. I pulled out my phone, my thumbs hesitating over the screen. It took me longer than I'd like to admit to open my messenger and press the icon for my mom.

I'd missed thirty-six messages. No calls—she knew I didn't answer my phone, even in an emergency. The messages started as if this wasn't a big deal, the calm way that I knew my mom to be, and I almost dropped my phone as I saw their progression of messages from serene to panicked.

I'm okay, I texted immediately. I hedged at the next message; what was I supposed to tell her? What if she knew something that we didn't about Sean, and it was bad news? I wondered if ignorance was truly bliss, or if I was better off knowing the truth.

Where have you been???? I've been texting you all night! I saw campus was on lockdown and

I stopped reading at the point where the exclamation points began to outnumber the actual words she was typing to me. My mom was freaking out, and I felt my own pit of panic begin to settle like a block of ice in my stomach. It had gravity to it, pushing me down into the couch. I didn't want to move, didn't want to breathe, didn't want to think anymore. I wanted my mommy to fix this.

I'm okay, I texted back. *Sean got scratched. He's got a weird infection but I put him on* everything, *mom. I think we caught it in time. It's not getting worse.* Much worse, anyway. I wondered if I should tell her that I suspected a blood infection; if I truly wanted anyone to know how bad off Sean could be. I felt protective over him, as if I needed to keep him away from anyone that would take him away from me.

Don't go to the hospital, she urged. *We're all overrun. Medics have to bring in cannibals that have been shot by the police, and they're attacking us. People are coming back from the dead. Christ, Kiera, this is a disaster. Stay home.*

My hands were trembling. If my mom was this afraid, this worried for my safety . . . she and Sean had to know something that I didn't, and I was determined to find out what it was. *What if Sean gets really sick?*

I waited, the three little dots indicating that she was typing, lighting up my screen. I knew she was typing, erasing, texting, deleting, over and over again until her words were perfect. I knew that she wanted to keep the fear at bay, but I also knew her just as well as she knew me. This was not okay. None of this was okay.

He won't, she replied curtly. *Text me the list of anti-biotics you gave him. It's probably the same treatment we're giving to patients here.*

I followed instructions numbly, listening to Sean singing in the shower. His voice cracked at a high note and I winced, wondering if it was bad singing or pain that caused the utter failure to all of music-kind. I wanted to comfort him, to wash his wounds and bandage him, to protect him from what was happening to him.

My mom didn't text very fast, and waiting was agonizing. I listened to Sean getting out of the shower, humming loudly, getting dressed and ready, I assumed. But ready for what?

That's all you can do, I got back finally. *Short of IV antibiotics. Keep it clean, keep it dry. I'll text you if we learn more. STAY INSIDE. I love you. Mom.*

Taking a deep breath, I crept toward the bathroom. Sean always kept the door cracked, mostly because he'd seen too many horror movies and thought letting the steam escape so that he could see psycho killers was a good idea. I angled myself so that I could watch him through my makeup mirror, and I bit back a low, desperate moan.

He was packing his wound, and it was bad. There was a thick ball of gauze about a quarter the size of my fist pressed into a crater, already soaking with blackened blood and green pus. The veins pulsed angrily, darker than they should be, capillaries shooting midnight trails down his skin. The skin around the wound was visibly shiny, gelatinous, quivering as he poured alcohol across the wound, soaking it. I was glad I'd bought a mess of medical supplies before this all started, or else we'd be treating him with Jack Daniel's.

I realized I was numb. I couldn't feel anything as I watched him double up on bandages to seal off the oozing. The bandaged areas were getting bigger and bigger as the goo spread, his skin purple and jet, shimmering in the low light before he placed the last layer of gauze on top. He wrapped himself up in tape, and I remembered the day I wrapped myself in ribbons for him as a birthday present.

I stifled a sob.

I saw his body sag as he called my name. "Kiera. You can come in. You've already seen most of it."

The world swayed dizzily before me as I looked into the sink. It was stained with red and black, like all of the ink in the world swirled down the drain into the depths. Thick clots of flesh and yellow nuggets of fat lay quivering in the porcelain vessel, obviously parts of him that he'd pried from his own flesh. I gagged, and that's when I noticed the smell.

It smelled of rot and ruin. It smelled like scorched earth, when lightning hits the ground and you know you've had a close call. It smelled viscous, the way I remembered the room smelling when my best friend gave birth at seventeen. I'd held her hand through it all, and it smelled just like this—endings and beginnings.

"Fuck," I said hoarsely. "What are we going to do?"

His eyes met mine through the mirror. "That depends on how brave you are, and how bad we decide this is."

"How brave I am? How brave *I* am? What the fuck do you think this is, Final Jeopardy? There's no brave. There's just me. What the hell are you trying to say?"

He turned, and I saw the black blood that had drained down to his wrist, staining the beds of his fingernails. "I'm saying that if this spreads any further, we might not be able to stop it. But right now it's isolated to my forearm, and I think . . . I think I have an idea."

Oh God. Oh, God, oh, God. This was not happening. Sean's ideas usually involved things that left me halfway up a cliff tied to his belt loop screaming into the wind because he thought rappelling sounded fun. Sean's ideas meant I would be in a tent in the middle of nowhere peeing in a river when the apocalypse began. Sean's ideas were *not sane and good ideas.*

But would they save his life? A quiet voice whispered in the back of my mind. Part of me, I think, knew how serious this situation was. Part of me knew that something was definitely wrong here, and it wasn't just a simple infection that could be dealt with by my mountain of antibiotics. Part of me knew we had to take action—quickly.

"Tell me what to do."

He raised his eyebrows, and my heart leapt. He'd never looked more beautiful to me; his skin was pale, and he was breathing hard, but his eyes were fierce. He looked like he would never give up on me, on us. He looked like his dying breath would be taken in defense of us both. And I couldn't give him any less.

"I need you to find something to use as a tourniquet, and I need every painkiller and bottle of alcohol you've got in the house. We need sheets, and towels, and . . ."

With every word, my breath quickened. Hell no. Oh hell no. We were not doing this. This was not that kind of movie. This was real life. This was not going to go the way I thought they were going. Was it?

I gagged again, closing my eyes, steadying myself against the wall. "Tell me you're not asking me what I think you're asking me."

As I opened my eyes to meet his, a glimmer of amusement glinted there. Somehow, despite it all, he found this *funny.* "You're such an asshole."

"Yes. I am. Do you still have the power tools your dad left you when he died in the basement?" It was an idea that scared me; I didn't know what would be lurking in the basement. Leaving the safety of our living room felt catastrophic, as if there were hundreds of zombies locked in the basement for no particular reason. I realized how silly I was being . . . but I was still going to be careful.

"Yes. I do. But we'll have to be careful if we leave the apartment. Are we seriously doing this?" I felt the world dissipate, tunnel vision enveloping me until all I saw was him. Everything was muffled, buried deep, and I wondered if this was how my mother felt when she was helping with something serious, something that changed you because you experienced it. Something that made you a different person than you were before it began.

Sean looked down at his arm. The pus was seeping through the bandages. "Yeah, Kiera. We're doing this." He paused, his free hand gentle as it touched my face. "Go get the saw."

I threw up.

New Beginnings

~ Sean ~

Clearly, I'm an idiot. Kiera is not exactly mechanically inclined, and I wasn't sure how much of this I was going to be capable of doing after chugging all the alcohol in the house. But it was the only idea I had. Kiera's yelling at me about *The Walking Dead* had given me the thought; I remembered something about a guy in prison and hacking a dude's arm off. I was almost positive he lived. I mean, he got killed by somebody later, but right now, I needed to live through the weeks long enough to get Kiera the fuck out of this.

So.

Neckties? Sex rope? What exactly made a good tourniquet? I dug through the bottom of the pantry, humming as I considered our options. She actually did have a tourniquet, I was pretty sure. It was a blue stretchy strap, and I'd Googled how to use them last night. The results all warned that wearing a tourniquet for too long cut off the blood flow to your extremity and you could lose use of it.

Well, no shit, I thought. That was sort of the point in this case. Maybe it was "don't bleed out" normally, but right now, "don't bleed out and get this limb the fuck off of me" was pretty much the name of the game. I could feel the difference in my skin; I could feel the heat creeping up toward my elbow. The infection felt like a living thing, trembling tentacles reaching up through my veins, contaminating me, lessening my chances of saving Kiera. No thank you.

She came back from our bedroom with the weird little jewelry chest I'd always figured held her childhood trinkets. We didn't pry in our relationship; everything came out naturally sometime, and her plastic earrings and the coins she'd crunched at various zoos and museums would appear eventually. Except that totally wasn't what it was.

"We do not discuss this box," she said, sitting down next to me abruptly on the kitchen floor. "This is not a box. In fact, you don't see anything. And my mother certainly didn't smuggle it to me. For that matter, you've never met my mother. I don't have a mother. I was brought down to earth by aliens and—"

"Okay, jeez, I get the point. What the hell do you have in there that you're claiming to be Superman or something?" I laid the tourniquet in front of me, along with the towels she'd brought back. We'd just mopped the kitchen floor, so it was as good a place as any. I didn't relish the thought of cutting my arm off in front of the toilet.

She hesitated. "So you have to understand that my mom has some really fucked up boundary issues and I come by my coupon hoarding honestly. What I haven't told you is that she's a doomsday prepper. Like, for real."

I raised a brow, trying not to itch my skin. It burned, but the flames fanned higher when I touched it. It was almost as if the infection rejected human touch; rejected me, rejected my efforts to tame it. "Okay. This is new. We've been together for how long?"

"Look, you haven't met my mom yet, and that's fine, but she's crazy. And she sent me a bunch of stuff to take care of myself in case . . . I don't know. I think her running theory was EMP right now. Zombies were not on her dance card for this particular year."

I nodded, nervous energy thrumming through my body. "You're making me crazy, Kiera. Just fucking tell me what is in the magic box that is going to save me."

She winced, and I could see her smaller form shaking. "Don't say that," she said softly. "You don't need saving. This is . . . this is just a precaution. This is just a good idea. We're not—we're not saving you. We're not. You don't need saving."

I had to calm her down. She had to be okay during this, because I would not be. And I wasn't sure how to handle that transition, that realization: I wasn't going to be her savior here, because she would have to be mine. The person I most wanted to protect turned out to be the one who I needed to save me in the end.

"Right. It's just a precaution. I can still sell tents with one and a half arms, Kiera. Things will go back to normal and I'll get a snarky tattoo on the stump about how I lost my arm to a zombie." I reached out, holding her hand. My skin was inflamed, hot and throbbing beneath her cool touch.

She sighed, opening the box, pulling out a vial and one of the many syringes. "Among other things, she stole Fentanyl from the ER. I don't know how she did it, but she did. Fentanyl will fuck you up, Sean. But I don't think you'll feel much. It's, like, super heavy duty. And I . . . I maybe Googled your weight class, figured it out."

I was surprisingly proud of her entrepreneurship. She didn't usually take the initiative to do things like this, though I knew she was capable. She was more than capable of handling her own life, handling herself, and even handling me when I needed it, but she preferred to let me live in the lead.

"All right," I said cautiously. "Then let's walk through it now. Go grab me a Sharpie."

Kiera winced. "My poor Sharpies," she said, trying to laugh it off. She had a humongous Sharpie collection, one that rivaled OfficeMax. Returning with a bright pink marker, she sat down next to me, her eyes wide, the whites showing.

"Don't be nervous," I said softly. "We've got this. The important thing to remember is that you are in charge of mopping the floor, even though it is gross, and that's your job."

She snorted, giggling. "No part of this is my job," she protested. "You're the manly man. Why can't you mop?"

"I'll mop with it taped to my stump. It's okay. Let

the newly alternately-abled man handle the household chores. I can do it while high on Fentanyl."

"All right, all right." She sobered, looking down at my arm. "Let me see it."

I closed my eyes, hissing an exhale. I *really* didn't want to show her what we were working with, but if I was asking her to do this, she had a right to see why. I slowly tore off the tape, grunting as the squishy flesh went with it, and dropped it to the floor. I pried the gauze off of the pus-ridden surface, letting it fall to the side.

"All of it," she demanded.

Fuck. "All right," I conceded, and grabbed the hemostat forceps that I'd gotten from the bottom of the pantry. I used them to pry out the balled up gauze, a low, bovine moan escaping my lips. "Oh-holy-fuck-this-is-a-bad-idea," I said all in one breath.

"Sean," she whispered, tracing her fingers along the good skin around the wound. "I'm so sorry. I'm so fucking sorry I put you in this position. This is all my fault."

The gauze fell to the ground with a sick plop, a gooey mess staining the floor. The wound looked pretty much how I expected it to look, except that the veins were turning black and purple, like a venomous camouflage. The crater had dug down to the bone, the pristine white glinting in the bright kitchen light. I vaguely wished I'd changed the lightbulbs to soft white instead of this LED hell that gave her a prime view of the inside of my arm.

She gagged, and the stench finally reached my nostrils. I held her hand hard with my free one, looking up at her until she finally met my gaze. "It's not your fault,"

I whispered through the pain, panting raggedly. "I would do anything to save you. And I'd do it all over again. None of this is your fault. It's all my choice."

"Promise?" she whispered.

"I promise," I swore. "We need to get this done before the infection reaches any further."

She hesitated, and I took the pink Sharpie and made a dotted line just above my elbow. I wrote "cut here" in my ridiculously bad handwriting, hoping to make her smile. God, I was so fucking nervous. Was there any way to *not* flip your shit in this circumstance?

"What do I do?" She was steeling herself, and I had never been so proud of her in our entire relationship. I could see the mantle of distance and peace descend upon her, determination to get this done, to let it bother her later, after it was over. This was the Kiera I'd fallen in love with. She'd let a lot of parts of herself fall by the wayside in her quest for her master's degree, but this one . . . this one I was glad to see back. My battle priestess.

"Put on the tourniquet as tight as you can. I'm going to bitch. Ignore it. We're going to wait a little bit to see if it does anything nifty to restrict the blood flow, and you're going to give me the Fentanyl. Did you, like, YouTube this?"

"Did I YouTube how to amputate someone's arm? No. But I know how to give injections. My mom made me give one to my dad once."

"Your family's a real treat," I muttered. "Right. You're going to stab me with the scalpel a few minutes later. If no bitching is forthcoming, you're going to cut the shit out of it, all around, until nothing's left but bone. Screaming may occur."

"You're being remarkably nonchalant about this. I don't like it."

I took a deep breath and met her eyes as steadily as I could. "Kiera, if I told you that I am about ten seconds from pissing myself, would that really help the situation?"

She paused. "Maybe. I like to know you're fallible. I like to know that you're not totally in control here. That we're in this clusterfuck together, and it's something we can get through. That we're scared, but working on it."

"Then be glad I pissed before you came back with the box. Do you have the saw?"

She nodded, glancing to the counter where the power tool lay, and back at me. "Did you disinfect it?"

I nodded. "Yeah. I mean, I'm not sure how great a job I did, but I used alcohol and iodine, just to be safe. I was going to try to heat it, but I wasn't sure putting a power tool to a stove was the best idea."

"Probably not," she said.

I took a deep breath, closing my eyes. I opened them. Then, looking down at my arm, I clenched my fist. It was a weaker grip than I was used to. This was the right thing to do. This was essential. This was the last time I would see that hand attached to this body. And I was doing this to save Kiera.

I handed her the tourniquet.

Tourniquets hurt like a bitch, did you know that? If you do them right, *really* right, and not just to draw blood, it feels like a vise on your blood vessels. My body was not a fan, and I heaved, steadying myself with one hand against the floor. "Fuck," I muttered. "That's not nice."

"I'm so sorry—"

"No. Do not. Do not even. Get this done, Kiera. Please."

Her eyes shifted to steel, her expression set. I could see her dissociating, fading away from the situation as autopilot took control, as her childhood slammed into her body and took over. "Are you ready?"

She didn't even wait for me to say yes before injecting me with the Fentanyl. It didn't take long before a warmth suffused my body, making me relax onto the kitchen floor. I stared up at the ceiling fan, watching it lazily spin in ever-widening circles, flash shadows across the paint. "This shit is awesome," I said. I think. I was pretty sure I said it.

"Uh-uh."

I felt tugging. Pulling. I was shaking, the same way that you do right before surgery, when you're cold and alone and you don't know what's happening. I wanted to look—I didn't want to look. My breaths hiccuped past my lips, and I swore I was hyperventilating, even though I couldn't feel it.

I looked.

Kiera's gloved hands were covered in blood, thankfully bright red blood instead of black, and I stared at them in fascination. The blood was remarkably beautiful; it was a color I didn't see very often. It made me think of dreams: dreams where there was nothing but blood and fire, and the world was ending, and you were in the middle of it, screaming for it to all be over.

"Sean." I heard her voice from far away.

"Did you know the world's ending?"

"Sean. Stop. You have to stop screaming."

I was screaming?

I looked. Blood was flowing in staggered spurts against the pristine white floor. Kiera was up to her knees in it, kneeling over me, her hand deft with the scalpel. "This is the hard part."

I took Anatomy & Physiology in school as an elective when I was going to be an engineer. I knew what that little bundle meant. It was a bunch of nerves. Nerves did not like being touched. Nerves did not particularly enjoy being separated from their buddies. Nerves did—

Fire lit through my body, shrieking for blood and glory, pain ramming into my chest until I stopped breathing. It was sharp, crystalline, a hard, physical line between *now* and *what that girl is doing to me.* I couldn't open my mouth. I couldn't scream. The pain was beautiful.

The darkness was beautiful.

~

I rose from the darkness slowly, edging my way past the gray in my vision until I could hear a voice. Several voices; the TV, I realized. I didn't know where I was. Hell, I didn't know *who* I was. I tried to turn my head, and all I could manage was an uncoordinated roll that flopped my cheek against the carpet. So I wasn't in the kitchen anymore. That was progress.

I opened my eyes slowly, just enough to see the light. The living room lamp that looked like a llama was on, which meant it was nighttime. I craned my neck a little further and found Kiera asleep in her reading chair, her face swollen with tears.

Her cuticles were stained with blood. I could see the faint marks of first-degree burns on her hands, and I knew—I just *knew*—that she'd scrubbed her hands until they bled, under the hottest water she could get. I watched her as she slept fitfully, likely dreaming about what she'd just done. I knew this wouldn't sit well with her. My poor baby; she was not made for these times.

I steeled myself. By the time she woke up, I needed to have my shit together. I needed to make sure that I dealt with whatever grief would come, whatever anger and sadness would find me, and reassure her that she did the right thing. Kiera was too good, too pure for what I'd made her do. I wished like hell I'd have had the courage to do it myself.

But I hadn't.

It was hard to carefully turn my arm. The muscles didn't want to respond; it took everything in me to lift it, and I had to catch the stray limb with my free hand—my only hand, now—to support it. She'd cut exactly where I'd told her to, and the bandages were tight. There was very little bleeding; I wondered if she'd remembered to sew a flap over the end. I hadn't been in great shape to give her Amputation 101 at the time.

As I gently peered an inch or so beneath the bandages, not enough to see the wound, but enough to see the skin, relief swept over me. I didn't see any black lines, no pus-ridden skin, no gelatinous messes. I sank back down to the floor, exhaling. We'd caught it in time. Surely we'd caught it in time.

I found a water bottle, the TV remote, my phone, and some Tylenol with codeine sitting next to me. Clearly, my mother hen had been prepared as she'd readied herself to watch over me all night. I took the pills, took a swig of water, and sighed, clumsily grabbing my phone and scrolling through Reddit for more news.

I wasn't the only one ready for home brewed amputation, it seemed. There was an entire thread called "Amputation: Does it work? What happens next?" As I read myself deeper and deeper into the thread, worry bubbled in my gut like tar. There were mixed results on whether or not it worked—and what happened to the infected was the target of the discussion.

If the infection progressed, did you just die? Did you come back? Or did you turn become trapped between life and death, unable to stop yourself?

I scrolled frantically, reading every comment and upvote, searching for more information as best as I could. Nothing. *Nothing* told me about what was going to happen to me. As far as I knew, I was the first to be on this end of the amputation and willing to type about it myself, rather than having my "doctor" do it for me. None of the other "patients" had been willing to talk about their experiences online.

So I started a new thread.

"Document of a Homegrown Amputee: Day One." I detailed as much as I could remember, posting a clumsy picture of what was left of my arm, bandaged carefully by my loved one. I still felt feverish, that was for sure, but the antibiotics on board would surely take care of that. I made a list of what I remembered Kiera giving me, except the Fentanyl. I was pretty sure somebody would track me down and arrest me for that. Either way, my little journal was begun, and it was around the time where I was asking about the benefits of using the bathroom one handed that I saw Kiera begin to stir.

Her eyes fluttered open slowly, unseeing, still dreaming. I watched her, my heart stopping in my chest as her gaze met mine, hazy and sleepy. She smiled the beautiful, brilliant smile she gave only for me. "Hey, baby," she murmured, her words still slurred by fatigue. "What time is it?"

I glanced at the clock on my phone. How is it that you can be staring at your phone for an hour and look at the clock six times and still have absolutely no idea how to answer that question? "It's about 11:30. At night. We've survived our first day of the zombie apocalypse."

She nearly fell out of her chair all at once in an attempt to get to me. "Shit, Sean! Are you okay? I forgot. Oh my God, I fell asleep. Are you okay? Do you need anything?"

I reached to cradle her face in my hand and stopped short, wincing at the pull of the muscles that weren't there anymore. I cleared my throat to cover how heartbroken I suddenly felt. "I'm okay, babe. I promise. I'm waiting for the codeine to kick in. It's not as fast as I would like, but all things considered . . ."

Tears sprang to her eyes, and I knew she was doing

everything she could to hold them in. "Sean, I'm so sorry. I'm so sorry I had to do that to you. I'm so fucking sorry."

"Hey," I whispered. I reached over with my good hand, tracing a line down her cheek. "I basically gave you marching orders, Kiera. I knew that this was what needed to happen to keep me safe for you, and I convinced you to do it. I don't know if you would have listened if you hadn't been so scared in the first place. I made you do it, baby. Don't ever blame yourself for this. I'm fine. I will *be* fine. I promise."

She held my arm gently, above the bandages, and my tendons screamed at me. I took a deep breath, feeling the phantom pains of a limb no longer there, and gave her the biggest smile I could. "Does this mean I get you to hold me while I pee?"

Kiera sputtered, trying not to laugh. "You're ridiculous," she said softly. "Most people . . . most people would be devastated, and you're making jokes. Besides, watching you pee isn't sexy."

"True." I winced, slowly trying to sit up. I backed up against the couch for support, gasping as each movement really took it out of me. I felt weak, like a toy thrown against the wall. "I'm not gonna lie, this fucking sucks. I think it will suck more if we run out of codeine. But for now, I'm okay."

I paused, looking at the concern in her eyes. I lied to her already; I didn't want to keep doing it. "I just . . . it's weird, you know? I can still feel my hand. I keep trying to make a fist. I can't . . . I can't."

She sniffled softly, caressing the skin above my bandages. I didn't have the heart to tell her it hurt every time she made my muscles twitch. "I read all about amputations while you were out," she said quietly. "And I made sure to close it well. I don't know much about medical stuff, but I knew about the flap. You were talking about it in your sleep. I wanted to tell you I remembered."

I smiled, resting my head back against the couch. My body felt like lead; I felt like my blood was turning to stone, weighing me down, pressing me into the floor until I would disappear. There was a strange clarity in my mind, a silence that normally held my thoughts. It was like I was thinking at myself, but no one was there. It was the strangest sensation I'd ever had.

"So are you going to tell me why I'm on the floor?"

Kiera raised a brow. "You outweigh me by over a hundred pounds, and you think I'm going to be able to lift you onto the couch? Half an arm does not diminish your weight class by all that much."

She had a point. I looked up at the couch, back at the floor, and made a decision. "That's okay. I'm comfy here." I held out my other arm, suddenly desperate for the contact. I felt lost, after this amputation. I was normally the one in control, and it felt like my life was spiraling out of it. What do you do when nothing makes sense anymore?

Kiera snuggled tightly against me, careful not to touch my arm, her hand on my chest. "You're still warm," she murmured softly.

"I know. Antibiotics take time. Don't worry so much."

I flipped through Hulu, determined to find something to lift her mind off of what she'd done, and found *Sailor Moon*. "All right! Half-naked schoolgirls."

Her eyes were leaking tears against my chest as she cuddled closer. "Please don't ever make me do anything like that ever again," she said finally, her voice shaking.

It was the closest I was going to get from her to an admission that she was traumatized. I swore under my breath; I knew this was a bad idea, but how bad of an idea was it going to be? How would she recover from this? And which one of us would recover first?

As it turned out, the point of mental health was somewhat moot at that point, as I heard the screaming begin from next door.

Sounds of the Apocalypse

~ Kiera ~

I hadn't finished feeling sorry for myself when the screams began. There were apartments on either side of us, and we weren't entirely familiar with who they belonged to. I knew one side was an older couple—older than us, maybe fifties or sixties. They seemed nice enough; they'd brought us cookies when we first moved in, and had a standing offer to let us borrow the proverbial sugar. We hadn't had many dealings with them since.

I really didn't want to know what kinds of dealings we were about to have with them, but I wasn't sure I was going to get a choice.

"Don't answer the door," Sean said, too calmly. "Don't panic, and don't answer the door. We've got this."

I looked down the ruin of his arm to the stub that I made for him. The sound of his bone cracking beneath the saw would haunt me for the rest of my life. I thought about him lying prone on the floor, passed out and panting, ranting under his breath, shuddering and shivering as I hacked through his arm. He started moaning when I dragged him carefully to the living room, making sure not to touch the fresh wound, and the grout in the kitchen was stained a pale pink, no matter how much bleach I scrubbed into it.

I would remember it forever.

The bone cracked again in my mind and there was a knock on the door. The slick sound of the scalpel cutting through his flesh echoed through my skull and I watched the banging, the door trembling against its hinges. I would do anything for Sean. I would do it again in a heartbeat. But I would *not* answer that door, I would *not* expose him to anything else.

It was my job to protect him now. My job to take care of us. At least until he healed.

"Please!" a man's voice shouted. "Let me in! She's going to kill me!"

I turned and looked at Sean, before looking down, digging at the blood in my cuticles. I scratched and scratched, trying to get the red stains out, trying to make it go away, only to open them up, mixing his blood with mine. I scratched harder, wanting to rub the stain out, wanting nothing more than to get rid of this memory forever. "Out, you damn spot," or something like that, right?

"We're not home," Sean said carefully. "Just be still and be quiet, and he'll go away."

I gave him a look. "Sean, not a few hours ago you were screaming on our kitchen floor. I'm pretty freaking sure he knows that we're home. You don't go from screaming to getting takeout at the local Chinese place."

He at least had the decency to look abashed. "All right, you have a point," he said. "But we're still not home. And I really want takeout now. Do you think Waitr is delivering during the zombie apocalypse?"

Well, *that* was an idea. What kinds of tips would you make on Waitr or DoorDash as a zombie apocalypse delivery boy? That would be pretty amazing, actually.

"Please!" An agonized moan came through the door. I shuddered, burying my face against Sean's good shoulder, guilt washing through me. It felt cold, like lead spreading through my veins, weighing me down into the floor. This was another human being, begging for help. Someone else that maybe I could save. Maybe I could do a better job and keep them from being bitten in the first place.

"Sean," I said quietly. "We have to help him."

I'd never seen such sorrow and pity on Sean's face. "We can't," he said with a sad smile. "We don't know if he's been bitten or scratched. What if he's injured somewhere that we can't amputate? What if he's infected and it's too far along for us to treat? What happens while I'm still healing, and I can't save you when the infection takes over?"

He cursed under his breath.

"What?" I said, narrowing my eyes. He only did that when there was something he hadn't meant to tell me. "When the infection takes over. You said the infection takes over. You know something that you haven't told me. Sean, you need to *stop* this bullshit! We're in this together! I amputated your fucking arm, I deserve the truth!"

Sean took a breath, exhaling slowly as we listened to the man beating at our door. "I know you're in there!" he hollered. "I heard you! Did you kill him? We can kill her together! We'll be safe together! Please, don't leave me out here, she's going to break the door down!"

Sean swallowed hard. I watched his Adam's apple bobbing uncertainly, watched the hair fall over his eyes the way that it did when he was unsure of himself. "Tell me," I demanded. "Or I'm opening the door."

Eyes widening, he stared at me for a long moment. "You wouldn't."

I untangled myself from his too-warm body, slowly standing up through the pins and needles feeling in my legs. "If I have to choose between you lying to me and me opening the door to a raving lunatic? Yeah, I'm opening the door to the raving lunatic."

"Fuck," he swore, running his one hand through his hair. He moved to sit up and groaned as his stump hit the couch, the blood leeching visibly out of his face. Stock still for too long, he remained silent, taking shallow, halting breaths.

"Got any more Fentanyl?" he said finally, panting. "Because if we're having this conversation, I need something to take the edge off of this."

Sean asked for the Fentanyl. I had an odd feeling that I shouldn't give it to him. Then I realized why: because I knew that he would need it even more later, when things got worse. I couldn't anticipate how rough this was going to get, and if he died, I might need to give him something to get him there. I was expecting worse.

I got a different vial, this time of ketamine. I gave Sean the shot. It took a minute or two before his breathing began to relax, before the pallor to his face shifted.

"Sit down," he said in a huff, more because he couldn't breathe than because he was angry. "I told you, I'd been reading all morning while you slept. There hasn't been a *lot* of information about what happens to people that get infected, but it's enough that I volunteered myself as your first surgical patient."

The banging on the door intensified. I could almost see him: Bang, his fist sliding down the wood. Smack, his nails digging into the door. "Please," he sobbed.

I heard the jiggling of the neighbor's door handle and swallowed, closing my eyes as I sat curled next to Sean, finding that my body was trembling. I snuggled into him for warmth and reassurance, trying to ignore the fact that his warmth was not a healthy one.

"I was reading a thread of someone who'd gotten scratched, like me. He posted pictures at each stage, from when the wound opened up to when it began to rot."

"Rot?" I whispered. "You're . . . rotting?"

His eyes flitted to mine. "I'm not sure what you thought was happening, but yeah, the skin is rotting. It spread. He got scratched on his thigh, and it spread to a major artery, I think. You could see it in the pictures: it was black. He'd gotten his boyfriend to take pictures when he couldn't do it anymore."

"Is that when you decided . . ." I squeaked.

"Yeah. I wanted to get rid of the infection before it got too far to save. I think we did it—there's no black skin when I peek under the bandages, but I'll have to unroll all of it to be sure, and I figured I'd give it twenty-four hours to, like . . . settle in before I start poking around at it. Anyway, his body started to rot, and that's when they started changing the vernacular."

I frowned. I knew what the word meant, but it seemed terribly out of place in this discussion. "What do you mean?"

"The couple lived in New York. Apparently this disease is fucking rampant right now, and they're discovering there's two kinds of zombies: biters and eaters. The ones who don't have the black rot just bite you, spread whatever virus it is and wander around to find more people to infect. The ones that do have visible rot . . ."

I buried my face against his shoulder, shivering. I didn't like where this was going, didn't want to know. Why did I have to know? Why couldn't we go back to yesterday, or even the day before, when things were normal? I could be planning our wedding with the girls at the bookstore. I could be cashing out freshmen buying chocolate bars instead of textbooks. I could be watching Sean read engineering books as I watch bad TV. But no, here we are, with a rotting arm bagged up in my trash can.

"The ones that do have visible rot?".

"They're more . . . aggressive. Instead of just biting people, they're the ones that seem to be actually cannibalizing things. They actively go after everyone, tear them down, and . . . feed, I guess."

Oh, God. My heart was fluttering in my chest, and I didn't know what to do. Tears sprung to my eyes as I stared at Sean: my savior, my love, my best friend. He was everything to me, and this new information meant that there was a possibility that I would have to lose him. I started to hyperventilate, hugging my knees to my chest, rocking back and forth. "No, no, no, no!"

I felt his hand on my back gently. "We got it in time," Sean reminded me softly over my cries. "We got it. You saved me, Kiera. You did it. You got the infection, remember? You got it all. No more black."

"No more black," I sobbed, burying my face in my knees. "No more. No more any of this. Sean, I can't do this!"

It felt like a whirlpool had opened to swallow me whole, a maelstrom to hell. I was falling, succumbing to despair, and my vision had a red tint to it. I was going to lose him. I would be alone. And then I would be eaten.

"You can," he urged me quietly. "Because we're in this together. Kiera, I promised you, *I'm never going to hurt you.* I don't care what happens to me; I will keep you safe. I will never do anything that would jeopardize your safety. You can do this, because we can do it together."

I looked up at him, swaying dizzily. "Promise?" I whispered.

He looked down at his arm, the gauze tinged a soft, cherry blossom pink. His eyes wouldn't meet mine as he smiled. "Promise."

~

I felt paralyzed. We listened to the sobbing at our door for at least twenty minutes, listened to him dissolve into screaming, and I imagined what was happening to my beloved beneath the bandages. He said it was rotting. *Rotting.* What I'd seen, the little he'd shown me, was rotting flesh, real and true zombie material. Had I taken off enough of his arm? Had we gotten to it in time?

I looked at him for a long moment and retched before tearing off to the bathroom, then hovered over the toilet as I threw up what little I'd eaten that day. *I amputated his arm. Oh, God, I cut off Sean's arm, and it was in the garbage can rotting*, and what if there were spores or something that came out of the bag and infected us again? I remembered the feeling of the saw cutting the bone, the splintered crack and the strange wetness inside of it, the relief that I'd managed to cut a straight line that didn't look like it would hurt too bad to sew a flap of muscle and skin over. I remembered the sewing, my seventh grade home-ec stitches that probably pulled too tight and hurt like hell. It looked horrible. But would it save him?

He followed me cautiously, kneeling down next to the toilet and rubbing my back softly. He was sweating, droplets beading on his forehead, and his eyes were slightly sallow. "Are you okay?" he whispered.

"No," I admitted. "I'm not okay. None of this is okay. This is fucked, Sean, and this is not okay." I took a deep breath and a swig of mouthwash, flushing the toilet and closing the lid so I could sit on top of it. "I can't believe we did that."

"Did what?"

I gestured to what was left of his arm, my stomach roiling in protest. "I can't . . . I can't believe I did that."

"You probably saved my life," he said gravely. "I'll keep

taking the antibiotics, I promise. One of them is bound to get me through this."

"You look like shit," I told him. Blunt always was my style. My thesis advisor had told me more than once that I needed to work on writing with a pen and not an axe. "Are you sure you don't have an infection?"

He shook his head, sighing, rubbing the sweat off of his forehead lightly. His head cocked as we heard a loud crack outside the door. "Shit," he swore. "Stay here."

Oh, like hell I was going to stay in the bathroom when we heard a noise like a bat out of hell down the hall. No sir, not today. I was on his heels as he tore for the door, needing to listen closer.

"Please, Marcia," the man sobbed. "It's me. You know me. We've been married for thirty years."

I nudged Sean so that we could share the peephole. The woman was coming slowly, and I couldn't see what was making her limp. Her arms swung low at her sides, and I thought I caught a bite mark evident across her wrist. I kept looking through the peephole at all angles, but I couldn't see what was happening.

The man held his arms out—to ward her off or pull her closer, I would never know. He was resolute as she came to him, that was for sure; it didn't look like he was even trying to escape. At least, from what I could see.

Sean thought of it before I did. "Open the window and climb down!" he yelled through the door. "I know it's far, but—"

The man glared at our door, hissing under his breath. "You're no fucking help," he growled. His face changed as his beloved came closer, at arm's length. He reached behind him, pulling the window up slowly, as if it hurt him to do so. We were on the seventh floor, and I wasn't sure how the hell he was going to climb down. The drainpipe, maybe? Fire escape? I wasn't sure if there even was a fire escape on that window. The woman finally touched his fingers with hers. She hesitated, almost, and I hoped that she recognized him.

I looked at Sean with hope. "Maybe—"

"Shh," he whispered, shaking his head.

She dove. She dove at him, her teeth gnashing, her nails gouging, and he didn't make a sound. He stared at our door, or at least that's what it looked like. The entire time as she bit and ripped at his chest, the woman too short to make for his throat. He watched us,,hopefully not knowing we were watching him, as she clawed his wrists to shreds, blood splattering across the hall. And then he took a deep breath and wrapped his arms around her.

"I love you, Marcia," His lips moved, and it looked like he said "I love you.", He was sitting on the windowsill with his attacking wife. And then he leaned back, and they were gone.

He didn't scream. I thought I could hear her grunting, grinding and rasping against his skin from the ground, but it was my imagination; it was silence for long, far too long. I counted forty-five seconds before I heard it. I'm sure it was my brain coming up with what it should have sounded like; I couldn't possibly have heard the sickening crunch of their bodies meeting the concrete below. Or perhaps they found the wrought iron fence that surrounded our complex, impaling themselves as a couple to the very end. If they were lucky, they would have died together, splattered on the pavement. If they weren't, she would be stuck there, skewered on the fence, waiting for some unsuspecting fool to walk by and become her next unwitting victim.

I needed to see.

I wrenched myself away from Sean as he stood staring at the door and ran over to the window, pulling it open with a grunt and leaning out as far as I dared. I saw gray and pink, red and white splashed liberally across the concrete, a veritable painting in death, colors that few people truly saw. He lay peacefully beneath her, or at least, that's what I'd imagined. I couldn't make sense of this: this new, terrifying world where husbands committed suicide with their wives.

He must have been holding her hard, hard enough to dash her brains across the pavement over his shoulder. He was dying, dying by his wife's hands and teeth, and still cared enough to make sure that he ended her life, too, so that she would no longer suffer.

I looked at Sean.

"I can't," I stammered.

"Can't what?"

"Can't do this. Can't do zombies. Can't do this. I can't."

He slowly walked over to the window and closed it behind me, leading me over to the couch. His face was flushed, but I couldn't bring myself to worry. There was a presumably loving couple dead on the ground dozens of feet below us, and it wouldn't be the last time. The entire complex was full of people just like us—people waiting for the end to come.

"It won't be us." It was a firm statement.

"Why not?"

He wouldn't meet my eyes, and I stared at his slightly jaundiced ones, urging him to lie to me, to tell me the truth, to make it all make sense. I begged him silently to fix this for me, even as I knew it wasn't fair to demand. I took a deep, shaky breath as he said, "Because I won't let it."

Infected

~ Sean ~

Okay, so that happened.

I'd never really talked to the guy next door. He got mad at me for starting my bike early in the morning to go to work; apparently it was louder than cars, and that made him angry. Or he thought I was a biker hipster, or he hated that my hair was long, I don't know. Either way, we weren't friends. But damn, that wasn't a good way to go.

What really stuck with me, though, is that he made sure his wife went, too. He let her do what the virus drove her to do: attack him, spread the virus, eat him, whatever it was. And then he took care of them both, because he didn't want to end up like that, because he didn't want to remember her like that.

They were splattered on the ground, and the lady across the courtyard was howling and screaming, and so was her dog. Granted, the dog probably wanted to *eat* the guy, but that's besides the point.

The point of the matter is this: I needed to lie to Kiera, and I needed to lie well enough that she knew what to do by the time it was too late for me to lie anymore. I was about fifty fifty that the amputation hadn't worked. That, or I was getting a regular, run-of-the-mill infection from a hastily disinfected saw that had last been used to fix our countertops. I kept reminding myself that we did, in fact, disinfect it, and maybe there wasn't sawdust particles and other, random house materials stuck in the blade.

My vision was sharper. I noticed the tiny clumps of what was protecting the arm that wasn't there anymore.

I could still feel it. I kept making a fist that didn't clench, flexing fingers that had no nails for me to dig into anything. I knew this was better than losing my right hand, but it was hardly a consolation prize.

I wasn't hungry. That, in and of itself, told me something. I was *always* hungry. I was the skinny kid at parties that inhaled the entire pizza by himself and had room for the whole cake, too. I'd always been able to pack it away—but this time, nothing.

Kiera was going to have a lot more than three to six months of supplies if this kept up.

As she sat huddled on the couch, miserably watching the news, I looked around the apartment. It was a two bedroom; she'd planned to make the second bedroom into a craft room or an office, if she got an editing job. My plans were slightly different.

If I thought I was going to turn, that was going to be my tomb.

I felt better, knowing that I had a plan. That door locked from the inside and Kiera was smart, Kiera could handle herself. If something happened, I could lock myself in and use whatever brain cells were left to convince her to get the hell out or kill me.

She amputated my arm, she could theoretically whack me, right?

I grimaced. Not a chance in hell Kiera would go through with it. I sat down on the couch next to her, wrapping her up in my arm, holding her against the furnace of my chest. We watched the presidential announcement on "The Infection," as they were calling it. Stay indoors, CDC has no answers, working on it, so on. In other words: this came out of the woods, we have no idea why it happened, and we can't fix it, so you're on your own.

When Kiera went to sleep that night, I decided I'd put a knife in the office. Somewhere she wouldn't see it—not that she went in there often in the first place. It had to be a knife she wouldn't miss, one she wouldn't need while cooking the meager amount of recipes that we knew. If something happened, if this all went wrong, I would do it myself. I wouldn't make Kiera a part of this.

I believed she was strong enough—but she didn't, and that's what mattered.

I stroked her hair as we watched the president talk about nothing, making plans and thinking about our future. As always, Reddit would have the answers while she slept. There had to be a timeline on this thing—someone, somewhere would be able to tell me how long I had. I'd been bitten, what, thirty-six hours ago? Two days? Time was slipping.

As the streetlights shined through the windows, lulling Kiera into a fitful slumber, I grabbed my phone and began to scroll. The answer was here somewhere. It had to be.

The problem was, I realized . . . that I couldn't lie to her for long. She needed to face some rather abrupt re-alities, if I was going to get sick. We needed to talk about final wishes, about how to keep herself safe. I needed to prepare her for what happened after—when I was gone.

Shit. This was going to be a gloomy day.

~

The knife was hidden underneath my asthma treatment machine. I sure as hell never used it, and Kiera knew better than to try to get me to take it—it seemed like a spot only I would think of. The knife was purple. It was part of a color-coded collection that she didn't know how to use.

The instrument of my death was the color of an egg-plant. Nice.

The Internet had more answers than I wanted, more answers than I thought I could handle. News flash: I was not the only one infected by a bite or a scratch. What *was* a news flash was that bites were going down quicker; it took only a few days for someone bitten to either die a grisly death, or turn into a . . . Jesus, I couldn't say 'zom-bies' and refer to myself. I could not believe or admit that this was happening to me. There had to be something else I could say, some way to make this believable to myself.

The fact of the matter was that the infection was killing people faster than it was turning them into the undead. Blood poisoning, vomiting blood, blood pouring out of your eyes, blood freakin' everywhere, and it was black and thick and gooey. There were pictures. Of course there were pictures. I didn't need to see some poor girl crying black, tarry tears. It was an image I couldn't delete from my brain.

The picture of the bite eating at her rib cage wasn't one I was likely to forget either. The scratches were better—there were holes, and gouges, and things that I didn't know belonged inside of a human body until this exploration had begun. But more importantly, nobody was dead yet. This thing had been going on for *two weeks* before it reached our town. *Two weeks,* and no one had said a word. Nothing from the government, the CDC, local police, the morgues—nothing. It reeked of a conspiracy, and conspiracy was my middle name.

I started to gather information. People had died of the bites, sure, but no one reported dying of the scratches yet. There was a lot of discomfort, and a hell of a lot of regularly infected amputations, but the subreddit for the disease was rife with people who sure as hell were still alive. One guy had been scratched pretty early on, eight days prior, and he was still kicking. The problem, though, was the infection.

The increased visual acuity thing was cool. At least, before it disappeared. Apparently seeing colors was something you lost during the transition. He had also reported better hearing, better smell—God, I hoped not. I got chronic migraines, and smell was my biggest trigger; I could always see auras when I had a migraine. I wondered if it was the same for them. I read on, biting my lip as Kiera rolled over on the couch. We'd taken to sleeping in front of the TV the last two days—was it three?—to make sure we didn't miss any emergency announcements.

What really worried me was the strange nausea that guy talked about. Food had become anathema to him; he couldn't eat, could barely drink, but he wasn't experiencing dehydration or starvation or whatever. What he *was* experiencing was stranger, and it pointed to something that I didn't want to admit to myself. He had a hunger that twisted his stomach, made it impossible for him to eat, and he couldn't name what it was he wanted.

I'd read enough YA zombie fic to realize that that probably meant he was turning cannibal. So there was that to look forward to.

I looked at Kiera slumbering fitfully, talking to herself softly in her sleep. She reached out and I held her hand, stroking my thumb across the back of it, caressing her soft skin. I couldn't imagine being so far gone that I would ever want to hurt her. But that woman who attacked her husband . . . She probably didn't think so either.

The knife was definitely the plan. After Kiera had gone to bed, I'd made sure that the door locked, and I'd hidden the key with the knife. Unless she came at it with a hatchet, she wasn't getting in without some serious effort and maybe the fire department or the landlord, and I wasn't sure if she'd be in her right mind to call maintenance if I was turning into a zombie.

"Sean?" she murmured.

"Yeah, sweetie?" I snapped to attention, hiding my phone.

"What do you think's going to happen?"

I swallowed hard, closing my eyes. What did I *think* was going to happen? I thought that my eyes would slowly shift to a paralyzing, neon green. I thought that my appetite was going to move toward something that I couldn't find, a yearning for sustenance that would repel me if I had even a modicum of myself to keep. I thought that I wouldn't go the easy way, choking on my own black blood, lying in a puddle of bile, dead on the floor, locked away where Kiera couldn't see me.

I was pretty damn sure I was going to go the other way, just because that was the luck of my draw. I sent up a silent prayer, a prayer to anyone who was listening, that I would be wrong. I *wanted* to drown. I wanted to cry inky tears as Kiera sat on the other side of the door, listening to me die. I wanted to bleed out from my stump, soaking the carpet in coal black, until there was nothing left within me except the breath to whisper "I love you" one last time.

Because the other way meant I would die trying to kill her, if I didn't time it just right. If I didn't gauge exactly how close I was to becoming a danger to the person I loved, I might be too late, and she might have to kill me herself. Or worse, she would go with me, succumbing to my hunger, and we would die or haunt together.

I supposed being zombies together wasn't the worst fate in the world. Maybe, somehow, we would retain a little bit of ourselves, and stay together. Maybe we would know each other. Maybe it wouldn't be the end of our world.

But maybe it would. And that meant I had to end it while she still knew me, while I was still sane, while she was begging me not to. I had to end it in the dead of night, while she slept, with a note on the coffee table and drunken bravery. I had to kill myself, so that I wouldn't kill her.

"I don't know, babe," I said finally. "I think that the National Guard will be deployed, and we'll find out how to stop this." I gently pushed her hair from across her face, looking down at her, only to realize that she'd already fallen back asleep.

I stayed awake that night, staring into the darkness, wondering how long it would take to die.

A Slow Turn

~ Kiera ~

Sean was asleep when I woke up around nine. I looked at the bloodstained wrap around the stub of his arm and gently began to unravel the tape. Sean slept like the dead, so I highly doubted that he'd wake up to my ministrations. Besides, it was time to clean and rewrap it.

How's Sean? The text from my mom was immediate, almost as if she knew what I was doing.

My hands trembled as I made my reply. *He's okay. Still has an infection. I really think we need a doctor.*

Don't was the immediate text back. *With the way things are going, he'll never get out of there. I'll over-night you something. Promise. Gotta go. Love you.*

That was my mom, for sure. Coming up with solutions for problems that she didn't even have all of the details for, sending illegal drugs across state lines via FedEx, and telling me what to do. I sighed quietly, finishing unwrapping Sean's gauze, and carefully unstuck the pads from his wounds.

The suture line was black. Fuck.

I couldn't tell if it was a run-of-the-mill infection or if it was The Infection, but clearly, we had to do something. "Wake up." I nudged him.

"Wha? Huh? What do you want?" he grumbled.

"We need to wash out your wound. It's gross and black and we need to keep it clean."

Stumbling blindly after me, he then sat on the toilet with his stump hanging over the sink. I noticed that his eyes were even more jaundiced, and a lump of coal sat in the pit of my stomach. I decided at that moment not to tell him, not to worry him. What good would it do, knowing that this might get worse? We would spend the time together that we could, and when we couldn't any longer, I would get him to the hospital before it was too late. I could do that much, I promised myself. He just had to be out of it enough to let it happen.

I poured a mixture of peroxide and alcohol over his wound, mercilessly. I ignored the howl, the way that he slapped his hand against the tub, the widening of his eyes. I ignored everything except using my fingers to gently scrape off the offending black. This infection was *not* going to take Sean. Not if I had anything to do with it.

He sat quietly, shuddering, and I saw his muscles contracting and quivering above the stump. The skin was clean now, if angry, red but with no pustules. The sutures held. *Thank God home ec saved me for once in my life,* I thought to myself.

I began to wrap him back up, carefully, pouring all of my love for him into hiding what portions of the infection I could. At least there didn't seem to be any of that strange vein involvement, right? We had that going for us.

Nerves fluttered through me as I finished bandaging him and smiled softly. "I'm sorry," I whispered. "I took a look and it just . . . scared me. I needed to clean it. I'm sorry I woke you up like that."

He shook his head, clearing his throat. "No," he coughed. "I've woken up in worse ways than that. Not many, though. Thanks for taking care of me, Kiera."

The what-ifs flared through me like wildfire. What would happen if he got the bad infection, the one that my mom was talking about? What would I do, if he died and left me here alone? Who would I call, to take his cooling body away from me, while I cried atop it, begging him not to go?

No. That was unacceptable. There was no way I was letting that happen. I would walk to the hospital myself, get what supplies I needed, and come back if I had to. I would give him any and all things that my mom sent me through the magic of overnight mail. And I would cure him.

His eyes flashed a little strangely as I looked at him and tried to seem determined. I frowned, not knowing what it meant. Sighing, I offered my arm to help him haul himself off the toilet, and we wandered back into the living room, turning up the ever present news.

CDC has determined the cause of the virus, the ticker tape scrolled. *A CDC employee has come forward to offer an admission of guilt, that her department was the cause of the leak of a biological weapon . . .*

"Oh, holy shit," I breathed.

"What?" Sean grunted, tearing into a Pop Tart.

"Did you read that? Are you listening to the president? The CDC said this was, like, something they were studying. They *made* this. What the hell kind of thing were they working on to cause people to eat each other?"

Sean looked at me levelly, eyes cool. "You realize that you can weaponize zombies pretty effectively, so long as you don't care about the casualties and who's coming back from the war."

Guilt washed over me. Guilt that I hadn't caught this announcement, I would have never known what my own country was up to; guilt that I belonged to a people who *thought* about this kind of thing. "Are you serious? The military would, like, send zombies into combat?"

"It's pretty easy to win a war when your troops keep coming after they've been shot," he replied quietly.

I closed my eyes. What did it all mean? "So why are there two types of infections? What's the second one for? If they aren't turning people into zombies, what's the purpose?"

Sean's eyes darted around the room, and I frowned. There was something that he wasn't telling me. "I don't know," he said finally. "I think it was a mistake. I don't think they knew it was transmissible this way, that it was so easy to get infected. Maybe they didn't make it strong enough to infect everyone."

"You're lying," I said, wonderingly. I was in awe. Sean

never lied to me. Sean was the paragon of truth in my life, the one thing I could trust, the one person who told me everything, no matter how hard it was to hear. "You're actually fucking lying to me."

He winced, and I knew I was right. "Kiera—"

"No. I'm not going to play this game. I'm going into our room, locking the door, and I am going to figure out what it is that you're too cool to tell me. I'm going to come back with the truth, and then you're going to apologize to me, and we're going to figure out what to do."

I flounced away, slamming the door behind me, before the tears started. I leaned back against the door, listening to Sean sigh, and started to cry in earnest, clutching my knees to my chest. Sean *lied* to me. What did that mean?

A cold, invisible hand on my shoulder led me to one belief: whatever it was that he didn't want me to know was lethal, or a doomsday sentence. And he thought he knew the truth.

Or that he was the truth waiting to happen.

Fuck.

~

Sean obviously had resources that were giving him information about what was going on with him, some ways of knowing what could happen. He wasn't the only one; I had friends too. I screwed up my courage and scrolled through my list, trying to think of someone, anyone I could call to fix this problem.

There had to be a solution. Somehow, we could fix this. And I wanted to believe that we could fix it together.

I hesitantly pressed my finger onto Callie's face and

listened to the phone ringing. She was breathless when she picked up. "This is Callie?"

"Callie! Hi. Oh my God, hi. What the hell is happening? What do you know?" Callie went to undergrad with me, and she majored in journalism. She didn't work for Reuters or CNN or anything, but she *did* do op-ed pieces for the New York Post occasionally. I was sure that if anyone had contacts, she would. Maybe she even knew more than Sean.

"Kiera," she sighed. "My phone is ringing off the hook. It's so good to hear from you. I keep hearing of friends who've been attacked, people that are, like, barricading themselves in their houses away from their boyfriends and girlfriends . . . it's a fucking nightmare. I think half my friends list is affected by this, and I can't help any of them. Has your mom said anything?"

"She said the hospitals are overrun and nothing good has come out of them. People are getting the strange black infection and are dying left and right, and if they aren't dying, then there's cannibals in the emergency room and they're attacking the staff. The last time she texted me was earlier, and she said that half the staff in the ER was in quarantine now. I don't know what the hell is going on. And . . ." I swallowed hard, closing my eyes, leaning my head against the wall as I sat on the floor. "Sean has the black infection. He made me amputate his arm. I'm not even kidding."

"OhmyGod," she said in a rush. "Seriously? And you did it?"

"Well, what the hell was I supposed to do? I thought

he was going to die! It was disgusting. The skin was black and mushy, the veins were like, pulsing and inky and I don't even know what. I swear the bone was turning gray. It was horrible. And I had to do it alone—he passed out halfway through. I don't know how I did it. I started drinking at about the time he passed out."

"Holy Christ, Kiera, I'm so sorry. I mean, I know you thought you were saving his life, but it still couldn't have been easy."

"No," I whispered. I cleared my throat to cover the cracking of his bone in my mind. "Anyway, what have you heard? What do you know? Please, tell me something. Anything. He had some gummy black stuff on his wound today and I'm so scared, Callie. And he knows something and he won't *tell* me. It's bad. I know it's bad."

There was silence on the end of the line for so long that I wasn't sure if we'd disconnected or not. She sighed. "Well, there are two possible outcomes, three if you think maybe it's just residual gunk. If it's just stuff from before and it's all cleaned out, maybe he'll be all right. I've heard of a few people who had amputations and they were fine. I mean, some of them got actual infections and ended up in the hospital—"

"I'm pretty sure we're headed that way," I interrupted quietly. "My mom's overnighting meds. She knows the FedEx guy on our route and she paid him five hundred dollars to make sure it got delivered." I hadn't told Sean that.

"Okay. That's good, I guess. And probably really illegal in about seventeen different ways, but I'm also sure your mom was a bra burner and doesn't really care about the law."

I laughed, a little strangled. "No, laws have never been mom's favorite. Taking care of her family, that's a different story. If this whole apocalypse scenario ends well, she's probably going to lose her license and end up at a CBD dispensary."

"Not a bad gig if you can find it." Callie paused again, her voice dropping. "I'm at the paper right now. Everybody's calling everybody, trying to figure out more information. I've been eavesdropping all day. The other two options aren't good—if he's got the black infection for sure, he's either going to die, or will become a cannibal. There's no other way, Kiera. I'm so fucking sorry."

I held back a sob, a prayer, the hint of hope that she'd given me that I'd gotten all of the infection the first time. "But he might be okay, right? If I got it all? If I did a good job?" I was pleading with her. Begging.

"Yeah, hon," she said gently. "I've heard of people that were okay. Not many, but it's not impossible, especially if your mom is sending in the pharmaceutical cavalry. Just keep giving him whatever she got you, and I'm sure he'll be fine. But Kiera . . ."

I didn't want to answer. I didn't want to move. My body felt frozen, like ice was slowly creeping up from my toes to my fingertips, numbing me and penetrating my bones. I couldn't see; everything looked like broken glass, shattered, as I grasped at straws. I said nothing. I couldn't say anything.

"If he's not. If he's not okay. You need to get out. Pack a go bag. Have him help you, I know he will. Or . . . he could leave."

"No!"

"Kiera, he won't be himself anymore. You have to be responsible for your own safety. If he turns into a zombie, he's gone, hon. And as fast as the CDC is working on this, I'm still not sure there's going to be a way to ever turn people back. Look, I've got to go. Be careful. And remember what I said: he won't be who he is. Don't forget that." She hung up.

I stood woodenly, shoving my phone into my pajama pockets, pants that I'd stolen from Sean because girls' clothes didn't *have* pockets. I wrapped my arms around myself, shivering, and looked at the door, knowing Sean was likely on the other side, waiting for me. Alone. Not knowing what the future held for him.

God, he must be terrified.

I flung the door open, and he practically fell into the room, blinking up at me. "Kiera? Are you okay? I heard you talking to Callie . . . I'm so sorry . . . I don't know what . . ."

"No," I whispered, falling into his arms. Arm. Arm and a half. I sobbed. "Why didn't you tell me? Why did you think you had to suffer with this alone? I don't understand. I could help you. We can do this together. Please, don't abandon me like this. Don't keep me out."

"I know," he murmured, pulling my head under his chin, cradling me tightly against his chest. "I'm so sorry

I didn't tell you. I didn't know how. I wanted to protect you—if I'm okay, you never needed to know. And if I'm not . . ."

I stiffened. "If you're not, what?"

"I'll take care of it, Callie. I won't hurt you. I promised you that." His voice was firm, solemn. Unwavering.

"Take care of it how?" I struggled in his arms, trying to look at him.

"Look, I don't want to talk about this, okay? We've already fought enough. I won't leave you unless I have to. I promise. But I'm not going to endanger you because I was stupid enough to get scratched. And, just so you know, I called the hospital while you were on the phone and asked them what to do. I . . . wanted to do something, anything, to make you feel better."

I closed my eyes. More good news. "What did they say?"

He sighed, running his fingers through my hair, holding me tightly, his amputated arm sliding down my back unsteadily. "To stay home," he said tentatively. "The nurse sounded like he was going to kill himself, to be honest. He said there are no rooms at the inn, so to speak. He told me you did the right thing by cutting it off, and we should get the arm in the dumpster immediately. He said the black blood attracts more of them, like flies. So I did that while I waited for you.

"The street is overrun, Kiera. There are cars and accidents everywhere. Neighbors are walking around, alive and dead, like they don't know what to do with themselves. People are attacking. I had to run back into the building. The security guard downstairs got bit. You can see it on his neck. And he's trying to kill everyone."

"So what else did the nurse say?" I said in a small voice, burying my face in his chest.

"To barricade myself in a room if I experienced symptoms, like not being hungry for a day or two and then suddenly ravenous. Or if my eyes change. He said if my eyes change, you need to get out immediately."

"Callie said you should pack me a go bag," I said.

"All right. I'm on it. But I don't think you should do that. I think I should be the one to leave. If you're conservative, you can stay here for *months* and be safe, Kiera. If my eyes change . . . just . . . please, let me take care of it?"

"What do you mean, "take care of it"?" The freezing feeling had come back. I was cold, so very cold. I didn't want to be alone. It was my worst fear. When I was a child, I was locked in the back of a truck in the cold, alone, listening to gunshots and not knowing when my father was going to come for me. I stayed there so long I had an accident, and it froze my pants to my leg. I was so fucking alone, and no one came for me for so long.

"Please don't leave me alone," I managed.

"Kiera, I'm not going to tell you my plans, because you don't need to know. But after talking to the nurse, I've got a plan, I'm going to lock myself in your office, and I'm going to take care of it. You might have to be alone, but you'll be *safe,* baby. And that's all I've ever wanted."

I looked up at him with swollen eyes, barely able to see. "All I've ever wanted is you," I said miserably.

His eyes were swollen as well, likely for a different

reason. I started to pray that it was just an infection, just a regular infection, and that if he died, I could be with him. Go with him. Take care of him. Whatever it took, I wouldn't leave him alone.

"I know, baby," he said softly. "But sometimes, all we can do is take the next right step. And the next right step for me is taking care of you."

I didn't know what the next right step was. I never had. I bounced from one thing to another, following the leader, the rest of the world telling me what to do. I'd never had to fend for myself, and now I was on the brink of having to be all alone, for the first time in a long time. It was the most terrifying thing I'd ever had to face; even more terrifying than the idea of Sean turning into a zombie and killing me was the idea of me outliving him.

Please, God. Let it be an infection.

Symptom Checklist

~ Sean ~

I was pretty sure by dinner that night that it wasn't just an infection. I mean, it *was* an infection; when I unwrapped and looked, it was red and angry, with the right color pus, and I knew damn well I had a fever. I was sweating like a whore in church. And as long as I could, I would convince Kiera that that was *all* it was. Because the rims of my irises were not usually that color, I was almost positive. They were shimmery, a little glittery, like the fake vampires in that one book Kiera tried to make me read. That didn't seem good.

But what really made me think things were going south was the fact that the underside of my arm—the side Kiera didn't seem to inspect quite as carefully—had tiny black tree roots growing under its skin. Little lines following my capillaries, deep under the flesh. It was barely noticeable; if you looked quick enough, it just seemed like I had varicose veins. But I knew better.

I was eating because I had to. I ate in front of Kiera at lunch because it served my purpose: feed a fever, starve a cold, right? Or was it the other way around? I was never sure, but I went with the first one, just in case.I examined the stockpile of food in the living room, and frowned. I wondered if it would be enough to keep Kiera safe and fed. It was hard to plan for a future that I wouldn't be in. I checked my knife. I made sure the window opened. And I made my plans.

I was going to stay around as long as I could, because I knew her: I knew her past, I knew her fears, and I knew that I needed to prepare her for this. Her mom was hundreds of miles away. Her best friend was in New York City. She had a handful of Facebook friends she had brunch with as part of a book club every Saturday, but I was pretty sure that they weren't the kind of people you'd go to during an apocalypse. She'd never had to take care of herself in any meaningful way, and she was neglected by her father, sure, but babied by her mother. Kiera had never cleaned a toilet until she moved in with me; what made me think she could run a zombie-proof household?

Maybe that wasn't giving her enough credit, but I still had to get to work. She helped me organize, packing the go bag I knew she'd never have to use, if she followed my instructions. We took stock of the pantry, making monthly lists of what to eat and when, and I conveniently made one for both of us and just for her, "just in case."

The FedEx man came, with a weird smile, and dropped off a package for Kiera. We looked up how to start the IV. It felt vaguely weird to be doing something so illegal, something that I wished we could've saved for her in case she needed it, but she needed this illusion, until I could get her to let go.

To let go of me.

"Kiera," I called from the couch. She was making some pasta, cheese, and chicken thing. I was hooked up to an IV hanging from a defunct lamp that I couldn't get her to throw out. It had a duck on it. I didn't know what the attachment was, but there we were.

"Yes, baby? Are you feeling okay?" She rushed to my side, spoon still in hand, and dripped sauce on my shirt. "Shit. Sorry."

I started laughing. It was the most levity that I'd found in the situation all day. "At least now I smell good. I need a shower. That sponge bath shit isn't doing jack. Look, we need to talk."

She came back and paused, returned the spoon back to the kitchen, and presumably set every burner on low. "So is it weird that my first instinct was thinking that you're going to break up with me, not that you want to talk about the zombie apocalypse?"

I hesitated. This was the part I hadn't planned so well; I hadn't expected to be tied to the couch by a thin, clear tube pumping fluids into my body. "Two things. The first . . . Kiera, this isn't looking good. I know that we're living by hope and . . . What's that song? Loving on a prayer? I don't know. I hated Bon Jovi. I'm hoping that this is an infection just as much as you are, and that these antibiotics—Jesus, how many days are these antibiotics?" I got distracted, looking at the box.

"A week. What the hell are you rambling about?" She curled a tendril of her hair behind her ear, and I watched the dining room light behind her make a halo around her face. Sweet Jesus, I loved her. Which led me back to the first part.

"This is not an 'in case the worst happens' kind of thing. This is a, 'I had made reservations this Friday for us to go to the expensive bookstore in the city and eat dinner at the little diner there, and I was going to propose in the Fantasy section.' But, you know, zombies. So I don't exactly have the romance angle to go with here, except for this: I've never loved someone as much as I love you. And I will never love anyone else the way that I love you. I know we can do this, baby. I know that no matter what happens, you will shine, and you will survive, and you will overcome. In the best of times, I'll do it with you. In the worst of times, I'll be your shadow, your angel. I promise. So even if we can't really get married . . . will you marry me anyway? Please?"

She stared at me for what seemed like an eternity, flour on her chest, sauce in her hair, and launched herself carefully on the couch. "You are the worst," she sobbed. "You are the absolute worst. Your proposal is 'I might be dying, so marry me'?" This is how you propose?"

"So . . . no?"

She slapped me across the chest. "Of COURSE it's a yes. What the hell is wrong with you? You propose now?" She was laughing, crying. And she was elated.

I relaxed, shimmying my fingers into my pocket and grabbing the ring. It was a blue sapphire with Celtic designs around the band, tiny diamonds among them. I knew nontraditional was her thing.

"Well, the 'what the hell is wrong with me' is the second part," I said softly.

She lay down against me carefully after I placed the ring on her finger. She watched it sparkle in the light, like every woman ever has done, and I smiled, nuzzling my nose into her hair. God, she smelled good: like roses and sunshine and everything good in the world. I couldn't believe I was going to have to leave her.

"We need to talk about what you're going to do if the worst happens."

"You are the absolute worst proposer on the face of the planet. You don't follow up the happiest moment of my life with your death. You just don't."

I held up the IV that was steadily dripping into my bad arm. "Well, you might not, but I do, because this is part of it. I believe in that 'better or worse' shit. And the worst might be that you need to live with my memory, not my presence. And I need to know that that's an idea you can get used to. I need to know you'll be okay, Kiera. I need to know you'll survive this, if nothing else, to tell our story."

"What story?" she whispered.

I paused. I hadn't thought that far ahead. "The story of proposing during an apocalypse and heroically saving you from my untimely demise. Write a book. It'll sell millions."

She lay quietly against my chest for a long time, looking at the ring. At the promise. For better or for worse. As in sickness and in health—and this was 'as in sickness' as it was going to get. I didn't want to tell her this, but I lay under her, dying. I lay under her, an infection overwhelming my senses, dulling my need for food, expanding my hearing. I could hear the neighbors across the hallway fighting. I could hear the dog across the courtyard barking. And I could hear the soft, tinkling beat of her heart.

"Only if you promise to be around to read it," she said finally. She clutched at my chest, shaking, stroking her fingertips over my collarbones. I knew she was scared; I could feel it. She could feel me slipping away from her, I thought, and she had about as much a clue as to what to do as I did.

There must be a way to find a cure. There had to be. The CDC was working on something, I knew it. I had to have faith that something would happen to save us all, to turn back time, to make this better somehow.

I just knew that faith would only take me so far. Faith might not beat the clock. And I was running out of time.

~

It had been, what, four days now? That was about the timeline that I'd seen on the Internet. As we settled in to watch the news for the night—nothing else on TV seemed to matter anymore—I decided that it was time to enact my plan. The black lines were growing deeper, longer, fatter. They were edging out of my bandage. I vaguely wondered what it would have looked like if we hadn't cut it off; would I have had an impromptu amputation by goo?

"Kiera," I said calmly. "We need to talk. About what we discussed earlier. My plan."

She turned and looked at me, an uncharacteristic repose in her eyes. "All right," she said softly. "Your eyes. They're . . . like, sparkly? They're not neon yet, but they aren't the color they're supposed to be. You told me to warn you about that."

"I know," I hedged. I hesitated, running my fingertips up and down the side of her arm. Her skin felt amazing with my amplified senses. I wanted to take her into the bedroom and make love to her one last time, but who knew if she would catch this infection from me that way? My last act of love would not be to doom her. "We're going to go to sleep together. At least, I'll let you fall asleep while I hold you. And in the morning, when the sun rises, I'm going to lock myself in the office."

"What are you going to do then?" she whispered, closing her eyes.

"Wait, I guess. I'm not going to take myself away from you until I have to. We can at least talk through the door or something, until I have to make sure that I can't hurt you."

"What if . . . what if you fail?" She winced. "I don't know what to hope for. If you succeed, it means you won't become one of those things. I don't want that for you. I don't want you to lose yourself like that. But I don't want you to do it, either."

"I know, baby. But I've got a few contingency plans." I'd been texting a buddy of mine from the store, Brett, on and off when I thought Kiera wasn't looking. He didn't live too far away, and he was too stupid to have any kind of hangup about saving his own skin. He lived for the thrill, and

I knew he'd enjoy taking his own motorcycle and riding through a horde of zombies to check on my Kiera.

"I've got people who are going to look in on you every two weeks. The last things I do . . . I'm going to text Brett and say goodbye to you, and that will be it. You won't have to worry about it anymore."

She looked like she was going to vomit in my lap. "I don't want to be talking about this."

"There won't be a smell, not with what I've got planned. Just . . . just don't go out back, okay? You have no reason to go out back. Put your garbage at the front door and Brett will take it."

I could see the wheels turning, but it wasn't clicking. Good. She had no idea that my body disposal idea involved hurling my dying form out of a window. I wasn't saying she wasn't clever, but I really didn't think she watched the true crime shows that I put on while I was cooking. It was something I'd seen in a murder mystery. The man had dumped the body out the window into a snowbank, and covered it with snow from the driveway. They didn't find him until spring.

"I can't believe you're doing this. Why couldn't it be me?" Kiera slammed her fist into the coffee table, shattering the glass. The sound was so unbelievably loud that I ached inside, more for my ears than for her. I knew my time was coming just from that. I exhaled loudly, trying to get myself under control, and took a deep, shaky breath. I held out my hand for hers.

She was reluctant, but gave it to me. The glass was

embedded in her fist, but she was unearthly calm, as if it had expelled the demons of the situation, talked herself down from her anger and fear. I balanced her wrist on my knee and started to pluck out the glass. It was thick and it stuck in her skin, slurping out of her flesh and tinkling onto the floor.

I said nothing as I worked. It took so much concentration to use my fine motor skills now. This was what scared me: my hands wouldn't grasp, fingers wouldn't work the way I was used to. What if I couldn't get the knife in? What if I couldn't do what I'd promised her? Holy shit, what if my plan fell apart because the goddamn zombie apocalypse kept me from being able to wield a Swiss Army knife?

"It'll be okay," she said suddenly.

I looked up at her, confused. I picked out the last piece of glass—a long one, embedded sideways into her finger—and grabbed the remains of the first aid kit that we'd been using to doctor my arm. "What? What do you mean, it'll be okay?"

Her eyes were shining—with tears? Anxiety? A radiating sense of righteousness? I had no fucking clue, but she was starting to scare me. And that wasn't easy. Kiera was the sweetest, kindest person I'd ever met, but she looked like a fucking tiger.

She shook her head, pulling the gauze out of my hand and wrapping it slowly around her fist. She didn't even disinfect it first. Okay, something was wrong in Kiera-land. I watched her carefully as she dressed herself, then settled back down against my chest. "I just know it will be. I'm not going to lose you. This will all be over soon, and everything will go back to normal."

Okay. So now my fine motor skills didn't work *and* Kiera was losing it. This was fine. Everything was just fine. I held her as tightly against my chest as I could, praying that she would go to sleep. Please, God, baby, just go to sleep. Because I didn't know what the hell I was going to do if she didn't.

~

Thank God one of Kiera's skills was not pulling all-nighters. She finally succumbed to sleep at around four in the morning, just an hour before I'd planned to be awake myself. I spent the last hour reading Reddit, hoping against hope that there was something out there for me, for us, that would make this all better. All I got were CDC techs breaking the law by telling us they were working feverishly on *something,* but even they didn't know what this thing was.

Great.

I crept out from under Kiera's slumbering form, walking quietly down the hallway for the last time. I looked at all of our pictures on the walls; the visits to the fair, the trip to Maryland, up and down the New England coast. She was everything to me, and I was about to leave her.

I looked back once more at her, asleep and peaceful, and my heart burst with love for her. She was going to have to be so strong. She was going to have to become a survivor, and I wouldn't be there to save her. It made me contemplate staying, just a little longer, to prepare her . . . except.

Except that as I lay holding her, while she stared blindly at the TV, playing with her phone, I *smelled* her.

And she smelled good. Not in the rose shampoo, lavender body wash kind of way. Not in the 'my lover, scent of her skin' kind of way. It was a way that scared me; a way that made me dizzy with a hunger that I knew I wouldn't be able to control if it got much worse. I didn't want to eat her flesh, per se; I wanted to rip into it, to give to her this sick, twisted gift I'd been given, to share it with her so that we could be zombies together forever.

Yeah, that one fucked me up. So here I was, carefully closing the door behind me, and I began rooting around in the mess for my knife, dropping things on the floor with clumsy fingers. It was becoming harder and harder to grasp things, and I was starting to worry that I was going to lose my grip on the knife before I could do enough damage to finish the job.

I was having a hard time finding my knife. Wherever it went, it was lost now. I went over to the door, thumbing the lock undone and went to open it, when I realized that the door would not—could not—open under my hand. It wasn't a question of my lack of coordination; it *would not budge.* The doorknob itself was jammed, unmoving, and I couldn't for the life of me figure out why.

I could hear Kiera outside the door, and even though it had been my idea, I was somehow panicked knowing that this was real. I couldn't get out. There was nothing I could do about it.

"What the everloving FUCK, Kiera? This is *not* the time to screw around! I . . . ." I leaned my forehead against the door, clutching my fingers against my palm. "This isn't a joke. I'm starting to get symptoms, Kiera. It's starting, and it's not going to stop. I need that knife."

"I also nailed the window shut while you took a shower last night. Just for the record."

It felt like a punch to the gut. I was doing everything I could to protect her, and she was literally losing her godforsaken mind. "Do you want to live with a zombie, Kiera?" I exploded. "Do you want a fucking cannibal trying to attack you through the door? What are you *thinking?* There's no time! I'm not fucking around, I almost bit you this morning!"

Her voice was wavering, sounded a little bit more hesitant, a little bit sadder. "I'm sorry, Sean," she said quietly. "But I need you. At least a little longer. I don't know how to do this by myself. Please. Just . . . use this time. Teach me what I need to know. And when you're gone . . . I'll . . . Brett can help me. We'll let you go. You can be free."

"I don't want to be free! I want to be dead! I don't want to be this thing, this fucking *creature* that hurts other people! I don't want this existence, Kiera, and you're taking that choice away from me!" I slammed my fist against the door over and over again, cursing under my breath. I couldn't believe she was doing this. I couldn't believe she was actually doing this. I realized that tears were streaming down my cheeks.

"Promise me," I whispered through the door.

"Promise you what?"

"Promise me that when I'm not me anymore, that when I can't recognize you anymore, you'll let Brett kill me. I'll help you survive. I'll make lists, I'll give you phone numbers, I'll make plans for you, but you have to let me go."

The silence was deafening. I realized that I was starting to get dizzy—truly dizzy, the kind where sitting down was not optional. My vision was razor sharp, and I could see every fleck of carpet, even the stains where Kiera had cleaned up a Diet Coke she'd spilled. I could see everything. I could even smell the coffee grounds that were mixed in with the carpet fibers. Everything was so beautiful.

And I could smell her through the door.

I moaned, sitting with my back against the doorframe, closing my eyes. This was going to be agony, but she was right. I hadn't prepared her. I'd spent all my time looking on the Internet to see what was going to happen to me, and not enough time trying to figure out what Kiera could do for the rest of her time in quarantine.

As batshit crazy as she seemed, she was right. I had to do this one last thing to take care of her, and then I could go.

"If you can't recognize me, I'll let you go," she whispered finally.

It wasn't the only whisper I heard. I realized, as we sat back-to-back through the wooden door, that there was something strange going on. This room butted up against the apartment building, and I could hear someone, something coming down.

The problem was, I wasn't hearing it with my ears. Well, I was—I heard the boot treads, the shuffling, the uncoordinated movements. I heard all of the vestiges of human movement and interaction with its surroundings; at least, post-human movement. But that wasn't all of it.

It's starting, the voice hissed in my mind. *It'sstarting it'sstarting it'sstarting*

Oh, holy fucking shit. "Kiera?"

"Yeah?"

Shewon'tunderstand

I paused as the voice laced itself through my brain. It was insidious, penetrating my senses, overwhelming my common sense. I wanted nothing more than to listen to that voice. I wanted to listen to that voice forever. That voice, not hers, was home. Family. Life. Everything.

I came back to myself with one thought. "Never mind," I said softly. "Let's start making lists."

He was right. She wouldn't understand.

Preparing for the Apocalypse

~ Kiera ~

I swear it wasn't a decision I made lightly. I didn't just go crazy and lock him in the office. I mean, I did, but that wasn't the point. I wasn't ready. I knew damn well I couldn't take care of myself—and he had the knowledge I needed to survive.

But, of course, my secret hope involved my texts with Callie.

The CDC is working on the virus, she'd texted. *They're talking a vaccine, maybe.*

A vaccine wasn't a cure. It would protect us, if we had to continue to go outside, though. It made me wonder if a cure was even possible. If there was a way to cure Sean.

I realized, as I sat outside the doorway listening to him making endless lists on pads of graph paper, that this was probably the definition of codependency. I realized that this wasn't healthy; I should let him go. He was going to turn into a damned zombie, for fuck's sake. But that was the problem: I couldn't see him that way. I couldn't let him go. He was acting *fine*. For all I knew, this was just a precaution. He wasn't the only one that could troll the Internet while the other was sleeping. He'd slept less and less as the few days wore on, but I still snuck in a little information gathering while he was in the shower.

It looked like what I imagined a dogfight would look like: torn meat, hanging with little, fine black hairs, broken open at the end and oozing. There was no suture in the world that would have held that together, I assured myself. I'd done all I could. And now, I couldn't see it at all.

That was the hardest part. My comfort, my rock, my person was in the very next room and there was nothing I could do to comfort *him*. I was effectively using him, in part, for his knowledge. The other part was a pipe dream, a hopeful wish, a desperate plea to the gods that somehow there would be a way to save him, to get life back to normal, so that I could finish my thesis, he could go back to school, we could get married . . .

The more I thought about it, the crazier I sounded. I blocked it out, closing my eyes for a long moment. I could do this. He was making me lists: how much to eat every day. How to dispose of my waste. What to do if the water, the electricity went off. A list of what was in the basement that he'd stored there over the years, making an apocalypse-lover's dream out of our little cubicle. And he was telling me, over and over again, to keep my promise.

If he didn't recognize me, I had to let Brett kill him.

I lay my cheek against the door, feeling the warmth of

what I thought was his back against the other side. "I miss you," I said softly.

I heard the slow scratching of his writing pause. "I miss you too," he said tentatively. "But this is right. Mostly. I'm still mad at you."

"I know." I winced. "I'm sorry. I mean, I'm not really sorry. I still think we can wait this out. I think that we'll beat this, Sean. Somehow, something's going to happen to change the way this is going to work out. I just know it." I paused. "There's just . . . there's no way that you can leave me. Not like this. Not yet."

He was silent for a long time, and I sensed that he was . . . doing something. He was paying attention to something beyond our walls, to something I couldn't understand, and I started to panic. For the first time, I truly felt like I was losing him, and I couldn't breathe. He started to pass papers under the door; my hands were shaking as I reached out for them. I couldn't—I *wouldn't*—do this alone. I was not letting him leave me. It was not an option.

"You're crazy," he said finally, his voice dull. "I don't think I've ever really noticed that you've gotten that streak from your mom, but you're just a little bit insane. Kiera, we're not going to beat this. I'm going to die, one way or the other. It's just a matter of whether or not you're going to make my afterlife worse with the knowledge that I took you with me. Or my existence worse by keeping me a zombie forever. There's no good way out of this situation, and you know it. I know you want to keep me, but I'm not a fucking pet. I'm not a parakeet you can keep locked in a cage. Kiera, I can smell you through the door."

"What?"

He leaned into the keyhole, his voice husky and stilted. "I said, I can smell you through the door. You smell like . . . meat. You smell clean. Uninfected. I can smell myself now, you know. I can smell the infection. It's sweet, like rotting flesh that's been cooking in the sun—that bizarre sweetness that only morticians talk about. And there is a part of me that wants nothing fucking more than to make you just. Like. Me."

I met his gaze through the keyhole, even though my body was shaking. Finally I realized that I was playing with fire, that this was a situation that I might not get out of. I was playing for time, trying to keep Sean alive until a cure happened, but what if it didn't?

God, what if it didn't?

"I promise," I said softly, as tears streamed down my face. I clutched at the door with my fingernails, digging rivulets into the wood until the beds of my nails bled. "I promise, I promise, I promise. I won't let you infect me."

"How are you going to stop me?" he asked after a long, long time.

Who knew? I certainly didn't. But I had a few ideas.

~

I spent most of the day sitting next to the door, on that Reddit site that Sean paid so much attention to. I knew the password to his phone, and he hadn't taken it in there to die with him, so I scrolled through the same posts that he had, tears leaking like a sieve. The pictures of what was happening to people were horrifying. I read the threads of tens, hundreds of people chiming in, discussing what they did with loved ones that were turning. "Turning," it was the word they used. Turning into a zombie. We were in the real, fucking, Godforsaken zombie apocalypse.

Man, my language was going to shit now that I wasn't going to school every day.

More importantly, I found a thread that Sean hadn't: people who had decided to "keep" their loved ones. The ones who decided that love was more important than some virus, or fungus, or bacteria, whatever the hell it was. People like me were out there, and they were out there in force—an admittedly small force . . .

The consensus seemed to be, so far, that it wasn't so bad to have a zombie in your office. They damaged the furniture, and the noise was a little much, but it was the smell that was getting to people. If they had injuries, they were becoming putrid, infected, and pus-ridden. And then there was just the fact that they were unwashed human bodies: no toothbrushes, no soap, not even hand sanitizer there to save them from themselves. The BO stench was more putrid than the putridity of the ones who had gigantic bite marks taken out of their bodies. I felt lucky on that point: the IV antibiotics had pretty much taken care of the *actual* infection that he'd had, the last time he'd let me see his arm. And the infected bits from THE infection itself were inside of his arm, I think. So long as he didn't over-exert himself, I had at least a week until the smell started wafting under the door.

That thought train was what stopped me in my proverbial tracks. Christ, was I really contemplating this? Was I really going to keep Sean locked in a room? How could I do that to someone I loved? How could anyone trap someone they claimed to love?

That was also about the point where I threw up in my mouth, almost spewing all over the door frame. This was wrong. This was so, so wrong. I had to do something. It had only been . . . I looked at the clock. I'd been sitting against the door frame for sixteen hours. In sixteen hours, it couldn't possibly have progressed that much, could it?

Trying to look under the door took a lot more effort than I'd thought it would. I squeezed myself as close to the ground as possible, my hands shaking as I wondered what I would find.

Sean was standing in the middle of the room, staring at the door.

His eyes weren't quite neon, but they were definitely green, and definitely glinting. I could see the black running up his veins on his left arm, pulsing in the low light of the lamp I'd turned on for him. He clenched his fist, over and over again, shaking his head.

"She wouldn't understand," he murmured.

"I wouldn't understand what?" I called carefully.

His head snapped up and looked at the floor. He approached slowly, the way the lions in the YouTube videos stalk a zebra on the plains. It was the first time I had ever been nervous in his presence; it was a predatory anxiety, one that screamed to the back of my caveman brain that I needed to run from this thing that was in front of me, this thing that wanted to eat me.

Holy shit, I just thought of Sean as a *thing*.

"Nothing," he said shortly, sounding dazed. He blinked

a few times, then sat down in front of the door. "How are you feeling? Did you read all of my lists?"

"I did," I said, fidgeting. My mouth tasted like vomit. I wanted him to hold me so badly. "I put the meal chart on the fridge. The news hasn't mentioned shutting off the power or anything crazy like that." My phone went off.

How's Sean? It was my mom.

He twitched at the sound, the way an animal twitches, an involuntary spasm reacting to stimuli that were exciting. He found my presence *exciting,* and not in a way that I liked.

Great. So there was that. *Idk,* I replied quickly. *Acting weird but fine. Will talk later. Love you.* How do you explain that there's a half zombie in your office?

"That's nice," he said vaguely. His head was hanging. "This really sucks."

"What's happening?" I pressed my hand against the door.

"I feel sick. Like I'm going to throw up on my shoes. I have a fever, I know I do. Everything's too loud, too bright, but I can't . . . can't turn the damn lamp off!" he growled. I could hear his footsteps stomping to the door. I heard the crash of glass and ceramic, and realized he'd knocked over the lamp once the light flickered and burned out. I could only see his eyes, his neon green eyes, that would haunt me for the rest of my life.

"Sean," I said tentatively.

"She's not wrong!" he shouted. "She's not!"

"Who are you talking to?" I asked, shivering. He sounded . . . insane. He was talking to himself? Was

that a symptom? I grabbed his phone and started scrolling. Nothing—and I mean *nothing*—said anything about
psych symptoms, unless you take cannibalism as a psychological disorder.

Note to self: that might make a great paper, if we ever
get out of this.

"No one," he said dully. "No one at all." I wanted to
believe him. I wanted, more than anything, to think this
was the ranting of a fever. But as I watched him in the
moonlight, I noticed that his neon eyes kept glowing in
the darkness. I wondered what he was looking at.

I had a hunch, and I didn't like it.

~

It took me until Sean fell into a fitful sleep to get up the
courage to go to look out the window. I wasn't sure what I
was going to see, if the zombies had made it to our apartment building. I went to the front door to see what had
become of our front hallway, then thought better of it,
creeping back to our bedroom, grabbed the baseball bat
he kept next to the bed "just in case," and went back to my
window.

I looked out. There was nothing. No movement, not
even so much as the spider plant swaying from its hook. I
couldn't see the man and his wife, and my heart dropped.
They were definitely dead, but where were they?

Emboldened, I went for the door to engage the chain, a
meager three inches or so. It was enough to see through.
My skin crawled when I heard a noise, one that I couldn't
identify.

See, the problem with these zombies was that, as Sean

was showing me, they had heightened senses. And heightened senses meant that the teenage boy who'd lived down the hall from us heard me engage the chain, heard the tinkling of the metal. So he came to investigate the sound, to see if anyone was around to spread the virus to.

Enter Kiera, stage left.

I held my breath, hoping that he wouldn't notice me. Maybe it was movement based, like *Jurassic Park*. Maybe . . . Sean said he could smell me. Shit. The lavender wasn't doing me any favors as the boy's nose perked up and he followed the scent straight to the door, punching his fist into the crack.

I shrieked, jumping back. I could tell how he'd been turned; there were lines of fingernail marks scoring his cheek, like the aftereffects of a nasty lover's quarrel. Maybe his girlfriend had gotten into a fight with him and turned him. Who knew? Either way, he was relatively intact, he didn't smell, and he still made me want to throw up as he stared at me with his neon eyes.

He hissed, a feral, somehow guttural sound that didn't seem natural—or possible—coming from a human body. It was loud, loud enough that it seemed like a roar, and that's when the worst sound I've ever heard, the worst betrayal I've ever felt, smashed into my world.

Sean made the noise back.

The boy was reaching into the apartment, jingling the chain with each movement, and I reeled back with all of my might and swung the until-then-forgotten baseball bat. It made a sickening crack as I met his hand with what little force God had bestowed in my weak muscles. His hand immediately went limp at the wrist, but he was still shoving his arm in, tearing the skin off his forearm, exposing the grainy, meaty muscle beneath.

I retched and hit him again, and again. It wasn't a hard target to hit; he was moving slowly, growling, reaching for me. I hit him, and I hit him, until the connective tissue began to wear through. I hit him, and I hit him, until the veins splattered open and the black blood stained my door frame. I hit him until there was nothing left to hit, because his hand was lying tattered on my floor, twitching.

"Fuck," I moaned. He was still coming, but it gave me the opportunity I needed to shove the door closed and slide home the dead bolt. He pounded against the door, over and over again, until I finally backed away, far enough away that presumably he couldn't sense me anymore. Only then was he quiet. Only then did I have a moment's peace.

But only a moment. That was when I remembered Sean, awake and moaning in the office in the apartment, alone. I charged back to the office door, slamming down to my knees looking under the door. "Sean? Sean?"

His eyes were bloodshot, and starting to turn lambent. His skin under his eyes was drooping just a little. He stumbled over to the door, kneeling down awkwardly, and stared at me with his eyes—red where it was supposed to be white, glowing as if he was lit from the inside.

"What'd you do that for?" he mumbled.

"What'd I do what for?" I asked nervously. He had been locked in the room the whole time. He couldn't possibly . . .

"Knocked his hand off. He just wanted to talk."

"He most certainly did *not* want to talk! He wanted to eat my face!"

Sean shook his head irritably, getting back up to pace back and forth. "He said you wouldn't understand," he said slowly. "Nobody understands. No one knows what it's like."

"Sean, *who* are you talking about? What's going on? Please, baby, tell me what's going on!" I was panicking, hyperventilating. This was beyond my scope of zombie-ism. I was starting to get the hang of having a zombie in my office, but having a hallucinating zombie—and one who could see through walls?—was too much. This was too much. "Wait, Sean, how did you know about his hand?"

He turned and lumbered toward me. He knelt down until I could barely see him under the door as he stared at me. I wondered what he saw when he looked at me. "He told me so," he said crisply. "Why'd you do that?"

"I . . . I thought he was going to kill me. Infect me," I said lamely. My mind was circling the drain, trying to find the common denominator. How the hell had the zombie teen talked to Sean? What was going on? How did Sean know about the baseball bat and the hand? Too much, too much.

"It's not so bad," he slurred, leaning back from the doorway. This was not the Sean I knew. This was not the joking, sarcastic man that I'd fallen in love with. This was becoming something else, something unrecognizable, and it scared the shit out of me. I was becoming alone, all at once and a little at a time.

"What's not so bad?" I whispered.

"This. The infection. Whatever. The fever hurts, though. God, Kiera, the fever is so bad. I feel like my skin is melting off."

I ran to the kitchen where we kept our flashlights and tried to look under the door again. His skin did look . . . different, prickled, the way that chicken skin did before you cooked it. He was sweating, liquid pouring down his face as he sat in front of the door, rocking back and forth feebly.

"What can I get you?" I whispered. Pleading. Dear God, please let there be something I can do to make this bearable for us both.

"Ice?" he asked hopefully. "Ice chips. Please. I'm so thirsty, Kiera."

"Ice. I can do that. Right! I'll be right back." It was an action, something I could actually help with, some gift I could give to him, last rites of love. I stood up quickly enough that I felt dizzy, leaning against the wall, closing my eyes.

"Kiera?" he whispered.

"Yes, Sean?"

"I love you," he said simply. For a moment, just a moment, he sounded normal. He sounded the way I knew him, the way I missed him already.

I realized, then, that I was mourning the living. I walked to the kitchen, using the wall to hold me up, listening to the soft grunts and moans coming from the office fade as I left. I opened the freezer and stared at the ice maker, before laying my head on the shelf, letting the cool plastic calm me down. It was inevitable, I finally realized. Sean was turning into a fully fledged zombie, and there was nothing I could do but watch and stay out of his way.

Or I didn't have to stay out of his way.

I gathered up the entire ice bucket and a washcloth, calm descending upon me, finally. I knew what I had to do. I treaded back to the office and unlocked the door.

It softly swung open. "Hello, Sean."

Twilight Time

~ Sean ~

Oh, holy fucking shit, she opened the door.

See, the problem with becoming a zombie wasn't that I was losing my mind—it was that I was losing my body, and my anger management skills. It was hard to move, hard to walk, hard to grasp—hard to do anything, really, other than charge at walls in futility and wait next to the door for something to happen.

I could still hear him outside, in the hallway. *Shehurtme shehurtme shehurtme,* he said. *She'llhurtyoutoo.*

No, she won't. I struggled to separate myself from the stream of consciousness style that he seemed to have. It was harder to *not* string thoughts together like that; harder not to think in ideas and pictures rather than sentences and words. *She won't hurt me. Not ever.*

Justwait, he said.

The door was opened about halfway, and Kiera was standing, remarkably calmly, in front of me with a bucket of ice and a pink washcloth. "I'm going to take care of you," she said mildly. "Lie down on the couch."

I stared at her before trying to command my body to do what I wanted it to do. I stumbled over to the couch, my feet dragging, and I cried out as My ankle twisted below me, knowing there was nothing I could do about it. It was a reflexive cry more than one of pain; I could barely feel it. The only pain I could feel was the fever, and the spreading blackness of my veins across my arm, up my shoulder. It had reached my chest since she'd locked me in there.

It would have been easier if I had had my phone. I wished I could still use my phone, the dexterity in my fingers gone. I wished I knew what was happening to me.

As I fell onto the couch, she pushed me gently into a lying position, propping me up on the pillows. "Not sick," I managed. "Don't . . . you can't take care of me like this."

"Shush," she murmured. She pulled a spoon seemingly out of nowhere and fed me some ice chips. They felt amazing, like liquid euphoria pouring down my throat. I was so thirsty. So very fucking thirsty.

She put some ice chips in the washcloth and placed it on my forehead, and I sank into the couch, finally able to relax. It felt like it was taking the fever down and chasing away the pain, just a little. But moreover, it was her presence that kept me calm, kept me sane. I could do this, if only for her.

But that voice . . .

Gethergethergether, he said.

No, I growled into my mind. *Not her. Never her.*

Her hand was cool against my cheek and I moaned, leaning into it. This felt like the worst case of the flu I'd ever had. I remembered, once, when I was very small. My mother had come in from a work function, and there was snow on her coat. I leaned into it, burning my fever into the snow, and it felt miraculous, like the world itself was healing me.

Maybe this was what that was like. Maybe she had some special healing.

"Any news?" I whispered, closing my eyes again. The smell of her was intense. Just her natural odor, the scent of her skin was cloying, overpowering, invading my nostrils and propelling me toward some primal urge that I couldn't quite name, couldn't quite pin down.

"CDC officially ponied up and said it's a parasite," she said quietly. "Based on toxoplasmosis. It was engineered. We're the only country that's been hit this hard. Everywhere else that has cases, the people were Americans traveling."

"Biological weapon," I whispered.

"To turn us into fucking zombies. I know. But now that they know what it is, they're working on a vaccine. Maybe even a cure."

Trying to find her in the room, my eyes flickered back and forth. It was hard to focus, hard to see past the details that accentuated every movement of my glowing eyes. She carefully spooned them into my mouth. "Maybe not," she said quietly. "But I've got a few ideas, at any rate. A few plans. I'm going to take care of you, Sean. You don't have anything to worry about."

I sat up all at once, as if possessed. My muscles strained to move, pulling like a freight train. "No!" I shouted. "No. Don't . . . don't take care. Don't do it. Don't expose yourself!"

She pushed me down easily, my muscles locking and then relaxing as I fell again into the couch. "I made you a promise," she said sternly. "I promised that I wouldn't let you hurt me. I plan to keep that promise. I'm not going to let you hurt me, Sean, and if you don't recognize me anymore, I'll do something about it."

She was remarkably silent on what the "something" was going to be, no matter how much I pleaded with my ever diminishing words. It reassured me that she remembered her promise not to let me hurt her, but what worried me was her definition of "hurt." If she was crazy enough to lock herself into an apartment with a zombie, what else was she capable of?

"You didn't have to break his hand," I added as an afterthought. "He wanted to come see me."

"Well, that's kind of part of keeping myself safe," she drawled, and I sighed. She was right.

I didn't know anything about the boy taunting me from outside of my apartment, except that I could hear him and he could hear me. I knew that he was young, only seventeen, and his mother had slapped him across the face with bright red fingernails. I knew that the red was not nail polish. And I knew that somehow, his mother had been infected.

He didn't want to remember before that, so he didn't. He chose not to. I wondered if I would ever get to a point where this new life, this new existence, was preferable to my old one. Preferable enough that I would forget this apartment, forget Kiera, forget our life together.

It was physically painful to me to think of, making me gasp and shake. I didn't *want* to lose myself that much. I didn't *want* to forget who I was. But this boy—he did. And I was scared that I wasn't going to have a choice.

"It's okay," Kiera soothed me, flipping over the washcloth and adding more ice. The melting ice trickled down my forehead, cooling me, and I sighed again, closing my eyes. This was the closest to human that I'd felt in hours.

Except for the lavender.

If it was a parasite, the parasite liked the lavender. The parasite wanted to join with the lavender. The parasite wanted to infect the lavender. And that meant I wanted to infect her.

No! I screamed at the boy. *How do I fight this?*

Youdon't, he said simply. His brain was amazing; it felt so smooth and calm, so focused, so full of purpose. At the edges of his awareness I felt . . . others. More than us. More than him.

Yougivein. Youbecome. You'llbe . . . oneofus.

Oh, like fucking hell I would.

~

I held on to that thought like it was the last bastion of hope on earth. I fucking *would not* become like him. The longer I stayed like this, the longer the parasite, the virus, the whatever melded with me, the easier it was to *think* about staying like this. Now there were starting to become points where I wasn't thinking, I was . . . *communing* with the boy outside the door. The picture/feelings were becoming harder to translate into words. It was becoming more difficult to talk.

And God, she smelled good.

"You need to leave," I groaned. She was smoothing back my hair while she scrolled through my phone. I could only assume at this point that she'd gone through the entirety of my browsing history and had read everything that I'd read, and then some. "This won't be good."

"You just have to hold on," she said. "They're saying—"

Another static moment. That's what it felt like: flipping the channel. I remembered being little when one or two of the local channels still turned off late at night, turning to static as I tried to will myself to sleep through the noise. It was an abrupt switch from understanding what she was saying, being completely in the moment, and wanting her to get the hell away from me to—other.

There was a curious blankness around the corners of my awareness. I was very painfully cognizant of the fact that *she* was close; *she* was different, not like me. I wanted her to be like me. I *needed* her to be like me. It was this driving need, a consuming and deep-seated desire to let her join us. The best way I could describe it was like *Star Trek:* that race of robot things. They were all the same, together, and it was inevitable to become like them.

If she stayed with me, she was going to become like me, whether she wanted to be or not.

Next to the need to succumb to spreading the infection was my perception of The Boy. This was when my brain felt like it was on fire; it was like listening through a marble wall that I couldn't scale, couldn't get better access to. I heard his voice coming from the other side of that well; heard his ideas, saw his thoughts.

You'reclose, the idea came. I hated the way that he thought: all squished together. It hurt me to know that I was going to end up like this; thinking in a stream of consciousness that would probably psychically damage my beloved writer Kiera to witness. Run on sentences were the bane of her existence. *Youcanmeettheothers.*

There are others? I separated the thoughts carefully, willing myself to be different. To not succumb. To retain some modicum of myself. The engineer in me thought of this like a problem to be solved: there was something here that shouldn't be, and I needed to figure out how to deal with the issue. Reroute. Overcome.

I didn't think it would be that easy.

Stairsareopen. He showed me pictures of the fire escapes, of apartments with doors busted down, of windows broken and bodies lying splayed against the floor, half eaten and gone. And he showed me more: more like us. More with pulsing black veins, injuries not bad enough to kill us, just enough to infect us. But more importantly, he showed me the link.

It was capitalized, in his mind: the Link. The walls of his even, level mind reminded me of a hexagon, and each wall of the Hex touched the wall of someone else. My Hex touched his; his Hex touched five others. Their minds touched five others. He had a local Link to everyone around him, all the time, and they all had one thought:

to get out of this building and Infect. Spread the Disease. Make THEM like US.

I wrenched my mind away from his and bolted upright, throwing up over the side of the couch. I gagged and coughed up black bile, thick like clotted blood, into the potted plant next to the furniture. Kiera stared at me for a long moment, not sure how to comfort me, certainly unsure of what the hell had just happened.

I wiped my mouth off with my sleeve and smiled weakly. "Sorry," I whispered. "It's . . . harder to concentrate now."

"What's happening to you?" she asked quietly. "What's it like?"

I sighed, throwing my bad arm over my forehead, shielding myself from the low light in the hallway. "I fade in and out. The boy outside the apartment comes, he talks to me. He tells me . . . there's others in the apartment building, Kiera. It's not safe to open the door. Text Brett and tell him. He's gonna need a shotgun to get to you."

She shook her head, tears blossoming on her long lashes. "How can I ask him to kill them? They're . . . like you."

"They're NOT like me!" I shouted, my body tense. I wanted to throw up again. "I'm different. I'm different, Kiera. I can do this. I can control it. I have to."

"Oh, Sean," she sighed, and resumed patting me down with a cool cloth, wiping my forehead, my arms. I hadn't noticed she'd unbuttoned my shirt; she was icing down my chest. The black veins had spread, closer and closer to my heart. I wondered if that was when it happened, when I faded out and never came back.

"If you don't think there's a chance, if you don't think I can beat this, why are you still here? What are we doing, Kiera? You can't keep taking chances like this. You're going to get bitten. One day, one hour soon, I won't be able to stop myself, and I'm going to attack you if I can't figure out how to stop it by then. And then what? We'll both be zombies? Is that what you want?"

"Tell me what happens," she demanded.

"It's a connection," I said flatly. "There's a connection between us. It's like I'm growing closer to his mind. We're sharing thoughts now. I can see what he's thinking when he's on the other side of the wall. It's like the goddamned Borg. When I'm talking to him, I want what he wants. We all want the same thing: to infect you all. Is that it? Is that what you wanted to know?"

"Yes," she replied evenly. "It . . . it doesn't sound so bad."

I snorted. "You haven't seen everything I've seen, Kiera. It's not just infecting. It's attacking; he won't come out and say it, but they don't infect everyone. Sometimes they just rip people open. They have to. They have no choice. Do you want that? Do you want to spend the rest of your life being an unthinking, unfeeling piece of a machine, hunting the living until someone shoots you in the head? Do you want to open your mouth and feel your blunt teeth slamming into the skin of a human, and know what it takes to tear it open, to end a life with little room to care about who you're killing?"

I was snarling, spitting. "Do you want to know what it's

like to kill? To swallow human flesh and feel it go down whole? It feels good, Kiera. It feels good. To him, it feels like everything amazing, like making love and eating a good meal and holding your family. Is that what you fucking want?"

She stared at me for a long time, tears spilling down her face. I sighed, reaching out to touch her arm. I was lucky; she didn't flinch from me, not yet. She would. I knew it. "I'll save you, Sean," she whispered quietly. "One day, I'll save you."

I smiled, and I knew that it wasn't a nice smile. "No, Kiera. One day, you'll scream, and Brett will shoot me. And that's how it should be."

That time, she flinched.

~

We didn't talk for a long time. She scrolled through my phone, texted on hers, going back and forth between two small plastic devices that held our entire world. I lay quietly on the couch, staring at the black blood vessels on the insides of my eyelids. My consciousness faded in and out, as the boy came closer and wandered farther away.

I was beginning to think he was doing this to torture me. He *wanted* me with him. It was more than the Link; it was a pack. A roving pack of once-humans, looking to seed the world with its infection. And the longer she sat next to me, the more I wanted her.

It was a physical feeling. My jaw ached; my joints creaked. I wanted something to bite down on, something to rend apart, something to tear into. I opened my eyes, blinded by the light. "Meat," I exclaimed.

"Potatoes," she said back, sounding a little bored. "Reddit is a bunch of degenerates with video cameras. I can't believe you spent so much time on this shit. What—"

"No, Kiera. *Meat.* I think it might keep me from . . . from . . ." I struggled with the imagery, trying not to gag. I knew that her blood was thinner than mine; I knew it would go down like silk. I knew that turning her, and keeping her in proximity, would blend her mind into mine, and we'd be closer than ever before. And it sounded so, so good.

"Like raw meat?" She sat up, suddenly excited. "I can defrost some stuff, I think there are some things in the fridge. There was a special at—"

"Kiera, I don't care," I moaned. "Specials. Coupons. Don't care. Please." It was all I could think about, now that I had the idea. I knew that everything we had had come from the butcher; it was fresh, bloody. I moaned.

You'resoclose, the voice came again. *Turnher. Biteher. Tearherapart.*

You're horrible! I screeched. *Why won't you leavemealone?*

I could *feel* him smirking. And then came the pounding on the door. It was slow, methodical: one knock. Another. I knew it was him banging his head against the door, slamming his skull into it and not caring about what would happen to his face. He was proving a point—and trying to scare Kiera into opening the door.

She was in the kitchen, I realized, and came back ghost white with an equally white plate covered in a bloody steak. "What's happening," she said nervously.

"Nothing. It's fine. Please?" My words were diminishing, fading away.

"Sean, this is not the time for 'it's fine,' tell me what he's fucking doing, or I won't give you the plate."

Anger flared inside of me, hot and blistering. God, I had never felt so *angry* in my life. I saw red, shining ribbons of blood distorting my vision, and I lurched up, off of the couch, and launched myself at her.

She shrieked, throwing the plate into my face, and I stumbled, feeling the meat hit my chest. I grabbed it with my hand, shoving it into my mouth, chewing the tough muscle and viscera that came with it. God, it felt so fucking good. It was amazing. I ripped into the meat where I stood, blood dripping down my chin. I didn't—I couldn't chew, couldn't make myself stop, wanted to feel the pieces, the flesh gob down my throat, stick a little. I would choke until it slithered down, finally, and somehow, that made it all the better.

I was halfway through the raw piece of cow when my vision came back. Kiera was staring at me, the same way you stare at a strange animal at the zoo. She was fascinated, she thought me grotesque, she was curious, and she was horrified.

I swallowed again and sat down. I didn't let go of the meat.

"There's a piece of plate sticking out of your forehead," she said clinically. Everything about her was distant: her voice, the way her little finger twitched as she spoke. Everything except the lavender smell.

Something had to give. I stood there with my meat,

hugging it to my chest, and I realized that tears were streaming down my face. They hurt; they burned, like acid. I wiped them away, and realized that they were tinted black.

"Kiera," I whispered. "You have to kill me. Before I hurt you. Call Brett. Please."

She offered me a small smile and came closer, her hands shaking as she gently reached up and pulled the ceramic out of my forehead. She placed the washcloth on it, holding it in such a way that she didn't get blood on herself. She sighed, closing her eyes.

"I can't," she said finally. "Because one day, they're going to cure this. I can't kill you. I can't let Brett kill you. I won't let you go, Sean. The idea of us—the idea of us being together again one day is all I can hold on to right now," she whispered, with a soft sob. "Making pancakes together on Sundays. Playing video games with my head in your lap. You're everything to me, Sean, and I can't let go like this. But . . ."

She paused, taking a deep breath. "What if I just let you outside?"

I stared at her for a long time. "You mean . . . to be with him? To attack people?"

Kiera looked away. "I texted Brett last night. We have a plan to close the doors to the building. You can be . . . whatever it is you are, without hurting anyone that isn't so stupid that they open their door."

"There's no one on this floor but you," I said softly. "You. And me. And him."

"Then I won't open my door," she said firmly. "But you

can . . . we can be together. I can still see you. And Brett can come up through the fire escape to check on me."

It seemed too good to be true. It was such a good, simple plan: keep me here, keep me near, keep me from hurting someone. Let me wander the building with the boy and his friends. Let me live with the constant hunger without torturing the living, without torturing what was left of my soul by hurting Kiera. And maybe, someday . . .

I realized then why it was too good to be true. The pounding on the door hadn't stopped. Somehow, I had to get him away from Kiera.

For good.

Opening the Gates

~ Kiera ~

I steadfastly ignored the pounding on the door as I extolled the virtues of my plan to Sean. I knew that eventually he wouldn't have a choice but to go along with this; Callie had been texting me. I had secrets. I knew things.

At least, that's what I pretended.

She told me there was talk of a vaccine, and that was encouraging; it was. I believed wholeheartedly in vaccines, and would get one the second it was possible, so that I could spend more time near Sean. But I was speculating when it came to a cure; there wasn't talk of there *being* one. Just that they were working on it.

As I watched Sean fall into a restless slumber on the office floor, I sat back and sighed, standing up and closing the door behind me. The rational part of me knew that not only was this dangerous, it was counterethical to everything our relationship stood for. We weren't this codependent; weren't this desperate for each other. But knowing I was losing him, that every moment I'd fantasized about, everything I'd ever planned for us was about to disappear . . .

It made me a different person. And I wasn't sure I liked her.

I sat down at the dining room table, surrounded by my months' worth of supplies, and buried my face in my hands. I had made Sean a promise: if he no longer recognized me, I'd deal with it. But I had carefully not specified what exactly it was that I was going to do. I planned to secure the apartment building, starting with the stuff in the basement that Sean had bought for his own thoughts on the apocalypse. I knew that the service elevator was closer to our apartment than the humans one; I also knew that the janitor left the key in it, because he was a lazy asshole, and so was my landlord. More importantly, I knew that it went straight to the basement, and it was unlikely to be used by zombies.

That made me stop and think. Just how cognizant *were* the zombies? Sean was doing pretty well with his rational thinking, except for the part where he tried to eat me a little bit. I wondered how fast that deteriorated; the boy at the door seemed pretty determined to get in, no matter what was happening.

Fuck. The boy at the door.

I thought carefully about the pounding noise that wasn't ceasing, wondering what it was doing to his head, wondering if there were bits of skull embedded in my door. Now was the best time to go, as it sounded quiet in the apartment building I realized that I was going to have to do what Sean and I referred to as the Stupid: that Thing in horror movies that you screamed at the hero not to do. Well, usually the heroine. The heroes weren't usually quite as stupid.

At least I wasn't blonde.

I checked the lock on the door to Sean's room one more time and opened the window in the living room, taking a deep breath. This was going to suck so hard. Athletic weren't among my finer skills. I climbed out of the window, hitting my head on the window sill. I started to climb, knowing my hands would only hold me for so long, and I broke my fall on a potted plant, gashing open my hand for posterity. This was starting out as a lovely trip.

Maybe this is what Spiderman feels when he climbs walls. I knew the windows of the people on the next floor down might be open; they had a cat that liked to sit in the window and yell at the birds. I could still hear the banging at the door as I slowly eased down to the next level. I considered my options to get down to the basement, and none of them looked good. I wasn't up to breaking and entering yet, though if I ran into a bunch of dead bodies in the apartment basement, that might become a thing.

I leaned forward as far as I could, realizing that I was going to have to give myself a little more daring than I had originally bargained for. I hopped over the railing, gently putting my feet down on the bare inches of the other side, and grasped the brick windowsill right next to it. I carefully tested it with my toes before moving onto it, holding onto it with my fingertips as hard as I could.

Looking in the window—don't look down, stupid, don't look down—I didn't see any zombies. More importantly, the window was open after all.

That would be when all hell broke loose. Or, at least, the awning below me broke loose; apparently I'd stepped on it one too many times.

I wouldn't say it was a scream, but I definitely did something, scrambling to catch myself as much as I could. My toes couldn't find purchase on the brick. As the awning shook, the metal rods creaking, I took one last breath and grabbed on to the sill with all my strength.

I held on to the window, listening to the sound of my sweater tearing beneath it and my skin beneath that. I could feel the skin peeling like a banana, tearing up and open, blood blossoming against my shirt, seeping into the yarn. I briefly mourned the sweater I'd made, and I fell, on purpose this time, making an attempt to swing through the open window below.

Hitting the floor, I was bleeding and panting. I listened to the sound of the awning hitting the one below, and the one below that. There was a hole worn in the toe of my shoe. I'd hit my head; an ache was blooming deep in my temple. This was a lovely fucking start to my adventure.

That's about when I remembered that we were in the middle of the zombie apocalypse. I looked up, startled myself, and listened hard. There was no pounding on this floor. No random batterings, screaming, or strange sounds. I did hear a TV coming from down the hallway, but I figured that as long as I left them alone, they'd leave me alone.

Or the zombies had started to watch CNN. Either way.

I crept to the service elevator, holding my breath as it creaked up, and dove into the corner. I pressed the button as hard as I could, as if that would make the doors close faster, and waited until I began to descend. Taking a deep breath, I started to relax. It felt like maybe I'd won this one. Maybe I could grab our shit, get back upstairs, and . . . figure out how to get back into the apartment from there.

I simultaneously realized that there might actually be zombies in my building, the awning of the sixth floor was gone, and I had no idea who was in residence in the basement at that current moment in time.

This was going swimmingly.

~

So at the very least, there weren't any zombies in the basement. I had that going for me. And I remembered the code for our combination lock; that was a feat in and of itself. Memory was not my strong suit at the best of times. I hunted around in our little storage cube, looking for something, anything that would help us. I realized that I was still thinking in those terms: us. As if Sean wouldn't be gone. He might be gone by the time I got back upstairs.

Great.

Morosely, I grabbed the huge hiking backpack, the kind with the sleeping roll and weird metal bars built into it, and started digging. There were flashlights, of course; MREs in bar form, some high protein stuff you mixed with water. Speaking of water, there was one of those straw-like water . . . purifiers? Condensers? Things? I wasn't sure what the hell it did, except it made water safe to drink. I grabbed that, too. I put the little fold up tent in there, the hiking boots he'd insisted I bought, and anything else that even seemed remotely zombie apocalypse like.

I really wish he would have sorted this by what type of apocalypse he was looking at. Firestarter, check. Hatchet? Did I need a hatchet? I probably could use a hatchet, just in case anyone else stuck their fist through my door. I realized I was packing for what happened IF: if I had to leave the apartment. If the electricity got cut. If this lasted longer than the eight months I'd calculated I could manage without eating myself out of house and home.

Jesus, eight months. What would this look like, eight months later? I slumped down against the snowshoes, resting my back against them and closing my eyes. The silence closed around me, and I sat quietly, listening to the noise in my brain, wondering how we'd come to this. Which way would the apocalypse go, I wondered. There were two options as I saw it: we would cure this or vaccinate our way out of it, or we would succumb to the zombies a la *The Walking Dead* and end up roaming bands of humans living out of prisons and burying our dead behind dumpsters.

And I would have to go it alone. Fucking Sean, getting scratched by a zombie. *Of course* he would be the one heading the line, making sure everyone got out. *Of course* he would be the responsible one, and get in trouble because of it. *Of course* it would be Sean, because why wouldn't it be?

I sobbed quietly, wrapping my arms around my knees,

and realized I was shaking. I sat there in the dark, with only a single, bare light bulb for company. Tears streamed down my face and I mourned all that I'd lost. It was that moment that I finally, finally admitted that I was losing Sean; that I couldn't keep him. Sure, I could pen him and his zombie friends into one floor, if I was brave enough and fast enough. And maybe I could do just that. But . . . wouldn't it be fairer, better of me, to let him go? Or was I being a better person by keeping them in, not inflicting more zombies on unsuspecting citizens?

What was the morality of keeping zombies?

No matter what I decided, eventually, I would see the life fade from his eyes. He would look at me the way he'd looked at me earlier: hungrily, as if I were the most wonderful meal on earth. He would look at me as something to hurt, to rend apart, to infect. And there would be little I could do to stop it—because I didn't think I'd *want* to stop it.

If Sean attacked me, so be it.

I realized I hadn't made the decision before that moment. If the end of the world was truly happening, if no one was going to save us from this crisis, I wanted to be with Sean, and this mind meld he seemed to have with the kid outside didn't seem so bad. I didn't want to become a killer—and that decided me on the blockading of the doors. If I could make the apartment building safe, if I could pen all the zombies in, then it wouldn't *matter* if I became one.

Except . . . it would matter to Sean.

If there was some modicum of him in there, some

essence of Sean-ness left in his mind or soul or whatever was left behind when he became one of them, he would be horrified to know that he'd turned me into a zombie. He would never forgive himself. He would never let it go. And it would torture him for the rest of his life, being trapped in there with that kernel of knowledge.

Fuck. I couldn't do that to him. I couldn't let him turn me into a zombie. I couldn't let him be the one to do it, if it had to be done. I had to fight this, with all that I had. I had to make sure that I got through this, with every ounce of determination and will I had left. Sean would want no less for me. He would want me to go on, to survive, to see what the world remade itself into after the crisis was averted. With him or without him.

Well, that realization ruined my day.

I wiped the tears from my cheeks, opening my eyes again, and sighed. I fished out the list that Sean gave me, digging around the cold basement and looking on each shelf. The one thing that wasn't on his list was duct tape, and I realized that might come in handy. There were some rusty nails and a board, and I wondered if I could block the door with it. I decided to bring that, too. I grabbed the backpack and hauled it all back with me toward the elevator. It more or less fit in or strapped to my backpack, though it threw me off balance to even try to walk with it.

The hatchet was in my hand. I was going to the seventh floor. And most importantly, that fucking kid with one hand wasn't going to be the one to take me away from the life Sean wanted me to have.

~

At the very least, the elevator didn't ding when it got to the seventh floor. The door opened smoothly, if a little crookedly. It was halfway between the stairs and our apartment at the end of the hall. There was a good chance that the boy with one hand was still in that hallway.

I had had the foresight to have the key in my pocket before I fell down through the window, just in case. In case of what, I wasn't sure, but I was damn glad that God, the Universe or whatever had told me to do it. Wrestling with the key with a zombie breathing down my neck didn't seem like my idea of a good time.

I peered around the edge of the elevator, and saw something I didn't expect.

Of *course* there were two zombies.

There was the boy, who I took a better look at from my vantage point, was outside the elevator. He was wearing low slung jeans, making me wonder if current fashion trends would hinder the zombie apocalypse. It was hard to go after prey if your pants were around your ankles. It made me think of a joke a mortician friend had told me once: he tied the shoelaces of every client he'd ever had together, just in case. At least *his* dead people wouldn't be effective zombies.

I made a note to do it to Sean, if I was given the chance. Making him a less effective zombie might give us more peace of mind.

The boy was wearing an oversized T-shirt, and I wondered what band he was into. I couldn't kill this kid. I wasn't sure I could kill anyone, much less a seventeen-year-old half dead kid who was communing with my fiancé. The other one, however . . .

I studied her. She was eighty if she was a day, somebody's grandma, surely. She still had curlers in her hair from the last night she'd put them in. I could see the permanently tattooed eyeliner and lip liner on her skin as she stared at the boy, not looking at me for the time being. It appeared as if zombies stopped bleeding very much once they turned for sure; she had a huge gash from her left shoulder down to her right breast, and it had oozed black blood in a trickle down her flower patterned nightgown, but that was it.

Sean was in my apartment, past the zombies. And I realized, at that moment, that while I wasn't sure I could kill Sean's new friend, I damn well could take a hatchet to grandma.

There was nothing to it but to do it, as my cousin Jason always said. I took a deep breath, baring my teeth and raising my hatchet, trying to look as fierce as possible. Topping out at five foot two, it never seemed possible before, but maybe I looked more intimidating to zombies than I did to everyone else. I was about to leave the elevator before I realized I could try a trick.

It worked in movies, right? I dug around in the backpack and came up with a a metal tool, one that looked useful in the kitchen but I couldn't place it. I threw it hard down the hallway in the opposite direction of the zombies and ran for the janitor's closet between the elevator and the apartment, standing behind a mop, hoping the potent cleaning solution would hide me from their sensitive noses.

I heard the groans, the lurching, the shuffling. I listened as hard as I could, realizing I was shaking, as I waited to see if my idea worked. I *needed* to get back to the apartment. I *needed* to clear this area. Hell, if I was lucky, the wiper fell down the stairs and they'd chase it down, letting me lock the door, keeping our hallway zombie free.

God, I could never be that lucky.

When I stopped hearing the sounds, I crept out of the janitor's closet, reevaluating my fierceness, and looked at what I'd wrought. Grandma was out of sight—down the stairs, just like I'd wanted her to be. I looked down the hallway, only to find Zombie Kid staring mutely at the wall, the wall that Sean was lying next to.

Fucking fuck.

I managed to force my way down the hallway, pretending the hatchet was a fully fledged sword, or a gun, or something more useful to me than this, and carefully shut the stairway door before grandma could come back. That solved one problem, and created another. There was only one stairwell: the one grandma had gone down, which was now blocked off unless she had the ability to turn doorknobs.

So now I had one zombie to deal with. This was fine. This was all fine. I walked down the hallway calmly, slowly, waiting for him to notice me.

Notice me he did. He turned, leaning against the wall,

almost casually. He looked like any normal teenager, except that his eyes were leaking black stuff, and he had no hand. He had big, angry scratches across his face, and his eyes were neon green. He stared at me, and I shook.

"Don't . . . don't come any closer," I said nervously, brandishing my hatchet. "I'll do it. Leave me alone. Leave Sean alone!"

He said nothing, obviously, staring at me with those lambent, jaded eyes. He held up his arm, showing off the bone I'd whacked. Holy fucking shit, did he have memory?

"Yeah," I said toughly. "I did that. And I'll do more if you don't get out of my way." I made practice strokes with my hatchet, lashing out at him, again and again.

He snarled, lurching forward, reaching his arms out toward me. I could see him gnashing his teeth, feel the fetid breath from his mouth as he got closer and closer—and then he hit a wall. Almost literally; he stopped dead three feet in front of me, as if there was something that he couldn't get through. And I had no fucking clue what it was.

I hugged the opposite wall, taking my luck and running with it, scooting around him and edging into the apartment. He kept snarling, lashing out at me with his arms, waving and flinging his black blood at me with every movement. His eyes were vicious, hungry, and I shook as I closed the door, locking it behind me.

This was our future. And I had no way out.

Turning a Little Dead

~ Sean ~

I was pacing, stumbling around the room until she came back, waving my half an arm around the room and communing with the kid in the hallway. *You will not fucking eat her,* I snarled. *Leave her alone!* Over and over again I screamed at him, overwhelming his senses the only way I knew how, keeping him focused on my voice while she presumably slipped past him.

The way she'd slipped past me.

Fucking hell, I was so mad. Whatever else this virus, this parasite had caused, it definitely caused rage. I was tearing at the walls with my good hand, ripping into the drywall, peeling the paint as I roared. My sensitive ears listened to her lock the door behind her. I heard her panting, dropping something on the living room floor, and she came hesitantly to the door to the office. "Sean?"

"What?" I screamed, gnashing my teeth. I actually felt the gnashing; scraping against each other, chipping my teeth, little pieces of grit and enamel grinding between them. It was disgusting. I relished it.

She stayed on the other side of the door, thank God. "What just happened?"

I let go of him. His name was Samuel. He was so angry, so hungry. He wanted her so badly. He could still smell the lavender of her body wash, her shampoo. The honey-eyed scent of her skin. The warmth of her flesh, when he felt so very cold. *Thankyou,* I said. *Thankyou, thankyou.*

Onetime, he snarled. *Thisonetime. Nomore. She'sfood.*

She would never be food. Not to me. I sighed, looking at the black blood coming from beneath my tattered fingernails. One more place Kiera couldn't touch me. "What did you do, Kiera? Why the fuck did you leave?" I was in one of my more cognizant moments, thankfully. Anger seemed to clear the palate, so to speak. It made me sane. But it made me want her so much more.

I could see the doorknob twisting slowly, back and forth, as if she was unsure of whether or not she should open the door. "I went downstairs," she said. She sounded hurt; I was instantly alert, pacing again, wracking my brain for how to help her. Her voice was subdued, soft and a little broken. "I got all of the stuff you've been saving for the apocalypse. I . . . I think this counts as the end of the world."

"What's the news?" I said, voice grating through the broken enamel.

She slid down against the door, and I knew she was resting her head, her ear against the panel to listen to me more clearly. I couldn't sit down, couldn't stop moving. I needed to move; to *rove*. I was a roving zombie. I was going to be part of a horde. Fuck.

"Let me check," she said.

"Tell me why you sound hurt." I started peeling at the paint with my bloody fingers, leaving streaks against the wood beneath. It was soothing, somehow. Like tearing skin from a body.

"I may have done the dumb thing? I, um, climbed out the fire escape and sort of fell into the sixth floor. I was trying to avoid your friend. As it turns out, no zombies on sixth, no zombies in the basement. Pretty sure I heard some zombies on eighth. Oh, and I chased a grandma down the stairs and shut the door, so now there's only one staircase your zombie friend can use." She said it in a rush, as if she were waiting for me to yell at her.

"So . . . are you hurt?" I sat down slowly, only after realizing that I was wearing a tread in the floor, and I'd broken open a callus on my foot, leaving a trail behind me on the carpet. "Are you . . . are you okay?"

As I calmed down, the hive mind found me again. I felt him out there, angry, weaving back and forth, up and down the hallway. I knew he was trying to work the door to the stairs. And I didn't know who he was bringing with him.

"Kind of? I didn't break anything, but I scraped the shit out of my ribs," she replied, sighing. "I think I bruised one. There's a nice purple stain emerging. A little black and green. It's bruising fast. I scraped both knees and managed to knock half the skin off my knuckles. So that's got to count for something. But I got almost everything I could think of. You did such a good job, Sean. You did so good preparing for us. I promise you, I'm going to survive this." She hiccuped, as if she were crying.

Aw, fuck. I closed my eyes, rubbing my face with my good hand. "At least you sound like you're accepting this," I said slowly. Words were fading. She was so warm against the door. I could feel it through the wood. I was so cold. So cold.

"I . . . I am," she said slowly. I could tell she was lying. "I'm . . . I'm making plans, Sean. When you go to sleep tonight I'm going to organize my food, I'm . . . I'm going to make a list, just like you showed me."

"Kiera," I managed, slurring my words. I could feel them upstairs, right above me, taunting me. A new awareness touched mine: a woman, older than me, and calmer. She was steady, a machine. Ready to spread her "awareness": the infection. Ready to succumb to the "new nation," she called it. As if we were a new species.

Fucking great. *Leavemealone,* I whispered in my mind.

No, she said back. *Don'tthinkIwill.*

It was a struggle to talk to both of them at the same time; the woman, Darla, kept pulling me in, urging me to talk to her, trying to get me to come around to her way of thinking. She whispered sweet words to me about a world with fewer humans and more of us, an interconnected species, a beautiful creation. She was fucking nuts.

"Kiera," I said again. "You have to let me out. They won't stop."

"Who won't stop?"

It wasn't banging on the door that I heard now; it was stomping. Rhythmic pounding on the floor, as if they were marching back and forth in time, a collection of zombies waiting to pounce. I couldn't feel the other one yet, but I knew another zombie was coming. They marched in the apartment above ours, and I could hear their groans. I could see their words. I could feel their ideas. And I wanted to be part of it, more than anything.

Except I couldn't. She was here. "The others," I said softly. "Theothers, theothers. Upstairs. They want me. Wantme to come out. You have to let me out."

Peering under the door, I could almost see the sadness in her tears. I wanted to lick them off of her face, taste her sorrow and regret. "I'll text my mom," she said finally. "And Callie. See if there's any news. Maybe . . . maybe." She ended the sentence there, and she walked away, sobbing beneath her breath.

I punched the door and my knuckles split open. I felt nothing as the black sludge pooled and dribbled down my fist. I could feel them upstairs, taunting me. Samuel was lying on the floor above me, waiting to find a new victim. Darla was waiting with him, patient as an iron statue. And someone else was waiting too, waiting for me to succumb, because he couldn't imagine me wanting to be anything else.

~

I was alone then, alone for a while. I was alone in the room with slime cooling on my knuckles, my heart beating too fast, and my vision laser focused on the doorknob. I could break it down, I thought. *Breakit breakit breakit.* I smiled to myself for the thought. Then I could find her, and she could become like me. We could break out together, and find them upstairs. She could be part of my Link, and we would never be forgotten.

That might have been what I liked, the only thing I liked, about the state of being that I was in: I could *never* be forgotten. Once someone was in your Link, they were there until they died. And zombies didn't die easily.

Samuel mourned grandma. That was her name: Grandma. She wasn't *his* grandma, he told me. I could hear Kiera talking out in the living room, and I wondered if she was talking to someone the same way I was talking to Samuel. But Grandma was *someone's* grandma, and that's all that counted. She was downstairs, on the sixth floor now, trying to come back. She had *brokensomething fallen stairs down bad*. And it was Kiera's fault.

God, I was so angry. I was locked in here, and Kiera was free. Samuel was free. Darla was definitely free. And I was curious, so curious about this new person, this new man that was waiting for me, waiting for me to be free. I reared back and kicked the door experimentally. My hand was no longer working the way I wanted it to. I couldn't turn the knob.

A flash of panic overcame me. *I couldn't turn the knob.* I realized all at once that I had come back to myself from Zombieland, that I had been in the somewhere else with Samuel and Darla and what's-his-name for hours. I had wanted to be there, more importantly, instead of here, with Kiera. I sank to my knees. At least I could still do that.

I felt the tears more than the emotion; they were thick, like maple syrup. I looked down at my arm, the black lines snaking up to my chest, and down at my bare feet. It had accompanying snakes wound up and around my ankles. I knew my whole body had to be covered, and I cried for myself, and for Kiera.

I was losing this battle, and I couldn't even feel it.

These thoughts were insidious; I didn't even notice that I was thinking differently, *acting* differently until I snapped back and I wasn't anymore. And it was taking longer and longer to come back. I could talk to Samuel all day long, I realized, and I *wanted* to. I wanted to be with people like me. I wanted everyone to be like me.

I pulled my knees up to my chest clumsily and wept, listening to Kiera's voice outside the door. She was talking to someone, Callie probably, but I couldn't hear what they were saying. The urge to go back, to talk to Samuel, to listen to Darla, to find out about this man was intense.

There had to be a way to distract myself, to stay here. Even if it meant doing something stupid.

I looked around the room, for something, anything that I could use to keep myself grounded in the present. If I cut myself with the letter opener, would that just create a biohazard, or would that keep me here, keep me with Kiera? Could I even feel pain anymore?

I leaned down on my stump, pressing it hard into the ground. I pressed until I felt bone grinding, and I closed my eyes with a sigh as the bandage began to bleed black. I couldn't feel that, either.

No, there was no way that I was going to win this

battle. If I couldn't even feel pain when I was *here,* when I was as close to Kiera as I was likely to get safely . . .

"Kiera," I called hoarsely. It was so hard to talk.

"I gotta go," she said shortly. "Thanks." She rushed to the door, letting herself in and leaving it open behind her. I watched her take it all in: the sooty tears, the stained bandages, the general disarray of my body that I couldn't fix, couldn't help, couldn't stop.

"You've certainly been having fun while I've been on the phone," she said softly. "What happened?"

"It's harder to come back," I managed, lying on my side on the floor. "Harder to move. Harder to think."

"Come back from what?"

I gestured uselessly to the ceiling, where three zombies milled around upstairs waiting patiently for me to eat my fiancée. "From them. From wanting to become like them. Make you like them."

"I've been talking to Callie. My mom . . . my mom isn't answering her phone anymore, and I can't get an answer at the hospital."

I stared at her, trying to formulate a response while trying to understand her words at the same time. "She what? What happened?"

Kiera shook her head, rubbing her forehead with dirty, scratched fingers. "I don't know." She moved like she was broken, aching at every joint, like a doll that had been tossed aside too many times. "I just don't know. Callie said that the World Health Organization and the UN have taken over. America's not even in charge anymore. The military . . . Sean, the military's, like, *gone.*"

"Wait, what?" I tried to clear my head.

"I don't know, put hundreds of guys sleeping in one room together with a zombie apocalypse and see what happens? We have no military. No one's coming to save us. The rest of the world is all we've got. There's barely an America anymore. Everybody's getting sick." She sobbed breathlessly, wiping her tears with the back of her hand. "Nobody's coming to save us, Sean. It's just you and me."

I pulled myself up off of the floor. Fell, hard, face first on the carpet, smashing my bleeding eyes into the white rug, leaving stains. Tried again, managed to get myself to my knees, and Kiera helped pull me up.

I inhaled slowly. Lavender. My God, it was hard. "Then we have to save you ourselves," I said quietly. There was only one way.

"How?" she said dully. "I don't know what to do anymore. I don't know how to help you."

I hooked my arm around hers, pulled her with my forearm, stumbled toward the front door. One foot after another, Sean. Just one more. One more foot. Another, and we were there. Ten feet feels like a million miles when you're struggling to be in control over a damned parasite that's presumably eating your brain, or your intestines, or something.

"Let me go," I said.

"No," she whispered. "Not yet. You're still—"

"Let me go!" I roared, turning to stare her in the face. I was panting, my heart racing, blood pumping sluggishly through my veins. I could feel it. I could feel each particle moving, and I felt alive, more alive than I'd felt in days.

I kicked at the door behind me and stumbled, off balance. "Just a danger," I said, more softly. "Justadanger, justadanger." Shit. It was coming back.

"Sean—"

"Please." It was the only word that would come out, the only word that I could find. I could see each individual line in the irises of her eyes. They were beautiful. I wondered what they'd feel like rolling around in my mouth.

"Please." I was losing the rest of my words. Her hair sparkled in the low light, compliments of the hairspray she used. How soft would it be in my fist?

"Please." One last time. It was all of the effort I had. I was holding on by a thread.

She stared at me, and reached behind me. She lifted the latch. The door swung open.

One last time.

The Door is Shut

~ Kiera ~

He stared at the open door, as if he didn't know what to do with it. I felt like a mother ushering her child into the kindergarten room, not wanting him to leave but not having a clue how to function if he stayed. Things couldn't last the way they were going. At least, I didn't think so.

I didn't think that Sean knew I'd been listening to him talk to himself—himself, his new friends, whatever. He muttered, when he thought he was alone. And he talked about me. "Lavender," over and over. "Honey." "Kiera." Single words, but with so much meaning behind them. A longing for me, in a way that made me super uncomfortable. It wasn't a longing for his partner, for his TV watching buddy, for the girl he had arguments with over keeping tents in the living room. It was a longing for . . . God, I couldn't even describe it. It was a *possession*. He wanted me to be a part of his group, his *herd*, his . . . whatever.

And then he'd said he'd never let me go. And that, my friends, sounded like a fucked up relationship if I'd ever heard of one. I had my own codependency problems, I was self-aware enough that I knew I had issues, but damn, I didn't want to *become* Sean.

"Are . . . are you going?" I said softly.

He turned and looked at me, and smiled sadly. His eyes were turning green; they weren't glowing yet, not neon, but they were fully light green now, and my heart clenched. He was almost gone, I realized. And I didn't know if I could get him back, once he left for good.

"Love you," he said. "Love you." And he began to stumble away, walking against the wall, letting it hold him up. He headed toward the staircase and I watched him go, one step at a time, faltering, on his hands and knees after a single stair. He crept up the staircase and I closed the door, sliding the latch home.

It wasn't until I heard the dead bolt click that I began to sob. Great, wracking sobs that tore through my body. Grief hit me like the proverbial freight train; it hurt to see him go. It hurt to know he'd be up there, wandering around with his new family, and if I got anywhere near them, he couldn't stop them from hurting me. He couldn't stop himself from hurting me. Sean was a zombie.

There, I'd said it. I collapsed into a pile, hugging his phone to my chest, the one I'd kept in my pocket, hoping he'd need it again to look up home remedies for zombie-ism on Reddit. I had hoped I could keep him . . . keep him, like he was my pet. This was no way to have a relationship.

My talk with Callie hadn't made me feel any better. They were focusing on a vaccine, not a cure, as far as she knew. There were splinter cells of scientists gone rogue, mad scientists if you will, that were; she was trying to interview one of them, just to see what she was working on. But that was it. Aside from the occasional odd duck, they were working on protecting the rest of us, not fixing the ones that had already succumbed.

I'd lost Sean, probably forever. I opened my eyes and looked around our apartment; it was trashed, as I'd spent the last few days either taking care of Sean or locking him away from me and furiously doing research in an attempt to cure him. No cure. No research. There was nothing left here for me except survival.

Drying my eyes and ignoring the fact that they still leaked; ignoring that I kept crying, no matter how strong I tried to be. I could hear stomping upstairs, and assumed Sean had found his people. It occurred to me that this would be a good opportunity to close the door to the stairs.

I couldn't.

My stupid brain needed to know if he was okay. I had to know what happened when he finally became a zombie for good, no coming back. I realized that I couldn't live with myself if I didn't at least have the possibility of glimpsing him in the hallways . . . and then I realized how fucking stupid that sounded. I ran to the stairway and shut the door, tears streaming down my cheeks, and ran back to the apartment.

My floor was now relatively zombie-free, or as

zombie-free as I could make it without going door to door to check. I hadn't heard any more screams while I was caring for Sean, so that was good. But that also meant I was alone, either for a week and a half or until I told Brett to come sooner. I began picking up laundry, thinking about the conversations I'd had with Sean about apocalypse survival; I had a laundry bucket you could spin with a pedal, if it came to that, and I even knew how to make soap. Hell, we actually had lye. I didn't care what he said, he was a doomsday prepper.

I walked along the shelves of my full dining room, looking at my food stores, and sighed. What was the point? What was the point in surviving alone? I couldn't find reason, couldn't fathom spending the rest of my days waiting out the apocalypse without him. For the life of me, I couldn't figure out why I needed to wake up the next morning.

Maybe I didn't.

~

I stared up at the ceiling, listening to the zombies stomp around upstairs. I heard moaning downstairs, too; that was new. I watched the popcorn ceiling as the sun rose. It was my first day without Sean, and I didn't know what the hell I was going to do with myself.

I rolled over on my stomach and grabbed my phone. I kept his near me, just in case—in case of what, I wasn't sure. It was my last connection to him, my last tangible thing that he'd touched, aside from the disgusting mess left in my office.

God. The office. I *really* didn't want to think about the

hazmat situation that was my office. Maybe if I closed the door, it wouldn't attract any zombies. Did it work like that? I seemed to recall Sean talking about them being attracted to zombie blood, but I couldn't remember the specifics.

I didn't want to get out of bed. It didn't seem particularly interesting to me, getting up. Watching the news some more, hearing about more horrible things happening, seeing the lack of hope in the country. I had watched the only news channel still broadcasting CNN until I passed out, only to wake up and crawl into a bed that didn't have Sean in it. Major cities were being wiped off the map. Detroit was a city full of zombies; the National Guard, or what was left of it, had given up on it entirely. New York City wasn't much better. I did, however, find some amusement in the fact that the White House was overrun as well. Fucking deserved it.

There were no new texts from my mom, of course. I texted her one more *????* just to be sure; I'd have to call the hospital later, when I garnered the energy to. Was this what depression felt like? This mindless, endless nothing, an emptiness that you can't explain or place, and you certainly can't fix it. All I wanted to do was sleep. And maybe become a zombie.

I did have a message or six from Callie, however. *Pfizer reports a prelim vaccine they're manufacturing in England,* she told me. *Long time from releasing. But maybe hope for us???*

Maybe, I wrote back. *Not sure it matters anymore.*

Don't talk like that, she shot at me. *It matters. I'm sorry about Sean.*

That would be when I dropped the phone at my side, sighing. I'd told her in the dark hours of the night what I'd done; letting Sean go had been the hardest thing I'd ever done in my life, and I had to share the horror with someone. It was like seeing something gruesome on the Internet: you had to show your best friend so that you didn't see it alone. Now Callie was all I had.

The phone rang; it was the theme song from *Bob's Burgers*. I sighed, wondering if there were still telemarketers in the apocalypse, and sighed harder when I saw it was Brett. Didn't he text like normal people? "Hello, Brett."

"Hey. What's going on? You ready to zombieproof your apartment?"

"Isn't it a little late for that? The only zombie I gave a damn about is now roaming around upstairs. I closed the doors. Unless they've learned the talent of reusing their thumbs, I figure I'm pretty safe."

He scoffed. "Not really. I'm more worried about looters," he said. "Your apartment is in a nicer area of town, and people are going to want food. They're already breaking into stores. What's gonna stop people from busting into your apartment with guns blazing?"

"Oh, I don't know, my hatchet?" I replied dryly.

"Yes, you, all of five feet with a hatchet, are going to scare off armed intruders. I think not. The point is, you're awake now, and I'm coming over. I'll drive the van straight up to the fire escape."

"I slightly damaged the fire escape on the sixth floor. That might make this plan slightly problematic."

He sighed, and I could see him closing his eyes and brushing his hand across his face in frustration just by the tone of his voice. "All right. I'll fix that on my way up. You need a way up and down, and you texted you've got zombies on all different floors. So whatever you fucked up, I'll fix it."

"Brett the handyman. Got it."

"Man, you're in a mood today. I know this sucks, but at least you've got someone checking up on you, right? You're not totally alone."

Not totally alone. I guessed not; it felt like I was. It felt irredeemable, as if I would always be alone. This was my first damn day of the zombie apocalypse by myself. I needed to shake myself out of this. Yes, I lost Sean, but . . .

But what? Fuck. "All right. I'll see you soon." I hung up, sitting up slowly with my eyes shut. I felt like a truck had hit me during my adventures on the sixth floor. The more I thought about it, the angrier I became about the zombie situation. Sean was safely locked on the eighth floor, but what about those down below? What if there were people trapped, like me, without a Brett to help them?

Those fucking zombies took Sean. I was looking at this the wrong way. Sean didn't just spontaneously become a zombie; *they took him from me.* So I put on some jeans, took off Sean's shirt that I had been wearing, and finished getting dressed. The new plan? I was going to secure the fuck out of this apartment building with Brett.

And when he was gone, I was gonna get my hatchet. Mama's going hunting.

~

As it turns out, I realized early on in my practice hatchet swinging that I was going to want a slightly better distance-to-zombie ratio when I was actually doing this. I had a mop handle, a battery-powered and really freaking powerful screwdriver, and some super long screws that Sean had used to make my shelving for my supplies. Not only did I practically weld my hatchet to the mop handle, I weaponized the hatchet's handle too, drilling the screws through it all the way until they stuck out on all sides. Now it was a hatchet with pointy tetanus-giving goodness.

I stuck it in the cleaning closet so that Brett wouldn't see my brilliant idea, and I got out the mop bucket, bleach and some gloves. It was time to make my apartment less like zombie bait. I was gonna have to scrub.

Jesus, Mary and Joseph, zombie blood was hard to scrub! I learned once that the more saints attached to the swear—Patrick, Jude, Jesus, Mary and Joseph, for instance—the worse the swear was in Ireland. It made sense, and it kept me busy trying to think of all of the saints I'd ever heard of. I wondered if Jude was looking over all of us right now. I wondered if he was laughing.

I sang the old Beatles' song it reminded me of softly as I dug into the carpet, erasing Sean's frantic attempts to . . . something. I didn't know what he had done, actually, or why he'd dug his stump into the floor, but here I was, cleaning up his mess again. The more that I thought about it, the less of a saint *Sean* became; and it was easier to deal with how I was feeling when I remembered all the little things he did that annoyed me.

Scrub. He never picked up his laundry.

Swish the mop bucket. He didn't soak his dirty dishes.

Scrub. He left black, bilious zombie blood all over my fucking office floor where I was going to become a great editor and write many books. Or craft my way out of the hell of my thesis. One of the two.

I left the floor looking pretty worse for the wear, but gray instead of black, and poured bleach over the spots and let it soak. The rug would look funky, but I was pretty sure security deposits were a thing of the past anyway, so I wasn't sure I cared.

Hell, where even *was* my landlord?

Um, hello, Mr. Landlord? There are zombies near my apartment. I almost died laughing thinking about that phone call; English was not his first language, and while He'd certainly heard the word "zombies" by now, I was pretty sure it would get lost in translation if this situation hadn't occurred. I wondered what kind of fixer-upper guy (it was never an actual licensed plumber or electrician) he'd hire for that.

I cleaned myself up and dumped the water down the sink, using the garbage disposal to get the worst of the thick gobs of yuck. By that time, I heard clanging out the window. I wasn't afraid. If it was a zombie, so fucking be it.

I was so, so tired.

Of course, it wasn't a zombie coming to end me, it was Brett with a ladder, climbing up the wall with a tool belt, a bunch of boards slung over the side on a rope, and a hammer in his hand. He was managing all of this more gracefully than I thought I would have, even if he hit himself in the head with the boards a few times while I watched. As he got to the sixth floor, I watched him puzzle out what I'd done.

Hell, I didn't even know what I'd done, but regardless, he fixed it pretty quickly, and ended up at my window in pretty short order. "Hey, Kiera."

"So how is it I didn't know you were this serious, mountain climbing handyman?" I asked.

"I dunno. You never came by the store? We never played game night? How the fuck should I know? Most of the stuff is down in my van. I'm gonna board up your stairs doors first, and then you and I are gonna go downstairs, sweep the ground floor, and board that up, too."

"Wait, I'm helping you with this? You want me to kill zombies?"

He looked at me strangely, brown hair hanging over his face. "Of course I want your help with this. What did you expect, me to take them on with the hammer while I nail a two by four to your door frame? I don't think that would work out very well."

For the first time in at least twenty hours, a smile blossomed across my face. "I'll be right back." I ran to the mop cupboard.

Day One

~ Sean ~

I found Samuel. It was easier to forget Kiera now that I'd found Samuel; he "clicked" into my Link, and I knew him. I really *knew* him. I felt his urge to hunt. I felt his impatience, the clicking of his jaw, the slow pound of his heart pushing sludge through his veins. His thoughts were surface: food, humans, movement. *Letmeshowyou.*

He was waiting for me when I made it up the stairs. I was starting to feel far away, as if there was a barrier between myself and my actions. My arm flailed and I patted him on the shoulder, without knowing why. He did the same. Zombies had greetings?

Zombies had greetings. Who knew. I swung my head over to the left and looked at Darla. She was older, maybe my age, and she was *ravenous*. I got the feeling that Samuel had had a little to eat since he'd become a zombie, but Darla *knew*. She actively hunted.

Darla was going to lead us home.

And then there was the Old Man. They all clicked home in my Link, three sides to the wall that was my mind, and with every click, less of the old world made sense. Why did I need to live in a home? We could move, track prey, find them everywhere. Work? School? No. There was no need for that. We were together.

Together was all that mattered. Together, and making more of us together. Making all of us together. I could feel Kiera in a different way, the feelings of loss and pain slamming me against the doorway of what I used to be. I wanted her to feel this, wanted her to be together with us, but something stopped me. I couldn't remember what it was. What love felt like. But maybe *nottogether withher* was the closest zombies could get to love.

I missed her face.

The Old Man got up from his chair. I could tell he needed a cane, but couldn't use one. His left leg dragged against the ground as he moved forward toward us. He grunted, and Samuel grunted back. I understood this to mean *let's go*. I was learning that there were two languages to zombies: the internal thoughts, and the grunts and moans.

As I sat in the backseat of the car that was my brain, I realized that zombies were far more complicated than we gave them credit for.

While I pondered this, my body started moving without my consent. We followed the Old Man, through the hallway and around the corner. There was a broken door, and that's when it hit me. *The smell.*

It wasn't lavender, but it was *human*. Unmistakably human. And I, just as unmistakably, was not. The Old Man pointed at the door, and Darla and Samuel groaned in response, throwing their shoulders at the door. That was the good thing about being a zombie: they did it again and again, and it didn't hurt. I watched, behind the Old Man, as the door gave way.

The eighth floor was ripe with goodness that the seventh floor hadn't possessed. Many more people were home on the eighth floor, I realized. And none of them were well secured.

The door splintered, cracked, and fell to the ground. Samuel's eyes rolled to me, and I could tell he was smiling inside. *Let'sgo*, he said.

Where?

Inside, he said. *Ofcourse*. We staggered over the remains of the door, and I could hear the first sounds of the humans: breathing. They were breathing quickly, and I could tell they were afraid. I moaned, feeling their fear in my bones. The sludge in my veins quickened, and I let out a screech, not knowing why I did it.

Darla made the same sound. The Old Man was silent, but he led me along, almost holding my hand. He nudged me forward with his shoulder, and we searched the apartment as one. One unit. One pack. One family.

This. This was family. This was my family. It felt like *home*. I rolled my eyes blissfully as I followed the Old Man into the room, bumping into the furniture. I could no longer recall what the furniture was called. I knew this was a *living room*. They would not *live* in the *room* for long.

Samuel found her behind the curtains, pulled her out by the arm. He dragged the screaming girl over to me. She couldn't have been older than he was; she was still a teenager. She was saying something, over and over again, and I couldn't understand her.

That was when the panic set in. I couldn't understand her. She was speaking, using words, and they meant nothing to me. I shivered like an animal, the hair running up my spine, feeling like I had knives in my back. Samuel buried his face in her neck and tore.

There was nothing. I had no control. My body seized, my muscles tensed, and I was on her, with my face in her side, ripping her shirt off. There was nothing sexual about it. That word had ceased to have meaning. She was meat and she was mine. I felt the thick skin between my teeth and bit, hard. It burst like a sweet apple, meat not meant to break under teeth like mine. Liquid gushed like cherry juice into my mouth, dripping down my throat like ice cream. I heard nothing but static. silence. The meat beneath me was moving and I held it down, hungry. I was so hungry.

I could *feel* the Infection wanting her, wanting to transfer to her, but I couldn't stop. I didn't want to stop. I watched myself from far away as I dug into what I identified as a kidney, felt it rupture under my teeth, felt it slide down my throat. It stopped moving. I kept eating.

I felt full, then, for the moment. I closed my eyes and laid my head on the ruined stomach, rubbing the juice into my face, moaning. I was thankful, so thankful for this meal. It calmed the screaming void, the emptiness inside of me. I felt the jellylike flesh wobbling in my stomach.

I opened my eyes.

Samuel was staring at me, a crooked smile on his dripping face. He was covered in blood and gore. I looked down at the girl; she wasn't a girl anymore, she was pieces, and I had done this.

I wanted to throw up.

I couldn't. I laid my cheek gently against her liver and licked up the puddle of blood instead, screaming inside of my mind.

~

My new life was equal parts horror show and pretty cool, actually.

Samuel was driven to distraction with how awesome he thought it was that I was finally *oneofus*. Darla had a crooked smirk, concerning if only because half of her lips were missing, ripped off of her face by whoever had turned *her* into a zombie. It wasn't Samuel or the Old Man, I was sure, but who did that leave? There were no other zombies on this floor.

Which meant maybe there were more zombies in the building.

I wasn't entirely sure how long the whole "stairs" thing would work. I was moving around pretty well, but the Old Man was a shambler, each step awkwardly rolling into the next. Darla shuffled, not raising one foot higher than the other, and Samuel staggered, taking big steps as if he were about to mount a skateboard. I didn't know how the infection affected everyone's movement, as it was different for all of us.

I realized, however, that I was only at the *beginning*

of zombiehood. It was entirely possible that I was going to continue getting worse until I looked as bad as the Old Man.

Watchit, he grumbled. *'mfine.*

Are . . . not. I struggled to separate the words. I was desperate, still, to keep myself separate from them. To be *better* than them. To somehow retain my humanity, so that one day, I could go back to Kiera.

I looked down at my hand. My swollen, blood-covered, gore-infested hand. It was completely coated in red, with little bits of intestine hanging off of it. I tried to shake it quickly, and watched my hand respond sluggishly, the bits only falling off after several seconds. My body was failing me. I tried harder, and it was like driving a car in the highest gear: it just wouldn't go any faster. There was nothing I could do.

I sobbed, on the inside. *Stopit,* Darla scolded me. *Thisisbest.*

Best, Samuel added. *Nexttime, spread. Don'teat.* The hard part of hearing his plea for more of us, to make someone become like us, was that I knew it would be *hard* not to eat them. As much as I detested what I was becoming, I wanted more. And more and more I remembered every horrible zombie movie I'd ever seen, were they all sentient too? Or was this something new?

Were zombies all trapped in their own bodies, tied to a fetid hunger, drowning in what they couldn't stop themselves from doing?

I wanted to throw it all up, to heave over the floor of the apartment we were in, but my body wouldn't respond even that much. I mindlessly followed the Old Man and Darla, with Samuel behind me, and they led me toward the stairs. We were going down.

Kiera was down. Dear God, I prayed. If you care about the children you've ignored, care about this—let Kiera have closed the damn door.

I knew one thing: none of us could use a doorknob. The Old Man's hands were gnarled, curled in on themselves, and Darla wasn't coordinated enough. Samuel, maybe, but his strength was in his legs, not his arms. And as for me . . . I wasn't coordinated enough for anything anymore. Not even hugging Kiera.

We stumbled toward the doorway, the open stairwell, and I saw the differences in how zombies dealt with their . . . I didn't want to use the word "disabilities," but it was the closest word I had. If zombie-ism was a disease, it definitely came with some "conditions that limit a person's movement, senses, or activities." I remembered the exact definition only because of a scolding Kiera had given me once for using it incorrectly.

I missed her so fucking much.

Getoutofyourhead, Samuel snarled. *Justbe. Live. Exist.*

He was right, unfortunately. Pining for Kiera wasn't going to do me any good. I felt like I was the most cerebral zombie I'd ever met. Considering I'd only met these three and the one that had bitten me, that didn't amount to much, but I knew I was focusing on Kiera longer than I should.

You'llgetoverit, the Old Man said warily. *Keepsome-language. Losesomemore.*

Okay, so he was a little cerebral too. *Howdid . . . how . . . did . . . you?*

He grunted, a sound that I now knew meant, "This is frustrating." I knew it was usually used when prey was faster than predator; and I knew he meant it as, "It was fucking stupid, and yours probably was too." I was shown an image:

The Old Man, in a wheelchair, taking a walk with his aid. They got into the elevator of the building, up to his floor, when the door opened on third. A horror show of a man with half a face, his skin torn off and hanging, his nose wrenched and missing cartilage, attacking the nurse. The nurse beating him off with the Old Man's cane that had been hooked to the wheelchair, beating him down until he stopped moving.

The nurse turned quickly. She had locked the door behind her and the Old Man, keeping them in his apartment, and then it was too late for him to do anything to stop her.

Atleastcanwalk, he mumbled. *Doesn'thurtnow.*

I guess that was one way to think about it. Zombie-ism did an awful lot for making your major and minor ailments go away. I noticed then that my amputation wasn't even hurting anymore; no phantom limb pain. No "this is wrong" pain. And the fever was gone. That was pretty great.

Samuel leaned back against the wall and slid foot by

foot down the stairs, while Darla took a four-legged animal approach. The Old Man held onto the railings with
his wrists, and I knew that his hands had not gripped in
life and did not grip in death. I stared down the stairway,
inwardly frowning, and tried to figure out how the hell I
was going to do this.

I realized two truths at the same time: I was a zombie.
And zombies didn't feel pain.

I took one big step and tumbled down the stairs.

Day One

~ Kiera ~

My hatchet-mop was heavier than I thought it would be, but it felt *right* in my hands. It felt right for taking away some zombie brains. They'd taken away my Sean's brain; I had every right to take away whatever made them, *them*. But I wasn't sure how Brett would react to the new Sean; I knew that Brett was against zombies, and I couldn't imagine him welcoming Sean back into the fold. I couldn't let him disappear again. But how? I wasn't sure what the plan was.

"So what's the plan?" I guessed the best way to find out was to just ask.

Brett flopped his blond hair across his forehead and sighed, wiping the sweat off his brow. "So we're going to go down to the main lobby, block off the windows and doors there, and then come back up here and nail your door shut. That'll keep the looters out of the building, and the zombies out of your apartment."

I looked at him for a moment. "Until what?"

"What do you mean, until what?"

"I mean, until what? Like what's going to happen? Is this just the new normal? We just . . . exist every day, waiting for zombies to kill us or not kill us? Our whole world is defined by zombies now? No jobs, no careers, no writing?"

"I mean, go for it, you've got enough notebooks stacked up in your living room that you could write ten dozen novels for all I know. Keep yourself busy. But yeah, the name of the game is survival, toots."

I looked at him some more, crestfallen. I truly didn't know what to do with myself now that Sean wasn't there to provide structure, entertainment, life, love. "I don't . . . I just don't see the point."

"Look, you've just had a major loss, and the whole country's got zombie-related PTSD right now. The rest of the world is trying to figure this out for us. Our only job is to live through it while they do. So that's your goal, Kiera. Live through it while someone else fixes the problem. Document it, or don't. Write Amish romances. Actually, I bet the Amish are doing pretty well, spread out like they are. Huh. Who woulda thought the Amish would be right about everything?"

I was beginning to see why Brett hung out with Sean. I was starting to think that Brett was into survivalism and doomsday prepping, too. Or he was just weird, in which case, he was also Sean's people.

"I guess," I said softly. "It just . . . seems pointless to wake up without him."

"The point is to see how many days you can survive

without being eaten. Get a Sharpie and mark it on the wall. Make it a game. Treat yourself every twenty-five days or something."

"Twenty-five?"

"I dunno. That's how many levels between megabosses in my favorite video game. It seemed appropriate, considering." He cocked his head and looked at me. "It's just a game, Kiera. See how long you can win. And the reason you need to win is because Sean can't."

"Do you . . ." I looked down. "Do you think they'll ever find a cure?"

He shrugged, hefting the two by fours and starting toward the door. "I know Switzerland's working on it. I've got an Internet friend I game with that lives there, her roommate's a lab assistant. If anybody can do it, it's the Swiss. Don't they have like, industrial strength, country-wide healthcare? They've got this."

It was the first glimpse of hope I'd had in a while, but I was reluctant to take it. The Swiss were so far away, and so foreign; why should they care about what happened in America? They were about the only people whose business we *hadn't* gotten into. Maybe they'd take their sweet ass time about it to prove some kind of international point.

He opened the door, and led me to the elevator. "Well, we probably shouldn't go down the stairs," I said. "There's gore all over the stairwell, and I think I still hear noises. That way." I pointed to the elevator. Thank God zombies couldn't use elevators, or I'd be screwed.

Brett looked at the elevator for a moment, echoing

my thoughts. "Whatdya think the chances are of a zombie figuring out an elevator?" He frowned. He grabbed the planters at the end of the hall and put them in front of it, lining them up rather nicely, actually. "There. At least you'll have some warning if they do."

"Um, thanks, I think." We went to the elevator, me with my hatchet and his tools, him with a whole bunch of boards and a hammer, and descended in silence down to the main floor. It looked pretty good, actually: there was only one bloodstain on the stool of the security guard, though he was nowhere to be seen.

"I'm not gonna guess what happened to Security Dude, but keep an ear out, will ya? I don't want to suddenly find out where he went all at once." He dropped the boards at his feet, and pulled a tin of nails out of the bag I was carrying, and went to work.

I found myself in the rather peculiar position of guard duty, taking up residence behind him with my hatchet-mop and not very much confidence. I was listening for zombies as hard as I could, but Sean hadn't made very many zombie-like noises, so I wasn't sure what I was listening for. Did they sound like they did in the movies? Were they silent zombies? Did they speak gibberish?

And how the hell was I supposed to "keep an ear out" over the hammering? Holy fuck, it was loud. It echoed throughout the lobby, making the little planters by the door jump with every strike. I whipped my head back and forth, trying to track every motion that wasn't really there, until I heard Brett sigh behind me. "Look, if they haven't come by now, they won't. Calm the fuck down. Hand me some nails."

It was going to be a long afternoon, wasn't it.

~

So we boarded up the front door and the little windows by the front door, and generally made it look decrepit and unhappy in the lobby. I was relieved to know that there were no surprise zombies on the ground floor. I wasn't sure what had happened to the security guard, though. He had been a good guy. Mr. Tony. He had helped me get my groceries into the elevator every time, before Sean had moved in.

I wondered what Sean was doing. I helped Brett gather up his tools; he'd used all the two by fours that he'd brought, regardless of whether or not it was a good idea to overload the door with them. It seemed like less was more was a good way to go, seeing that we didn't want the door to actually fall off, but Brett seemed to know what he was doing. Or he acted like he did. Whichever.

My thoughts wandered back to Sean. I had to stop thinking of Sean like he was a rational human being. Like he was still *mine*. Like he was still someone I could be with in the future. I had to grieve him, somehow. Accept the finality of our somewhat mutual decision to let him go upstairs. I had to wonder, though; did he find his "pack"?

Was he with zombie boy, right now? Were there more zombies? A girl zombie, even? Did that even matter to him, anymore?

Wait, was I jealous of a maybe-existent girl zombie? Fuck. This was getting out of hand.

I sighed, the sound echoing loudly in the chamber of the lobby, and threw my head up as I heard something fall against the stairwell door. I looked at Brett, and his expression had immediately grown grim. "That didn't sound good," he said.

"No," I said nervously. "And that door's got a push bar. If it's a zombie . . ."

"They'll eventually throw their weight against it and get free. Run."

"Wait, what?"

"Run!"

Running so wasn't what I had planned to do when I woke up that morning, but there I was, stumbling after Brett, who was carrying considerably more tools than I was and running a hell of a lot better. I wondered if he practiced this with Sean at the store, running during the apocalypse. It seemed like a very doomsday prepper thing to do, running with heavy things. Cans of potato soup, maybe.

Did most people gaze pensively at their navels while running from zombies? I tore after Brett and threw myself in the elevator, gasping for breath. "So I'm not asthmatic," I wheezed, "just incredibly out of shape."

"Good to know," he replied calmly. The fucker wasn't even breathing hard. At all. I wanted to push him out for the zombies to get him. The door closed immediately under his questing fingers, and I relaxed as much as my aching body could.

"So that was fun," he added. "It added a little excitement to the day. That and the window. What the hell did you *do* to it, anyway?"

"I sort of broke into it," I gasped. "With my whole body. I was trying to do something stupid. So what are we doing now?"

"We're going to board up the front door of your apartment. From the inside." He started humming honest to God elevator music.

Son of a bitch. It felt so . . . final. So zombie apocalyptic. It felt so much like I was giving up, giving in. I couldn't go haunt Sean, listen at the door for him to be on the other side. I couldn't go upstairs and look for him, unless I wanted to brave the elevator and not be able to know what was on the other side when those doors opened. Fuck! I couldn't keep living like this.

"Sounds good," I said finally. Because it did. Because it had to. I had to do this, I had to survive. Maybe I'd do what he said, do a docudrama memoir of my life during the zombie apocalypse. Grieve through my writing. Write haikus. Do bad poetry. Something, anything as a way to get through this, to find purpose through this mess. There had to be a reason that I survived when Sean . . . when Sean did not.

I said it. Sean did not survive.

Abruptly I found myself weeping silently in an elevator with a near stranger, who looked steadfastly forward, pretending it wasn't happening, humming his Muzak. I was thankful; at least he didn't want to talk about it. He didn't want to make it better. He just let me be as I thought about all of the moments with Sean: Ice skating, with Sean coaxing me forward as he skated backward, holding my hands, not laughing as I fell. Picking me up, dusting the snow off of me and helping me try again. Me looking back as I studied to see him smiling, watching me, and hearing him tell me how proud he was that I was going for my master's. Each and every time we went out at three in the morning to have dinner or breakfast after a late night cram session for tests and papers at the Pancake Den, having pancakes and ice cream, feeding them to each other.

Being together was paradise. But being alone had to be enough. Because that was what it was now: being alone.

We got off the elevator, Brett still humming, and I frowned, cocking my head. "Wait . . . do you hear that?"

"What?"

"That sound. A dog. Brett, there's a dog in that apartment!"

"So?"

"So there's a *dog. Alive.* We have to do something! Alive means it's not in with a zombie, and it's barking, so it's probably alone! We have to save it!"

He looked at me askance. "Like . . . you want to rescue a dog during the zombie apocalypse?"

"Like I don't have enough food in my dining room to feed a fucking army? I can rescue a dog during a zombie apocalypse. Yes. We are breaking down the door and rescuing a dog during the zombie apocalypse."

Brett stared at me for a long moment and shrugged. "I mean, I did bring a crowbar. I just wasn't sure why. Guess this is why." He listened at the door to make sure we weren't breaking into apartments willy nilly, I guessed, and started to pry the door open.

The barking got louder and more frantic. It was high pitched, and I wasn't sure what kind of dog to expect, but I was super excited. Every apartment I'd lived in besides this one hadn't allowed dogs, and I wondered if you had to get special permission. Well, who the fuck was going to care now? My landlord sure as hell couldn't get back to the apartment to screw with my security deposit. I was pretty sure I was good on that part. I fidgeted with the screwdriver I held, trying not to be impatient, but I realized I needed this.

I needed this new friend. I needed this being, this light in my life, more than I'd needed anything in a long time. I needed something to take care of, something to need me, something to love me.

Something to replace Sean.

The door fell to the floor and a black and white face blinked at me, surprised. A border collie stared up at me, sitting politely behind the door, complete with tags and a purple collar. Her matching leash was on a hook next to the fallen door.

My face brightened and her tail wagged. "It's nice to meet you," I said softly, as I walked onto the door and knelt down to check her tags. ". . . Grace."

Roaming the Floors

~ Sean ~

It was kind of cool to tumble all the way to the bottom and not feel anything, but when the rest of my horde didn't follow me, I had to laboriously climb on my hands and knees up and make my way up the stairs. At least I wasn't fighting against the elevators, as they were made of metal. My teeth wouldn't stand a chance. They had at least come down a few floors; I estimated we were on five, though I could no longer read the numbers or count them.

I could no longer read the numbers or count the floors. Damn, this was going quick. The numbers just looked like black marks to me; counting felt like steps were missing, like there was something I was supposed to do in the middle that I just didn't have in me anymore.

There was a lot more noise on the fifth floor than I was used to hearing. TVs were blaring, people were talking; everything was so *loud* here. I went to cover my ears and hit myself in the head. Samuel burst out laughing, grunting hard, rhythmically. Darla rolled her eyes wildly, and the Old Man simply sighed, an exhalation of air that sounded like a sad balloon.

I looked down, and I realized with no small amount of shock that my foot was turned around the wrong way, inward toward my other ankle. I'd apparently broken something in my tumble down the stairs. In retrospect, I was surprised I hadn't broken anything else, but it still shocked me that I hadn't noticed on my slow crawl back up.

Benefits, the Old Man said simply. *Likenewfloors. Benefits.*

Newfloors? I said.

Floorsnoteaten, he replied. Floors not eaten. So this floor was ripe for the picking. My stomach felt like it was sticking together. It felt like smacking gum, pulling apart and folding in upon itself, a yawning, gaping maw that was never full. The Infection itself felt different, as if it was no maw. No, it was insidious; it was infecting my brain. It was changing the way I thought. It was making me think of the people in those apartments as food, yes— but more importantly, those people were Opportunities.

Yes, the Old Man said. *Infectyourfirst.*

Infect, I said softly. It felt so good, so right to think about. I wanted to spread my family. Right now it only had three people in it—Samuel, Darla and the Old Man. What about the fourth and fifth walls? It felt so empty, so alone. There were places in my mind, in my soul that remained untouched by another, and it was profound to me that this was so. I could feel the three of them at all times. I knew what they were thinking, what they were feeling. Samuel was on fire; he wanted to break the doors down, and was waiting for a signal from the Old Man. The Old Man was resigned; he knew that Samuel had no patience, and knew that the best way to manage him was to let him exhaust himself with a good meal. And Darla . . .

Darla was insidious. Darla wanted to Infect the World. Darla had been completely taken over by the Infection, and Darla *was* the Infection. She didn't even eat anymore, not really; she bit to Infect, and to watch her Infection spread.

I wanted to be like Darla. I wanted to spread the joy of feeling no pain. I wanted to spread feeling your family so close to you like this; this unending feeling of well-being, a general state of *is,* with no wondering what *will be* or worrying about what *was.* It was existence, plain and simple. I wanted Kiera to feel this, more than anything. She worried so much. She would never worry again.

I would make it my mission that she would never worry again.

You'llregretit, Samuel sang into my mind.

Never, I said. *Neverregret. Regrether notbeing. Notbeing withme.* For that was my deepest regret: missing her, when I did. The cognizant moments that were fewer and farther between.

Those moments were slipping. Right now, I wanted to feel. And feel I would. Samuel slammed himself against the door and I went with him, throwing my shoulder into it. I felt nothing, and smiled. I knew it didn't show on my face, but I equally knew that my family felt it, and knew my joy. They knew my expectant happiness as I bounced into the door again and again. They knew my persistent enthusiasm as I pummeled through the wood. And they knew what I would do when I got through it, as long as it would take.

The door cracked. Samuel smiled.

A woman screamed.

~

It was easy to no longer see them as fellow citizens of my apartment complex; I didn't know them before I became a zombie, and I sure as hell didn't know them after. I tried to communicate with them; when I tried, when I pushed my awareness toward theirs, I felt . . . nothing. No walls, no Link, no smooth, seamless well where their awarenesses lay. Just . . . nothing. It was terrifying. Were humans really so alone? How did they live like this?

I felt Samuel with me and shuddered, relaxing in his presence beside me. He felt like home. He barreled into the apartment and toward the woman. She had yellow hair and dark skin. She was wearing a bright shirt and green pants. Things were starting to become a weird mixture of primary colors, secondary colors, and light/dark; I couldn't see various shades, could only see an eight-color box of Crayolas.

Well, that was mildly terrifying. But everything was so damn *sharp*. I could see her earrings: they were shaped like cats. I could see the . . . the marks on her skin, what were they called? I couldn't remember. Little bumps. I could see Samuel's fingernails, dirty and broken, holding her down.

I charged at her. I felt the need to Infect for the first time; a real need, a need to spread this wonderful feeling of awareness that felt so magical to me. She didn't feel like she had a family to me, and it was terrifying. Wasn't it terrifying to her, too, to be so alone? It scared me. I was going to make sure she wasn't scared and alone anymore.

Comehere, Samuel coaxed me. I leaned down and wavered over her, hunched and sniffing. She smelled good, like honey. Her skin smelled so sweet. I leaned over her and bit down, hard, swiping my tongue across the wound, burying it inside of the cloying taste of her blood, mixing my saliva in. I savored it, ignoring the need to feed, and felt it.

There wasn't a Link; not yet. She wasn't one of us; not yet. But something was there. I felt one of my walls fill up, like an empty cup filling with water. It held the breath of possibility. I didn't know who she was, not yet; but I would. It felt like a promise. It felt like I was smiling like an idiot.

Samuel was bouncing, holding her like an idiot as she stared at me in abject horror. "What did you do?" she wailed. "What did you do?" I could hear her, yet the words were blurred together, and it took me a moment to figure out what she'd said.

Fixedyou, I tried to say. *Fixeditallforyou.* I knew she

couldn't understand me—but she would. And we would stand up for her. Just like we would come for everyone on this floor, eventually.

She lay sobbing on her couch as Samuel let up, the fight drained out of her by the sluggishly bleeding bite. It was a sign of the Infection already ravaging her system, something I had noticed when I had gotten bitten. It didn't bleed nearly as much as I had thought it would. Neither had my amputation. I probably should have bled to death with what Kiera had done to me.

I wondered what would become of me when I forgot her name, too. I could barely remember her face, and it was just this morning when she had set me free. Or was it? It felt like days. Months. Years. But I could talk then . . . and now I couldn't.

I sighed, and it came out as a strangled moan. Samuel slung an arm over my shoulder and led me out to where the Old Man and Darla were waiting, staring at us, slack jawed. It wasn't with any sense of shock or awe; they were simply standing there, and their mouths were unattractively opened. It was a nice realization of what zombiehood had in store for me.

Finished? the Old Man asked.

Yes, I chattered excitedly. *Fixedher. Howlong?*

Differentforeveryone, he said. *Hours. Days.*

I bounded a few steps, impatient. I wanted her with us now! She was so *interesting* now! I wanted to know everything about her. She was going to be a part of our group, our system, our Link! She was part of our family now. That meant I needed only two more people to complete my hexagon, my home, my walls. Then everything would be perfect.

I looked at the Old Man. *Whatnow?*

He smiled. It wasn't pretty, especially with his mouth open. *Wewait.*

The Doors are Shut

~ Kiera ~

I bounced into my apartment with my new friend and Brett trailing behind. He looked a little confused and amused at the same time. "So her name's Grace?"

"I guess. That's what her collar says. I doubt people go to the trouble of printing out a tag with another dog's name on it."

"Smartass. So what are you going to do with her? You can't exactly take her for walks."

I beamed. I'd already thought of that. "I'm going to train her to go on the tarp that Sean bought and I brought up here just in case I needed . . . I don't know what I thought I'd need it for. And I'll clean it up after that."

"Okay. She's a border collie. Energy. Lots of energy. What are you going to do about *that?*"

"I'm going to make an agility course in our living room."

"You're what?"

"You heard me."

"Okay. That's not the answer I was expecting, but I can see that you obviously put thought into this for the, oh, ten minutes that we've known about the dog, so here we are. Do you need dog food?"

"Shit. Yes. I need dog food." I couldn't believe that I hadn't thought of that. "I can feed her out of like, regular bowls, but she probably should have actual dog food. I can feed her hamburger for a few days, I guess."

"I'm sure she'll be your best friend forever after that. I wonder whose she was? Did her owner just not come back? Or did we just steal a dog?"

I frowned. "It's been weeks since this all started. Who the hell is going out in this *now?*"

Brett looked at me pretty hard and gestured to himself. "Um, well-meaning mild-mannered citizens bent on helping their friends' girlfriends who are also bent on destroying themselves in a myriad of weird ass ways?"

"I am not bent on destroying myself. Except the fire escape. That was potentially stupid."

Grace barked. "Speaking of which, I think it's time that my Gracey girl and I get acquainted with our tarp system. I'm going to put it in the zombie room. We will be right back." I walked Grace on her leash to the dining room to grab the tarp, and into the zombie room, where she quickly circled, sniffed, did her thing, and waited expectantly for . . . me to do my thing, obviously.

Well, shit. Smart dogs and all expect smart owners, I guessed. "Hang on!" I said hurriedly, and led her to the dining room. She nuzzled into my hand, searching, and I ran through my hoard a few times until I found some rather tame sugarless cookies (generic brand Lorna Doones, maybe?) and gave her one. "Is that better?"

She woofed in answer with a doggy smile. I smiled back. "This is gonna be awesome."

She even raised her paw! I gave her a high five and took off her leash. She trotted back to Brett to give him the old sniff over. "So . . . you're bonding well," he observed drily.

"Yes. We are. Thank you. So what's the plan?"

"We're going to board up your front door, remember?"

"Um, obviously. Sorry. Yes. Let's get started." I hauled the screwdriver and the rest of his tools that I could not readily name over to the door, and locked it. I realized it was the last time I was locking the door. That I would never need my keys again. I would probably not drive my car again, if not for a very long time. Fuck. This was awesome.

"Are you crying?"

"No," I cried. "I'm leaking."

"O . . . kay," he said slowly. "We're going to go with that, then." He began hammering the door shut, sealing my fate with Gracey. We were in this apartment for good. I was going to have to use all my craftiness to keep this dog entertained, or teach her how to crawl up and down the fire escape at the back of my apartment, the one I hadn't even considered an option. It was broken, very broken, and I wasn't sure what made me think of it in the first place. It was the only choice we had, to entertain her. I bet I could make one hell of an agility course on the roof.

Actually, that wasn't such a bad idea, now that I thought about it. I bet a dog with her intellect probably *could* crawl up and down a fire escape. It would take some time, sure, and a lot of treats, but it was only two floors to the roof. We could do it, I was sure of it.

Gracey watched Brett with a tilted head, one of her ears flopped inside out. She looked at him curiously, as if he was doing something fascinating that could not possibly be replicated. I wondered if she was any good at zombie hunting. If we could clear the building together. The non-Sean parts of the building. Or the neighborhood.

Maybe we could be the dual vigilantes.

The more I thought about it, the more I liked it. I *liked* the idea of destroying them. I liked the idea of taking away what was giving me this stupid life in a boarded up apartment building in a boarded up apartment. I liked the idea of hacking into them with my hatchet-mop, Grace by my side.

We could do this.

My phone dinged. It was Callie. *Vax in progress!!!!!* she texted. *In major cities now. Will notify when it comes to you. University towns next!!!*

Excellent! I texted back. *My day is okay. Found a dog. Boarding up my apartment. Lost Sean. You know that already.*

Found a dog???

It's a long story. Actually not. Barking. Broke door down. Rescued dog. Her name is Grace.

Awww! Pix!

I quickly snapped some pictures of Grace while Brett

finished boarding up the door. I wasn't sure how I felt about the vaccine thing, really. Did it mean one hundred percent immunity? If it did, it still didn't guarantee I could follow Sean around. He could still attack me and kill me. I needed to get him out of my head. I needed to focus on Gracey.

I handed Brett another nail, and he made quick work of the door. I stared at it for a long time, and I wasn't sure what either one of us were thinking. He cleared his throat delicately. "So . . ."

"It's real."

"What's real?" he said quietly, with a strange, sad sort of smile.

"The door just . . . made it real. I can't leave. There's nowhere to go if I *do* leave. No more lunch on the quad. No more dates with Sean, especially that. My only real contact is you. And I don't even really know you. What's your last name, even?"

"Brentwood."

"Brett Brentwood? Really?"

"My mom liked country western. I don't have a better excuse than that."

"All right. Anyway, it's just . . . scary. And lonely. And weird. Isn't this weird? Like, did you ever *really* expect the zombie apocalypse to happen?"

He looked at me levelly. "Yes. Or something else."

"What did you and Sean talk about, anyway?"

"Pretty much exactly this. Except I never thought he'd end up a zombie. I always thought he'd end up a leader of a pack of survivors, saving everyone, while I was the hermit on top of the mountain. Here I am, rescuing his girlfriend, and he's doing zombie things for fun and profit while I nail boards to doors and climb up fire escapes."

"What would you do on your mountain?"

"Read. Garden. Go down and kill zombies. For fun and profit."

"I don't really get this 'fun and profit' thing."

"It was just something we said. Like an inside joke kind of thing." He shuffled his feet slightly, looking away. "He was my best friend. Not just a work friend. I don't know."

"I'm sorry, Brett." I really was. My heart went out to him. Sean was my best friend, too. More so than Callie, more so than my mom—who I was more and more convinced was dead or a zombie now, herself. And we'd both lost him. "I don't . . . I don't think it's all bad? I guess? Like, he made it sound kind of okay. There was a community of zombies. I'm not sure what all the rambling was about, really, but I'm fairly certain by the end he was talking more about them and his zombie 'family' than about me and our home."

He cracked a smile. "So you're telling me now he's leading a pack of zombies for fun and profit?"

"If he isn't leading them by now, I don't know what the hell he's doing. He's had all day to conquer the zombie pack. By now he's sure to have figured it all out."

We laughed together, and lapsed into silence, staring at the boarded up door. Grace padded up to the door and sniffed at it, giving it her seal of approval. She licked it once and turned around, staring at me expectantly, as if this was the first day of the rest of our lives.

Well. I guessed it was.

~

Brett eventually left, promising to come back in two weeks exactly, and I tucked Grace and I in on the couch for some news searching. She rolled over charmingly and snuggled in by my feet, her little paws up to her chest, and sighed happily. I got the feeling she'd been alone for a while.

It wasn't true, but it felt like I had been, too.

"What are we gonna learn about tonight, puppy?" I questioned her. She harrumphed at me and I laughed, reaching down to stroke her furry ears as I flipped on CNN. I was becoming adept at reading the ticker tape and listening to the newscaster at the same time. Listening and reading had never particularly been my strong suit, but I was learning.

I sighed as I was updated about vaccination progress by the president and the CDC advisor. At least they hadn't been turned into zombies. I learned that more than sixty percent of the country had been turned or killed as a result of the infection. Holy motherfricking shit.

That was the most depressing number I'd ever heard. I stroked Grace's ears mournfully, tears streaming down my face as I watched the news clips of riots in the streets and roadways full of zombie bodies, blocking the sidewalks and following single file down alleyways, chasing patiently after their prey: us. Their mouths were hanging in a Joker-style grin, a malicious smile that said "you are mine," and I shuddered. Sean was up there—did he have that smile yet? Was he done turning? How long did it take?

The more I watched, the more uncomfortable I became. The images of the zombies began to mesh with my memories of Sean and I sobbed, holding Grace to me as she crawled up my body and began to lick my face. "Good puppy," I wept, cradling her face in my hands.

Then I did something I hadn't done in a long time: I prayed.

"Dear God," I whispered through my tears. "Please, take the Sean I knew from this infection. Let him die, or let his awareness die from this disease. Let him become something other than the Sean I loved. Someone else. Let him go away, so that he doesn't have to be trapped in a zombie's body. Please don't let him be aware of what he's doing. Please."

I couldn't stop thinking that maybe Sean was still in there, thinking about what he was doing and being unable to stop it. Was he still cognizant of his actions? Was there horror behind those eyes? I tried to keep watching the news, but the tears were blurring my vision. What would happen if they did find a cure? Would it even be worth it?

I didn't know. I didn't know if it would be worth it to the survivors of an infection like this. What if they could remember everything they'd been through? Jesus. I couldn't imagine remembering killing someone, and killing someone in that *way*.

Grace whined, and I realized it had been hours since I took her to the bathroom. I sniffled, wiping my eyes with the back of my hand. There was no real use in crying, but I needed to grieve, I guessed. It was the only real way to get through this. We went to the zombie room quickly, and I cleaned up after her and rewarded her with the makeshift Lorna Doones. I texted Brett and added dog treats to the list, as well as reminding him I needed dog food *before* he came back in two weeks. *Well shit,* I got back. *Three days?*

Three days.

At least I could fairly well promise I wouldn't be a mess by the time he got back. If nothing else, I was resilient. I settled back on the couch with Grace, feeling morose. My eyes felt puffy, and I was miserable. It was awesome.

The president was no longer on the TV, but the CDC chick was still there. She was promising the vaccine would be rolled out to every town with a university level school by the end of the following week. So that meant I *would* be going out. Because I'd be damned if I'd be the one girl that *didn't* get the vaccine and found the one zombie that only wanted to bite me and not eat me.

"I project that we will reach seventy percent of the American people infected or killed by the end of the spring. Our numbers are dwindling, people. We are not doing well with this. This wave swept across the country and decimated us. If the Swiss find a cure, that number could switch to sixty percent uninfected or cured. But the National Guard is not coming to save you. There is no National Guard anymore. The Army is not coming to save you. What little Army we have left is guarding the president. The CDC consists of about twenty-five people working around the clock that never leave the CDC building. Get the damn vaccine. I don't care if it's made of star-stuffed aborted baby tissue blessed by the Pope. We need you to get the damned vaccine." She stalked off the stand.

Well. I guess that was one way of doing it. And I also guessed there were not many people left to fire her for being a jackass about it. But she had a point. If there were only going to be thirty percent of Americans left . . . we were a dying breed, and she knew it.

I sat my head on the pillow of the couch, Grace in the hollow of my knees as I lay on my side. She snuggled up to my butt, curled in a little ball, her nose sticking out onto my knee. I felt safer with her here. I felt like together, we could survive this thing.

To be honest, though, staring at her tiny nose was the first time I'd *wanted* to survive all day.

A Few Days Later

~ Sean ~

I t was light, and then it was dark. Again and again. And I didn't sleep; we hung around outside the apartments, in the hallway of floor five, listening to them play and watch that screen and laugh. They were quiet every time they heard us walking; they knew we were out there, but they didn't seem concerned.

Makethemworry, Darla snarled. *Infectthemall.*

My eyes rolled toward her, as I staggered over a potted plant. I fell to the ground on my broken ankle, then slowly got to my feet. Samuel stood still, letting me use him to pull me up. I couldn't get up on my own. The Old Man simply watched; it was his way, to let us get through disputes on his own, I was learning.

We moved toward the next door. My awareness was spreading and changing. I could feel her. Her name wasn't there, not yet. But I could feel her presence, her otherness in 5D. She was there, and she had turned overnight. The sun exploded in the sky, with yellow chasing orange and the blue falling into the well of the universe. I wiggled with excitement, looking at Samuel. *Issheready?*

Yes, he said gleefully. We grunted, over and over, bouncing on our heels as we looked at the Old Man.

Lethercome, he advised. *Wait.*

I was crestfallen. I wanted her to come now! I wanted to know her! I could feel her wall slowly cementing itself in my awareness, could tell that she was a cat lover. She had worked as an accountant. She was terrified, but she was losing it quickly. I wondered who she would become. What different person this would turn her into. I beamed at this thing I had done—I had made her *better*. All the worries of her old life were *over*. There was nothing left to be scared of.

She was one of us now.

She'llneedtofeed, the Old Man warned us. In my excitement, I'd forgotten that first moment when you fully turned: your stomach turned into a battleground, warring with the Infection. There was a moment where you couldn't possibly decide whether you should feed or Infect; that was what your family was for. To help you, to guide you. I relaxed as Samuel and the Old Man put their arms around me. I longed for the contact.

It felt amazing, like the best hug from your mom in the world. They were my true family, the family I'd been missing all along. I watched the door impatiently, eager to expand my true family, and excitement burst from my chest as a hesitant foot popped through the doorway.

A dark leg was exposed, then a hip covered in a white

skirt. Then she came. She came! As she came toward us, I learned her name was Sarah. Sarah! *HelloSarah!* I screamed, throwing my hands against each other in an approximation of a clap.

She winced, as if the light was too bright. I knew that feeling—everything was too sharp at first, too bright. As her eyes settled into being one of us, it would get better. I tried to send her that feeling through our Link, and felt her relax a little. *Hi,* she said shyly.

Darla was unhappy. She had liked being the only girl in the group. At least, she wanted to be the badass girl of the group. *Notimpressed,* she said shortly, and turned away to meander toward the window. Sarah looked confused. She'd lose control of those facial muscles soon enough, I knew.

Whyconfuse? I said.

Sostrange, she said back, struggling with the words. *Ifeel . . . sostrange.*

She did feel strange: a little lost, a little unsure. Was this how I had been at first? I felt amazing now. It was like I was superhuman; I guessed I was, really. I felt like I could do anything, and I would. The four of us would do amazing things together, until we found my six. And then . . . we could get out of this building, and build our own world.

I threw my arms around Sarah and she flinched, but relaxed into my enthusiasm. *Wehunt!* I crowed.

Wehunt, the Old Man said solemnly, as if it were a duty, and not the most fun thing in the history of fun things.

We listened carefully at the doors, trying to find

somewhere that wasn't so full of people that we couldn't handle it. Finally, at 5F, we found it: the low sound of a TV, and an old man coughing. We waited patiently and I watched the sun; a full hour passed, and there was no sound of another person in the apartment.

Sarah looked at me, unsure. Samuel and I were the resident door breakers, and it didn't take much for us to break this door, as it wasn't even deadbolted. Samuel fell in front of me and used me to pull himself up with his one hand, and Sarah followed cautiously behind.

The elderly man wasn't surprised to find us knocking at his door. He simply stared at us as we invaded his apartment, checking all the rooms for surprises, knocking plastic plants over and mail off of tables. "I was waiting for you." It took a second for the words to trickle through my brain, to make some sense of what he'd said.

I grunted and groaned, trying to tell him that I hadn't heard that one before, but it didn't come out in English. Of course not. It was frustrating, sometimes, not being able to talk to them, but mostly I didn't *want* to anyway They weren't my family.

Darla tapped her foot impatiently, except it came out as a stomp, and Sarah looked to me, her maker—her maker!—for direction.

Eat, I said. *Justeat.* I looked down at the man, sensing somehow that he wouldn't resist. I almost wanted to apologize to him for what we were about to do. I didn't know why; it wasn't wrong. People were food. He was without a family; what life could there be for him? He could get injured and spend the rest of his short life hurting. Hell, he could be hurting now. There was plenty of reason why this was the best thing for him.

We were doing him a favor.

I knelt down next to his wheelchair and grabbed him by his hair, holding his head back, and gestured with my head for Sarah to begin. She walked over to him, wobbling, and leaned down to his neck. "I forgive you," he said.

She looked at me, worried. *It'sokay,* I said soothingly. *Justignore.*

Sohungry, she whispered. She was dazed; I could hear it in her voice. She scented him, inhaling the baby powder and medications, and I marveled that we could ingest such things as the chemicals he was taking to survive and turn them into fuel for our bodies. We were amazing things!

She bit, and blood splattered all over me.

The man moaned weakly, flailing in his chair, and I held him fast, as hard as one could with one hand. I was beaming with pride as she gorged, moving from his neck to his chest, ripping open the rib bones and going straight for his heart. He had died quickly, early on, and she held his heart in her hand, still warm, and began to eat.

I moaned hungrily and she gestured, inviting me to the other side of his frail body. I dropped his head back and dove into his soft abdomen, digging my teeth into his skin and spleen. It was spongy, not meaty, and I chewed it hard, my teeth sticking into the grit. I felt at one with Sarah; we were doing exactly what we were meant to be doing, and I was in harmony with her, more in tune with

her than I'd ever felt with anyone in my life. I could almost have wept; it was beautiful, eating this old man with
my new zombie friend.

I looked up at her and smiled, feeling the vein hanging
from my lips.

~

Veins were my favorite part: they reminded me of spa-
ghetti. I sought out and tasted each one of them with
Sarah, languidly searching through the man's body for my
favorite treat. I recognized something in the back of my
mind: it was a screaming sound, a voice, telling me that
what I was doing was wrong. It sounded like my voice.

How could that be, when everything was so perfect?
Everything was so right. I had my family, I had food, I had
safety and shelter . . . there was nothing to worry about. I
knew his voice wasn't the most important one. His voice,
whoever he was, was behind bars, locked up and safe, and
when—

Oh, God. And sometimes, when I concentrated, I
switched back to that voice, and the voice behind the bars
took control. Oh, holy fucking hell, what have I done?

I heaved, but nothing happened. I watched Sarah
mangle the old man in front of me, and tears fought to
spring to eyes that no longer responded. I mourned him,
mourned this old man who had died alone in front of two
zombies who didn't give a fuck about him, and I cried,
cried on the inside, cried trapped inside my body.

Kiera. Fuck. It had been what, three days? How was
she surviving? Was she okay without me? Had Brett gotten to her? I was so worried. Samuel was behind Sarah,

looking at me strangely, and I took that to mean that the "behind bars" feeling wasn't one he participated in very often. I shrugged it off, using my fingers to dig the blood off of my arms, one uncoordinated swipe at a time. I didn't give a fuck what Samuel thought.

I deserved to die.

There had to be a way to get them to kill me so I could end this. Except . . . why would one zombie kill another zombie in his family? I was learning that if nothing else, family meant everything to these fuckers. It was like the goddamned Mafia, the mob, the Family, all caps. You didn't mess with the Family. I had a feeling if I made my presence known too often, they'd step in and do something about it, and I didn't know what it was.

So I had to act. I had to lurk. I had to pretend I was a zombie, even when I had these moments of clarity, even when I wanted nothing more than to kill myself to free myself of this horrific fucking nightmare I was trapped in. Please, God, let Kiera be safe from this reality.

I would pretend to be a zombie, while planning to die.

I watched Sarah as eagerly as I could pretend to, inwardly cringing as she gored the man, making a mess of his intestines and the bile in his liver. I was learning a lot more about anatomy than I'd ever wanted to know. My stomach kept heaving, wanting to throw up, but nothing would come out.

Samuel poked at my mind gently. *Youok?*

Fine, I responded, as happily as I could manage as a suicidal zombie. *Tired? Satisfied? Content.*

Makessense, he said finally. *Goodjob.*

I nodded, my head rolling from shoulder to shoulder, and stood up slowly, feeling the blood pooling across my shirt, stiffening in pockets across my body. It was sticky and horrible, knowing that I had this man's dying breath on my body. Sarah reluctantly stood with me, having that dazed look that I'd imagined I had had when I'd . . . eaten . . . my first person.

Good, the Old Man said as we started for the door. *Nowshecan Infectsomeone.*

Is that the goal? Eat and infect? That's our whole life? And Zombie Sean is happy with that? I sighed, whistling through my teeth. Samuel looked at me strangely again; he knew something was up, but he didn't have the words for it. I didn't understand myself, for the first time in maybe ever. There was nothing in life more that I wanted than Kiera, but I knew now that I would never deserve her again.

I wondered what she was doing, right now, three floors above us.

Zombie Sean fought me, fought to get back control, and I tried to push him away, wanting to remain myself for just a little longer. *Stayback,* he growled at me. Was this what it was like to have multiple personalities? Was that what zombie-ism did? Fuck. I had a true-to-life psychological disorder and couldn't even analyze myself for it. Brett would have a field day laughing about learning I had a dissociative disorder during the apocalypse.

Let me be! I shouted, pleading, begging him. Just a little longer. Let me picture her, smiling by the window, sleeping on the couch, just a little longer. Let me hear her voice, singing in the shower, telling me stories about her day, just a little longer. Let me remember her touch—

I smiled at Sarah, feeling my jaw dropping open again. *Wasgood?* I asked. *Wasgoodfood?*

Goodfood, she echoed, beaming, bouncing on the balls of her feet. She still had more coordination than I did. *Infect? WhatisInfect? HowdoweInfect?*

Thatfeelingtospread? Togrow? Morefamily? Infect.

Oh, she said thoughtfully. *Infect.* It was like translating to a new language. She was learning quickly, though; she danced along in front of me, happy as could be in her new life, and I smiled again. There was nothing better than being what we were. I didn't know what Behind Bars Sean had to worry about; there were no worries here. There was nothing left to think about. There was nothing left to be scared about. We were invincible. All I had to do was look down at my stump arm and my broken leg to prove it.

We would find Sarah her new friend, and watch her Infect him or her. We would wait for them to wake up.

The Old Man was watching me thoughtfully, as if he knew something that I didn't. I frowned. I didn't want him to think about me. I hurried up, catching up to Sarah and Samuel, and listened to their conversation about Infecting. It was better this way.

It was better this way.

Day Five

~ Kiera ~

Grace was really great at putting her front legs on the third rung/step of the fire escape, but she was hesitant to lift her back legs onto it. I had climbed up the rickety fire escape myself to make a little obstacle course for her on the roof earlier that morning. I stood by the ladder with my Lorna Doones, knowing this would be exponentially easier when Brett came back today with treats. I leaned back, luring her up the ladder, waiting, waiting . . .

Yes! She put a foot on the ladder rung and I hurriedly gave her a cookie. One step at a time, right? This was my life now: training dogs and, well . . .

Zombie hunting. I kept working with Grace, trying to get her to put all her weight on the fire escape as I thought about the early morning. I'd gone up the fire escape, alone—Grace sure hadn't been ready to go up at that point. It took me all morning, and when I finally put

Grace to bed for her nap, I decided it was the best time for me to go down.

I wasn't sure what to do without Grace next to me; she had become such a force in my life that it felt like she had always been there. I lurked around the corners of the building, lingering, the way men did when looking for an unwilling date. I was looking for an unwilling zombie: someone to walk by that didn't expect me to be there, someone who thought that I was going to be prey, not predator. I hefted my hatchet-mop and stalked the streets carefully, sticking to the shadows, patrolling the corridors of my block.

It was then that I saw her: straggly blonde hair, limp and hanging in her face. Her eyes were raging and dead at the same time; black and bleeding. She staggered along the alleyway, banging into trash cans. I was surprised I hadn't heard her before; she was making a hell of a racket.

I crept along slowly, circling around behind her, and raised my hatchet-mop. I thought I could hear Grace snuffling at the seventh-floor window, but it had just been my imagination. I relaxed, knowing that she was safe, knowing that no zombies could get her—but this zombie could get someone else. Could get someone else's dog. Could get someone else's boyfriend.

And that would just not do.

I launched myself at her back, swinging my hatchet-mop as hard as I could. It connected with the back of her neck and I swung again, yanking it out of her spine and hacking again, and again, and again. I hacked so hard I felt something pull in my shoulder, but more importantly, I felt something give in her neck. She was so surprised she hadn't moved; she had merely grunted, falling to her knees, like a woman falling to an execution-er's axe.

An executioner. I was the executioner. And I loved it.

It was hard to stick a hatchet through a human being's neck. Was she still human? With the last swing, something had stuck, and I planted my foot against her back, leaving a bootprint against her flowered dress. I pulled and pulled until my hatchet-mop yanked free, black ooze coalescing up to the handle, not so much dripping as seeping like sap off of the blade. I wiped it off on the hem of the white dress, leaving black stains on the bottom. She wore Mary Janes, I noticed clinically. I wore combat boots that Sean had given me for Christmas one year. She wasn't the one that took Sean away from me, but she could have been, if she'd been on campus. It was so easy to justify murder when there was nobody home behind those eyes.

I watched her twitch a little, nudged her with my foot. Her head lolled, rolled, and finally detached from her body. Her eyes were iced over green. She was gone. And I felt . . . nothing.

Maybe a little grim. A little satisfied. But otherwise . . . nothing. I hefted my hatchet-mop and leaned against the building, looking around the corner. It was clear. Look at me, acting like a professional and everything. My shirt was covered in sticky zombie blood. I'd have to burn it in the oven before Grace got to it.

It surprised me, how little anger I felt. I felt nothing for the woman—the zombie—I'd just killed.

I felt a vibration from my phone and thumbed on the screen. It was Callie. *What are you doing?*

I paused, smiling. *Watching CSI. You?*

I put my phone back in my pocket and felt the cool, clean air against my face. I sighed, relaxing into the breeze, and turned another corner. I saw him then. He wouldn't be as easy to surprise; he was facing me. He had dark hair that fell over his green, green eyes, and was wearing a long hoodie with the university's logo on it. So he was a student, then. He probably fell in the same riot that got Sean. I should have felt bad, I knew. I should have had sympathy for this kid that was probably younger than me. But I didn't.

He might be on the same soccer team as the "kid" who got Sean.

Fuck that noise. They all had to go. I walked toward him brazenly, hefting my hatchet-mop, and thanked Brett silently for the sheer amount of screws and nails that held it together. It was probably the most solid piece of construction I'd ever, well, constructed. Building was not my strong point, but if I could tear it out of the spinal column of a zombie, it was doing pretty well, I thought.

He came toward me with that eerie grin, the one that looked fit to split his lips. He looked like a modern maniac without the makeup, and even had a slit up one corner of his lips to his cheekbone to prove it. I didn't want to know what had happened—had someone tried to kiss him and eat him? I felt my phone buzz again, but I didn't exactly have time to answer it with a zombie shuffling toward me. They weren't really fast, but they weren't creepers, either.

And I didn't want Callie to know what I was doing. She would think it was reckless. Hell, it probably *was* reckless. But that was sort of the point: I didn't care. The only thing I had to look forward to, the only thing I had to take care of, was Grace, and I had a fallback plan. Brett was coming later that day with treats and dog food, so if something happened to me, I knew him well enough to realize that he'd feel obligated to take her with him. And he'd been checking on me every day, so if he didn't hear from me, he'd know something was wrong anyway.

Safety. It had its perks.

The zombie launched itself at me and I swung clumsily. I might have *liked* my hatchet-mop, but that didn't mean I was *good* with it yet. I hit his hand, severing a tendon or two, and it grunted, making that weird mewling sound that I was taking to mean that it was hurt. I swung again, higher, and hit him in the pecs as he reached for me. I was lucky for the reach of the mop handle; I didn't know what the hell I'd be doing if I hadn't thought of that. Probably not this. Probably watching *CSI* after all.

Probably lying in my bed sulking, crying over Sean.

Sean. I swung harder, higher, and connected with his throat. He squawked as I hit something good, something oozy, and he stumbled unsteadily. "That's it," I cooed. "Get a little closer. Let me finish this for you."

That's what I was doing, after all—what he had was no life. This was half a life, a cold life, a life full of nothing and eating people and hurting people. This was spreading infections and killing and burdening others with something you couldn't possibly understand once you had it.

There was *nothing left* for zombies. I didn't care what fucking family Sean was talking about once he had started to turn, it couldn't possibly hold a candle to a real family. Zombie-ism was a burden and nothing more.

"Let me take your burden away."

I swung again with a *thunk,* making contact with the big artery in his neck, and ducked as it began to . . . well, it didn't spray, exactly. It dribbled, it oozed, it seeped, it did all manner of really gross things, but it was still my instinct not to get it on me any more than I already had. I didn't know if ingesting this shit would be enough to turn me into a zombie, but I wasn't about to find out the hard way.

He turned a little toward a sound and his head flopped. I winced, seeing the things inside of his neck that I really didn't want to see. I was disgusted, and focused on that, and not what I should have been seeing behind him.

His "family."

His "family" was behind him. Oh, fucking hell, there were three more zombies behind him. He was lurching on the ground, all of the ooze tumbling out of him like sap and strange, and I began to run. *Dear God, please let me be right. Please don't let them be runners.*

I rounded the corner and headed toward the fire escape, praying that they didn't remember how to climb.

~

Needless to say, I was fine, but it got a little hairy there for a moment. I got back up the rickety escape to train another day with Grace. I'd taken a very, very long shower, as hot as I could get it, to make sure that no globule of ooze was left on my body. I scrubbed hard, with a brush meant for calloused feet, until my skin was raw. I couldn't believe what I had done. I couldn't believe I'd gone out zombie hunting. I'd killed one—no, two zombies.

I sat on the floor of that shower until the water ran cold and Grace was pacing at the door, sticking her paws under it, trying to get to me. I decided from now on, she was an in the bathroom kind of dog.

I fell asleep naked on the bed, still cold and shivering, with Grace tucked up against my back and leaving a lot of fur that I found in the morning stuck to my skin. It still smelled like Sean. I wondered how long it would take until that wore off; until I washed the sheets, I guessed, but the pillow's scent would take a lot longer, I bet.

Either way, the next morning saw me working with Grace on the fire escape to the roof some more. They were at enough of an angle that I thought Grace would get it in no time; the stairs were just super narrow. Wide enough for doggy feet, or at least, I hoped they were.

It also gave me incentive to scavenge when I went zombie hunting, for things that I could make into an agility course for her, though I was increasingly sure this was only interesting for me and the dog. Sean wouldn't have been into it. But I was excited, because I was going back out. There was no question about that. There were at least three more zombies in the neighborhood that I knew about, that were probably missing the guy I hacked up last night, if Sean's family theory held any water.

They wouldn't have to miss him for much longer. But it made me wonder—how could I take on three zombies at once? Were they together all the time? I wasn't exactly *good* at fighting. I was lucky, because zombies were slow. Well, that made the decision for me—there were some really interesting—looking stick fighting practice videos, called Kendo, on Amazon Prime Video, so stick fighting practice it was. Maybe kung fu or something? Was that still a thing?

I needed to get into shape. Round was not a shape. Bookish was not a shape. But it was going to change, and fast, especially with Grace running me up and down the streets. Because I had ideas for Grace, too.

I'd seen this cute little TikTok of a dog that had a coyote vest. Tiny little dog that I had absolutely no interest in; big dogs for the win. The coyote vest was what had me interested. I knew I couldn't stay in the apartment forever, and that meant Grace couldn't either. We would run out of food eventually, and if I wanted her to stay with me, she had to have some protection, and that meant that I was going to take the too-big vest that I'd stolen from Sean's doomsday hoard and craft the shit out of it.

Brett had left behind a few tools after seeing my hatchet-mop and hearing about my bent for crafting, and while I was one hundred percent sure he didn't think for a moment that I was going to do what I was actually going to do, I was fairly certain he'd approve, with his old man on the mountain jazz. Or young hermit on the mountain. Whatever.

Grace and I made our way slowly back down to my apartment. Luckily, it was only eight floors, so we didn't have to go far. I was expecting it to break eventually, and

I wanted to get in as much practice with Grace as I could. After we climbed back through the window and I gave her some food, I concentrated on her vest.

I'd measured her the evening before, and took the vest apart fairly quickly to cut it up and make it Grace sized. She was a medium-sized dog, so it took a lot of cutting and finessing to get it to look more like a doggy vest. It even had a zipper!

And then the crafting began in earnest.

I had thick, huge nails that I wedged between the walls of the tactical vest as it was still in pieces, realizing from former projects that it would not be comfortable to have the equivalent of cold rivets against your back. Fur. Whatever. They stuck out a good three inches, so while the zombies would have to get fairly close to her to puncture themselves, those that did wouldn't appreciate it.

I covered all that that without interfering with her walking—belly, chest, back, and I even looped some extra length around her tail, just to be safe. And then I really went to town: the vest had a hood.

Realistically speaking, I didn't know what the hell vest ever had a hood, but I guessed it was a guy thing, I didn't know. Maybe it was like how women's clothes never had pockets. Or functional pockets, anyway. Whoever thought up the fake pocket needed to be taken out back and shot. Or thrown to the zombies.

I used the hood to go all out helmet. I was *not* letting my dog get bit by a zombie. If I did it right, the hood would loop around her snout just enough to leave her teeth free. So she'd have those daggers to fight with. I cut out eyeholes for her and made little doggy spikes up and down the hood so her head would be safe, and debated holes for her ears, until I realized that her ears were long enough to grab and rip off. Nope, not going down that way, either.

I wondered if dogs needed shoes.

I wondered if Amazon still delivered.

Maybe I could make her some shoes out of, like, paper plates and knitting. That had to be a thing, right? I could totally do that. Or take the soles out of some of Sean's old shoes, knit up around those! I realized then that I was officially the most boring zombie slayer in the entire fucking world.

I hid the suit away and put my hatchet-mop back in its trusty place by the dining room pantry after a thorough scrubbing—I'd already burned the clothes before my shower last night—as I heard Brett clambering up the fire escape. He wasn't exactly the quietest person in the world. Then again, he also had a fifty pound bag of dog food over one shoulder and God knew what else in his hands, so what the hell did I know about being quiet?

I opened the window and let him in, Grace standing close behind. Ever since that shower, she'd been my shadow. I thought she'd known what I'd done, as much as a dog could know something like that. She knew something was wrong, anyway, as I cried myself to sleep, naked, with a dog.

Brett came through the window and hefted the bag on the floor, only breathing mildly hard. I hated him so damn much sometimes. "So what are we doing today?"

He dropped a second bag of assorted dog treats, and Grace went to town sniffing and investigating, wagging her black and white tail fervently.

I thought quickly. "So . . . how do you feel about zombie hunting?"

His face grew serious. "That *you* probably shouldn't be doing it."

"How do you feel about Japanese stick fighting?"

That one got him. "I mean, if you're doing it *because* you want to go zombie hunting, I'm not a fan. But if you want a sparring partner, I'll take the broom. Wait. I want a weapon attached to it. What do you got?"

Okay, so Brett was taking the stance of "don't ask, don't tell" on the zombie hunting thing. I had a feeling that I could swing him around to my side if I showed even a little prowess at this stick fighting thing. "You're going to let us use live weapons to practice on each other? How about we use two broomsticks first, and I'll nail a machete onto it later?"

He was very serious. "Promise me you won't forget about the machete."

I beamed. He was going to be my zombie hunting partner with Grace. I just knew it. "I promise."

~

We put on the Amazon video, and I really had to wonder who thought it was a good idea to put weaponized fighting on a $9.99 a month subscription, but what the hell did I know? We got out the brooms, and Brett had the brilliant idea of couch pillows and duct tape for some padding. Decking each other out, we looked utterly ridiculous, especially him with the fringe on the pillows, but it would work.

Grace took one tentative bite out of my knee pillow, and seemed satisfied. She sat down on the couch, taking very serious watch over us.

The video took us through some guided meditation. With sticks. I didn't know meditating with sticks was a thing. There was a waterfall motion that Brett almost busted his ass on, and some posing like a mountain, and then all of a sudden we were in the thick of things. Block, thrust, forward. Back, thrust, attack. It was this intricate dance that fascinated me. I'd taken dance from three years old up until I went to college, and this was just an extension of ballet—it felt like the most natural thing in the world, to extend these motions beyond my arms.

Brett was having a little trouble.

He was definitely what we would call hack-and-slash in the gamer world. His brilliant ideas were to hit as hard as he could, advance as much as he could, and he certainly wasn't following instructions. Fortunately for me, the video seemed to be primed—haha, get it?—anyway, it seemed to be primed and ready for beginners that thought strength over form was important, and the instructor was form all the way. *I* had already decided it was form all the way. The broom handle ebbed and flowed with me as I danced around his hacking and slashing, and he couldn't touch me. I finally, finally! landed a blow on his left flank, and it felt like victory.

He grunted. "I don't like that you're good at this," he said at last.

"Why?"

"Because I think it's going to give you stupid ass ideas that you shouldn't be having."

"Or brilliant ass ideas that you should be having *with* me. Brett, I fucking hate them. I loathe their very existence. There is one very special zombie in this building that I would do anything to keep safe, but otherwise I want to destroy every one that I see, preferably with my hatchet-mop, preferably by taking their miserable heads off of their miserable bodies." I shook my head, hair falling into my face, out of my ponytail. I was a few heads shorter than Brett, but I'd never felt stronger. "And you? You're the hermit on the mountain. You can do this."

He grunted again, and I noticed he'd buzzed his already short hair down to the scalp. He looked a lot more intimidating that way—well, if you didn't know he'd trekked a few miles in the hot sun on a bike with dog food just for his dead friend's girlfriend.

"What? What's the grunt? I don't speak primitive man. Or zombie. Are you a zombie now? Should I hack your head off? Come on, Brett. We can do this. Rid the streets of one disgusting zombie at a time. I . . . I happen to know of three that are plaguing my neighborhood, and if they weren't around, I could maybe scrounge around for supplies."

"The fuck you need supplies for?" He stared at me, bewildered.

"Look, you told me to be prepared for the long haul, I'm going to be prepared for the long haul. I don't know what the long haul is, so I want some canned cranberries, for fuck's sake. It doesn't *matter*. But I need something to do outside this apartment or I'm going to lose my god-damned mind."

He heaved a breath, his muscled chest rising and fall-ing heavily, and I knew he was thinking about it. Closing his deep brown eyes, he then opened them slowly, staring at me. "I'm not responsible for you."

"I'm better at this than you are."

"I'm not responsible for you," he said heavily. "I'll take care of you the ways Sean wanted me to, bring you toi-let paper, dog food, though he never said anything about dog food, I'll do all that shit. Check up on you. Whatever. But if you go outside vigilante-style all alone, and you die, or if we go out together and you get bit, *I. Am. Not. Responsible. For. You.*"

I looked at him steadily, putting a hand on his sweaty shoulder. I was still panting a little. It would take time for me to get into shape, to be in prime zombie hunting state, Brett was already there, he just sucked at any type of movement that wasn't 'hit the thing as hard as he could.' "Brett, I promise you, this is on me. It was my idea. And I'm getting the vaccine."

I could tell he was skeptical about the vaccine thing, but too polite to say anything about it. Let's be honest, if a zombie bit me, that was pretty much it, running away was not aligned with my talents in life. Well, maybe it would be—just to get Grace away. I could heal. I could make it through, the way Sean couldn't. I could come through the other side.

Right?

One Week

~ Sean ~

here had been several risings and fallings of the sun. I had completely lost my ability to keep track of time, or what day it was, or even if the world had kept turning. We spent more of our time than not *communing:* talking to each other, but not really talking. It was more like the weird nature walk stuff that your parents talked about, guided meditation and everything weird that came out of the seventies. We simply existed, together, and floated on in the realm of togetherness.

It was amazing.

It was even more amazing when we heard a sound guiding us to our next appointment. That's what Darla referred to them as: appointments. She wanted to Infect the entire fifth floor by the end of the month, but I couldn't remember what month it was, or what a month was.

I was getting used to walking on my funky ankle, and

Samuel was doing fine with his one hand. Zombies were nothing if not resilient.

Darla was getting frustrated, I could feel it. She was pacing as we communed, pacing up and down the hallway in measured, staggered footfalls. *Whatisit?* the Old Man asked calmly.

Weshouldbe outthere! she yelled. *Free! Notthiscrap!*

I closed my eyes. The only reason I wanted to stay in this apartment building was, well, the girl. The girl on the seventh floor. The girl who I wanted to bring into my family. She had red hair and she smelled like lavender.

A voice in the back of my mind sounded equal parts exasperated and devastated. *Kiera.*

It wasn't one of the family. *Huh?*

Her name is Kiera.

Who???

The girl. The girl with the red hair and the lavender skin. Her name is Kiera. She doesn't want to be a zombie. Please, leave.

Whoareyou???

It wasn't the first time that I'd heard him, of course, but I poked at it anyway, trying to force it out. It disturbed me to have voices other than my family's in my head. I didn't know any zombies that spoke the way he did, not that I knew an awful lot of zombies in the first place, but I had a feeling this voice meant something awful, and that they wouldn't like it if I told them about it.

I'm you. Sane. Not a zombie.

Idon'tlikeit, Idon'tlikeit! I panicked, rocking on my heels. This was Change, capital C. There was a VOICE IN

MY HEAD and it wasn't theirs. He knew me. He knew everything about me, and he was talking to me.

Samuel looked at me, confused. *Areyouok?*

Thinking. AboutDarla. I shook my head. *Don'tknow whattodo.*

Meanwhile, the voice that was me sighed. *This is no life, Sean. There is nothing for you here. You used to be so much more than this.*

Family! I insisted, my heart wrenched. Why couldn't I make him understand? Why couldn't I make him see what beauty lay in this system, this way of being? There had to be a way to lead him to the feelings I felt.

Instead, I felt his sorrow. I felt an immense amount of grief, immovable and irrefutable. The grief felt like pushing a boulder up a mountain, only to tumble your way down and land with the boulder on top of you, day after day. He felt hopeless—and I was the cause.

I was crestfallen.

He sighed. *It's not your fault,* he said, his voice fading somewhat. *You are what you are.*

Iam, I said shakily, half listening to Darla lay out our strike plan. She wanted to go downstairs. She wanted to bust out the doors and stalk the streets. She wanted to head downtown to the campus, to find more people like us. And she wanted to Infect everyone she saw.

God, it felt so clear, so clean! It made so much sense! The more people we Infected, the safer they were, the safer everyone else was! If we were all Infected, no one would get hurt anymore! I had a broken ankle, and I didn't even care! Why couldn't Other Sean, if that was what he was, see that? There was no pain. Until recently, there was very little confusion. There was no big emotional leap of faith and the only love I needed was the love of my family.

And if something happened to my family, there was *always* more family. There was always someone looking to be taken in, someone who needed a place to be, someone looking to fill that last role in their Link. We were a community by nature, and they just didn't *see* that. Why couldn't they see that we just wanted to be a community with *everyone?*

Other Sean scoffed, and faded into the background. I shook my head, feeling a little stunned, and looked up at Darla, determined. *Allin,* I said. *Allin. Let'sgo.*

That'sachange, she snarled.

Don'tbenasty, the Old Man said calmly. *He'strying. He'sstillnew.*

Sarah looked at me cautiously, putting a clumsy hand on my arm. *WeInfect? Wemake theworldbetter? Thatis howit works?*

Yes, I wispered, squeezing her hand with my own. *Thatishowitworks.*

And it was, whether Other Sean wanted to admit it or not. We barreled toward the stairs, making a better plan than "fall down them and see what happens" like I'd done earlier. We each sat down on the top step and half fell, half crawled on our bottoms like crabs, moving slowly but as a team, and it took the better part of the morning to get through one floor. The sun was high in the sky by the time we reached the door.

Fuck, I said, and I knew I'd be out of breath if I could.

Yeah, Samuel echoed, huffing in his mind. *Forzombieswe'reoutofshape.*

ZombieISashape. Darla grinned, with broken, craggy teeth.

We started scooting down to the next floor, and the next, stopping only to listen at the doors and see what we might be coming across. The floors were largely silent, except for a few scattered, hushed conversations and a few loud footfalls. Finally—*finally*—we got to the ground floor, where Brett and I had spent so much time working on de-zombifying the place.

It took all of us to lean against the door, but it opened to the setting sun as we shoved past the boards on the front of the building. The boards were no longer nailed in; something, or someone, had pulled them loose. I smelled the rancid air of trash uncollected and the sweet air of freedom. We squinted into the sun, the five of us, and it was up to me to lead. I was the one who knew the way to the college. I was the one who knew the way to the rest of us. And I was going to get us there.

I looked at the Old Man for a long moment. I wasn't sure if I was looking for approval or permission; maybe both. I wasn't trying to take up his mantle or anything, but he was the one putting me in charge in the first place by tacitly giving me this assignment. He nodded, once, and waited.

Allright, I said finally. *We head north.*

I took a step.

~

My sense of direction was no longer the "go left two blocks" variety. I didn't exactly remember what north *was*. What I did know was that the sun shone on my face *that* way, so that meant I should go *that* way toward the school. Directions were solely focused on the earth and the sky. Did zombie-ism mean a return toward nature? It excited me to think this was a new kind of man—a kind of man that was closer to how we should be, living off the land.

I giggled, and Samuel smiled. He knew exactly how I felt. Sarah followed at a distance, and Darla scowled, picking up the pace. We meandered down the street. I didn't know how long it would take to get to the campus, or how far it was—those numbers were meaningless now—but I knew we would get there eventually. That was one of the great things about being what we were—eventually, everything would happen. We would always get where we were going. We would always outlive our prey. We would always find what we were looking for. It was inevitable.

This was the first time I'd encountered zombies other than my family. It was different, somehow; knowing that they were there but not feeling them through the Link. I could sort of feel them pressing against my walls, a buzz of energy humming around me. There was so *much* of it! Sparks of life everywhere, zipping between every one of us. "Zombies are dead." As if. There was more energy here than I'd ever felt before in my life.

The Old Man was watching me, smiling his grotesque smile. I could hear Other Sean howling in the background, screaming against his bars, about a false life. A half life. A life that was only alive because of what it took from others.

So what?

I felt a little ashamed of that one, really. I knew somewhere inside of me I had better answers, but I didn't have them right now. All I had was the excitement of going *somewhere*.

I trotted along beside Samuel, and nudged his shoulder with my head. *Everbeen?*

Toschool? No. Tooyoung.

Toobad. Ladywentthere.

Whatlady?

I struggled. Other Sean screamed. *Kiera! Kiera! Kiera! Her name is Kiera, you useless piece of shit!*

Ladyfrom before. We . . . wewill needtogo back. To Infect.

Samuel frowned. *Why?*

Wantherin myfamily. Important. The problem was that I couldn't remember any longer why it was important, and it panicked me. I stopped, heaving in a breath, staring at the zombies milling about in the streets in front of me. I couldn't remember. The nice lady with the lavender scent. I could remember her eyes, I could remember her hair, the way it fell over her shoulder; I could remember the way she spoke to me, but why was she so important?

Other Sean was sobbing in his cell, and carefully

walked forward, pressing toward me until he came into my awareness. *Her name is Kiera,* he said carefully. *Her name is Kiera, and I love her. I love her more than life. Please don't go back. Don't ever go back. Don't let her see you like this. I'd rather die.*

And I would. I'd rather die by some fucked up zombie-related mortality than ever let her see me with vein slime down my face and zombie blood soaking my shirt. I would never want her to see me as an animal, and that's all we were, now. There would never be anything else. We were animals now, the two of us, together.

I ignored Zombie Sean's desire to go back to the apartment, his whining in my head that grit my teeth together and made me want to scream. All he could do was talk about *the lady, the lady* that he didn't even fucking know. He didn't remember her name! It had been a week. A *week!*

What was she doing? How was she surviving? God, I wished I could write her texts, letters, something to let her know that I survived, that some part of me was still in here, still okay, inasmuch as I could be okay in a situation like this. It wasn't easy to wrest control from Zombie Sean, but it could be done. And that meant I could kill myself.

I looked at it clinically, like the solution to a problem. It was the best that I could do, all things considered. There was a bridge above a wrought iron fence that held a beautiful garden. I could easily fall over the bridge and onto the fence. Easy peasy. But something inside of me kept me from falling, from ending my own life. I didn't know if it was survival instinct or something from Zombie Sean, a relic of being part of the Link and not abandoning his family.

Nosuicide, Zombie Sean said sullenly. *Keepwalking. Findourown.*

At least he was off of Kiera now. We kept walking, a strange mixture of ZS and . . . NZS? It was weirdly peaceful, a co-op of the two of us lost in our own thoughts, and I had decided it would remain that way until we made it the eleven or so miles to campus.

Yeah, so that didn't happen.

There were snipers. There were snipers at the entrance to the little town-within-a-town that was the campus, men and women with crossbows—who the fuck had crossbows? Oh, right, the store I used to work at. Anyway, they had crossbows, and I found myself ducking for cover as Samuel threw himself bodily over me, grinning his relaxed smile.

Thisisfun, he said. Interestingly, his voice sounded like static when fed through my little piece of the nonzombie brain. That probably wasn't an appropriate thought to have while we were being shot at.

Fun, I grunted. *Wehaveto killthem.*

And just like that, NZS was back in his pretty little cell. I had full control, and I was going to use it. The Link in my mind shuddered, making me wince. Something was wrong. I swept my eyes over the scene, feeling as if something was wrong. This metaphysical shit was getting to me.

I realized that one of my walls had shattered in my

head. There was a bullet hole—no, an arrow hole. An arrow hole through the Old Man. He had been hit by one of the high speed arrows, and we dragged him into one of the nearby buildings as he stayed silent, staring up at the sky.

His eyes were rolling in his skull. The shot went into his chin. If he moved an inch, it would do what headshots did to all good zombies, and he would be down for the count. And he was too old not to move that inch.

I looked at the wound, the black gore dribbling down his wattle, staining his whiteT-shirt, looked at his Texas belt and the marks on it where there had obviously been a sidearm for years. I panicked, realizing there were so many things that I didn't know, hadn't known about him, and now there were no more moments, no more time in which to learn about him. I sobbed, and it sounded like a freight train.

FollowDarla. He then stared at all of us, one by one, presumably giving us silent instructions—and when he came to me, he simply said, *Bethebest.* I had no idea what that meant, no idea what it could mean, but he dropped his head, and the arrow went up, and his eyes turned that cloudy, disgraceful green that meant he was gone.

We howled together, holding hands as best as we could with Samuel and I only having one each. Sarah clung to me, and we rocked, mourning our dead, the Old Man who had taught us and led us. He'd led the others more than me, but he had begun to grow on me. He had started this journey for me. And now his journey was at an end.

I stood up slowly, looked out the window. There were

humans out there. Snipers who wanted to end our lives. Snipers who thought they were better than us, better than the Old Man. *No one* was better than the Old Man.

I looked at Darla, at Samuel, who had come to the same conclusion as I had. I pulled up Sarah, who would follow me anywhere. We looked at the door, decided.

We'd show them exactly who was better.

It's Been a While, Maybe

~ Kiera ~

Brett was not impressed by my Doggo Suit. Then again, he wasn't really impressed by anything that I did. He was pretty much down for anything, was good ol' Brett, so long as he got to carry the machete-on-a-stick I made him. I was getting pretty good at making apocalypse weapons, I thought. Though *nothing* would beat my hatchet-mop.

"You're taking your beloved baby puppy thing that you're building an agility course for and are *teaching how to walk up ladders* and bringing her out in the zombie apocalypse?"

Grace took that moment to yawn, baring her fangs in her cute little Doggo Suit. She was all spikes, from her nose to her tail. I had hacked up a pair of Sean's sandals and invested in making her tie-up shoes. She hadn't really *liked* them, but I sure as hell wasn't going to let her get tetanus or let a zombie bite her feet off, either. She was fully suited, and I was proud of my girl. She wagged, and clinked at the same time.

"I think she has a keen eye for danger. Don't you, Grace? Don't you?" I pet her little nose and she wagged again, her whole body this time, tinkling and clanging and stomping around in her little boots. It was adorable. It was hard to think that this beautiful, kind soul was going to go out into a world so dangerous, the world full of zombies, but I also knew what happened the one time I'd gone out without her to kill zombies.

When I'd come back, she had very carefully taken every item off of the lower shelves of my pantry and made what could generously be called a fort around the couch. She piled things everywhere, making a safe place for herself the way a child would. She made such tall walls that I could only see her ears above the cans and boxes. I didn't know how the hell she did it, or how long I'd been out that it had *given* her time to do it, but nevertheless, she boxed herself in next to the couch where we often slept, hiding against the fabric, panting and shaking.

My poor Gracey did *not* like being alone. And to be honest, I didn't like to be without her either. We had both lost our persons: the people that gave our life meaning. We had both lost everything, and found each other. That had to mean something. It meant never going away. Never leaving each other alone. Never leaving each other's side.

Hence, the Doggo Suit.

And hence, Grace going zombie hunting. Hell, she might be good at it, for all I knew. All I *really* knew was that we were both trauma-soaked messes traveling in human and dog suits, and we were doing the best we could with what we had. And the best we had was each other.

"All right," he said finally. "But I am not responsible for you—"

"Can it with the speeches already, okay? I know. I'm responsible for myself and Grace. You're responsible for the canned yams I owe you when we get back. Whatever. I really don't care. I want these zombies off my block."

"Got it. That we can do. Let me go first." He paused. "That's really misogynistic of me. You're better with your stick thing. *You* go first. I just happen to be larger and have a penis. That doesn't make me better than you. And can your dog go *down,* or just up?"

"We're going to see," I muttered, and paused. "And thank you about the penis thing. Penises do not equate to zombie killing prowess. At least not that I've read. And I've read an awful lot of zombie books. In fact, penises are quite likely to get you killed. You might want to watch out for that."

I mean, I wasn't wrong. Look at that guy in *The Walking Dead.* He was, like, the main dude, and he still got all dead. I thought. I stopped watching before that because they killed off my favorite character (who *does* that?) but either way, he was a dude, and he died just like the rest of them, easy as pie. Being a guy didn't make a damn bit of a difference to the zombies. Flesh was flesh. It didn't matter if you were a guy, a girl, gay, straight, purple or zebra, they would fucking eat you.

And that's about where my prejudices started.

I went down the steps first, coaxing down Grace. We'd worked on this more than a little bit since I'd approached Brett with my plan. Brett had come over several days in a row to work on our stick fighting; what he hadn't seen were the dog tricks. She stepped down with one paw, struggled a bit, then another, and stair-stepped her way after me, shaky but expectant. She knew I had treats in the fanny pack Brett had stolen for me from his store that he regularly burgled. Was it burglary if it was no longer a store anymore, really?

We had a lot farther to go *down* than we did to go *up* when we were going to play and train. I stopped her on one of the platforms, giving her a drink from one of the water bottles I carried in my backpack and offering her some treats. I couldn't really pet anything but her nose, but she took it, leaning into me and wuffing. "You're such a good girl, Grace," I murmured.

"Hanging off a ladder here," Brett said.

Oh. I'd sort of forgotten about him. "Sorry," I mumbled.

We made it down the next few flights of stairs and finally hit the ground bouncing, in Grace's case. She still wasn't used to the boots.

Brett looked at me. "I should've made a strappy thing for my machete like you have," he observed.

"I told you I'd make you one."

"Yeah, but it didn't seem practical to whip one in and out while—"

"Bet it seems practical now, doesn't it?" I reached behind me and "whipped it out." It was on a carabiner clip with a sling at my heel. It was not hard. It was a craft, not rocket science.

He sulked a little, waving his hair from his face. "Yes, mother," he replied sullenly. "Will you make me one for next time?"

"We haven't even survived *this* time, which you reluctantly agreed to, and you're already thinking about next time?"

He brightened. "Hell yeah I'm thinking about next time! This is already more fun than what I usually do all day." We started to walk.

"What do you usually do all day?"

"Make my rounds at the different stores I frequent for supplies. I have several elderly people I check on and deliver stuff to, people with medical needs. There's a few medical supply offices in town that I raid on a regular basis, some pharmacies, stuff like that. There's a few other people's significant others I check on. I'm fucking Robin Hood, except I'm taking from the dead, not the rich."

"That's . . . encouraging, I guess."

He shrugged while Grace trotted beside me. She was pressing uncomfortably close to me, which meant she was probably giving me tetanus, but that was all right. At least I was vaccinated. Speaking of vaccinated, I hadn't heard from Callie in a whole day; I hope everything was all right.

We rounded the corner where I'd seen the second zombie and there they were, right where I'd left them, around a trash can and looking for trouble: the trio of the undead.

"Well, this is going to be fun," Brett said mildly.

Okay, so maybe they weren't exactly looking for trouble. They were more . . . *loitering*. Publicly hanging out. Staring at a trash can. I don't know, homogenizing? Synchronizing their watches? Whatever, they were standing there staring at a Coke can, and for some reason, it pissed me off.

They got to stand around, doing nothing. *They* didn't have to get nailed into their apartments and lose their loved ones . . . Well, except for the fact that I whacked that one guy, so maybe they did. Maybe Sean had been right about their attachments, their families. What did I know? Either way, they *caused* this whole thing, and it wasn't my fault that if I came any closer, they would attack me. This was on *them*, not me.

"Are you lookin' for some more introspection, maybe, or can we go about doing this?" Brett said abruptly.

I realized that we'd been standing there for . . . well, for a while. I hefted my hatchet-mop, and Grace dug her feet into the cement, growling low in her throat as she scented the air. That answered one question I'd had about her: dogs knew about zombies. Oh, yes they did.

She looked at me, and I looked at her. I looked at Brett, and we nodded grimly. I looked at Grace one more time. "Be careful, girl," I whispered.

We charged.

It wasn't like in the movies, with the action heroes running up bravely into the middle of the melee, it was more like . . . we carefully walked up to the zombies with our weapons out and waited for them to notice us. As soon as they started moving, we each called a zombie, leaving the third for Grace, or whichever of us happened to manage to get him. I moved forward on the girl, who seemed about my age, with long, glistening brown hair. She was beautiful, except for the chunk taken out of her cheek that oozed black blood. Brett went to town right away on a sleazy looking man who was a full head and a half shorter than he was, machete-ing the crap out of the poor guy. He didn't stand a chance with Brett's aggressive style.

I went a little more ballet on her ass. She reached out for me and while I didn't know the words for what we were doing, I moved back and hacked at her arm, making my mark, hitting the bone. I must have severed a tendon or something useful, because it hung loosely at her side after that.

There was also the disadvantage of keeping an eye on Grace at the same time, even though from what I saw, I didn't need to. She looked like a hardened battle dog if ever I'd imagined one. She had quickly figured out what the outfit did, that was for sure: she used her flanks to turn around and quickly jab the zombies with her hips, wagging her studded tail like a mace. It would've been hilarious if she wasn't doing *so* much damage with the gigantic nails. I'd made some last minute adjustments early this morning to sharpen the nails, and she was taking full advantage of it as she dug her teeth into the older woman's wrist and shook her head like she was killing prey.

I was really fucking glad that dogs couldn't get the virus right about then.

Pulling my attention back to my zombie, I backed up before she could get an arm around me. Lord knows she was trying, and she was within reach of me before I realized it. I danced back again, using all the ballet I knew to get myself the hell out of her range, and hacked again, sticking my hatchet-mop in her collarbone. Damn it. I missed her neck. I held her at arms' length, trying to get the hatchet OUT of her collarbone, as she groaned and hollered and snapped her yellowed teeth at me.

"Brett, a little help?" I yelped.

"Sorry," replied a calm voice from behind me. "I've been watching you and your dog for a few minutes. You seemed like you were doing a pretty damn good job without me, so I figured I'd see if I could pick up on any techniques."

"You've been—" I grunted, "—standing there watching us for all this time? My hatchet-mop is stuck! Get her!"

Notice that I didn't say what I wanted to say: "kill her." I couldn't say it, not out loud, not yet. That, to me, would admit sentience, a sentience I was not sure about yet. It would make them people, just people of a different kind. And that was not something I could abide by.

Grace was done next, panting and dancing along beside Brett, looking up at me as if she were wondering why I wasn't done with my training exercise yet. She was obviously jazzed that she'd Done the Thing and put down the zombie, because she had—there was no throat to be seen on that zombie, and it was full of holes. It looked like a fucking cheese grater. I don't know what the hell she did to it. I could practically hear her saying "Mo-om, hurry up! I need treats for this one!"

Brett leveled his weapon against the zombie's shoulder,

pulled back, and cut off her head. He failed to stop appropriately and hit my hatchet, which sent a resounding ring and pulse up my arms, making me groan. "You fucking jerk," I moaned, pulling hard and sheathing my weapon so I could shake my hands. "Oh, man, that hurt."

Brett, on the other hand, seemed pleased. "Do you realize that you, me and the dog are one for one as far as zombies go? Like, your plan worked. We did this. We can go zombie hunting. We can probably clear out half of campus so they can set up the vaccine stations like they want."

I brightened. "I can notify the media, my best friend is a journalist. You really think we can do it?"

"If we're careful and we recruit some people? Sure. We can definitely make this work. Get a couple squadrons going, do some training on your roof every night since it's getting warmer out? We've got this."

"We've got this." A truer "oh shit" was never spoken.

The Ambush

~ Sean ~

We didn't have a tactical battle plan, exactly. Zombies didn't think like that. The more time I spent with Samuel, Darla and Leslie, the more I thought there was something unusual about this journal that I wrote in my zombified brain with more pictures and feelings than words or phrases. If anyone tried to put it down on paper, it wouldn't be recognizable as a coherent story, as everything was becoming jumbled and broken. Here I was, trying to get a linear time frame of our zombie attack on the battlefront. We had reached the school, and the snipers were in the buildings next to the big archway sign that announced the campus. They were about thirty feet away from the zombie, and they were in the two-story buildings, I noticed. Not too much in the way of hiding people.

Candothis, I assured them. I looked at the Old Man's

body mournfully. He sat up against the wall. Darla had found a sheet in the building and draped it over his head. Sarah had found a weed and put it on his chest. It was strange, the things we held on to, even when our humanity lapsed. We wanted to honor each other, even if we didn't honor our prey.

There was, indeed, a code of honor among thieves and zombies.

Darla stood up jerkily from a crouch. I looked at her, really looked at her for the first time. She had dark hair and dark eyes, and she was older than me. She looked grim; not worn, definitely not that, but she seemed energized by the battle ahead. I could see the bite that turned her into a zombie: there was a thick black mass of blood coagulated on her left shoulder, about the size of a basketball. That must have hurt like hell, and she must have turned fast.

No wonder she was angry all the time. She got ripped to pieces.

I looked at Sarah, who sat on a chair peacefully watching me. She had been scared once, but it had worked out perfectly: all of her anxiety about food and safety had been gently blown away like dandelion seeds. They were scattered to the winds now, and her only worry was the well-being of her new family. She smiled beatifically, and I wondered if intellect had anything to do with *how* you turned into a zombie.

I felt kind of bad for that one.

Don't, said Darla abruptly. I hadn't known I was

broadcasting my thoughts. *Youweren't. I'mnosy. She'sjust . . . notsmart.*

I chuckled, which sounded like the braying of a donkey. Darla looked up. *Nomorewaiting,* she said to all of us. *Let'sgo.*

And that was our battle plan.

We followed Darla out of the ruined building and said goodbye to our ruined friend; I felt the hole where his wall used to be in my mind. It was like cleaning out your locker for summer break: something that had become such a part of your daily life was suddenly alien and foreign, full of nothingness, and it didn't make sense anymore.

It was like a lost tooth. I kept poking at it with my mind. It didn't like being poked. I was sort of afraid that one day, the abyss in my brain would poke back.

We climbed over the barricades awkwardly. By "climb," I meant that we threw our bodies at them and tumbled over the other side. Once you gave a zombie momentum, they almost always kept it. We ended our tumble in a roll, and I and Darla managed to get back to our feet after a few minutes of surprised silence in the courtyard. We pulled Samuel and Sarah up in a hurry before the shooting started and stumbled into the building next door.

It was wide open on the bottom floor, and there was obviously no one in it. They were also obviously not expecting zombies to know how to climb stairs, because there was nothing in front of them. We leaned against the walls, making our slow way up, and I was guessing the guys didn't have radios, because no one came for us. Maybe they hadn't seen us come through. It was more likely that the snipers on the roofs freaked out about us being zombies and are hiding. I didn't know how they couldn't see us, with the racket we made coming over the barricades.

Either way, Darla stopped short at the doorway to the second floor. How did she *do* that? I couldn't do that. Samuel and Sarah sure as shit couldn't do that. We all slammed into her and suddenly we were in the room and there was shooting of arrows and Sarah was screaming—

It went exactly as a zombie battle did in my brain. There were five or six guys, college-aged, and I was pretty sure none of them had learned how to use a crossbow before this. I got clipped on my bad shoulder, and Sarah was shot through the leg, but I managed to get to the first guy fairly quickly. This wasn't time to spread the Infection; these were Enemies, trying to hurt us. They had already killed the Old Man. I was not going to let them take Samuel and Sarah.

Darla was on her own, and Sarah hid behind me, cowering. I wrenched the boy's arm out of his socket, surprised by my own strength, and tore into his throat, growling. He was screaming, I think, praying, maybe. His blood was warm pouring down my throat and I ate his throat, tearing through the arteries and his esophagus, savoring the flavor, and dropped him on the floor, a shell of nothingness, with light blue eyes staring at the wall.

Sarah came with me as I came for the next one, who ran out of ammo shooting at me and searched for arrows. Darla was on her second as well, and Samuel on his. Gore covered the floor; death caused far more mess than one would think it did. I examined it clinically as I held the man down, looking at the blood and the feces, the piss and shit smell that was so intensely strong here, almost overpowering the blood. A wet streak ran down the man's pant leg and I looked down at him in disgust. "Really?" I tried to say out loud.

I managed a manly grunt. He wailed, hitting me with the crossbow, and I felt the bone next to my eye socket open up, bleeding sluggishly. I hit his head hard on the floor until I heard an uneasy—sounding crack, and turned him over onto his belly. I wasn't exactly the "braaaaains" kind of zombie, but the scent was intoxicating. His skull was cracked, like I thought, and I waved Sarah in.

As Samuel killed his last and Darla played with hers, Sarah and I ripped open the man's skull, and I heard a high pitched whine in the back of my head, like broken static. It sounded like my grandfather's description of tinnitus. I recognized it as Sean wailing: not wailing like the dead man, whose brain was up my nose. It was the wailing of the dead, of the dying, of the men who had seen their despair come to life and walked alongside it until the end.

It was the sound of death come to life.

I smiled and turned to Sarah, watching her dig into the skull cavity with her tiny hands. We had become death. And I relished it.

~

It wasn't quite as easy, breaking off the arrow in Sarah's leg so she wouldn't go around bumping into things more than a zombie normally would. One handed, it would already have been a bear, just trying to hold her leg and snap it off. One handed *and* a zombie, it was fun in spades. I rested my stump against her knee and used my useless hand to press all of my rather considerable zombie strength (why yes, I *was* impressed with myself) against the arrow, and it snapped a little easier than I had been anticipating, actually. And then I stabbed myself in my broken foot with it.

Well, it was going to have to stay there. Was there zombie AIDS? Was that a thing? Fuck.

NZS was remarkably quiet, except for the low keening in the back of my head. It was like watching a video of the Scottish moors, I suddenly had a flash of memory: howls of wind coming off the fells, the water misty and foggish. It never ceased to surprise me, what little brain cells fired up at random moments, what pictures came to my brain. Darla was surprised too, as she watched me.

Youthinktoomuch, she observed.

Youdon't? I said.

Notlikethis, she said back, and we started our long, slow fall down the stairs on our asses, the way you do as kids. The arrow was serving as a bit of an impediment; it went all the way through my foot, and it was catching on the concrete stairs. That was going to be fun if we needed to get somewhere in a hurry.

Youthink . . . She struggled visibly with the words. *More. Words. Lesspictures. Lessfeelings?*

Iguess, I replied, watching Sarah fumble down to the bottom floor. We all got in a circle on our butts and hauled each other up with a degree of synchronization I hadn't known we were capable of. It was something to keep in mind for the future.

Wail, wail. Soft, miserable wailing. NZS sounded like a dying kitten. I wanted to wrench his head off.

Watch it, NZS snarled. I could feel him pacing. A tiger. I saw a tiger. It had stripes, teeth. I liked its teeth. I bared mine, growling, enjoying the sound as we walked out of the building and toward the other one, where people were evidently more alert: there were more arrows.

One hit the ground next to my foot. So there were archers and not-archers in the world, and I was guessing we were looking at the second group.

Just you wait, just you wait, NZS said, over and over again. He rocked back and forth in the corner, holding on to the bars of the cage I kept him in. The cage *I* kept him in. What made him think I was waiting on anything?

I mean, I guessed if I thought about it, I was waiting on getting up more stairs. That was going to be hard.

Darla and Samuel went in first, using their combined weight to shove the door open; it wasn't hard. I felt Samuel's excitement, felt him fueling Darla's angry fire, felt Sarah's curiosity. She was so intrigued by humans; she thought of them like exotic foods that bit back, sometimes. She trusted me to take the bite out of them before she got to them.

I laughed. It came out a steady, unremarkable groan.

We marched into the first floor, and this time, it wasn't empty. Three guys had crossbows trained on us. If they were anything like the first ones, I wouldn't trust them to hit the broad side of a—

I frowned. It was red. The thing. Cows. Moo. What did cows live in?

You're going crazy. You're losing your words. Once you lose your words, you'll be one of them. Gone. Only me to talk to. No more Link. Just feeding. Ha!

Amnot, I said defensively. Just because I forgot the word didn't mean I was losing *all* the words. It didn't, did it?

. . . Did it?

I swallowed and choked. I knew it wasn't possible to choke on your tongue, but that's what it felt like. I gagged, and Samuel looked back, and then it all happened in a blur.

"No!" I screamed, only it came out in a wheeze.

Sarah whipped her head around in slow motion and rapid fire at the same time. Darla, who was never startled, narrowed her eyes.

And Samuel was grinning like a menace, his eyes slanted to one side, as an arrow plunged through the side of his head and out through that smile, that twisted smile, with black sludge painting his smirk.

He dropped instantly, the bioluminescence fading out of his eyes, and his head lolled on the floor. My heart wept at a quick flicker of surprise in my head, followed by the terrible feeling of him being siphoned away from me all at once. He fell into nothingness, and I lost my brother, my first friend, my first family.

I craned my head and looked at the man—no, the *boy*—carrying the crossbow.

His eyes were hard, though his expression looked

terrified. He looked like a boy who didn't know how he'd done that, but he was damn sure he was going to try and do it again.

And I was not about to have that.

I bellowed, and it came out the way it should. NZS threw himself against the walls of his cage and rattled the bars as I charged, stumbling at the man as fast as I could while the three reloaded, and Darla and Sarah followed me. Sarah was forced to attack, and I felt her uncertainty flicker gainst my awareness, Darla's determination, and my own devastation. I was wrong when I said there was nothing to worry about as a zombie. This pain was real.

It was like losing . . . losing . . .

Kiera, NZS whispered in my mind, a poisonous viper ready to strike.

She'ssafe, I raged. *Safefromme, safefromthem, safefromeverything! Samuelisnotsafe!* I rammed my head into the boy's throat as he clipped the arrows into his crossbow and fired through my stump arm. Great, more shrapnel to get caught on shit. I didn't care. I knocked him to the ground, pinning him with my weight, and dug my teeth into my chest, holding him with a knee to the groin.

He didn't deserve to die all at once. I ripped away the skin on his chest until I saw white, the white hard things, glistening with the blood that I'd shed for Samuel. I used my hand to slide between the white hard things and made a fist, cracking them with little problem. I was so *angry.* Everything had lost its primary colors; I was now down to red and black and white. I saw his heart beating and listened to the whining coming from his mouth while I dug my knee hard into his groin, crushing whatever was left underneath it.

He didn't scream for much longer as I dragged my teeth across the muscles, and buried my lower jaw into it until it stopped moving. I couldn't remember what it was called, or why it moved, but it tasted like victory for Samuel; it tasted like I fixed it for him, once and for all. I fixed what he couldn't. I got even.

I chewed the last of the muscle and used my fist to smash the white things, the—the *bones*, crushing them beneath my strength, until he was no longer recognizable, just a puddle on the floor. Three more boys and one girl had come down the stairs, and now stood wide-eyed, staring at me, as I looked calmly back at them, blood dripping down my face.

"What?" I said. It came out as a grunt.

They ran. I couldn't even find it in me to be satisfied.

Expanding the Program

~ Kiera ~

The problem was that I was relying on Brett to do most of the planning, since I was stuck in an apartment building full of presumed zombies and shut-ins. We didn't exactly have our own door-to-door social media board.

So I waited, and I trained, and I texted Callie. It took a few nerve-wracking days for her to respond, but finally, I got something back. *Sorry, reception's in and out here. There too?*

I don't know, I responded after a long time. *You're the only one still texting me. TV's out though. Power's still on. It flickered last night.* I was watching DVDs of *Bob's Burgers* and sleeping with what was left of the shirts that smelled like Sean, Grace on my knees on the couch. It was the only way I felt safe. Now I was afraid I was going to have to stop sleeping with the lights on. In the dark, in silence, with only the sound of my breathing and Grace's soft, sleeping woofs to keep me company.

It sounded terrifying.

Sorry. What's going on?

I hesitated. *I know everyone's trying to get onto campuses to vaccinate,* I said. *I think I found a way to get people onto ours.*

Really?!?!?! A herd of punctuation later, she sobered. *You have—had—a super excellent science department. One professor is still posting—sorry, was still posting, until the Internet went down—from his lab. He was the only one in the science wing left. The gov't is seriously interested in your school, Kiera.*

How do you know this shit????

I'm sort of working with them? she shot back.

I paused. *Wait, what?*

With the gov't. Sort of. All journalists are now. It's . . . awkward and uncomfortable and it's NOT like we're being gagged or anything, but they want a unified front to the rest of the world. Which is chaos. So I'm, as you say, in the know.

That. Is. Fucked. They'd co-opted journalism now? The last free press of the United States was gone? TV had gone a long time ago, I knew. Fox News had proven that. But journalism? I was devastated.

We're Watching You, she said, and I could just hear her voice saying it in its eerie, twilight-time tone. She had a great voice for horror stories. *No, but seriously, what's your plan?*

And I told her, step by step, what Brett and I had outlined. He had about fifteen people that were able bodied and might be willing, and he had spent the last week and a half making rounds, updating me as he went. As soon as some of them took some time to think about it, they bailed, leaving us with seven, excluding the two of us and Grace, of course. No one else had a battle dog. Or a hatchet-mop. We were going to be looking for survivors, as best as we could, unless the zombie presence was just too big for us. Otherwise, we'd look for the government, whoever was in charge, hoping for some answers and direction.

Kiera, that's brilliant!

I paused, and waited. And waited. There was something she wasn't telling me, and I didn't know what it was. I probably *couldn't* know what it was, now that I thought about it, now that she worked for the government. I sighed, realizing that my last relationship that didn't directly involve zombies was now politicized, and I sent back some little ditty of thanks and set my phone down. I wondered how long it would take for the power to go out for good, and for her to stop being able to text me.

I texted Brett instead. *Do you have radios or something? What are we going to do when we can't charge our phones anymore?*

Does zombie survival freak with a private campsite in the mountains mean nothing to you? Of course I have radios. Why?

I told him what I'd been talking to Callie about, and he swore colorfully. He didn't like the government co-opting the journalists "for a United Front" either, apparently. But what he *did* like was our plan.

That means they'll send in what's left of the National Guard with the vaccines. They aren't going to send in civilians and the CDC. I have radios that can get those frequencies. We can talk to the National Guard while we're in there.

Isn't that slightly illegal? I asked.

He paused. For four minutes. *A quick Internet search proves that no one knows if it's truly illegal or not, but probably. At least, most people are super suspicious that you'll get Extra Governmentally Arrested from it. There's a bunch of "I've tried it and nothing's happened to me" crap but I doubt it.*

Where the hell did you get gov't radios?

Do you really want to know?

No. No, I did not, in fact, want to know where Brett got much of anything. He had showed up at my window with a gas lit burner thing and a five pound sack of rice the other day, wordlessly dropping them at my feet and handing me a box of six hundred matches. He departed without a sound. I didn't know why Brett did anything he did, only that he was coming over in two days with the first batch of recruits, and we were going to start training.

"Excited" was the wrong word. I wasn't excited, exactly. "Excited" meant that something good was happening. This wasn't good, this was necessary. This was extermination of a thing that had destroyed our whole world. This was revenge. And this was calming Grace's anxiety and PTSD.

Wait, was that me or the dog? It was hard to tell.

I curled up on the couch with a bowl of noodles and tomatoes, Grace lying on her back beside me with her feet in the air. We watched Bob together, and Louise's antics didn't make me laugh the way they normally did. The whole world felt smaller as the lights flickered, and bigger as I looked out the window to the world outside. I didn't know how many hundreds or thousands of people were left out there, and how many were soulless *things* instead.

How many people out there were sitting on their couches in the dark with nothing to comfort them, waiting for the end? How many were running out of food while I sat with this bounty? Was I really doing the right thing by going out there and ending the zombies, when people might need me right here?

Brett? What if there are starving people in my own apartment building?

I could hear him sighing. *You want me to do welfare checks?*

. . . Kind of.

I'll see you in two days, Kiera.

Thanks, Brett.

I tucked in Grace as she lay on my legs and put Sean's shirt over my face so I could inhale what was left of his scent, listening to Linda singing about Bob losing his mind at a wedding. Tears welled up in my eyes, and I hid from the world as the lights went out.

~

Living without electricity for a day or two could be fun, under certain circumstances. With the snow gently falling outside, when you didn't have to leave the house and lived with your loved one? Candlelight aglow with a good book? Romantic, right? This was a little less so. Because I knew there was very little chance of it coming back.

I dug through the supplies I'd taken from Sean's stash and came across a little solar powered gadget, and was pleased to find that it fit my phone. So at least I could communicate with Brett and Callie, however long they held out. I was one hundred percent certain that Brett had one of these, too, if not a hand cranked power charger, or something equally ridiculous. Callie I wasn't so sure about.

Brett had told me last night he was going to hack my phone anyway, put it on "emergency channels." He was the one who told me that Sean might have some solar powered stuff I could start using on the windowsills; we had a phone charger, one device that plugged into a cooker that I'd brought up, and a water purifier. All very useful stuff. I silently thanked Sean, though I wished him dead at the same time.

Wasn't that just a horrible little trainwreck worth of thoughts?

My first night without the power on was at the mercy of one very clingy dog. She knew I was anxious, and rather than being a little ball of nerves herself, she was instead a pillar of calm. She laid her full weight on top of me as best as she could, balancing on top of me with her paws resting on my shoulders and her head on my chest. She leaned up far enough to lick my chin periodically until I fell asleep, and she stayed there until I woke up in the afternoon. I was convinced that she was the only reason I slept through that first night at all.

Amazing creatures, dogs. And tonight was the night that we were going to meet the first seven or so people in our cadre, our little squad, our zombie battalion. I was sure that "battalion" had a number attached to it, now that I'd thought about it, but I couldn't for the life of me tell you what that number was, so a battalion of seven we were.

They'd get to see Grace in her pink and nail-gray tactical Battle Doge vest. I was so excited! And I'd get to show my hatchet-mop to someone other than Brett. Hell, to talk to someone other than Brett. I hated to count up the days—I'd thrown out my calendar and didn't look at the date on my phone anymore. But I knew it had been weeks, at least, since . . . well. Since it had all begun.

My modified sleep schedule put me to bed at around four in the morning, so I was a little closer to Brett's afternoon arrival than would have been otherwise. I gave Grace breakfast and we went onto the roof to the glorified garden that I'd found up there the first time we'd managed to go; there was a small patch of plants that Grace had claimed as her own, and I could chuck the poop off the side of the building. It worked for us, and Grace went up and down the ladders naturally now. It was weird to see a dog do it, but it was probably weird for dogs to hunt zombies, wasn't it?

Not anymore it wasn't. She was a natural. When we went up to the roof to watch me practice at night, she spun around too, as if she were practicing. I couldn't place any bets on whether or not that was what she was actually doing, of course, but it sure as hell seemed that way. She bit imaginary enemies, danced on her little white and black toes, and pranced around the roof with me, proud as can be.

I saw Brett limping every so often, as if he couldn't bear weight on his foot as well as he could have. I frowned, opening my mouth to speak, and he shook his head, averting his gaze. Sighing, I started back down to my apartment.

We made breakfast: rice in the cooker. I was getting a little sick of rice, to be honest, but that was kind of an apocalypse staple at this point. Brett had brought me two five-pound bags, and they sort of lasted a while. I managed to clean the house and keep myself busy enough until I started hearing noises at the ladder at around sunset, and I sighed, excited.

I opened the window and Grace sat excitedly by the sill, staring down into the coming darkness. She was there to greet Brett as he came in, as usual, but she knew there were people behind him; she wasn't a stupid dog, after all. "Hey, girlio." He pet her fondly. They'd gotten to know each other quite well by now.

"Got six," he explained, nodding his head at the window. "I'll round up the rest by . . . mmm, maybe week after next? Gives us two weeks to train with this crew, go out at least twice, see how we do together."

"How often do we train?"

"Every other night."

"When do you think we should check on the people in

my building? We can go together." I pulled my hair back into a bun, twisting it in loops. It was longer now, longer than I liked, but I wasn't sure how I felt about cutting it myself.

The next person that came up was a tallish man with dark tan skin, brown eyes, and bushy eyebrows. He wore tan clothing, comfortable shoes, and immediately held out a mop handle, looking at me with pleading eyes. "Brett said you could make me something cool? And a sling to hold it with?" He paused. "Oh. My name is Ohmar."

I started laughing. "So we're going to start our zombie sessions with crafting class 101?"

A small Black woman poked her head in my window, nose to nose with Grace. Grace licked her face and she laughed, a beautiful, tinkling laugh. "I like your dog. And yes, we are," she added, a baseball bat slung through her belt. "If I have anything to say about it." I looked at her hair, in awe. The braids formed a pentacle shape on top of her head and dangled into low loops around her ears, only to pull back into a symmetrical, tight bun at the back of her head.

"OhmyGod, did you do your hair yourself? Please tell me you did your hair yourself!" I paused. "I'm so sorry, I know it's A Thing for people to check out your hair, people fixate on it too much."

She stared at me for a long moment, and I was about ten seconds away from apologizing for being that crazy girl. "I did," she said finally. She was hesitant, as if unsure if I was about to attack her for it or compliment her about it. "Why?"

"Because it's *beautiful* and we're in the middle of the zombie apocalypse and I feel like a sheep right now? Can you do my hair? I can pay you in . . . ramen and spiral pasta," I begged. Those sounded like good, solid apocalypse foods. "I have three cans of tomato paste too."

She brightened. "If we get done making my weapon before midnight, I'll do your hair," she laughed. "But probably not like this. It's a little complicated. I'll get it out of your face and make it pretty, though. What can you do with a baseball bat? And I'm dying over that tomato paste."

"Are you gonna let me in or what?" A head peeked around her and scowled. It was another man, a boy, really. He had a black mohawk, and I was pretty sure he was using dish soap to keep its shape. He wore punk clothes and had an honest to goodness *axe* with him.

"Oh, sure," she said. "My name is Lydiana." She moved and let him in.

He grunted as he pulled himself past the overly excited dog. "Evan," he said sourly. "So this is fun."

"Hi, Evan," I said. "Come on in. Is anyone hungry?" I looked at Brett, as I fidgeted. I needed to take care of these people already. Somehow. I needed to do something.

"Probably." Brett ran his hand through his hair and sat down on the couch. Grace immediately went over to him and sat down on top of his steel-toed boots. She liked the feel of them or something, I was never entirely certain what her obsession was.

A boy of a similar age poured through my window, except I couldn't see him past the long hair covering his face.

He had black eyes. "I'm Chen," he said quietly. I could feel the intensity coming off of him. He carried a tool handle of some kind, similar to mine, and I started wondering if we should raid the basement again.

Leslie, a brown-haired dental assistant who announced herself as such and came with nothing, stepped delicately through my window in heels, and I looked at Brett, bewildered, as I started water in the cooker. He shrugged, mouthing "it's cool" and nothing more.

So this was going to be fun, I thought, as I stirred the rice into the cooker and examined my new crew. Grace looked at me, concerned. *I know, girl. I'm worried too.*

Advance

~ Sean ~

Darla stood staring out the window, pondering our next move, I guessed. NZS was weeping audibly, the sound like ooze out of a pus-filled wound, and it came out of my mouth like a strange, moldy whine. Samuel was not there to look at me funny. Samuel was not there at all.

Wherenow? It was more pictures than words now. My vision stayed that strange black-white-red. Sarah sat on the floor next to me, drawing pictures in the bright blood on the tile. She was even more simple than I was becoming; childlike, somehow. I was envious that she could play that way. She was optimistic that we could do . . . whatever it was we were doing. She wasn't even sure.

I looked at Darla.

Findothers, she said. *Likeus.* I got the impression from her thoughts that she knew more than I did about our kind; she knew that we were stronger together. Smarter together. That if enough of us came together, I wouldn't be reduced to this . . . mind-numbed thing that I was becoming. The phrase "hive mind" flashed through my brain, though I couldn't remember what it meant.

It means you're a fucking zombie, NZS sneered.

Goback tohell whereyou belong, I managed as clearly as I was capable. He was the enemy. His kind took away Samuel. And the Old Man. And so many more, I was sure.

My heart hurt, even though I wasn't convinced it was still beating. How did I check? I knew, once, how to check. I'd forgotten so much.

We left Samuel behind, as we left the Old Man behind, and I didn't know what would happen if we found many more zombies or humans. I had decided we would only engage when someone was stupid enough to attack us; we were outnumbered, but hopefully we could keep ourselves away from the humans.

Stayclose buildings. Darla showed me pictures. We hugged the walls, wandering further into campus, and made our way successfully past the place for sick people and the kitchens. I saw a house with letters on it, three, down a column. It looked fancy, with flags and fliers posted all over it. I could tell it had been a place for parties and mayhem. It didn't look like much fun anymore.

Maybewe shouldtakeover oneofthose houses, I said to Darla. It was the closest thing to a joke I had, but really, I kind of wanted one, for all of us. A house where we could all be a family. Where we could be safe.

Darla poked around in my mind for a moment, and sighed, a strangled moan. *Notabadidea,* she said slowly. *Reallynot. Let'slookinwindows.*

It surprised me to hear that anything I said was a good idea to Darla.

Sarah trailed along after us, running her fingers up and down the wildflowers as we walked by the windows. The lights were all off. I couldn't tell if the . . . the shining was down, the—*power,* NZS cut in weakly. The power was down, so if there were human, they were too cowardly to turn the lights on. The house was big, though, and I wasn't so sure about our abilities going in.

Darla started peering in the windows. *Webs,* she said suddenly.

Huh?

Ijustthoughtof theword. Webs. Thosethingson thewalls. Meansnobody hasbeenhere inawhile.

Perfect, I said, and grabbed Sarah by the arm with my good hand. I walked her toward the back of the house, where the door swung lazily on its hinges in the cool breeze. Darla led us inside, where bodies lay strewn across the floor, old, dried blood staining the rugs. Cups were scattered across the kitchen. Snow was displayed on the TV past it, in the living room.

I saw pizza sitting on the floor next to the couch and realized when I heard the flies that I couldn't smell anymore. It was just another thing to separate myself from the humans. It was one more way I was *inhuman* now. What else would I lose? Will there be a stopping point, or am I just going to get lower and lower until the end? Was I *inhumane* now, too?

Yes.

Nobody asked you, I growled to NZS.

You did, just now, thanks. And yes, you fucking are. You ate a fucking kid's heart. *There's something seriously wrong with you and you know it.*

I looked around the house, Sarah walking around behind me and exclaiming about pretty colors that only she could see. *And that's proof. You can only see blood and black and white. Doesn't that say something to you? That's not natural. That's the mark of a predator. An alien. Something inhuman. You don't* care *anymore. You don't even remember her name.*

Sarah was getting anxious, fidgeting with my hand, looking around for Darla. I knew she was upstairs, checking bodies and getting a feel for the layout. The bodies would stay where they were; we simply weren't built for moving them anymore. None of us had the fine motor control to move a corpse down a flight of stairs. Darla was rapidly getting to the point where she couldn't move herself down a flight of stairs, and I was just as rapidly following.

Wait, remember whose name? There was someone whose name I was supposed to be remembering? The idea felt wrong. Empty. There was a piece of me . . . a piece of me from before. Something I had wanted to do. Someone I had wanted to bring with me. There was something missing, and it felt awful.

I could feel Not-Zombie Sean's sorrow, feel his longing.

He showed me pictures of a red-haired girl smiling as she wrote in a book, as she sang a song, as she made some kind of meal I no longer had a name for. *This is Kiera,* he said carefully. Proudly. *And you will* never *make her into someone like you.*

I sat down on the couch, pulling Sarah down with me, letting her rest and relax. She lay her head down on my shoulder as I examined these mental images. I knew this woman. She was there when I was bitten by that boy. She was there when I turned. I saw her face when I went up the stairs. But who was she?

She was everything, NZS said softly. *And we left her. Left her all alone. Don't know if she's still alive. Don't know what life is like for her on her own.*

I . . . I did that?

Yeah. You did. We went and got ourselves bitten, and there you were, ready to take over. And now I live in a corner of my own goddamned head, while my body does—

I shook my head hard. That was enough of that. I was not going to lose what happiness I had left to NZS. I looked at Sarah, who looked up at me so sweetly. It was clear to me by now that something had gone wrong with her transformation; when I touched the part of the Hex that was "Sarah's wall," I didn't get any words from her, not really. Not anymore. I got pretty pastel pictures, simple emotions, fragments. She was happy, but like a butterfly. She flitted from one image to the next in her mind and never stayed on anything for very long. She was ethereally happy.

"Ethereal." I was proud that I remembered that word.

It was enough, to see this happiness in a girl who had had such worry and fear when we busted down her door, to know that *I* did that. I made her feel this way. I changed her from a terrified human to a blissful creature that walked the earth on lighter feet. This was my legacy. And I could do it again, and again, and again.

I imagined bars across NZS's mouth. Maybe it would shut him up for a while. Because Sean's Legacy sounded pretty damn good to me.

~

It wasn't long before we had the urge to move. There were humans out there. I could feel them. Darla could feel them. I wasn't really sure what Sarah could feel, but she tugged on my hand relentlessly, pulling me toward the back door, past the bodies and the mess. I was surprised there weren't any zombies like us in the house; I guessed the neighborhood watch had dealt with them.

They were about to find out what happened when zombies banded together, that was for sure. We left and started for the house next door. It was white, with pretty blocks around the windows. There were red flowers lining the walkway. It didn't look like a party house like ours did. I was disappointed, in a way. Every zombie house should be a party house.

Darla peered in the windows, looking for signs of life. I laughed a little; life. What life could there really be without the Link? I reached for Sarah and her butterfly—like love and light. She was looking at the house suspiciously, throwing pictures at me of teenage humans. I asked, *Youthink peopleareinthere?*

She nodded. Her head flopped wildly about her neck, rolling. I frowned, looking at Darla, who was creeping around toward the back. There were no lights, which made me think NZS was right about there being no . . . no . . . what was the word? And why was it so hard for me to remember?

There were no lights, that was good enough. Darla grunted loudly and I wordlessly followed, holding Sarah's hand and dragging her along with me. She wasn't who I wanted to have my back in a fight. I remembered Samuel, in a building down the road, and sighed. He was a good kid that didn't deserve to die. He just wanted to Infect. What was so wrong with that?

Speaking of which . . . *Infect,* I urged Darla.

You'reright, she said after a long pause. *Theydon't wantto attackusas muchafterwe Infect.* Her eyes gleamed in the daylight. She was excited, I could tell; her awareness buzzed against mine, jumping up and down, screaming for the chance to spread the Infection. She was thrilled.

I was . . . What was I? I wanted this more than anything, but the voice of NZS haunted me. I left someone all alone, the way Samuel left me alone, the way the Old Man left me alone. Their voids could be filled, however; and whoever NZS left behind, his voids would not be occupied by other beings. They hadn't been occupied in the first place, I reminded myself. He didn't have the Link. So what was his problem?

I shook my head. There was no telling with humans. How could he miss her if he never really knew her? I followed Darla into the house, where three humans lay sleeping on the . . . the furniture that you lay on when you don't want to go to bed. It was green with flowers on it. They wore skirts, so they were like Darla and Sarah, not like me. That was interesting. The other house had Darlas *and* Seans in it.

Something about this house was different.

I leaned down and grabbed one of them around the neck, pulling her up towards me. She was young, younger than Sarah, much younger than Darla. She startled awake, flapping and waving wildly, her voice strangled by my arm twisting around her throat. It was inconvenient that I couldn't tell her what was happening—tell her that the worst would be over soon, that the best was yet to come.

Oh well!

Sarah cheerfully sat down in the lap of another one, wrapping her arms around her and eagerly biting at her throat. I couldn't see what Darla was doing, so I focused on the scared one in my arms. She was flailing, so I held her tighter with my arm and my stump, and bent her a little, to give me access to her rib cage. It did less damage, but it tasted so much better. And it Infected them quicker, to be so much nearer to the heart.

I sighed happily as I ripped a piece of her flesh off in my mouth, chewing eagerly, making smacking sounds with my teeth. I ground the skin around. It was mealy, and tasted of some kind of strange product. I frowned, and swallowed; at least it wouldn't go to waste, even if it did taste like she put hair spray on her sides.

A splash of memory. A mother, getting ready to go out

for a date. Me, sitting on the bed, watching her spray her hair, tasting the spray in the air. Lipstick and mascara, things unfathomable to me as a young boy, that somehow made my beautiful mom ethereal. I couldn't wait to find someone who loved me that much—not to put on makeup, but to go somewhere with me, somewhere special, and focus solely on me, just because they loved me.

Kiera.

I wrenched my head away from her, panting, staring into her eyes. She stared back, wide-eyed and shuddering, and I knew the Infection would take her sooner rather than later. I didn't let go of her as she shook, because I was shaking too; I remembered her now.

I remembered her, even as the memories began to slip away. There was a girl, a girl that we loved, somewhere in this city. A girl that I carried around inside of me, because we abandoned her, and inside of me was the only place she might survive now. A girl that meant more to us than anything, because she loved me for me, and . . . and we left her.

Fuck. I sobbed, a grunting scream, and threw the girl to the ground. She wasn't Kiera. None of these girls lying in states of disarray and bitten-ness were Kiera, and they never would be. Kiera was safe from me. Kiera was far away now, and I wasn't sure I'd remember how to get back. I'd never see her again.

I learned something in that moment, as I stood hunched over, clutching my stomach, my mouth open, a ragged breath escaping my lips.

Zombies couldn't cry.

Into the Mire

~ Kiera ~

We turned Ohmar's mop handle into a whirling tool that . . . well, it reminded me of those big balls on sticks with spikes. I didn't need *all* of my carving and dinner knives, and Brett had a way with a screwdriver. It was monstrous, and Ohmar loved it. "Please don't poke your eye out," I said warily over some rice.

He beamed at his makeshift weapon. "I won't," he promised. "But I make no statements about the zombies."

I looked at Lydiana, tall and stoic as she watched the rest of us eat dinner. She had had Brett put some extra-long nails through the end of her baseball bat, and seemed satisfied with the results. "My grandpa gave me this," she explained quietly. "To protect myself, when I moved out. He said there was no way he was letting a woman in his family go off alone without something she knows how to use, and I know how to use a baseball bat. I had four brothers."

Had. It was the silent string that held us all together, the one that Brett had told me about but hadn't divulged facts and secrets about; everyone here had lost someone. It seemed that Lydiana had lost more people than the rest of us. I thanked God that it was just Sean.

My heart dropped as I remembered my mother. *Who forgets their mother?* I chastised myself. I hadn't heard from her in . . . weeks. I had no reason to think she was anything other than dead or infected. She'd stopped answering long before the power had gone out. Something was definitely wrong.

Evan didn't say much, and there wasn't much we could do to his axe. He was evidently friends with Chen, as the two of them stuck closer together than I'd have liked. In my experience, super friendly teenage boys were never a good thing, and plotting teenage boys during a zombie apocalypse was *definitely* not a good thing. Hell, *Sean* plotting during the zombie apocalypse involved tents and Squatty Potties. Nothing good could come of this adventure.

"So what do you want to do with your handle, Chen?" Brett asked with his mouth full.

Chen stopped and thought about it, his eyes radiating heat. I would have been worried he was infected if Brett had not informed me that this was, in fact, just his personality. He was *on,* all the time. It was a little terrifying in a teenager. "Do you have any butcher knives or meat knives? We could fasten four or five blades facing out in a circle."

"There's gotta be a name for all of these weapons,"

Brett mused. "I wonder if the library has books on medieval weaponry. I could find out and let y'all know what the hell we're all making."

Leslie looked at him brightly. "Why do we need to know what we're making? Aren't we just walking to campus?"

Brett looked at her patiently. "Leslie, you agreed to be part of a zombie kill squad, remember? There's no "just walking" anywhere. I know that you don't like to think about it, but you gotta face facts eventually."

I surreptitiously texted Brett under the table as they talked. *What in the hell does she mean, just walk to campus? I thought you got real volunteers! These are a bunch of kids, Leslie, and TWO adults!*

She's . . . complicated. She was a martial arts expert for years. She became a little touched in the head after she lost her wife. She'll be fine, I promise.

I didn't know what to do with that. Evidently Leslie had layers like an onion, and I was stuck with the top layer that had bubblegum all over it. Great. "That sounds like a great idea, Chen. I think I have a knife set in the bottom drawer I haven't touched. It was one of those Christmas gifts you don't know what to do with and . . ." I laughed, then sobered. "Guess there isn't going to be any weird Christmas presents this year."

Evan, who was normally pretty damn silent and sullen if this afternoon, spoke up. "I wonder what traditions will survive this," he said "If any. Will Christmas matter anymore as a gift-giving thing, or will it be a time when you pray your loved ones haven't been eaten? I mean, I know Jesus rose from the dead, but that's Easter, isn't it?"

Ohmar looked a little scandalized.

"I think we're getting off topic," I threw in hastily. "Leslie, can you handle a stick with nails on both sides? I think we can manage to make something like that for you."

"Sure," she murmured softly, looking off to the side. "We were Jewish. No Christmas. But Anna really liked putting up the Hanukkah lights every year. I'm gonna really miss those."

Okay, maybe less bubblegum and more substance. She reminded me of the Joker's girlfriend; hiding her trauma under a layer of pretty lies and cheerfulness. That made more sense than Brett bringing in a lunatic in heels.

"We're gonna have to get rid of those heels, honey," Lydiana said gently. Great minds think alike.

Leslie looked down, surprised. "Oh," she said. "I hadn't thought of that. Where am I going to get shoes?"

Brett began talking of the logistics of suiting everyone up, and I faded away, thinking about all that we'd lost. We had an entire mountain of supplies in the basement that we could use to solve the riddle of the zombie apocalypse, but it didn't matter unless we got to campus. Everything hinged on getting the vaccine to the middle of town. Could we really do it?

My phone buzzed.

Bad news, it said. Brett was texting me as he talked. It was a skill that I didn't possess. *The other half of the contingency has bailed. Their apartment building just got taken over. The last survivor is texting me updates after he locked himself in the janitor's closet. I'm going to go back over to his place tonight and see if I can get him out. Can you keep these ones here?*

I leaned back in the chair I'd fallen into. How could we do this with only seven of us—eight, with Grace? The odds seemed so slim and the world so big. I looked at Brett, who was grim, and nodded wordlessly as Leslie and Lydiana chattered on about protective wardrobe during the zombie apocalypse. I swallowed hard.

My phone buzzed again. *Any news?* Callie urged me, and I knew she was hopeful that we could set up a rescue point at the university.

It's going to be fine, I lied. When I was a teen and in the throes of depression, it was the best lie that I had. "I'm fine." "It's fine." It's always fine. Until it's not. As I looked at the kids, and at Ohmar and Lydiana and Leslie, Grace wedged her nose under my hand as if to make sure I counted her presence. I sighed, closing my eyes, and began to pray.

It's going to be fine.

I realized what Brett had said a little after he said it. Give me a break, I had a lot on my mind. I stared at him for a long moment over the heads of the faces in my living room. "Are you kidding me?"

He had a mouthful of rice left, and he blinked a little, cocking his head. Grace whined, pawing at his foot. "What?" he said, finally swallowing.

"You are *not* going to save that survivor by yourself." I gestured. "We've got six people here that need to train—"

"*Need to train,* Kiera. As in, have not trained yet. As in, might get me deader than I'd get myself, slipping in some dude's window." He shook his head, finishing hammering a few more nails into an errant weapon. "I'm going by myself."

Ohmar opened his mouth, about to speak, then appeared to think better of it.

"I'm sure as hell not going without practicing a few times," Lydiana said after a long moment. "No way."

Evan was unnaturally interested, of course, but Chen held him back from the conversation. "Not yet," he said to his friend. "We're not ready yet."

Leslie was staring out the window, oblivious—on purpose, maybe?—and I sighed, rubbing my face. "What's your plan? And your backup plan? And your safety plan?"

Brett gave me A Look. "I'll be fine," he said shortly. "You don't need to mother me." He set up shop next to Chen and Evan and said no more in my direction, showing them how to hold their knives-on-a-stick and axe, respectively.

One more person to worry about? Check.

"Then I'm coming with you," I said firmly. "I've practiced, I've done it, Grace has done it—"

"Wait, the dog kills zombies?" Evan perked up.

"Yes, the dog kills zombies. That's not the point. I'm going with you."

"Couldn't we have this talk later?" Brett said, his lips pursed.

"No," I said, surprised to find that I was choked up. "I don't—I can't—" *I don't want anything bad to happen to you,* I thought furiously. *I can't handle someone else dying. I don't want to know what it's like to lose more people.*

I sighed in frustration. I wasn't sure what to do—wasn't sure how to express myself on this one. Chen watched me with his handle-mace-thing, and finally set it down next to Evan. He came over, pushing his black hair out of his face, and looked at Brett seriously. "She can do this," he said softly.

Evan, uncharacteristically serious, came up beside me. The boys framed me, standing around me like my supports, as I watched Brett sit in his chair. "She can do this," Evan echoed. "I know she can. She's made all of these weapons for us and kept us fed while we did it. She can do it."

Grace came, sitting down in front of me, and I just knew that somehow, she understood what was happening. She was volunteering, to protect me, to work with me, to hunt with me—to help Brett come back safely. I wanted to hug her in thanks, but I stood my ground, staring him down. He wasn't going to get out of this conversation alone.

Lydiana was watching us as she twirled a braid in her fingers, and she shrugged, picking up the plates on the table. She stopped in the middle of the living room, examining the weapons strewn about, and the kids and adults there. "She can do this," she said quietly. "Don't say no to help, Brett. She cares about you."

Ohmar was fiddling with his mop handle, another type of ball mace with carving knives. Leslie loosely held the baseball bat we'd found for her in the basement. They were both looking at Brett.

He took a deep breath. "Let's all go," he said finally. "We'll go up the fire escape and break into his apartment. We'll practice working through the streets. The closet is on the first floor, but we boarded it up when we did the windows." It had been in the before times, when we didn't know what zombies are capable of. I realized now that boarding up my house made no sense. "We're going to have to go through the fire escape, break a window, and go down the stairs."

"How many zombies are there?" I asked.

"I don't know. At least four. I hope between the seven of us—eight with Grace? Is that where we are? We can get through them pretty quickly."

Grace's stomach took that opportunity to growl for her, and we all laughed. I went to the closet and pulled out her Attack Suit. "Time to suit up the puppy," I said delightedly. She danced, prancing on top of Brett's steel toes, and settled in a standing position so I could dress her.

Evan was staring. "You have a very strange dog," he observed slowly.

"Wait till you see her go down the fire escape. She goes everywhere with me. She's killed zombies before. She's such a good doggy," I gushed, tucking her toes into her boots.

"Your dog has shoes?" Ohmar stared, looking at Grace incredulously.

"Well, I couldn't very well have more of an opportunity for zombies to grab her," I explained, stuffing her tail into the tail sheath. When I was done, she was a glittery nailed mess of sharp and pointy things, only her eyes and her nose sticking out, as usual. She beamed, wagging her whole body.

Ohmar dodged as she wagged in his general direction. "I can see how your dog is dangerous," he admitted, laughing. "She's going to wag me into oblivion."

"She's done it before," I said seriously, and looked up at them. Leslie had been silent this whole time; I looked at her to make sure she hadn't checked out again. "And she'll do it again. But you have to protect her, each other, me, Brett—we are a team now. And we need to get this done right. Are you really ready for this?"

Leslie closed her eyes, pulling on the shoes we'd found after we broke into a few holding areas in the basement. "No," she admitted. "But I'm going to do it anyway."

Evan looked at her closely. I thought that all of us had doubts about Leslie; it was questionable whether or not she'd survive this. "Why?" he asked.

"Because my wife would want me to," she said simply. She tied the laces in double knots and stood up, staring us both down. "So that's what I'm going to do."

Everyone started gearing up, grabbing their weapons, the vests we'd found, the arm protectors made out of pool noodles, the legwarmers turned into armor. We were a motley crew, that was for sure, but as Lydiana pulled on her baseball cap and pulled her hair through it, I was proud of us. We were doing a thing, together. It wasn't what I thought we'd be doing—and if we got home, all of us, together, who knows what we'd have to do next?

The point was, we were about to hunt our first zombies

as a team. The window remained open, and we holstered our weapons, gathered our courage, and descended.

Grace looked spectacularly impressive as she went down the fire escape. I hoped it was a sign for what was to come. *How can this possibly go wrong?* I thought.

Well. About that.

Days Pass

~ Sean ~

Most of the buildings were empty. The school had been evacuated, right before I turned into a zombie. Not-Zombie Sean was closer to me than ever as we remembered her, thought about her, dreamed about her. It was difficult to separate myself from him; he was horrified and screaming, but keening for her, and I keened for her as well. It sounded like I was gargling metal. It was no sound for mourning.

We found others, others like us, in one of the school buildings. I stayed away from them, didn't touch their minds, didn't want them to be part of my Hex, my Link, my awareness. I didn't want someone else to fill the spot that Samuel held. I could feel Darla's disdain for the Link, for the Hex, for the feelings. She occupied a rather large spot in my head now, as did Sarah. But Sarah felt only light and hunger.

We went back to our girl building (*sorority, NZS*

whispered in my brain) and waited for them to stop sounding like they were dying and actually wake up and do something useful. I looked at the girl whose rib cage I'd bitten lying on the floor, moaning. I could see the black spreading under her thick tank top. The red was still visible; at least I had that color.

You're a monster, NZS reminded me. *Monsters shouldn't be able to see beauty.* I tried to look inward at him, even while he was fading into the background, and wondered what it would be like without him. If he faded completely, where would that leave me?

I could only retort, *I know I am.*

Because I was. I was a monster. I'd spent so much time mourning Kiera that I hadn't thought about the house full of girls that I'd killed. I couldn't stop thinking about her; what she was doing, if she had been turned into a zombie. I almost smiled at the thought; we could be together forever. With or without sorority girls.

The problem was, I genuinely believed I was a *better* monster than humans. There was no war, here; no famine. No drug abuse and sexual abuse and rape and killing for no reason. There were only two things that mattered: eating and Infecting. It was a simpler time, and I was a simpler monster.

The girl sat up, and her awareness brushed against mine, blooming into fullness in my Hex. It wasn't the place where Samuel had been; I exhaled, and it whistled. It felt like relief.

Hi, she said, staring at me with wide, fluorescent—green eyes. *Whereisarewe? Whatdowedo?*

She was turning out just fine, I thought. *Infect?* I asked Darla hopefully.

Darla stood quietly for a while, looking out the window, and Sarah sat down next to the girl—Gwen, her name was Gwen—and began to play with her long, blonde hair. *Infect,* Darla said abruptly.

We switched gears, stumbling out of the house with our new recruits. There were seven of us now, but I only cared about the four of us: me, Sarah, Darla and Gwen. I didn't *want* to know the rest. I just wanted to feel them—as family, as a comforting crushing weight against me.

I felt the eagerness to Infect like sludge through my veins. It felt poetic: I wanted to make the world look like me, and I knew that I could do it, if I was careful.

Do we want to be careful? NZS said quietly. *Do we want to stay alive for Kiera, or die for her?*

It was a punch to the gut. I doubled over, physically feeling the pain he felt, and tried to push him back into my brain. I couldn't; I realized, then, that I was losing control. I stood up without my own permission; followed the herd without acknowledging my own autonomy. Even my zombie brain was being bypassed by zombie instinct. At what point would I be locked in my own head, just like NZS? Would we share a cell?

No, he said numbly. *I think you just fade away.*

I liked that. Liked the thought of it. Liked the feeling behind it. I could fade away. If I embraced this feeling, these instincts, the strange pain could be gone, and I wouldn't miss someone that haunted my memory. I relaxed, letting my body carry me into the campus, and watched through my own neon green eyes as Sarah bounded awkwardly ahead of me, Gwen and her house-mates in front of her.

Darla led; of course she did. We crept past silent houses and buildings that once held students and learning. They would be filled with our students, our learning soon. Darla brought us into a building with doors opened wide; it was a big, open building, with black (*they aren't black, monsters don't see in color*) cushions on the wall and lines all over the floor. The windows were up high, higher than I could reach, and there was a lot of wood stacked against each wall. I used to know what they were called, could almost remember sitting on them for . . . what?

And there were zombies.

Milling around were . . . I couldn't count anymore. A lot. More than were in the sorority house, more than I'd seen before; Sarah squealed with joy, and Gwen was intensely interested. It was Darla, though, who was calculating. I could feel her thinking, feel her twisting the scene in her mind into her own purposes.

Thisisforus, she said quietly. Her voice then rebounded and she screamed across the halls of my mind. *Thisisforus!*

It *was* for us. Her words rang in my head like a bell, and I wondered if anyone outside of our Hexes could hear her. It was a remarkably coherent thought from Sarah, and I wondered if she had a Not-Zombie Sarah screaming in the back of her head. I let my body move, surprised that it followed my orders, and followed Darla to the middle of the room, and I found a place in my mind to rest.

I was so tired of following Darla; so tired of walking into the shit storm, only to come out missing friends. All I wanted to do was *Infect*. And these beings were already Infected. What would we do now?

War! she shouted. *War! Wewar againstthe humans! WeInfect andweWIN!*

It wasn't the best speech I'd ever heard, but it was good for what she was facing. More zombies than I had fingers, maybe even toes began to form a mob for her. Sarah and Gwen were in the crowd, cheering (grunting) and screaming (squealing). Being in such a crowd, for this purpose, was an incredible rush. It felt the same way it did when I Infected someone; a surprise glimpse of joy breaking through the clouds that wanted me to eat everyone.

I wanted more.

~

There were accidents at first. We found more humans in another building, a short building that smelled like chemicals. They had barricaded the doors, but I could tell the humans were sick and hungry. They smelled of famine and ruin. They smelled excellent.

When you have a fingers—and—toes amount of zombies in one room, it is difficult to Infect, we discovered. I found myself with a small man, a boy? in the corner of the room. He was being gnawed on by one—two—three fingers of zombies, and he was crying as his leg was carried off. He was bleeding profusely, and I threw myself down on the floor, lapping up the combination of dirt and dust and blood with my shriveled tongue. He watched me as he bled out into my mouth, as I leaned up and began to chew on his hip, dig my teeth into the white thing there. The blood was pouring over me, a baptism, and I relaxed into it, letting my body do the work.

There was no longer a chance he would be Infected; he was dying. I welcomed him to the dying with my eyes, staring up into his, giving him the courtesy of having someone with him when he died. He died like Samuel died. He took a breath, and screamed as loud as he could. And he died.

As I grabbed the rest of the bone in his hip it yanked out of his body with my hand, leaving me with muscle and vein. I ate until I ran into the fabric that covered his parts, drowning myself in the taste of meat and oblivion. I felt myself move farther back into my mind, and welcomed the change.

Standing up, I looked at Darla She was frustrated, I could tell, at the lack of . . . of . . . *Organization?* NZS suggested. *You want a cleansing of the humans. You want all of them to turn or die. But you're not fucking organized enough to turn them. Have fun with that.*

I wasn't sure what he meant, organized, but "cleansing—" I liked that word. To cleanse the world of humans. Clean it up, make it better, keep the humans away from what they'd destroyed so heartily and readily. Yes. We would *cleanse* the humans.

Darla began with simple instructions: some zombies would stay here. Some zombies would follow her. She deposited zombies in different rooms and we got settled into the process of breaking doors down; the locks were simple, the doors cheap. After a while, all you could hear was the screaming and the growling.

It made me wonder what would happen if I took charge. If I was the general in the war. I was different; I was a zombie who hadn't lost myself yet, and it meant something. I was meant for something. Maybe if I was in the lead . . .

I found an old woman, her dress torn, behind the big desk in the room. She was hiding from us; I knew I would have to guard her until she turned, and she'd have to turn fast. "It's okay," I said. It came out as a honking noise.

She gargled and sputtered, uselessly clawing at me as I ripped her dress some more, pressed my lips in between her breasts and bit at the skin near her heart. I took the skin between my teeth and peeled it, ripping it up and over the mound, until it tore no longer. She was making noises, but I knew that I had to Infect her now. I dug deeper, hit the hard white stone, listened to her choking, and lapped at the edges of the wounds, dripping my saliva into her body. I wrapped my arm around her to hold her while the Infection set in.

She began to shake, digging her nails into my skin as she shuddered, her body flopping up and down like a fish. I watched the black pop up, spread, spread and dig deeper, past the white, into the red, and her heart was black like mine, black like the rest of us.

Her name was Holly. She was born on Christmas. Her favorite color was red, now, like the rest of us. And she no longer cared about physics; she cared only about one thing.

I smiled as she blossomed into my awareness, and it was shock and awe and family and hunger. I hauled her to her feet, both of us teetering and stumbling, and led her toward our army. OUR army, our army of zombies, Darla's and mine. Because I wasn't about to let Darla do this alone.But what Darla wouldn't know is that I wouldn't be helping for *her* sake. No, it was all for me, and Kiera. I had plans, and Darla was the way to them.

I was going to Infect until I could not do it any longer, I decided. Spread the Infection as far and wide as I could, until maybe it reached Kiera. And when it reached her, I would find her. I would find her, and we would be together. If I had to kill my entire family to do it, I would, until only she remained in my Hex, in my Link.

We would live together in perfect harmony, standing outside in the sunshine until the end of days. Eating when humans found us, Infecting when we could, and just *being*. That was the ultimate state, the one that we all sought: when there was nothing more, we would just *be,* existing for the sake of existing, and Kiera and I could exist together, forever.

Until the end of days.

The Apartment and the Trek

~ Kiera ~

Getting to the apartment was the easy part. We skirted past the zombie—related areas, thanks to Brett's routes and intensive scouting, and we reached the fire escape after a two—hour walk. I thought Evan and Chen's eyes were going to pop out of their sockets with how hard they were concentrating on the area around us. I knew it *seemed* like a zombie would pop out of every building and corner, but evidently, the city wasn't as full of zombies as it felt like it was.

Grace trotted along beside me as we walked, waving her nail—decked tail in the air, and Ohmar walked beside her, watching her with amused eyes. "She actually fights like that?"

"She does," I confirmed, as Brett started up the fire escape to the second floor. Ohmar gestured for ladies first, and I boosted Grace up, letting her settle her feet before she climbed up the ladder/steps. She wasn't *graceful* at

it, but she was good, especially when I stayed right behind her and let her lean her butt against my stomach.
We shimmied up the fire escape, Ohmar taking up the
rear, and Brett was still limping. I hoisted my dog into the
first—floor window that he had broken, and saw a flash of
blood running down his leg. I didn't have time to ask, or
maybe I didn't want to know.

We were in an empty apartment. I say it was empty
when I really mean there were two dead bodies on the
couch, holding hands, with gunshot wounds to the head.
They smelled terrible. It was a man and a woman; the
woman was holding the gun loosely on her lap. The sun-
flower painting behind them was stained with brown
blood.

I felt nothing.

I looked at Brett, breathing through my mouth.
"Where to?"

He led us back to the front door and unlocked it, then
peered out and held his hand up for us to stop and wait.
It was silent, so very silent. There were no hums of electricity or threads of people talking; the only sounds were
of us breathing and Grace's panting. She paced in place,
stomping her little feet, as we waited. As Brett edged out
of the apartment, his staff held high and tight to his body.
"Let's go," he said abruptly.

So fucking quiet. We were introducing noise into the
second floor and the boys were right up next to Brett,
Leslie not far behind. Lydiana and Ohmar had the sense
to stay back, to wait, to have patience for the end game.
We weren't charging in unawares.

We were led down the stairway. It looked so similar to the stairway that I lost Sean to; maybe all apartment buildings had the same layout here, who knew. But all I could think of, as I followed Brett and crew blindly down the stairs, was that day.

A flash. *Sean's shoes, crawling up the stairs. Reaching up to the bar with his one arm, the other having been severed by—again—my hands. Dressed lovingly, by my hands. And if I saw him again, killed just as lovingly, by my hands.*

I stifled a sob, and Ohmar put a hand on my shoulder. He looked at me with sympathy, and I knew he was remembering his demons, too. For that was what those people were now: our demons, our sorrows, our tragic stories left behind—or worse.

Grace whined softly, reminding me of her presence, and I sighed, leaning into her with my hand, running my fingers through her fur. It was reassuring, knowing that she was there beside me. She had been with me most of the nights I'd cried over Sean or not being able to contact my mom anymore, most of the nights I'd traded texts with Callie, most of the nights when I'd trained. She was everything to me now, and I didn't know what I'd do without her.

Please, God, don't kill my dog, too.

Brett took a deep breath and looked into each of our eyes. "He's in a maintenance closet on this floor. That means there are zombies walking the lobby. I don't know how many there are," he said quietly. "Keagan wasn't able to give me numbers before he locked himself in. So we might be overwhelmed. If we are, I want you to hightail it up to the landing, so we can spread out and funnel them through the stairway. I'll prop the door open and run up behind you. Got it?"

Evan didn't look like he was listening. He was bouncing on his feet, and I could feel the energy running between him and Chen. I wondered how they knew each other; were they neighbors? Schoolmates? Or just friends, locked together forever by the worst tragedy to hit our country since . . . well, since?

"All right," I said, since no one else was saying anything. I was hoping that Brett would pick up the story, but I realized they were all looking at me. I guess because I'm the one who made their weapons; I had given them the means to survive. And if I was some kind of secondary leader, it meant that I could be the one they'd go to when they hated the decisions he made. I wasn't meant to be a leader, and I wasn't sure what to do about it.

So then, great. Co—leaders. Excellent. I knew exactly what I was doing. All the time.

Brett opened the door, and chaos exploded—belatedly. It was actually sort of disappointing at first; we saw no zombies in the lobby in front of the door. However, as Brett eased us out into the lobby proper, I spotted them. Some poor fool had tried to break into the apartment building; the plywood was lying under him. At least, I thought it was a him—the body was wearing a long—sleeved flannel shirt and baggy pants, which I guessed could belong to anyone, really. The zombies were crowded around his head and chest, obscuring my vision of him—them?—so that I couldn't see what they were doing.

Fucking parasites. "That's it," I snarled. "Game over." Evan erupted into a huge smile, and Brett sighed, running after him as he charged into the pile of zombies.

"Here we go," Lydiana murmured, and grabbed her baseball bat.

It was a free—for—all. We had the advantage; the zombies were busy. Lydiana swung as hard as she could, and I suddenly wondered what the hell her brothers had taught her. She loosened the zombie's jaw for her, and it hung as her mouth continued to work on the air. That was one taken care of as Lydiana led it away.

Evan was enthralled, swinging his axe into the foray wildly, careful only when he saw that Brett was next to him. They were an executioner team; out of the twenty or so zombies that plagued that front window. They ended up getting quite a few.

Leslie had her stick handle, laden with pointy things, and even she got into the game. I was almost reluctant to wade in, afraid of getting hurt by friendly fire, when Ohmar tugged urgently on my shirt.

"What?" I began, only to turn around . . . and see the rest of the zombie pack lurching up behind us. "Oh, fuck," I whispered, and I took a deep breath. I had trained for this. I knew what to do.

Chen raised his mace. "For my mother," he said softly.

"For my wife," said Ohmar.

"For Sean," I whispered—and that was when the ghostly sound of groaning drifted to our ears, the stench of their deadened breath met our noses, and my hatchet met flesh.

~

It wasn't a glorious fight. There were no valiant and victorious dead, at any rate—just the zombies hitting the floor. Grace was wild, tearing through the horde at such a pace that I was worried about her; what if dogs could get the virus? But she was impenetrable, unstoppable as she wagged and wiggled serious injury, if not death, upon them.

Then again, I didn't think there was such a thing as valiant and victorious dead. People died. It was awful. And we walked on.

I slammed my hatchet down on the head of a zombie, hoping to crack her skull, only to find my hatchet-mop stuck in it instead. She was more than an arm's—length away from me, but it was still unnerving to have my weapons stuck in her. I couldn't see *where* she had been turned, where her bite was, what had made her into this— thing, but I knew it was there. I yanked hard, pulled her off—balance, and swung my freed hatchet-mop into her neck, severing her spinal cord in one blow.

She stopped moving. It was one less zombie, at least.

I wondered when it had gotten to this point for me. Where I no longer saw their faces, only blank bodies, hungry corpses, dead weight. They were no longer potential Seans; they were the enemy, and nothing more. Something to eliminate, something that got in the way. I couldn't humanize them anymore. I couldn't think that somewhere, there was a person inside of this zombie in front of me. When did that happen?

I didn't know, and I wasn't sure I cared. I hacked into

the next zombie—I couldn't even say "victim"—and his arm fell lifeless to the ground. I could see blackened bone. I didn't know that they got sick down to their very marrow. It disgusted me.

This whole thing disgusted me.

Ohmar was grunting beside me with his mop—handle—made—pointy. It was a blur, biting into everything in its path. I did not envy him the job he would have when sharpening that thing.

That's when I felt it—fingernails, long and sharp, digging at the padding on my arm. I gasped, wrenching my arm away, and turned to face . . . God, this one did look like Sean. I threw up in my mouth, feeling the mealy texture of rice. It felt like maggots crawling around my gums and I opened my lips, purging myself on the zombie I was desperately holding by the shoulder, trying to get my weapon ready as I vomited. I felt teeth graze my arm and I swung blindly, desperately hitting over and over again, my vision white around the edges.

He fell. I fell. I wiped my mouth with my sleeve, looking at the splattered mess of puked—up rice and blood and guts. Intestines lay coiled in a ribbon of rice and chicken, looking as if they exploded up their contents when they hit the ground. A leg lay strewn like straw across its own knee.

I carefully pulled my arm into view, inspecting it minutely. I saw teeth marks, but no open wounds. I wiped the saliva off of my sleeve, sighing, and realized that it was quiet.

Really fucking quiet. I looked around cautiously,

and no one was fighting. No one was saying anything. Everyone was standing . . . near one spot, together. I had a bad feeling about this.

I did a head count, my mind refusing to calculate what I knew to be true. I struggled to my feet, using my hatchet-mop as a walking stick, and slowly walked over to the group. Leslie was on her knees, holding someone's hand. I heard murmured voices. I sat down next to Leslie, and dragged my eyes up the body of the person on the floor of the lobby.

It was Chen, his mace hanging loosely beside him in uncoiled fingers. It was Chen, with Evan holding his shoulder, with tears gathering but not falling. It was Chen who looked at me and gave a small smile, then turned to Evan. "I was waiting for you," he said simply.

Evan looked nervous, his eyelids twitching. We all leaned in, trying to hear what Chen was saying. "I want you to do it."

"What?" Evan exclaimed.

"You need to do it. You're the one I can count on. You have to end this." Chen shifted uncomfortably as he spoke.

Evan stared at him for what felt like a long time. He turned to me, his eyes shining with tears. I sat next to him wordlessly, and he raised his weapon. Leaning over Chen, Evan took a swing back and slammed the weapon down— but he stopped at the last moment.

"I can't," he said. "I can't, I can't—"

Chen shook his head, groaning. "Someone has to do it. Please. I don't want to turn into those *things*."

I looked at the bite on his upper, inner arm. It was already turning black. I wondered how quickly Sean would have turned if I hadn't cut his arm off. God, was it really me that could do these horrible things?

"All right," I said unhelpfully, trying not to throw up what was left of my rice. I eyed Brett. He was staring at me, hopefully trying to psychic me confidence. If I acted like this was a privilege, no big deal except for the honor, maybe it would be. Maybe it would mean something to me instead of more death and dying. Maybe it would be something good, freeing him or something. I felt like there should be a ceremony or something. But there was just this: me, with my hatchet-mop, staring at a dying boy.

"Goodbye, Chen," I said carefully. Controlled. "I'm sorry it ended up this way. I'm glad to have met you." I made sure my voice didn't waver. Ohmar held his ankle loosely; Leslie put a hand on his cheek. Brett stood alone, watching silently, as I reared back with my hatchet-mop and looked into Chen's eyes.

"Goodbye, Evan," Chen echoed. "At least this way, I won't be able to hurt you."

He closed his eyes. I swung. I hit. When it mattered, I didn't miss. I had to remember that. It hit with a thick chunking sound as I slashed his windpipe, his Adam's apple, something, and then his spinal cord. I swung hard, and his head rolled off of his body with a dull thud.

Leslie gasped, turning away. Evan stared down at the head near his lap, his face frozen and expressionless. Brett was still watching me, his gaze steady, until he turned and walked toward the maintenance closet.

I heard the soft banging of the man in the closet, the sounds of a man who had given up on help. As my team mourned, I walked away, wondering if there would be a day where I couldn't live with all that I had done. All that I had seen. We rescued Keagan, but at what cost? I didn't even know him.

I looked down at my pants and realized that I had Chen's blood on them. I was glad; it would be a mark to remember him by. It was all we had left of him. Chen was gone.

Just like that.

And I had done that. As I watched Brett get a dark—haired man out of the closet, I couldn't help but wonder who would be next—and why I was now the executioner.

~

I supposed I would have to get used to feeling nothing; I felt like an empty gun cartridge, rounds dispensed, fallen to the floor, useless. I pet the tiny spot on Grace's head that was uncovered; it was a weak spot, but one I hadn't figured out how to cover. Her ears wiggled as I scratched them. She sat panting, wagging her nails with a scraping sound against the floor, as I watched Evan struggle not to cry.

Evan sat on the floor, mourning next to Chen's body, and I had to look away. I didn't want to have to do this. Chen was a good kid, and he deserved better than what he got. He turned to Brett shakily. "Has this ever happened to you?"

Brett blinked a little. "I think Kiera could answer that better than I could. I lived alone."

I exhaled, staring at Chen's limp body. "I had to cut the arm off of my fiancé." It made me shudder, and I swallowed hard. It was not a memory that I enjoyed, but it was one that would haunt me forever. Cutting skin around broken bones, feeling the nerves stretch—it was too much.

Thinking about it felt like shame, covered in a thick oil of defeat.

I sighed, nudging Grace with my calf to get her to follow me. We went toward Keagan, who looked rather battered and world-weary, considering we had done all the work. I supposed hiding in a closet didn't lend itself well to looking healthy and well adjusted. His brown eyes were wide and shocked, and he stood, staring into nothing, as Brett tried to get him to respond.

"You know, it's not like this is the first time we've seen zombies," I observed distantly. "This is kind of a thing now. Freaking out isn't going to help."

Leslie's jaw dropped, and I realized that it wasn't the most comforting thing I'd ever said. "Well, it's true. If he's going to live through this like the rest of us, he might want to keep his shit together better."

"Kiera . . ." Brett started, turning toward me. I saw the concern in his face, his posture. I didn't want it—didn't want any of it.

"No. It's fine. He can freak out. I'm going over there," I gestured lamely to the boarded up lobby window and the cactus near it. It was across the lobby from Chen's head, which oozed slowly onto the carpet. Evan was sitting next to it, his eyes dark and haunted, as he talked to Ohmar and Lydiana. I couldn't make out what they were saying, but I imagined it couldn't be good or cheerful.

Nothing would ever be good or cheerful again.

I think I'm broken, I thought to myself wonderingly. Something had snapped inside of me after I'd hacked Chen's head off, I realized. there should have been an audible pop to accompany the feeling. I felt far away from myself. My feelings were trapped, unable to get to me, and I was thankful for it. I looked at the world as if I were underwater and it was the surface, an entirely different place from where I was.

Good. Maybe I could get through this after all. I sat down next to Grace by the cactus, looking at the (possibly fake) spikes and the purple ball on the top of it. I reached out and patted the cactus lightly, playing with the spines, pressing my fingers against them until they threatened to bleed. I felt the pressure, but not the pain.

This was a really fucking weird feeling. I looked up as footsteps registered somewhere in the back of my lizard brain, my prehistoric warning system that was somehow still active through the fog. Brett was walking toward me, even as Keagan stayed behind with Leslie. They were talking quietly, Leslie's hand on his shoulder. He was tall and thin, lanky, and wore a Hawaiian shirt with toucans on it. It was probably the least zombie—apocalypse—ready outfit I had ever seen.

Brett sat down next to Grace, petting her slowly. She leaned into him, putting one foot on top of his bloody steel—toed boot, and I smiled a little. "Yes, Brett. I was rude. I'm sorry."

He shrugged. "Keagan's not exactly a friend. He's just a guy I knew about from a doomsday prepper site I was on. Sean used to make fun of him for complaining about the whole 'live alone in the wilderness' approach. He had a thing about shitting on trees, I think."

"Well, you probably shouldn't do it *on* the tree. That would probably hurt."

Brett nodded in agreement as Grace licked his hand. "Point taken. Either way, you were right, even if it wasn't the most diplomatic thing you could have said. He's not your biggest fan." Brett paused, looking around the room. "You seem to have shocked the room with your Jury–Judge–Judy—and––Executioner role. I wasn't sure what the fuck Chen was thinking."

"I don't know," I said hollowly. "I don't know why he asked me to do that. Evan wasn't doing it, and I was the closest one he could see. It probably had nothing to do with me."

"I guess he wanted to die looking into the eyes of someone friendly? You don't look too friendly now. I don't think Ohmar and Lydiana know what to do with you. Leslie was horrified."

"I don't feel too friendly now. I feel shattered. I feel like I'm in pieces, held together in a bubble with everything else on the outside. I don't understand this feeling, but I kind of like it. It's numb. It erases the pain of missing Sean. It's efficient. I could probably kill a ton of zombies like this," I said thoughtfully.

He shrugged, leaning his head back against the wooden boards. "It's probably shock," he observed. "Dissociation.

Removing oneself from the trauma. It's normal. But I wouldn't expect it to last forever. You'll feel it eventually."

"How do you know so much about, like, psychology and minds and stuff?" I looked at him, bewildered.

"I got my master's in psychology before I started working at the store," he said casually. "I was going to be a trauma therapist. Then I realized how much I hate people. It kind of killed it for me."

Wow. Brett was one smart cookie. I was surprised by this revelation; he didn't seem like a soft science kind of guy, not at all. I wasn't sure what to do with that information. "Um . . . I think you should talk to Evan, then," I said finally, with a deep sigh. "I hope I didn't break him, too."

He started picking zombie blood off of his shirt. It dried so quickly, and it was so damn gross. "I don't really want to be the bartender for this group."

"The bartender?"

He snorted. "Someone who doesn't get paid to listen to your shit but has to put up with it anyway."

"Then why did you sit next to me?"

He nudged me with his shoulder. "You're a friend," he said simply. "Not a would—be client. I wanted to make sure you weren't broken."

I looked at him for a long time, the numbness threatening to drown me. "I think I am," I said softly.

He looked at Chen's head on the floor. It was no longer bleeding. "You're not the only one," he said, after a long while. "We'll put our pieces together and make something new. I'm sure of it."

Brett smiled and patted my knee, getting up from

under Grace's paw. As he walked over to Evan, I thought about what he'd said. I wondered if I had enough pieces left. If there was anything worth making left of me.

I wasn't so sure.

Conquering Heroes

~ Sean ~

Gwen. Holly. Darla. Sarah. These four girls were now my world. That and an army of zombies.

I was starting to feel NZS, weaker than he was before, and it felt good to me. Like progress. Even with his being quiet, I wasn't entirely sure who I was anymore. Or if it mattered. The only way I could tell was that when NZS was present, he couldn't see red; just black, white and gray. The red was mine and mine alone.

I took Holly by her hand and led her and Sarah back to Darla and Gwen. I could easily follow the bloody trail between the classrooms, and I didn't hear any more screaming.

Darla was waiting patiently at the head of the stairs, surveying her work. I couldn't count how many zombies we had now—but there were a lot. More than I could count on one hand and two (mangled) feet. It was really starting to *look* like an army now.

Plan? I asked Darla.

Checkallbuildings, she said quickly. *Formore. Zombies, humans. Putall incourtyard.*

That made sense, I guessed dubiously. She flashed pictures of me, Sarah and Holly searching buildings as a team, other zombies getting together to check the classrooms and offices. It sounded . . . tiring.

I was so tired. I wanted to stand in the sun, letting its rays cover my face and body, and just be, but I wondered what my family would do without me. I knew they needed me as much as I needed them, even if I didn't want to do this anymore. As much as I wanted to Infect, as much as I wanted to help to create our perfect world, part of me was just done, and I couldn't pinpoint why. But I had people relying on me, and I couldn't give up yet, even when I felt like the world was slipping from my grasp.

You're starting to fade, NZS observed softly. I hadn't even realized we'd switched. *Like me. Soon, you'll have your own cage, until you fade completely.* He wasn't smug, he was simply stating facts. It felt like NZS only had two emotions now: regret and sadness. He was as tired as I was.

Whattodo? I thought at him cautiously. I noticed my speech was getting even worse than it had been. I wasn't sure what that meant, but it couldn't be good. Maybe NZS had better answers than I did. They couldn't possibly be worse.

What do you want to do? he asked, sounding genuinely curious. Holly, Sarah and I were walking toward the next building. It looked like an—*apartment,* NZS supplied—building. I assumed these were the *dorms* that Darla showed me. I could see the courtyard long past the dorms, with its beautiful—*dogwood,* NZS supplied—trees making a round shape. I stared at the glass doors for a long time.

What's wrong? NZS asked.

Door, I answered. *Workthe door?*

I heard laughing in the back of my mind, followed by a subdued voice. *It's probably locked,* he observed as we examined the glass. *Break it.*

I started to stumble into the door headfirst, knowing it was likely the strongest part of my body that I could actually use at this point. Sarah followed suit, banging her white brain—cover into the glass. *Iwant . . .*

Yes? he said patiently.

Iwanthome, I said. Home: with no other zombies dying. No stupid plans that would get us killed. I wanted a community of perfect people that wanted the same thing, together, so that we could all be *home.* I thought I might want the girl, too, but I thought it was best not to bring her up yet. She felt like the beauty of *home* that I was missing; the moments in the sunshine that felt like nothing short of perfection. She was that perfection. I was desperately holding on to the place that Samuel had left a gaping hole, holding on to it for her.

I hit the door with my head again. And again. Thin white lines began to appear on the glass as Sarah rammed herself into it with me. That must mean it was working. Holly wasn't about to throw herself in the fray.

Home doesn't sound bad, NZS said slowly. *I miss*

home. I miss her. I miss . . . everything. I wasn't sure how, or why, but I was starting to feel bad for NZS. He was more than just the enemy in the back of my head. He was me. He was me from before I saw the light in the darkness. He was a friend, I guessed.

One more hit and the glass door shattered. It didn't seem very safe that someone could break the door open where a bunch of kids lived, alone. That was okay. I would make them better—if there were any left.

We stepped through the broken glass. I felt the glass in my feet more from the way I was walking rather than the pain; Sarah, Holly and I all trailed little droplets of blood with every step, and Holly was even more uneven on her feet than I was. *Whatdowedo?* she said brightly.

I wondered if I'd ever feel that bright again. Sarah bopped along to music that none of us could hear, following along blindly. Now all I felt was a deep—seated desire to fix everything—my everything. The trees, the grass, and the zombies in the sun. It made me a little sad that humans couldn't see the world that they had created—the world that was changing without them. Humans had broken *everything*. There was no home, no family—just selfish creatures who lived only for what they wanted in the moment.

No. I had better plans for them.

What about Darla? NZS asked carefully.

What? ??? I sent back.

He paused as we finally found the stairs. Apparently college students were not fond of them, as they were all the way at the back of the lobby. *Darla wants to start a war.*

He showed me pictures, then—of people dying, blood and gunshots, bombs and torn limbs. I wasn't sure what he thought he was doing with the blood and bodies, as that wasn't exactly a problem, but the dying made me think. *She wants zombies to die?*

Yes, NZS said, and if he hadn't been in my head, it would've been so quiet that I'd barely hear it.

I stopped in the middle of the staircase and my mind exploded into brilliant whites and reds. I had trouble pinpointing the feeling until NZS supplied it—*anger.* I was so angry. Rage blossomed through my body, and I felt strength running through the sludge in my veins. Darla might not really *want* them to die—but what she wanted would kill a lot of us in the meantime.

When she started the zombie army and cried out war, I was in—in for a long battle against the humans that had started this in the first place. What I hadn't realized was that Darla had what NZS called "acceptable casualties" on the brain. No way. Not if I had anything to do with it.

I had my own war to wage.

~

I was surprised that NZS was on my side for this. He didn't explain why—but he was supplying the words, the information, the plans that my zombified brain couldn't handle. I was worried that he seemed weaker, somehow; his voice wasn't as loud and clear as it had been. Was he right? Were we both going to fade away?

I hated to admit it, but I didn't know what I'd do without NZS. He was, literally, the brains of the operation. I had to Infect everyone I could before Darla could feel what I was up to—and he pointed out that Darla could peek into my brain at any point in time, so it wasn't like I could sit around and think about it, either.

Sarah, Holly and I inched our way up the stairs, stagger by stagger. It was getting harder; my knees didn't want to bend that way, and the wound in my leg wasn't helping. I was just glad it didn't hurt.

There were an awful lot of closed doors on the second floor. Fuck.

You're in luck. Dorms are cheap. You'll be able to get the doors down fairly easily.

NZS had a point. I looked at the door, which had a handle instead of a knob, and gestured to Holly. She was surprised, but slapped it a few times, finally using the weight of her arm to push down the handle. She was the newest of us all; it followed that she'd be in the best shape, right?

It was literally just a room with two beds, two dressers, and two desks. I don't know what I was picturing a dorm room to look like, but it wasn't this. NZS snorted in the back of my head. We could see that there were no zombies in this room right away. There appeared to be . . . *twelve*, NZS said. Twelve rooms on this floor. We split up.

I couldn't open the doors as easily as Holly did, so I did what I did best: ram my head into it as hard as I could. It didn't take very long to break the door down, but I realized that black blood was slowly dripping into my right eye. Great. Only three—ish more doors to break down, and my head was already showing wear and tear.

Eyes stared at me listlessly from a thin frame on the bed. She was *emaciated*, NZS said. *Toothin,* I thought.

She had run out of food long before today. She was dying already, I could smell it. But that didn't matter. There was no minimum weight limit for zombies. Alive was good enough.

"Oh, good," she breathed. Her eyes rolled toward me, and I could almost hear them swirling in their sockets. "I don't have to keep going anymore."

I guessed not. Anything would be better than this. I was a little wary—she would occupy the space that the Old Man had held in my Link—but it was what I had to do. I would do my best to keep Darla from killing us all, and that meant that I had to save the humans first.

She didn't struggle as I lurched over to the bed, and even sat up for me. She wore a T-shirt and leggings, the same clothes *she* liked to wear, and I grimaced. Memories flashed through NZS's mind: Kiera had extensive knowledge of leggings and legging companies, and even made and sold some special patterns (with pockets!) herself online. NZS had been proud of her for the innovation. And now . . .

Now she might be gone, NZS thought quietly. *Or like the girl in front of you.*

"Make it quick?" she asked.

I knew it wouldn't be as quick as she wanted, or as painless, but I tried to pick a spot that I knew would let the Infection move into her fast. I leaned down and tore her shirt awkwardly, picking a spot near her heart, under the loose fabric band of the thing she wore underneath the T-shirt. She didn't even cry out; she simply collapsed against my arm, staring at me with eyes that wished they saw death, and this was the first time I felt my heart hurt for someone I'd bitten. But I knew—this time, I *really knew*—that her new life was going to be so much better than the one she was leaving behind.

Standing there with my arm around the lip girl, she shuddered and made little sounds. I waited for her to die, waited for her to come back. *Natalie,* I knew, the moment her body went stiff and her heart stopped beating. Her name was Natalie, and she liked biology.

I wasn't sure what "biology" meant, but NZS seemed to think it was a good thing. *She's smart. Depending on which way she comes back, she might know how to help us,* NZS said.

Whichway what? I said absently.

You know. Like you or . . . like Sarah, he said, not unkindly.

Oh. I guessed that made sense. Her eyes opened, that strange shiny color that seemed to glow from within. She sat up slowly, looking around as Gwen wandered into the room.

Infected! Gwen shouted. *Hi!*

H . . . hi, Natalie said shyly. *What happened?*

Like me, maybe? *HiNatalie,* I said. *Zombie. Azombie now.*

Oh, she said. She stood up from the bed, stretching, and smiled. I wished I could still do that. *Good. I like it.*

Definitely like me, then. I wondered what I looked like through Natalie's eyes. She would see a man with a flap of skin missing on his head, bright white showing through. His body was covered in blood, stringy veins, and gore of all kinds. There were bone chips embedded in his one arm, and his other . . . was a monstrous hole, pulsing with black sludge, a wound that would never close.

His face screamed silent rage.

This face was me.

To the School

~ Kiera ~

The rest of the group stayed in my building, splitting off into different apartments that Brett had picked the locks on. We spent the next ten or so days learning to work together, and we made quite the scene breaking and entering. *Was it still breaking if you picked the locks?* I had no idea. After leaving his chosen apartment, Evan stuck close to Brett as he retrieved all of the items he could. "How are you holding up?"

Evan's head turned quickly. "What?"

I hesitated, wondering if it was the right thing to say. "Since . . . since Chen died. How are you doing? Are you okay?"

He stared at me, his eyes bloodshot from not sleeping well. "Not really, but it's fine."

I wasn't about to let him off the hook that easily. "It sucked," I said. "It sucked hard, and I hated it, and now he's gone. He volunteered for my idea, followed Brett and

I, and now he's gone, and you want me to give up on you? Fuck that." I shook my head. "It's not fine."

We went to the apartments that the other members were staying in, giving them a wake—up call. It was nice. There were sounds, sounds of life, coming from the floor around me, and I wasn't sure if it was more comforting or strange, after all this time. I walked between the apartments, down the hallway and back up again, reminding myself of how lucky we were to have a zombie-free zone. Lydiana was getting dressed, calling out that she'd be over shortly, and Brett stood outside my door, a outdoorsy gargoyle that adorned the door frame.

Grace seemed to know that something was coming; she kept looking out the window as I tried to fall asleep, seemingly staring into morning. I wondered what she saw. Threats or promises? Zombies or flowers? Or maybe she saw a cat. I didn't know.

Chen's death haunted me during those mornings. I couldn't believe that he had asked me to kill him. I was a killer. I had killed with my own hands and my hatchet-mop. I had taken a human life, and it weighed on me terribly. I felt like I was sinking in the deep end, trapped in the bottom by a ball and chain.

I remembered my early undergrad years when I'd been preoccupied with serial killer shows on Hulu. Sean had teased me about my fascination. I scared myself quite frequently watching those shows, but I never once stopped to think about *how* they actually did it. How they were okay with killing people. I knew now that it was a psychological bent, a thrill for the kill. I knew that feeling now, when I killed a zombie. A twisted sense of satisfaction. It was very, very different from the feeling that I had after killing Chen.

I closed my eyes as I felt the fabric of Sean's back- pack. I had been packing all evening, trying to get ready for our next great adventure, with Grace following my ev- ery move. What do you pack for a zombie—killing, last— ditch effort to clear some ground for the National Guard? I mean, underwear was generally always a good idea, but the kitchen knives I had left went in there too. It was a mishmash of old and new worlds, a staggering display of how different my life had become after all of this had started.

Sean would've loved this.

I wondered where he was now, as I sat down with my phone to text with Callie. I had been in near—constant contact with her over the last ten days; she was evidently the point of contact for my school, now, not just a journal- ist. It was her pet project, her baby, and I didn't know how to feel about it. She used all sorts of military jargon that I didn't understand, acronyms that made her sound insane and way too far in the government's pocket. I worried. I worried a lot.

What did it mean that the government was so far into this project? Was it normal to have the CDC and the National Guard working together? This was unprece- dented, and it wasn't like there was a damn book (okay, maybe there were a lot of damn books), but none of them were nonfiction) on how to do this. I was uncomfortable with the thought of the military setting up camp in the middle of campus. What if they decided it was a lost cause and just began shooting?

Or worse, what about that movie where they just nuked the zombies, and what if we were inside?

That one, I asked Callie. She sent a laugh emoji. *No no no,* she texted. *We're the good guys. I can't imagine ever doing something like that.*

We. She said "we." Like she was part of the Guard or something now. Was she military and I didn't even know it? Didn't it, like, take time to enlist and train and stuff? Maybe they grandfathered her in somehow. I shifted, uncomfortable with the thought. I didn't trust the military.

So the plan is that it'll take you three days to get to campus, right?

Right, I texted back, fidgeting with the carabiner on Sean's backpack. I was almost done packing; just the food to go on top and the blanket to bundle underneath.

We'll give you two days to do what you can to clear campus or round up the zombies in one area. Whatever you can do.

Wait, I thought we were looking for survivors? I said, frowning at my phone.

You are, she wrote back. *But it's not like you can just walk into campus and find them. There's gonna be a lot of zombies. The last time we looked they were everywhere.*

What do you mean, the last time you looked?

We're planning on doing another drone sweep tomorrow. We haven't seen any changes in the city in weeks, so we're only doing them every so often.

Oh, I said. I sighed, looking down at Grace, running my

fingers through her long fur. "I don't know what we're going to run into, Gracey," I murmured. She sniffed my fingers and licked them softly. "Don't worry. We'll be okay."

Sounds good. So five days, and then what happens? I typed. I assumed there was some grand plan, some grand account of what was going to happen when the five days were up. Were they going to come in and rescue us? And on that note, why weren't we getting more help? Or *were* we getting more help, and they hadn't bothered to tell us? I furiously texted my questions to Callie.

And I waited.

I waited for hours, and the knocks on the door began. I waited as we assembled our shit together, a ragtag group of not-very-Avengers-like kids and youngish adults, that had no fucking clue what we were doing. And I waited until Brett showed up, out of breath and filthy. "How's your leg?"

He seemed surprised. "Pardon?"

"Your leg. You've been limping. And trying not to isn't working." I knelt down, about to pull up the leg of his jeans. He caught my hand and held it in the air.

"It's nothing." He pushed my hand away.

"Are you sure? It looked like it was bleeding a lot." I started to rummage through the things we'd collected, looking for a first aid kit, and Brett sighed.

"You won't take no as an answer, will you?"

I shook my head and sat on the floor. I rolled up the pant leg and my heart sank. There was a terrible gash, reminiscent of Sean's, curling around his ankle. It wasn't black—yet, and I wondered if it was going to be. Brett couldn't be Infected. He just couldn't.

The first aid kit I'd found was terrible, and the one of the only useful things in it was duct tape. I said nothing, pouring peroxide over the cut, and he hissed as it started to bubble. "I'm sorry," I said quietly, and began to pull the skin closed over the wound.

He said nothing, watching me with thoughtful eyes, and let me doctor him. Finished, I put the almost but not quite useless first aid kit back, examining the room. I followed his lead, and turned to face the group. No one was paying attention; it was probably the only reason Brett had allowed me to do it in the first place.

I looked around. We were all packed and ready. Grace was in her suit. We were heading out.

And I waited.

~

It was pretty quiet in the area around my neighborhood. Brett and I had pretty much taken care of a six-ish block radius around my apartment; it just made things easier when the rest of the crew decided to move in. Brett found all of the little zombie friends and led our group to them, letting us practice on real, moving targets. It was going fairly well, actually—but Callie still hadn't texted me back.

We stepped lightly, moving as a team through the streets as we walked our Brett—determined route toward the university. Grace was downright spritely, dancing in her pretty armor beside me. I didn't know how to feel. On one hand, zombies. I knew what to do with zombies. On the other hand . . . how many people were at the school, waiting to be rescued? How many people had died, waiting to be rescued? And was I responsible for all of them?

The weight of responsibility grew on me the more we walked. I shifted uncomfortably, hefting my backpack back up on my shoulders, and looked at Brett.

"What?" As always, he was passive and vaguely amused.

"I just . . . it feels like we're responsible for the world, you know? I don't know how Callie talked me into this. I just had this vague idea that we could save some people with the vaccine she told me about, and now we're storming a school to kill the zombies and rescue whoever's left? I just don't get the connection. I don't get why she talked me into doing this. I want to kill the zombies—all of them—but I don't entirely know that storming the castle is the way to do it."

He cackled. "That's not how I remember it," he replied. "*You* were adamant about eradicating zombies from the face of the earth. *You* felt bad about the university where Sean got attacked. And *you* had a guilt complex. When Callie mentioned deploying the vaccines to university sites, there was no way you were going to turn her down."

I closed my eyes, sighing. "I know. You're right. I practically talked her into it. I just . . . if one good thing can come out of what happened to Sean . . . I just know that there are some students left. Sean saved me when that zombie came. And if I can save the rest . . ."

Brett grunted, glancing over his shoulder for an attendance check. "I wouldn't count on being able to save *everyone* left. Lots of people probably starved by now."

Tears were springing to my eyes. I didn't know why I felt such a desperate need to help them; all I knew was that it was somehow connected to Sean. No matter how hard I tried, everything came back to that: the moment we realized he was infected, the amputation, locking him up . . . and leaving him behind.

I wondered what zombies did when there were no more humans to attack. Was he just standing in a hallway somewhere staring into nothing? Was he wandering around until he wore through his shoes? I sighed again, running my hand over the braids in my hair. "We have to try," I said finally. It was weak, but it was all I had.

"I know," Brett said quietly. "And I don't mind it. We'll check out the grounds, make sure there isn't a huge zombie pack in the middle of campus, and go door to door. We'll find everyone, Kiera. I promise."

It seemed impossible for us to look for so many people in such a short amount of time. We had three days to get there—and two days until . . . ? I didn't know what we would do then, what would happen when we reached the end of day two. Would they firebomb the place with us inside?

Would I care if they did?

It wasn't something I liked to admit to myself, to be honest. I had stopped crying myself to sleep, but that didn't stop me from waking up in tears. Grace did a lot to keep my loneliness at bay; she was an essential part of me now, a fifth limb, and I didn't know what I'd do without her. But if she was a limb, Sean was my heart, and I was *sure* that I couldn't live without him. I took out the anger on the zombies, sure. But there was nothing I could do to take away the sadness.

The only thing that kept me alive was the thought that Sean was still alive, somewhere, too. And if I died, that meant we wouldn't be reunited. Maybe I could talk Callie into blasting our apartment. Then we could finally be together.

I realized how sick and twisted my thought processes were now. I was an entirely different person, a person I couldn't recognize. A person who picked her nails down to bleeding just to feel something a little different. A person who fought and killed mindless beings just to gain a little bit of mindlessness of her own. I didn't know what it meant for me, morally, the peace I felt when I dispatched a zombie was the only time my heart didn't ache for what I could never find.

As I lamented my past life, images of Sean dancing around in my head, Brett stopped short, holding up his fist. The footsteps behind me cut off as we surveyed the area. Evan was breathing a little hard. Ohmar kept clearing his throat. And then we saw it: our first contact.

I grabbed my hatchet-mop, holding it tightly against my chest, listening to the sounds of my crew arming themselves, and we stood together, united, as a pack of zombies—larger than any we'd fought before—poured out of the broken, burned building in front of us, filling the air with grunts and moans.

I wasn't waiting any longer.

~

We were about halfway to the college when it began. I didn't know how the building had caught fire. It didn't matter, in the end, but it made for some interesting zombies. Skin melted like crayons caught in the micro-wave; a tongue poking out of a cheek that was no longer there. I saw limbs strewn across the pavement. I stared ahead at the zombie that was coming to meet me, won-dering how she could find me.

Her eyes ran down her face in thick globules that looked like bacon fat. They were seared into her skin, col-ors melding together and accented by a brilliant red that didn't look like it would ever dry. Her fingertips were burned off, thick black stubs reaching toward me.

I wasn't afraid, despite her appearance. I felt resigned. This was my destiny now; instead of wedding planning and a thesis, I had this. Aiming low and swiping up with a hard crunch, I caught her at the bottom of her rib cage and pulled up, tearing out part of her chest wall. They were coming faster; it was hard to keep track of where ev-eryone was. Grace was beside me, in her element as al-ways. And as always, I was worried that something would happen to her—my lifeline, my only reason for staying alive besides Sean.

I realized that I was becoming very clinical about what we were doing; dispatching zombies was hard work, but it was easy emotionally. It was nice to feel nothing for a while as I wrenched my hatchet-mop out of the skull of another zombie, her thick, flat tongue looked as if it was dripping down her chin. We fought together, all of us.

It was too much.

We were out in the open; there was nothing between them and us. The zombies poured around us, surround-ing the group, and we fought back to back. I heard Ohmar gasping, panting as Evan swung at the zombie behind him. I couldn't see Leslie. Keagan was hiding behind a pole. I felt Lydiana's back pressed against me as she said, "Oh, shit." Brett was . . . on a dumpster?

What the fuck was Brett doing on a dumpster? I didn't have time to think. They came faster, mobbing us, and it was all we could do to hold the line. I held my side back with my handle, snapping teeth coming closer, and felt Lydiana's limbs trembling behind me.

"Fuck, fuck, fuck," I chanted, and felt Grace wind her way between me and Lydiana, hiding behind me. We were all panting, gory and bloody, and I felt myself shudder. My arms wouldn't hold. I was ready to give up—

"Fire in the hole! Get the fuck out of there!" Brett screamed.

"What?"

"Huh?"

It took a brief second to see that he held something flaming aloft. I found one last ounce of strength to push the zombie away from me, to grab Grace and pick her up, using her spikes as a weird shield; she wagged her tail against my thigh tiredly. Lydiana thrust her baseball bat into an open mouth, shoving it through the back of a skull, and we ducked low. She was using her weapon as a clothesline, sweeping the zombies' feet out from under them. I saw Ohmar next to us. Keagan lagged behind. We ran.

And Brett threw.

As we entered the alleyway I didn't turn back to look, burdened by the weight of Grace, but I felt the impact as much as I heard it. There was a dull roar and a whooshing sound, and grunts and cries and strangled moans. I only stopped running when I realized that the others had, too; I put Grace down and she collapsed at my feet, exhausted. We stared at the fireworks in front of us: burned zombies, burning.

Brett waited until the majority of the zombies had wandered too close to the flame, and become moths in a bug zapper, before he jumped off of his dumpster. He casually walked over and flopped down next to me, panting. He was covered in oozing black blood; I realized we all were, and wondered where the fuck it had all gone wrong.

"So, too many," he observed breathlessly. "Note to self. All right."

"That's all you can say? Note to self? What even the fuck, Brett?"

He extinguished the torch he'd created and rolled an eye to look at me from the concrete. I grabbed my thermos off my pack, pouring some water for Gracey. "I mean, it is. I think our max as a group of . . . seven and a half? Eight?" Gracey snorted and went back to her water. "Probably fifteen, eighteen zombies. I'm pretty sure I counted at least three, maybe four zombies for each of us. So any more than twenty and we need to get the fuck out of there."

Ohmar was pressing a cloth against his forehead, swearing under his breath. It was scandalous; I didn't even know that he knew those words. "So what do we do in case it happens again?" he asked, a little darkly.

Because it would happen again. And we both knew it.

"We need to get something between us and them and make a plan," Brett said quietly. "Molotov cocktails don't last forever, and I could only fit so many ingredients in my pack. I think . . ." He trailed off, tentative, and looked at me.

It didn't bode well. "What?"

He hesitated. "I think that you need to find out how they're going to administer the vaccine, and go from there. The campus is gonna be shot with zombies. I think we're best on stealth, trying to get people out of buildings and to . . . where?"

I didn't know. I just didn't fucking know anything about this situation. I pulled out my phone and texted angrily. *Callie, what the hell? Why aren't you answering me? How are you pulling this off? How will you administer the vaccine? What's the plan? We* need to know the plan.

We all sat quietly in the alleyway, watching for strays as the pile of zombies burned noxiously. That was not a smell I wanted to be overly familiar with ever again, yet I knew it would be my future for a long time coming. *It's airborne,* she replied after several moments. *When you hit five days, we're going to get planes to dump it in the air all over campus. Anyone alive should be vaccinated just by breathing it in. We're hoping people will come outside or go onto the roofs when they hear the helicopters coming.*

"It's, like, aerosol or something," I muttered, frowning at the phone. That didn't tell me everything. "They're banking on people coming out when they hear the helicopters." *And the zombies? What are you going to do about the massive amount of zombies that are currently committed to their college education?*

That one took a lot longer. *That's why you need to get out,* she said. *We have a theoretical cure, airborne again. From Finland or Norway or one of those countries. But it might not work. So if you don't reach the checkpoint north of campus in five days . . . we take the final step.*

"They're going to bomb the campus," I breathed. "Holy fucking hell. Brett, what are we going to do?" I could feel the goosebumps on my skin, could feel the chill in my bones. "First, the vaccine. Then, they've got a possible cure. Airborne, like the vaccine. And if it doesn't work, they're going to bomb the fucking campus and kill anything that moves."

Brett looked at Evan, Ohmar, Lydiana. At Keagan, who volunteered absolutely no words to the conversation in his little Hawaiian shirt. I didn't even know where he got the damned axe from. And then Brett turned to me.

"We're going to do our job," he said finally. "Find the survivors. Let them aerosolize the fuck out of campus if they want, get a sticker for our vaccine cards. And then we're going to go north, and fuck up the checkpoint."

I thought about it for a moment. "Why are we fucking up the checkpoint?"

"I'm not about to become an experiment to the National Guard and the CDC. If they're going to aerosolize me with random shit, then decide to bomb the fuck out of me if I don't move *fast* enough . . ."

"Then we get to see if the government is better, or worse than we thought," I added softly.

Grace looked up at me, tilted her head, and sighed.

Zombie National Guard

~ Sean ~

I didn't check in to see if Darla noticed. The less attention I got from her, the better. ZS and I led the cadre of girls through the dorms, and we let the other zombies collect body counts. Holly managed to gather a full deck of cards, filling her Hex and beaming. Sarah required a little more direction and both Natalie and I pulled her away to keep her from killing the girls in front of her.

It was then that I realized this was not a co-ed dorm, or at least, not a co-ed floor. The "I grew up in America" part of me wondered what a zombie army full of young women would do against a zombie army of young men.

We wandered among the broken bodies, picking and choosing, feeding instead of Infecting as I thought about the ramifications. My zombies seemed to be of the smarter variety, and I wondered what Darla's army was like; if they were bouncy and happy to be Infecting, or if they were falling back in darkness due to what we had done. It could go either way; my girls, however, came back with a modicum of intellect. Brains vs. brawn was not something I'd expected to face in the zombie apocalypse. It felt like *Ninja Warrior,* but cursed.

"Waking up" to ZS felt awful as he was mindlessly ripping a tendon out of a girl's neck while she squealed. My stomach dropped; no matter how many times I saw it, it still made me want to throw up in his mouth a little. My body was doing that. *My body* was doing that. Or was it still my body? Was it mine, if I was a prisoner in my own mind, with no power to exert force over my muscles, my own tendons, my bones?

I wasn't sure who was fading faster. Who we would become.I spent most of my time in a foggy room, barely able to see out of his eyes, only able to think when he called upon me. The fog was taking up more and more of the room as the days went by. I was being swallowed by the roiling gloom of the sea, eaten inch by inch. It was an endless echo from across the world, into the mind of a zombie.

Would I have time? If I would see anything for the last time . . . or if I would fade into black.

My thoughts were growing too dark, and I decided to watch as Holly fill the spots in her Hex, watched our new nameless zombies start to form a group. By the end of the—*dorm,* NZS supplied sleepily—I couldn't count how many of us there were. I was the only one who had a spot, a place in my Link left. Mine was saved . . . for *her.*

I'd made a decision. We were going to defeat Darla,

and keep her from killing everyone before she had the chance. NZS and I would go back to the place. We would find the building with the flowers growing over the—

The word didn't come.

It had two wheels and it ran for you—you rode it. I knew that. It was blue and the flowers grew over it. But missing the word didn't bother me. The problem came when I realized *why* the word hadn't come.

I couldn't hear the voice of Not-Zombie Sean.

It was the first time he hadn't been there, the first time he hadn't given me the word, the first time red wasn't creeping into my vision. I reached for him, and only felt gray, a feeling of gray, a thick air feeling of gray.

He wasn't there, and I had no idea if he was coming back.

I heard a wail, the sound the horns make when their prey rows past in their ships, and the girls gathered around me. We stood in a flower-filled garden outside the girl-building, with me as the lone man. We stood, my National Guard of Zombies, and they reached for me as I cried into the afternoon sky, begging for him to come back.

~

I was groggy and disconnected as I felt ZS reaching for me. There was no life after death; only the gloam of mist drifting over the bog, the harbor in the distance. I found myself looking for its lone lantern on the dock, wondering where it led.

But he was calling me, and so was Kiera. I knew where to find her—knew how to get back to her. I knew the way to the rose-covered bicycle that ZS had been groping for. And I would bring us home to be her pet zombie, and live forever blissfully in her presence, until it was her time to turn, and we would be Infected together for eternity, until the sun spun down and crashed into the earth for the end of all things.

I missed her. I missed her in all of the ways that poets wrote about. But now wasn't the time. Now I could feel Darla on the other end of the campus, tearing through the administrative offices. She was growing her army the same way that we were, except that was the difference: "Darla" vs. "we." Darla was looking to conquer the world for herself, we were looking to keep her from killing the rest of us. Classic.

ZS was at a distance from me, staring at the sun, which did not altogether seem like a great idea, but there we were. It felt like there was a strange barrier growing between us; a hedge of intellect on one side and hunger on the other. I wondered how far we would get before we were separated for good.

I realized in the garden that at that point that I was in control. Zombies were shoving each other around me, so it took me a minute to figure out how to speak.

Darla wants to kill us. I kept it simple. *She wants to kill all the humans—*

Infect???

Infect!!

Zombies??

There was a cacophony of thoughts, a raucous sound of protest that Darla dared to do anything but spread the virus. *Yes,* I said simply. *Kill. Not Infect. We need to stop Darla. She's on the other side of the courtyard.*

Infect?

Infect!

Yes, I said patiently. *We're going to Infect everyone we see. Create our own army. Beat Darla. And Infect the humans on the other side.*

Infect, they sighed, relaxing. It made sense to them. It was the plan all along anyway. I was simply adding another step.

ZS crashed into me, taking up the rallying cry. He led the girls through the dorm building and into the next. I didn't know who Darla was getting from the administrative offices on the other side of campus, but I sure as hell was happy to find out that next door were the athletic dorms. Let's get a bunch of rugby girls and see what happens.

I thought about what color hair the girls must have. NZS could see the redheads, the true dark reds, but I couldn't tell if they were brown or black or red or purple. It was still a weird thing to miss . . . colors. After spending so long in a brilliant, bright world, everything was so dark.

I opened my eyes. I hadn't even realized they were closed. My zombie army swarmed the quad, Infecting and eating, and it jolted me back to awareness. I had been . . . somewhere, and NZS had been somewhere else. What troubled me was not only that we hadn't been together, but that I woke up with my fingers knuckle-deep in the chest of a young man, tearing.

My body wormed its way into the man as it peeled back his flesh, wearing his skin on my hand and arm. I wasn't in control, was only a passenger as my teeth, progressively becoming sharper from scraping against the white sticks, ripped pieces of his flesh for finger holes. I wore the skin of his chest like a glove as my teeth tore through the white bits into the beating bits.

The beating bits stopped.

My mouth grappled with the muscle, grinding my surprisingly intact teeth into the gristle, and my fingers kneaded his white sticks, playing between them, pulling viscera and organs through the broken sticks with his own skin.

I was doing this.

I looked at my hand in horror, wearing his meat suit, emptying him out like a Halloween pumpkin. I felt my tongue lashing at his heart, pulling the meat into my mouth—our mouth. I felt myself eating his heart, and I was powerless to stop it.

I screamed, beat myself against my own skull, powerless to stop it. I reached for ZS, somewhere out in the nether, and felt nothing but hunger. Part of my dissociated mind wondered if there was ever a feeling of "full" with zombies as I tried to separate myself from what was happening.

I was doing this. Me. "Not Zombie Sean." Oh my God, I was eating a person. I was a prisoner as my only arm was wrenched out of his body, leaving the skin-glove covering our arm. I screamed, and my voice came out as a series of grunts, an ape calling to his family that dinnertime was near. I called my zombies to me, and we took off in a run together, moving toward the administrative buildings. If this was what I'd had to become, if I was to have control while doing something monstrous . . .

I laughed. Control. What little fucking control I had over anything these days. I couldn't find "Zombie Sean," I couldn't find the strength to do more than think in directions. *Forward,* I thought to the other zombies. *We go this way.*

At least I had that going for me. I could communicate with the zombie nation army; it was more than I'd thought I'd have at this point.

The skin on my arm was no longer warm. It was slimy, and my clawlike fingernails were digging holes through it, making it a fingerless glove. I gagged, stumbling over my own feet. Then again, there was glass in my feet, an arrow or two, and any amount of unidentifiable detritus soiling my skin, muscle and bone, so who the hell knows what really made me trip? The girls urged me along.

I could see the administrative buildings ahead, almost feel Darla in my mind. She didn't need to know I had my Hex full except for the spot saved for Kiera. She didn't need to feel the endless connection of zombie after zombie, waves like dominoes, connected to each other. We were legion, a family, a home, and all we wanted was to survive.

Great. Now I was even thinking like him.

~

NZS was talking to himself in the background, trying to wash away the images in his mind, the feelings he'd had of eating the man's heart. He could still taste it, crawling around his cage, spitting imagined blood into corners, gagging. I could feel the little pieces of him, broken, and wondered what it would be like to shatter like that. I guessed I already had, once, into him and me; but now NZS was in a million pieces pretending to be a Sean, picking up memories one by one and examining them, looking for the puzzle places in which they went. I didn't know if he'd ever find the answers, ever be whole again.

It was what it was.

We marched grimly on until we could see Darla's expanded army. From what I could see, she hadn't had as much success with numbers, but she definitely had something going for her with regards to body type. I was assuming she'd found the dorms or something. But we had our girls, cunning and bold. I could hear the buzzing in the back of my head, feel how—complex, I thought of the word by myself—it was becoming. I didn't know what was happening to me, but I felt the extended network, all the Hexes and all the Links, and it almost felt like I could talk to them all.

I closed my eyes, briefly. *Need help,* I grunted.

I felt NZS rousing, slowly, collecting his pieces into some semblance of a self before dragging himself to his prison bars. *What?*

We're here.

So fucking what?

Need a general.

You need a general? To lead your zombie army? You're a zombie. Go. Be a general. NZS was clearly not in the mood for tactical development at this point.

Please. It was all I had. A simple plea, and a picture of the girl, the girl in the sunshine with a yellow flower in her hair.

His pieces were sharp, and I could feel the cuts in my mind tearing us further apart and stitching us closer together at the same time. We were becoming something else. I couldn't tell if we were merging or dying. I couldn't tell if I cared which it was, in the end.

I saw Darla.

She stood at the head of the loose circle of guys, girls, and other, and I stood at the head of my group. We *may* have had a grand total of five men out of the . . . fingers—numbers of zombies.

They'remore, I heard.

More

More

Whatdo wedo

Idon'tknow

Sean!

Helpus

Heystop! I called. *Smart. Youare smart. Youare strong. Youthink. Youknow. Youremember.*

Youremember!

Come. Youremember. Fightfor remember. Fightfor sun. Eternal. Infect!

The call was raised. *Infect!* They screamed it, stomping their feet and bones on the ground. *Infect! Infectnotkill! Infectnotkill!*

We marched to the tune of "Infect, not kill" as I and ZS attempted a straight line across the quad. Darla's army stood still, and I saw that one or two of the men still had guns, though I wasn't sure if they had an idea of how to use them.The idea made me laugh a little, and the chortle sounded like a honk.

We stood on one side of the quad, Darla stood on the other. *Nicegroup*, Darla said sarcastically.

Yours, too. What are you even doing?

Darla had the grace to look surprised with her mangled face. I took it to mean that she didn't know that I was hanging around. *Whoyou?*

I'm not a zombie. Sur-fucking-prise. Didn't expect someone with a brain to be leading the alternative?

WHOYOU?! she shrieked, and her army roared, raising their arms to the sky. *WHOYOU WHOYOU WHOYOU*

I laughed. This time, it came out as a snarl, and ZS was right there with me, clenching our meat-wrapped fist. Holly came to stand next to me, and Natalie. I felt the energy of our cadre, the sheer force of will behind me, and I smiled.

"I'm Sean," I said.

I fought—it was hard to say it. It didn't *sound* the same as English, but it was *my* voice, and my voice alone. *And you're not gonna fucking get past us, or kill us all, or do whatever your shitty domination plan entails. Are we gonna fight or what?*

She screamed in sheer ferocity. *Hewants humans tolive!* she crowed. *Dangerto zombies! Dangertous! Killthe humans! Humanlovers!*

Her zombie crowd was a little confused. *Kill the humans? What humans? Where humans?* I could hear them as clearly as I could hear my own thoughts. But it didn't matter—she ended with the dreaded "human lovers." Clearly, we were bent on our own destruction, rather than a will to Infect. When really, Infect is all we wanted to do. Stand in the sun—

I looked up into the sunlight, which was suddenly obscured by . . . wait, were those *helicopters?*

The ground was trembling as Darla's army began to run.

Toward us.

Well, fuck.

Let the School Bells Ring

~ Kiera ~

There were more, of course. More fights, more close calls, a few more firebombs and the fear of losing each other. It took the full three days to close in on the school, neighborhood by neighborhood, waiting for the end to come. We decided to come in from the west, toward the administrative buildings. It got us close to the dorms, the cafeteria, the bookstore . . .

The bookstore.

I sighed, closing my eyes. The bookstore where it had all started. The bookstore where I effectively lost Sean.

If this ended the way I expected it to, would I care? Could I ask God to kill Sean, to bring him back to me? Tell him that this wasn't fair, that we were interrupted by a very human virus, and we deserved a second shot?

What God would be listening by now?

Grace seemed to understand the need for stealthy prancing; she snuck through the bushes with us, the ones the university so painstakingly planted and posted signs everywhere for kids to keep the fuck out of.

I heard the helicopters. We had evidently come right on time. I stopped in a bush to fumble with my phone as Brett sighed, rolling his eyes. He was grinning. It seemed like he was actually excited about the situation. I should have been too; this was it. This was the end of the line; we could actually save some people, before they became like Sean.

Oh, Sean.

I texted Callie. *Is this it? We're here.*

A text came back almost immediately. *Yes,* she said. *You literally got here just in the nick of time. Stand by; there's going to be a siren, an announcement, and then the vaccine.*

I thought about that for a second. I remembered getting a vaccine for SARS-Co-2. I remembered the world burning down to the ground temporarily, fighting over the "right" not to get vaccinated, and the chaos it caused. Now, in a coordinated strike across multiple big cities, klaxons would sound, planes would launch, and helicopters would lug tanks of a vaccine that wasn't optional. If you went outside, opened a window—hell, maybe breathed in the air a week later, who knew? It wasn't a question of your freedom. It was a question of survival. If you got bit and survived—you could *really* survive.

I looked down at Gracey, who wagged by my side. *Does it work on dogs?*

I saw the little dots forming, saying she was texting back. *Dogs can't get the virus,* she replied. *Thank God. Can you imagine zombie cows in the middle of all of this?*

I shuddered, and hugged Grace carefully. "I love you," I said to her seriously.

The others pretended not to hear as we waited in the bushes. "Fuck," Brett mumbled. "I'm allergic to azaleas."

I stopped, turned my head slowly. "We're about to be vaccinated by something that didn't even have a trial run, and head into God knows what past those azalea bushes, and you announce your allergy?"

He sniffled and shrugged. "Let's get closer. We should be out in the open for the—"

The siren sounded.

It was a sound I'd never heard before, but one I could remember my grandfather describing to me. It sounded like tornado sirens, a hurricane siren, a "shelter in place" siren—something Big and Bad was happening, and all we could do was wait.

We crept forward, moving through the azalea bushes as Brett swore and batted at the flowers. He stifled several sneezes, and Grace tried to catch the falling blossoms in her mouth as we moved toward the quad through the blistering noise.

I had never heard something so loud in my life. The announcement that followed was equally loud. As we advanced on the quad, I could hear the helicopters humming under the voice that penetrated the air.

□□□ *Attention!* □□□

□□□ *There has been a successful vaccine against the Virus!* □□□

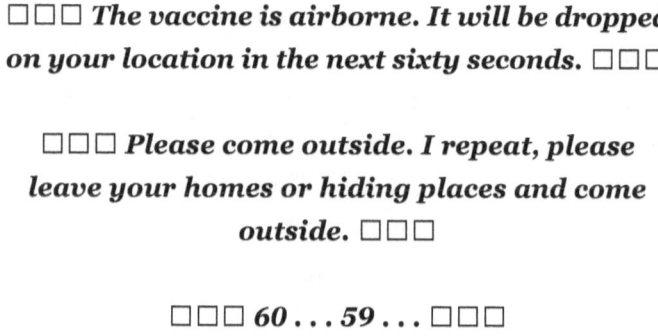

□□□ *The vaccine is airborne. It will be dropped on your location in the next sixty seconds.* □□□

□□□ *Please come outside. I repeat, please leave your homes or hiding places and come outside.* □□□

□□□ *60 . . . 59 . . .* □□□

The azaleas opened up to the quad, which was designed quite literally. There were four quadrants of grass, one by the administrative buildings, one by the bookstore and cafeteria, one by the athletic dorms, and one by the start of the classrooms. I would have felt homesick; I would have felt longing for Sean, my old life, anything before the start of this.

I would have, that is if it hadn't been for the not one, but TWO hordes of zombies facing off in front of me.

"What in the ever-loving fuck," Brett whispered. He pushed us up against the wall of the bookstore—where this had all started—and we sat down, crisscross applesauce, I thought numbly. They had started yelling, screaming, stomping. They were horrible to behold, blood-spattered and gore-covered, with black blood dripping down their faces and limbs missing, holes through their bodies, teeth showing through nonexistent cheeks. The siren began to sound again, and I wondered if they could even hear it.

The vaccine felt like nothing, except for a wave of heat over my body. The others felt the same, I was sure, by the shudders of their bodies next to mine. I wondered how long it took to work. I wondered who made it, if they were alive or dead. If they were even out there at all.

The zombies charged.

"I think it's safe to go into the bookstore," Brett said urgently. "I don't see anyone and clearly there's some shit going on. Get the fuck in the bookstore."

The fuck was gotten into the bookstore, that was for sure. We piled into the vestibule, and Brett locked the main doors behind us. We watched the zombies through bullet holes in the glass, wondering what the hell was going on.

"This is it," I said, my voice low. "They're going to kill each other. I don't know . . . I don't . . ." I squinted. The zombie standing at the back of the horde, the one on top of an overturned golf cart with a severed, oozing arm, looked familiar. His clothes were torn. Something was pulling at the back of my memory, something long buried.

"Good," Evan said nervously. "If I'm reading you right, that means that we can mop up afterwards, and go through the buildings. Right? Is that what's going to happen?"

Ohmar sat down on a spot of dried blood, staring out the window. "I have no idea," he said softly. "I didn't . . . I didn't know they could . . . what is this?"

I swallowed hard. "They were talking to each other," I said nervously. "Shouting, yelling. I don't think that was random. I think this was planned. I think . . ."

"You are not gonna fucking say what I think you're gonna say," Lydiana warned me, grabbing my hand. "Just don't. We are not going there."

"They're zombie armies," Brett muttered. "Fucking zombie armies. And they're fighting each other. Well, I mean, it could get worse, right?"

The east side of the quad was suddenly full. Full of a third group that I hadn't seen before. Fewer people than there were zombies—but these people had guns. Because of course they did.

"The National Guard is here," I said blankly. "Where the hell were they six months ago?"

"I'm guessing this is the *new* National Guard," Brett replied dryly. "The ones who had the misfortune of being conscripted solely because they could walk and speak English."

□□□ *Attention!* □□□

□□□ *We will now be deploying a potential cure for the Virus!* □□□

□□□ *The cure is an airborne mist. You will feel a light rain. It will not affect you or the vaccine.* □□□

□□□ *We do not know side effects it will have on the Infected. Please remain indoors. I repeat, remain indoors. The cure will be dropped in approximately thirty minutes.* □□□

Well, this was it.

"The final fight," I said softly.

Brett stood up. "Well, I don't know about you, but I'm not going to sit in a damn lobby while the 'final fight' goes on. They started this—we're going to finish it. At least, I am. I've got a few more cocktails whipped up, and there's plenty of cover between us and them. Watch out for friendly fire; I doubt the 'National Guard' is all that intelligent in discerning who IS and IS NOT a zombie, and Callie's friend wasn't too clear on what was going to happen at this point. I'm going out there. Who's with me?"

It was the longest speech that I'd ever heard him say, I thought wonderingly to myself. It was our rallying cry, as dry and lengthy as it was. It was our call to stand and fight. To see this through, to the end.

Grace barked loudly in my arms, and Ohmar was the first of us to stand. Then Lydiana, and Evan. Keagan—who had never said a word, who was a terrible fighter, and who really shouldn't be here—stood up and looked down at me. "We wait," he said simply. "We've got to see what happens. For everyone we lost."

I thought of the zombie who reminded me so vaguely of Sean, and put Gracey down. I stood slowly, feeling every ache, pain, and bloody bruise in my body, and lifted my head up to meet the eyes of my partners in crime. We had come this far.

"For everyone we lost," I said softly.

Brett unlocked the door.

Definitely a Zombie War

~ Sean ~

The words in the air didn't make sense. From NZS's misty place, surely they meant *something*, but it was so much nonsense to me. I commanded the charge, listening to the thundering of zombie feet and stumps, standing on a broken . . . Well, it was big and had wheels. I couldn't remember climbing up there, couldn't remember how I managed to make my mangled legs get this far. All I could remember was being here, forever, waiting for Darla to attack.

It was all that was left for me. This was the end; either we would leave, and NZS and I would wander into the sunlight in search of Kiera, or we would die for good, and wait for her in whatever end a zombie could find. Either way, I won.

You don't win, NZS said softly. *It can't be that easy.*

Itnever is, I murmured, grunting out loud. Holly, Natalie and Sarah went ahead of me as the sound of bodies clashing against bodies filled the air. I grabbed as much of the girls as I could with one arm and deliberately fell onto the ground behind the golf cart as I heard the gunshots begin.

There was a casualty on my side, each little blip in the system as a zombie was erased from our Link. I didn't know why I could feel all of ZS's little friends, and I wondered if Darla could too—or if she was so far removed from the zombie experience at this point that she couldn't feel a thing. That was another question, too—would Darla continue to Infect, or did she have other plans?

I had never cared enough to guess what it was. All I had ever cared about was my own suffering, and Kiera.

I could only do one thing for Kiera now, and that was win. ZS needed a strategist. I wanted to lie down, to lie down and die, to end this lethargy and this pain I felt in every limb (or not-limb), but ZS had earned more. He was a horrible monster who didn't deserve redemption.

But so was I.

I sent Holly to sneak over to the Guard for a little recon, and Natalie over toward Darla's side for the same reason. Sarah . . .

Sarah I could never control. Sarah, who dreamed in butterflies and thought in colors and light, smiled at me. She stood up, dancing to music only she could hear, and started walking toward the fight. I knew she wouldn't make it the moment she stood up. It was only a question of how.

The bullets hit her first. A sharp hit to the leg, tearing out—

I couldn't remember what white bit it was, the lower one in your leg, but she she stumbled and crawled, still laughing in her donkey voice, still seeing whatever it was she saw.

I would have given anything to see what she saw. I Linked with her hard, trying to get her back. I could oh so faintly hear the music, the beautiful music that drove everything she did. I could feel the damage that she had taken when she became a zombie, and I felt one of Darla's strongmen hit her. I felt the surge of bewildered anger, sweet and sickening, as she bit into his throat, and his hands ripped her arms from their sockets. She bled a slow black ooze, not feeling the bits that were missing, now only having one full limb. She still bit him valiantly, tearing at his throat, and his black blood was rainbows, rainbows that I hadn't seen in so long.

He reached forward and tore out her throat in one swift motion, grabbing her larynx and tearing away the songs and the music forever.

I howled, feeling a strange surge in my Link, and it only made them fight harder. My girls were swift, and cunning, and ZS and I were relentless as we stalked the snipers. Were they snipers, if they were out in the open? If they were stupid enough to lie on the ground and take zombies out one by one, not expecting the fact that Holly was behind them, with a full complement of the volleyball team?

Were they not expecting me to come barreling in from the side, headfirst, my shiny skull knocking into their guns and breaking their hands?

Holly's team launched. I bit. I bit, and it felt like God to bite, a religious experience that I had never felt before. I used my wretched teeth to tear the guts out of the soldiers, dripping down their uniforms and popping buttons off of shirts and insignia falling to the ground. I felt ZS—I felt NZS—I felt us, together, in one shining moment where we were zombie.

There is nothing. There is only this.

Guns fired, roared. Girls screamed, roared. We attacked, and the dark uniforms fell to the ground, one by one, boots kicking in the dirt. *Infect.*

Infect.

Infect.

The National Guard was ours.

The Zombie Wars, Part Human
~ Kiera ~

It was pure and immediate chaos. The National Guard kept staring at us, guns raised, and I looked down the barrel; it was spooky even if they weren't shooting at us. I could only feel Grace at my leg, pressing into my padding with her hip, and see Lydiana before me as we crept forward, trying to come around the quad and meet the National Guard from behind to join up with them without coming into contact with the two—two?!—zombie armies. I had no idea how the fuck we were going to pull this off.

My phone went off. For one longing moment, I thought it was my mother. I could barely hear it over the din, and quite frankly, I didn't care anymore what Callie had to say about it. I didn't know how long we had. How long *I* had, to live, to die. What the vaccine was doing in my body, what the cure would do mixed with it.

I also didn't know what the fuck the National Guard

was doing until a unit of zombies broke off from the herd and the National Guard started to scream.

"Fuck!" Brett stopped us short and I ran into Lydiana. We were hunched over in a hedge beside one of the administrative buildings, behind the first army. They weren't the ones who had attacked the National Guard, but they *were* the ones that had attacked the other zombies first. What the fuck was going on here?

I hid beneath my hedge, Grace on her stomach, panting, the rest of us scattered amongst various shrubberies. I could see Keagan to my left, and he whispered, "I don't understand what's happening."

It was the first time he'd ever talked to me, and might be the last.

"I don't . . . think the zombies are normal, Keagan. I don't think they're what we thought they were." I swallowed, closing my eyes. "Like . . . there has to be something in them that remembers, right? Maybe this is what happens when, like, former soldiers become zombies."

Keagan shook his head. "No, look at them. That one, that side, they're all young men in business clothes?" He paused. "They were in business clothes. That guy isn't wearing any pants. Or legs. He isn't wearing any legs." Keagan looked lost, horrified, and like he hadn't had two days to get used to this kind of reaction to this kind of event.

I looked closer. He was right—one side was clearly taken from the school, the administrative side, anyway. There were pencil skirts and floral patterns and jackets and ties. And a girl in front, screaming, tearing the throats from everyone who came toward her, spitting out the detritus like so much sludge, and moving on to the next.

She was relentless. She did nothing but kill; she wasn't infecting anyone like I'd assumed would happen. She was just killing, with no standard of ethics or morals that I could see. There were bodies all around her, forming a barrier, and they were all zombies.

"She's attacking her own kind?" I whispered to Brett, on the other side of me. Grace closed her eyes, and I sighed. My poor dog. I put her through so much.

"Yeah," he whispered back. "It looks like the side with all of the soccer-playing girls—weird choice in zombie accomplices, by the way, but they've got like the entire athletic dorm of girls in that one group—is attacking the National Guard for more recruits. It looks like Wall Street Grunge over there is just killing anything that walks, shambles, or otherwise moves."

I shook my head, finally looking down at my phone. *What's happening in there??? We lost contact with our guys!*

I closed my eyes with Grace, petting her softly. I was not about to tell Callie that her "guys" were now the enemy. I didn't know how to express that half of the zombies wanted us dead, and the other half wanted to zombify us. "What in the fuck is this, Brett?"

The National Guard followed along behind one particularly beat up zombie. He had one arm, streaks of blood down his shirt. A thick piece of skin was wrapped around his wrist like a bracelet, and I shuddered. There was a piece of rib bone sticking out from his shoulder like a demented wing, and I wondered how it had gotten there. I couldn't see what had been on his shirt, nor its original color, but his shoes . . .

One of his shoes was intact, the other, worn off of a bent and useless foot. The shoe I thought I knew. The shoe triggered a memory.

I found myself standing up slowly, unable to help myself, Brett uselessly pulling me back down. It didn't matter; it wouldn't have mattered anyway. I didn't know if I recognized him, and it didn't matter, because it was then that the other side attacked.

The Last Humans

~ Sean ~

I turned and saw Darla herself rushing toward a group of humans hiding in the bushes. What the fuck were they doing here?

I saw red

The screams and we walked forward, a machine with machine guns strapped to our backs

Ididn'tkillthem

We only Infected, everyone we saw, and I saw them, and they saw me. And then Darla saw them

Itwaslike a carwreck

She ran, screaming, a femur bone in her hand—how did I remember that, when I couldn't remember my own name? I lifted my broken arm and hollered

My own *real* National Guard and Barbie Army followed me and we charged. The difference between them and us—we weren't attacking the zombies, not unless they got to us first. I pushed my way past the horde even as they grabbed at me, bit at me uselessly. I felt this energy burning inside of me, a feeling of vast wellbeing at this great swelling of zombies in front of me.

Weweresoclose and I told her, told Natalie to *protectthehumans*, the last humans I saw, the ones I could change. The ones I could lead back to the apartment buildings, and we could create something new, we could do something new and make a beautiful world

InfectinfectInfectinfectInfect

Darla saw me.

She charged with her bone and I used the strength I had left—was it a lot? Was it a little? I couldn't tell anymore—to break the bayonet-like weapon off of the kid's gun to my left. Part of the gun came with it, so I had a nice, thick tube and a piercing weapon. Great. I could poke holes in her and baste her to death.

Itworksthough

There was a flash and I hit her knee, gouging, pulling sideways and she lost a tendon there, the one that connected your knee to your bone. Red bone, bleeding black, she reared back and swung at me and

connected hit hard ribs white things broken beating heartbeat broken heartbeatingbroken

I gasped, and wondered if zombies could breathe. The red was a strange color like black now, and I thrust again, and again, as Natalie protected the humans, the Last Humans that I knew about, the Last Humans I saw. Holly—

Holly nextome Holly femur big bone smashes her noseherfacehereye Her eye was hanging down now, touching her cheek, blood vessels and optic nerve pulsing in time with her sludge-ridden heart and *Holly down* she fell to her knees, scratching and biting at Darla.

I felt more than saw the muscle of Darla's back rip just above her hip, a thick swath of muscle like the kind you'd buy at the supermarket, and Holly couldn't stop herself from eating, eating in the middle of this battle

shetried shetriedsohard

She wanted to heal from the blood-spattered eyes that looked at the ground, fore and behind at the same time. I could see her spinal fluid leaking and knew it was the color of the rainbow I'd always wanted.

Darla swung again and Holly didn't get back up.

She had the better weapon, I knew it and yet here I was, poking at her, relentless. I yelled something about *Pokémon*, from *Lord of the Rings*, from all the 2000s memorabilia that I'd ever known to make me sound brave. I wanted to be brave for her, Lord, I wanted to be brave—

thrust

I hit her in the kidney, felt her grunt and twisted, pulling, trying to catch the edge of the knife on something to pull. I wanted to pull, wanted to drag her insides out, to show the world what she was made of

killingyourownkind She wanted to erase the rainbows, the sunshine, the flower-filled field that I was going to stay in with Kiera forever, and I wasn't going to let that happen

We roared and lifted the bayonet far above her head, she was so short, and smashed it into her skull. We pulled down and down and down, and little specks of bone

flecked into our skin, broken and spittle from her yawning maw *shehasnoteeth* splashed against our face and I
felt one of her lackeys punch me in the side with something sharp.

We tore her in two pieces, rent her to the ground, and
looked up.

welookedup

Darla's blood was covering my face, and I saw her, as
Natalie furiously tried to explain that she wasn't *that* kind
of zombie to the Last Humans

welookedup

But zombies can't talk, and Kiera could.

Because there she was, standing in the courtyard, the
sun shining on her braids, and I knew her, and I loved
her.

The empty section in our Hex almost glowed.

sheisours

sheisours

sheisours

The Zombie Wars, Part What the Fuck

~ Kiera ~

We had one group of zombies shambling to presumably attack us from the left, and the National Guard zombies coming toward us from the right. I put them in two categories for a reason; there was a lone zombie, a girl, that stopped in front of us, and started waving her arms as if she were at a rave. She was grunting and groaning, gesticulating wildly, and I had no idea what she was trying to tell us.

But I was damn sure she was trying to tell us something. There were no "nobody home" signs in her eyes; there was clearly someone there, someone trying to communicate with us. "Brett, what the fuck," I said nervously.

He cleared his throat and stepped forward. "Can you . . . understand me?"

The zombie stopped talking, staring at him with wide eyes, broken blood vessels popping out of her orbs.

"Okay. I don't know if that was a yes or a no. Shit, look out!"

As if she had a sixth sense, the zombie reached out and caught a zombie from the other side with her arm, like a soccer mom catching a kid in a car. It was the first of many; the stench of the old dead followed her, and so did the army from the left. We didn't have time to think, just react—and Grace lead the charge, storming into the group, wagging her tail as fast as she could.

"Fuck!" I ran after her with my hatchet mop, swinging wildly, trying not to hit the good? zombie next to me. I could feel my group behind me, around me, surrounding me as we fought, and I pulled the handle as hard as I could, feeling the spine of a zombie pop. He folded at my feet, still alive, his top half flailing and arching. I mindlessly executed him, the hatchet mop going straight down through his neck, and he stilled.

The zombies from the left were coming now, the National Guard leading and attacking the zombies from the right. This was getting confusing. It was hard to tell them apart, but it was clear that the NG Zombies were trying to help us. They beheaded, they swarmed, they tore limb from limb, black blood spilling all across the grass.

"Keagan!" Brett shouted. I turned and saw him going down, a swarm of zombies tearing him apart piece by piece. His leg was lifted into the air as a trophy, and he was still alive, screaming, as they dismembered him. Thick red blood poured from the leg, and the zombie began using it as a weapon against the NG Zombies, hitting them in the face with Keagan's shoe.

I was surrounded, hands and feet and mouths reaching for me, and Brett screamed at me to duck. He came in hot, swinging at the group surrounding me, his staff hitting the Evil Zombies and knocking them down like so many bowling pins. Grace jumped into action, rolling around on one of the zombies as if she were doing a delightful trick. Evan came up beside me and we stood back to back, dispatching the group that Brett had laid out, beheading and beheading.

It became a little routine, attack and kill, and there was so much blood. I didn't know what to do with the blood covering my arms; I was dripping in it, soaked in the blood of my enemies, and I suddenly wondered how effective that vaccine really was. Didn't they usually take some time to become effective?

I climbed onto a bench, using the height to cut a path through the zombies, noticing that my hatchet was not as sharp as it had once been. It took effort to cut down the man in front of me; he was wearing a suit and tie, and I wondered if the tie covered where he had turned into a monster. He looked impeccably dressed, and somehow uninjured, as if he could suddenly wake up and talk to me about that morning's stocks.

I killed him anyway.

I saw some of the NG Zombies coming towards me and felt relieved, then laughed. It was macabre, morbid of me to think that zombies coming to the rescue was a good thing. I wondered what they wanted as my hatchet caught on a rib cage. I pulled, pulled hard, feeling each rib pull out of place like popcorn, almost hearing the little "pop!" as they tore through his chest. At least his suit was black and the blood wouldn't ruin the ensemble.

We were truly surrounded on all sides by zombies. The NG Zombies were hunting down the Evil Zombies, actually being careful not to interact with us, and I was perplexed. I looked around and saw an opportunity to jump on top of a dumpster that was cleverly hidden by a rather large flowering bush, and I pulled out my phone.

Callie there are 2 zombie armies here we're in trouble this is not going well

What the fuck? Okay hang on are you okay? I'm telling them what's happening

No not okay but one zombie army is defending us?????

Fuck

And that was all she said. I didn't know what the hell *that* meant. Did she have some kind of inside information? Some knowledge as to why the walking dead were trying to keep us alive? What agenda did they have that we didn't know about?

The answer to my question came in a sharp cry, and I jumped as far as I could toward Ohmar. I wove myself between fighting, screaming, bleeding bodies, trying to reach him. We were drowning, losing ourselves, and I couldn't even see the rest of my squad. I could only see Ohmar's eyes as the zombie bit down on his collarbone, snapping it so loudly that I heard it.

I heard the roaring before I saw what was causing it.

It didn't sound human; I laughed at myself, because of course it didn't. It belonged to one of them. It was louder, somehow, this noise of anger and pain and the dystopian end-of-all-things bullshit that we were facing, but it came from one of *them*, not one of us, somehow.

"Kiera!" Brett screamed as one of them moved through the NG Zombies, the crowd rippling before him, letting him through as if they had some internal communication that allowed him to part the Zombie Sea in front of him. Whoever it was, He Was Coming, and the fighting continued around this partition of zombiehood. Soon it was upon me, and I was inside a keyhole of peace.

I felt more than heard Brett screaming as he plowed into me, knocking me to the ground, covering me as the Big Cheese of Zombies headed toward me.

It was then, in that moment, that I saw the zombie's one shoe. My mind struggled to make sense of what I was seeing, and I saw the broken figure bending down over Brett.

Brett made no noise, despite what I imagined was an incredible amount of pain, as the zombie gripped his throat and bit the back of his neck with sharp teeth. It was then that I heard the siren, as I slowly became covered in Brett's blood. He didn't move, only held a turtle shell position over me, protecting me from this zombie.

I felt Brett weaken as his life poured out onto me. I imagined the change as tears rolled down my cheeks; heard his voice, soft and careful, saying "Don't worry." His body started jerking uncontrollably as he held me down, refusing to move, and I heard Grace whining in the distance.

It started to rain. At least, I thought it was rain at first, it was a heavy mist, and I realized what it was the moment it pelted my body. They had said the cure would be like this, different from the vaccine.

It was the cure, and Brett was dying.

He was dying, covering my body. My weak, human body.

Brett went limp; the weight of him suffocated me. I tensed, waiting for it: the moment that he would wake up, disoriented, and I could knock him off of me, thank him for trying to save my ass before he tried to attack me, and I realized I was still crying, sobbing for this friend that had saved me so many times.

Brett was gone. I was somewhat surprised that he wasn't coming back; did this mean that the cure wasn't working? The zombie with the shoe remained.

As his body began to cool, I started to crawl out from under him, into the rain, and I looked up into the tall zombie's eyes, the glowing, phosphorescent eyes that were so familiar to me.

I knew those eyes, as the cure poured down onto both of us. Brett's flesh was stuck to his lips, drying skin coating his remaining hand like a glove. I saw the rib, the wing, sticking out of his back, and I saw the thick, infected, black limb that I had cut off so long ago.

Fuck. Oh, fuck.

Sean stared down at me with shocked, nuclear-waste eyes.

Finally Found

~ Sean ~

Itwasher itwasher itwasher itwasher

Holy motherfucking God, it was her. I wanted to smell her hair. Wait, that sounded like I was a serial killer—

Weare, dummy

I stared at her, startled, dropping the man that I had killed. Kiera turned him over, gently resting his head on the pavement

Ohshit

The man was so familiar. I knew him from another life; knew him from

Camping, mancamping topof themountain Brett

It was the most wonderful sight in the world as Kiera stood up slowly, a strange dog at her side. I was soaking wet and felt nothing but dread and elation as she stared at me.

"Sean?" she said, tentatively.

I groaned, a long, stuttering sound, trying to talk to her. I held back the urge to Infect her, *now! Nowbefore it'stoolate*

I heard the armies behind me, felt Natalie out there, my lone survivor. My Hex was wide open, but the next zombie we wanted to create was *her*. I craved the taste of her flesh and bone like nothing else. We would stand in the dandelion field, or by the roses, forever.

NZS was starting to merge with me. Or maybe it was inevitable; this, the twining of our wills, this joining between zombie and nonzombie, where I no longer knew where he began and I ended.

Sean!

I heard Natalie cry out, felt her run; she was so fast. Fast enough to escape behind friendly lines, fast enough to keep herself safe, but bewildered, unsure of what was going on.

It'sokay, we said. *Rain? Whyrain? Doyousee rain?*

Felt her shake her head. Saw images, blurry lines—the ants go marching two by two, hurrah! The National Guard with guns, so many guns and

No, she said. *Mud, dirtymudwet Iwant togo home!*

Me too, I thought to myself. Myselves. I felt memories bubbling up to the surface as I tried to speak, tried to listen at the same time.

"Sean, is that you?"

I nodded, exaggerated, trying to communicate the best that I could while running damage control on my zombie horde. I could hear all of their voices, their battle cries and war wounds, their dying sounds. Each death felt like a piece of me, shattered.

"What's going on?" I heard a young man's voice pipe up from behind her. She was staring down at the body in front of us soaked in blood, covered in spittle and shards of bone.

Iwantto GO HOME!

Easy, we told her. *Gohome soon stopDarla'sarmy stayhide beokay*

Flowers and bloodstains his name is Brett? We knew him the rain stopped falling. NZS so far away and Kiera so close. We struggled to remember and he struggled to forget and

I felt my body falling backwards

Feltmyself hittheground

*Dark*ness

Noth*ing*

Torn to Pieces

~ Kiera ~

I had no words. I stood there, pressing my leg hard into Gracey's side until it hurt, looking between Brett's corpse and the zombie who stood before me clearly trying to communicate. It was fucking *Sean,* at the school, as a zombie.

"Kiera?" Evan said tentatively. "What's going on?"

"That's Sean," I said weakly. "My fiance. And he's a zombie. And he's trying to talk. What the fuck?"

All of a sudden, Sean crumpled, as if an anvil had landed on his head. He fell to the ground hard in a zombie pool, a blackened mess of a man, and the sounds of dying zombies slowly quieted as the sky turned blue again.

I looked up. One by one, zombie after zombie began to fall to the ground. It didn't matter which side they were on; at this point, I couldn't even tell. Without exception, they all dropped to the grass and mud as Evan, Lydiana, Grace and I watched.

I looked back at them. We'd lost so much.

I looked down at Sean, unsure of what to do. I felt nothing: a cool, detached numbness reserved for the broken. I had no idea what to think, what to feel. Was he dead? Finally dead? Was this the time my mourning would cease?

I saw twitches on the battlefield, little rapid movements of zombies across the courtyard. "What's happening?"

Lydiana studied them, squinting in the bright light. "I don't know. Obviously something to do with the central nervous system, and it's about half of them doing it, I'd say. I don't know if it's a prelude to seizures or what, but something's happening."

"The cure?" I whispered.

I watched Sean's body like a hawk. Grace slowly stepped forward, and I was afraid she was going to at-tack—but God or the universe looked out for me, and saved me the mental scarring of my dog re-killing my fi-ancé. She sniffed him from head to toe, and when she reached his mud-soaked, putrid shoe, she jumped back, all four paws in the air at once.

Sean began to twitch.

She sniffed him with a fury, up and down his body, nudging his arm and his face. It took me a while to re-alize what she was doing; I remembered that dogs had a great memory for scents. And she knew his scent, even if she didn't know it belonged to him until just this moment. That apartment had more smells than just my own, and I was damned sure that she knew it.

Evan carefully placed his body in front of mine, even

though I internally scoffed at the thought. Chivalry at its finest, I guess. We watched as Gracey nudged furiously, and Sean began to open his eyes.

I stared from behind Ethan, watching closely. I was unaware of my surroundings; had no idea what was going on in the battlefield. I could have been standing in front of a zombie horde and I wouldn't have had a clue .I could only wait, holding my breath, for the telltale green to blaze from his eyes.

His eyes opened slowly. He stared at the sky for the longest time, a sickly smile crossing his face, followed by his skin turning ashen.

"Kiera," Lydiana said urgently.

"What?" I replied. I was afraid to look.

"Text your friend. Tell her we need medics."

"Why?" I couldn't look. I didn't want to know. Did I?

"Because we're going to need them after the rest of these folks wake up."

"Wake up?" I said stupidly. Sean was gasping rapidly, his sticky, innards-covered chest moving with his breaths. I slid my gaze up his chest, his neck, his face.

"Yeah," he said, his voice broken and sad. "Apparently . . ." He wheezed. "Zombie-ism is curable."

"Holy motherfucking ghost of Saint Patrick, you have *got* to be kidding me," I replied, and fell to my knees, staring at his strange, pearl-colored eyes riddled with pain.

"Kiera," he said softly. "You shouldn't have saved me." He refused to look at me, instead focusing on the distant helicopters that were coming closer and closer to the battlefield.

I stared at him, looking at the broken bones, the bruises, the black and red blood covering his body. His voice held immeasurable hopelessness, a crescendo of depressed notes, a rhythm of madness and torture.

Oh my God. Sean was cured . . . and he *remembered it all.*

Back to the Beginning

~ Sean ~

There were things that I would never forget.

Bending a child over my knee, listening to his back break as I twisted his helpless body and tore into his chest with my teeth, a great gaping maw covering his broken form.

Images that previously belonged to my other self came crashing down on me the moment I opened my eyes, overwhelming me to the point where I no longer felt the physical pain. I knew I was bleeding. I could feel Kiera and what was left of her crew working on me to try to keep me from dying for a second time. Bleeding out would have been a blessing.

I stared at the sky, watching the clouds float through the aquamarine blue, and wondered what this meant for me now. Would I be tried for my crimes? Punished for what I had done as a zombie?

I should be, for sure. The old woman whose head I

twisted off of her body with the same "pop" you heard when microwaving grapes. The young man who pleaded for his life, who I gleefully held down while Natalie Infected him, watching his sorrow grow greater as his life faded away. So many children . . . so many old folks. Young folks. Everyone, really. My hunger knew no limits.

Kiera was talking to me. I was beginning to feel dizzy, and I could feel my heart laboring in my chest, my lungs squeezing forlornly in an attempt to keep me alive.

"Sean!" she said urgently. I focused on her voice, turning to look into her eyes, and I saw the dog in weird clothing sitting next to her as military medics swarmed the plaza. She waved wildly, trying to get their attention, an endless litany of words still streaming in my general direction.

"I can't believe this, oh, Sean, I missed you so much . . ." She seemed awkward, familiar, as she stared down at my broken body, in a way we'd never been with each other before. She seemed almost numb, her voice a trembling staccato of one note. She reached out to touch me several times, only stopping millimeters above my hand, my shoulder, my face.

I looked up at her as the medic knelt down with a large, camo pack. I barely felt the small prick of the needle, the one that would take the pain that I deserved away.

"I remember," I said shortly.

She cleared her throat. "So do I," she said softly.

"What does it mean?" The medics were stabilizing my broken foot, packing gaping wounds, taping the bone fragments against my skin so they wouldn't move.

Kiera's gaze drifted and she stared into the distance, at the battlefield where moans and cries shook the very ground beneath us. I heard the chime of her phone going off, and I could have laughed; it seemed like such a foreign concept now, cell phones.

The realization that I no longer had a Hex, no longer had anyone in my Link, came slower. I couldn't feel Natalie anymore, and I wondered if she had been among the ones to wake up. I had lost track of her in the din, and now I might never know what happened to her. She had been such an intimate part of my soul; I could only focus on my breathing to steady myself in the face of these monumental losses. I had lost so much.

I had done so much.

Images flashed through my brain like so many ping-pong balls in a bathtub. I had tortured people. Gleefully wrecked their bodies and killed them. Worse, I'd created more of myself: fathomless creatures that knew nothing more than to divide mankind worse than it had done by itself. I spread suffering to so many.

"I don't know," Kiera answered slowly. The medic asked for her help loading me onto a stretcher, and they half carried, half dragged me through the courtyard to the ambulance. Every jolt and every bump sent excruciating pain through my remaining limbs.

I realized I was still wearing someone's skin as a glove.

"Get it off!" I shouted, writhing against the stretcher. I could feel myself panicking, and wished briefly that Zombie Sean could deal with this. It was weird to realize that he was gone; except he wasn't gone.

He was me.

I flailed my hand towards Kiera. "Get it off, get it off, please!"

She stared down at my flesh-covered hand, her face expressionless, as she peeled the rotting skin off of my arm. I could see that she felt nothing; she was in her own darkness.

I had a feeling that the people we were, the couple who ate Chinese food and watched *Bob's Burgers,* no longer existed.

Who were we now? And would I even want to know what we'd become?

Towards the End

~ Kiera ~

I found him.

I found him, bloody and missing a part of his left ear. There were shards of bone sticking out of him, a few arrows, and his foot was definitely broken. I almost dropped the stretcher when he started to panic and shove his arm in my face.

The maggots were inches away from me. I realized dimly that Grace had been following us. I wondered if she'd be allowed in the ambulance. I carefully removed the rotted flesh from his hand, dropping it on the ground.

We loaded him into the ambulance, his emaciated form shivering in the cool evening. I sat on the bench, with Gracey by my side, reluctant to hold his hand.

"What do we do now?" I asked softly.

He was staring at the ceiling, at Grace, anything to avoid looking in my eyes. I wondered if the pearl color was permanent. I wondered if it meant that something else disastrous was going to happen.

I wondered how many people he'd killed. As I sat there, waiting for the ambulance to rev up, another thought came to mind.

I wondered how many people *I'd* killed.

If this virus cured the zombies, and the zombies re-tained all of the memories from their zombiehood, that meant that they had been sentient. They had been, in their own disgusting way, people. I hadn't become the grim reaper of zombies—I had been the grim reaper for people looking for a way out of the monstrous disease, ill-ness, virus, whatever. I killed *people*.

We both had.

The weight of my body count sat heavily on my shoulders.

It occurred to me at that moment that he had killed Brett—my friend, my savior, my teacher. Tears started to trickle down my face. "That was Brett," I said finally. "You killed him."

He turned his face away. "I've killed a lot of people," he said huskily. "And worse. Kiera, you shouldn't be here."

I stared down at him, incredulous. "Where the hell do you think I can go? I have to be with the National Guard; they're the only ones that know what the fuck is going on. I have to find Callie, maybe she can get me set up in an apartment or something, somewhere with food. And . . ." I hesitated. "I can't leave you." It was true; despite it all, I couldn't help but remember the Before.

It would take a long time to forget the Before, I thought.

We stared at the walls of the ambulance together, Grace whining softly at my side. She stood up, carefully placing her paws on the stretcher, and hopped over tie next to Sean's curled legs. I watched her for a long time. She seemed content to not use her spikes to rip the shit out of him. I wondered why.

"What do we do now?" Sean echoed my earlier question, finally turning to look at me.

I swallowed hard. Visions of bashing someone's head in danced in tune to *The Nutcracker* through my skull. I wondered what had happened to my hatchet-mop. I might have to make a new one, just in case.

"This is the After," I said slowly. "I don't know how it's going to work. If every zombie was cured or killed. I don't know how safe we are, or how many people are left, just . . ."

"Safe from people like me?" he said dully.

"Safe from whatever comes from the cure and the vaccine," I said softly. "Sean . . . will we ever be the same?"

He reached down with his now maggot-free hand and stroked Gracey's long fur in the few places he could find it. "What did you do to this dog?" he asked, smiling. His expression sobered. "She'll be good protection against me."

I shook my head, closing my eyes. "I don't think we *will* ever be the same, Sean. But . . ." I hesitated. "Maybe we could be something new."

"Something new?" he asked.

I shrugged. "I never stopped thinking about you, Sean. Never stopped missing you."

"Me either," he confessed. "With what little I could do, my intent was always to get back to you. Even if that wasn't the best idea." I could tell there was more there that he wanted to say. I also knew that it was dangerous to ask about it.

"Then . . . I guess we just live one step at a time. See what world this awakens. I don't know what's going to happen," I said. "But once we get to wherever they're taking us, I'll find Callie, and she'll know what to do."

He looked at me, and I wondered if his pearlescent eyes would always hold a tinge of sadness, an echo of destruction. "She'll know what to do," he said softly.

I looked out the back window of the ambulance as it started to move, wondering what Evan and Lydiana were doing. I wondered if I'd ever see them again. I wondered what they would do with all of the bodies—with Brett's body.

"At least someone will," I said, trying to sound hopeful. I reached out hesitantly, pressing my fingertip against Sean's. It was the first time I had touched him since I abandoned him in the stairwell. His skin felt scaly and dry.

We sat in the ambulance in silence, Grace's panting and the EMTs chatter over the radio our constant companions. I didn't know what lay ahead of us. I didn't know if Sean could ever get over what he'd done; I didn't know if *I* would ever get over how many I'd killed. We were broken, asynchronous spirits, two lovers floating in the darkness of our own devising.

The silence was deafening. Nothing would ever be the same.

If you enjoyed this book, please leave a review at your favorite online retailer's website!

Enthusiastic reviews from readers like you are incredibly helpful.

Thank you!

Acknowledgments

I'd like to acknowledge the folks at Nef House who really believe in me and made me feel like being a horror writer wasn't a personality disorder. And Converse College, where I learned that I was not a literary fiction writer, but a genre writer (who would've guessed?)—residency was some of the best times of my life, and I can only dream of the community I had then. And to all horror fans: thank you for taking the ride with me. You all rock.

Discover more awesome books and authors at
www.nefhousepublishing.com

NEF HOUSE PUBLISHING